CHAOS RIDERS

As we rode side by side into the mountains, I could see that Eirene's horse—if, indeed, it had started life as a horse—had spent a lot of time in Chaos.

Black and orange lizard flesh covered the beast, though its mane and tail were normal. Its eyes were full of Chaosfire, and fangs protruded from either side of its muzzle. I had no idea what the creature ate, and no desire to find out, either.

Eirene, herself, was rather formidable, like most of the Riders. The green in her hair and the points on her ears were not the only changes Chaos had wrought in her. When she smiled, especially in the daylight, I could see fangs like those of her mount.

Books by Michael A. Stackpole

Once a Hero
Talion: Revenant

Star Wars X-Wing Series
Rogue Squadron
Wedges Gamble
The Krytos Trap
The Bacta War

A Hero Born*
An Enemy Reborn*

*Published by HarperPrism

A HERO BORN

Michael A. Stackpole

HarperPrism
A Division of HarperCollinsPublishers

HarperPrism

A Division of HarperCollinsPublishers
10 East 53rd Street, New York, N.Y. 10022-5299

ISBN 0-06-105680-4

Cover illustration by Paul Youll

First printing: May 1997

Printed in the United States of America

Visit HarperPrism on the World Wide Web at
http://www.harpercollins.com

❖ 10 9 8 7 6 5 4

DEDICATION

This book is dedicated to all the indoor soccer players I've ever played with or against. If not for my weekly jaunts into Chaos with all of you, I'd be as mad as a hatter. (And I'd have no idea what it feels like to have been in combat.)

ACKNOWLEDGMENTS

The author would like to offer special thanks to the following people, for without their contributions, this work would never have been created. Liz Danforth for listening to my mad prattling about this book. Dr. William F. Wu for asking questions that made me think about answers—ditto David M. Honigsberg in this regard. Dennis L. McKiernan and Jennifer Roberson for their help with horses and similar paradoxes of fantasy fiction. Ricia Mainhardt and Christopher Schelling for finding this project its various homes and Caitlin Blasdell for her patience as the book expanded to fill the time available to write it and then some. And, finally, Rick Loomis, the president of Flying Buffalo Inc., for allowing me to create and use this world.

Chaos began as a play-by-mail-game experiment I ran for Flying Buffalo Inc. (P. O. Box 1467, Scottsdale, AZ 85252 or http://www.flyingbuffalo.com) in 1984. For three months I created the world just ahead of a dozen players, fleshing it out in directions they forced me to explore. While we all had great fun, and the experience of having to write on demand each and every day helped me immeasurably in my career, the game died after the momentous occasion of the Bear's Eve Ball. Rick and I decided we could not pay writers enough to make writing up adventures worth their while, nor could we ever give customers enough stuff if we charged them what it really cost to prepare their adventures.

The players involved in the playtest were Phil Murnane, Liz Danforth, Scott Hagen, Steve MacGregor, Jay Dunkelberger, Mark O'Green, Chris Lancaster, Dave Pettit, Rick Shaffstall, Jim Walker, William Paxton, Jeffrey Martis, and E. L. Fredrick. To them my thanks for making the game incredibly interesting and challenging to run. Characters often take over stories, and such was the case with the game. While none of their characters appear in this book, their influence is everywhere.

A HERO BORN

Prologue

Standing high on the red bluff overlooking his grand project, the only sign of Vrasha's irritation came in the rhythmic, jerked twitching of his leonine tail. The sable-furred Chaos demon otherwise stood rock still as he watched his people labor below him. He felt some pride in their devotion to him, but their mindless and slavish adherence to his commands also repulsed him.

Even though this enterprise might kill me, not a one of them has tried to dissuade me.

In a hideous grin, black lips peeled away from darker, crystalline teeth shaped like daggers. Vrasha knew those Black Shadows below labored for him because they believed he would be able to restore his father to life were his mission successful. Kothvir was to him little more than a memory, but to them he was a legendary leader who had come closer than any other to making Chaos a place in which the rigid races feared to venture.

1

Out beyond the project, the opalescent Chaos Wall undulated like a curtain being caressed by a gentle breeze. On the bluff he could not feel its power, but even thinking about the creamy wall brought again to his flesh the sizzling tingle he had felt when walking close to it. Erected by the magick of those who lived beyond it, the Chaos Wall held back the forces of change in the same way a dike might hold the ocean at bay. Those born on the far side of it could pass through at will, but for anyone born in Chaos . . .

"Vrasha, for one final time I ask you to reconsider."

Vrasha turned slowly to face the Black Shadow who had spoken to him. "Rindik, do you so fear my success that you beg me not to undertake this quest?"

The larger Chaos demon shook his head. His black mane, unlike Vrasha's, had been shaved away from the sides of his head in the manner of warriors. It exposed his triangular ears, which flicked forward and back in a sign Vrasha knew from long experience meant Rindik was decidedly agitated. "You know, half brother, that is not my reason. If you succeed, I will bow to your will and support you. I may be a simple warrior, but I respect your dreams and will welcome their successful fruition. I would not, however, have you throw your life away needlessly."

"I do not throw my life away, Rindik. We have done tests."

"And in your tests, everything born on this side of the wall has died when you sent it through!" Rindik's solid gold eyes narrowed. "All of your theories have been proved wrong, yet now you are set to subject yourself to that which has killed all other participants in your experiment."

"You do not understand!" Vrasha pointed at the huge, steeply angled ramp that ended on a sharp upslope barely five yards from the Chaos Wall. "We have extended the ramp's height and have increased the angle to the point where the velocity will be nearly doubled when I reach the wall. Unlike the early, grossly unsuccessful trials, having the sphere airborne when it reaches the wall seems to lessen the damage. That held true for creatures and for the other demons we have sent through."

"Yes, but they died nonetheless."

Vrasha batted that objection away with a contemptuous wave of his left hand. "They were Storm demons who had neither the courage nor presence of mind to kill themselves when you captured them."

"True enough, brother mine, but they died doing what you will do." Rindik pointed back toward the northwest, where malignant green flashes of lightning darkened the bloodred sky. "And there the other *Tsvortu* come to war on us for your use of their kin. I need you and your insight to help control them. Use another of your thralls to test this new contrivance you have built. I want you with me as we fight them."

"Rindik, you surprise me. Were you not the one who has told me that the *Tsvortu* would never defeat the *Bharashadi*? You yourself pointed out that their power to influence storms was nothing compared to the power of the *Bharashadi* to defeat death. We, the Black Shadows, have forever lamented the fact that the key to our opening the Necroleum and summoning forth our long-dead kin resides there, beyond the wall. You ask me to fight the Storm demons at a disadvantage when, with incredible ease, I can bring us the power that will put them down forever."

The warrior folded his arms across his broad chest, and his right hand played with the leather strips hanging down from the hilt of the sword strapped across his back. "I know what you intend to do, and I praise it. However, you too must admit that to bring back those resting in the Necroleum at this time is wrong. Our father, Kothvir, is resting there, but he is incomplete. The other sorcerers say he can be made whole again— if he is not, you know he will not rise to lead us again. How can you even consider this course of action when he would not be returned to us?"

Vrasha hesitated as he recalled having once knelt before his father's enthroned corpse in the Necroleum. His father stared down at him with one good eye and a jewel-filled eye socket. The irony struck him that the *Bharashadi* power to return from the dead was as useful as his father's missing eye if the Fistfire Sceptre remained out of reach beyond the wall. That realization gave birth to his desire somehow to get his hands on the sceptre for the sake of his tribe if not for the power it would give him.

"You forget, Rindik, that the *Chronicles of Farscry* say Kothvir's eye will return to him when the appropriate ritual is performed." Vrasha pressed his hands together and let his claws slowly slide from their sheaths at the ends of his fingers. "You interpret that to mean we must wait until his eye has been returned, but I see it as a prophecy whose blossoming I can hasten by taking action. You know Kinruquel would never grant us the power were we to leave Kothvir out of the resurrection."

The sorcerer drew the barbed dagger he wore bound to the upper part of his left arm. "You and I are of a blood. We share a destiny. Know that I will not abandon our father." His thumb caressed the slender line of stars on the knife's crosspiece. "Join me in my dream."

The warrior's ears flicked forward. "Your dreams are my nightmares, Vrasha. You are obsessed with this quest of yours. You do not realize the danger in which you place yourself. Think, Vrasha, you could be propelling yourself into an ambush. You know little of your allies from Wallfar."

Vrasha let himself laugh lightly at Rindik's suspicions. "They are of the Church of Chaos Encroaching. They have chosen to believe that men only come to know their full potential under the influence of Chaos." He thumped his own chest with a fist. "They even purport to believe we Chaos demons were once men who have been living in Chaos for far too long. Ha!"

Even Rindik could not suppress a laugh at that idea. "Foolish may be some of their beliefs, but they could still be waiting on the other side of the wall to capture you and sell you to their Emperor."

"Nonsense!" Vrasha waved a hand at his ramp tower and the strange sphere mounted at the top of it. "They have labored day and night to send through the wood we needed to build this ramp and my journeycraft. They have supplied us with the animals we have likewise needed, and they have reported on our earlier successes. Even so, they are pitifully stupid. While professing to worship Chaos, their cult holds its membership in thrall with the system of ranks endemic to Wallfar. This behavior proves them to be fools."

"And you trust them?"

"Trust? Trust? Never and a day, not in the least." Vrasha pointed toward the southeast. "They believe I will be coming through the wall a league or two in that direction. That was the site of our previous tests and the point at which they sent the cattle through. They are also expecting me to come through in a week or so. Going tonight means I will be in Herakopolis well before their Bear's Eve Ball."

He waved his half brother before him, resheathed his dagger, then headed toward the catwalk linking the bluff to the ramp. Below him *Bharashadi* swarmed over the tower to bind its pieces together and reinforce the whole structure with more wood and rope. Others walked along the ramp's surface and stained its wood dark with smears of beef tallow. Still others, on a platform at the very top, tugged on ropes and hauled dripping buckets ever upward.

Vrasha moved from the catwalk to a ladder, which he quickly scaled. Reaching the top, he waited for his bulkier, slower half brother to join him on the crowded wooden plateau. As he looked down he saw the gore-spattered ground below, where a dozen Black Shadows slaughtered cattle and filled buckets to the brim with steaming blood and claw-minced flesh. Up there, so near his journeycraft, the scent of blood nearly overwhelmed him.

Turning back, he watched Chademons pass bucket after bucket of meat and vitals up to the hide-bound wooden sphere he and his engineers had worked very hard to create. They had tested many bits of wood from Wallfar and settled for oak. It had been cut into thin strips, then laminated together to form a strong yet springy spherical skeleton for his journeycraft. Even dropping from the top of the tower to the ground would not break it.

Rindik nodded as he studied the sphere that was half again taller than his half brother. "So you have chosen to cover the sphere with the skin of freshly slain cattle. You said that offered one of the *Tsvortu* some protection?"

Vrasha nodded. "We bound him up in one or two, then swung him out on a rope. We know he survived the journey out because he worked a hand free and came back through clutching a tree branch from the other side."

"But he was dead when he swung back here, correct?"

"A minor concern. He was *only* Tsvortu! He did not know what was happening to him, so he died of fright." Vrasha's pupilless-orb eyes became golden slits. "I have a mind, I have discipline, and I have a purpose. I *will* survive."

One of the blood-splattered Chademons knelt at Vrasha's feet. "Master, your journeycraft is filled to the point at which you must enter it."

"The skins are holding?" Vrasha looked past him and saw darkish liquid oozing slowly from the seams where the skins were bound one to another.

"Master, yes, they are. We are ready for you."

Vrasha nodded, and the Chademon rose to ascend some scaffolding to the top of the sphere. "It is time for me to leave, Rindik."

The warrior's hands balled into fists. "I cannot dissuade you?" Behind him green lightning again stabbed through the maroon twilight sky. "I have need of you here."

"There is more need for me there, in Wallfar." He grabbed the scaffold's crossbar, and Rindik boosted him upward. "I will return, brother mine, with the Fistfire Sceptre, and *then* I will be able to fulfill all your needs."

"Farewell, Vrasha. You are the last broodchild sprung from Kothvir's loins. May your legend be as great as his."

"No"—Vrasha laughed boldly—"greater. My legend will be greater."

Turning his back to his brother, Vrasha crossed the upper scaffolding and came to the top of the leaking ball. One of the Chademons held out to him a snaky length of tubing that ran from inside the sphere to a pinched orifice in the sphere's flesh. Vrasha took it in his mouth and blew out hard. A thin mist of blood sprayed up out of a puckered blowhole. Breathing in and out several times assured Vrasha he would have enough air while sealed in the ball.

Another of his minions approached him from behind and had him lean his head back. As Vrasha did so, he closed his eyes. He felt wet warmth that seeped into the fur on his face as the Chademon pressed two lumps of cow flesh over his eyes, then bound them in place with strips of hide. Vrasha tried to open his eyes, found he could not, and nodded his satisfaction to the others.

As they had drilled many times, two Chademons eased their blind master forward and positioned his feet over the lip of the sphere's round hatchway. Moving his feet forward and back, Vrasha quickly measured the dimensions of the opening, then worked himself closer and lowered his feet into the ball. The liquid, sucking sound he heard as his feet sank beneath the surface excited him.

Unseen hands steadied him and guided his own hands to the opening's rim. Planting his palms firmly on the latticework, Vrasha took his full weight on his arms, then slowly lowered himself into the sphere. The thick, clinging soup dragged at his legs. It squished between his toes and soaked through to his skin as, inch by inch, he immersed himself in it. It washed up over his thighs and groin to his waist, then he pulled his hands away from the hatch edge and plunged in fully.

The viscous gel closed over his head, and, instantly, he felt panic. His hands flailed through the blood and entrails, but his motions only sent him lower, not up toward the opening. His head jerked back as his breathing tube grew taut, then he sucked in a breath.

Concentrating on his breathing, forcing himself to inhale and exhale slowly, his mind overrode his desire to escape.

Thinking as little as possible about where he actually was, Vrasha reached out and felt through the blood and tissue for the harness that had been suspended from the sphere's cross bracing. By kicking his feet and drifting a little higher he found it. Twisting around, he lowered himself into the leather seat, then tied the straps that would keep him in place during his journey around his chest and legs.

The sticky fluid wrapped him in a cocoon that deadened all sound from the outside world, save what little he could hear through the tube leading to his mouth. He marveled at how, sealed in a womb made of and filled with things from Wallfar, he would be reborn in that alien place. *And through me will come the redemption of the entire* Bharashadi *race.*

Prepared for anything and everything he thought his journey would provide, he barked out a harsh order that echoed through his breathing tube to the outside.

Distantly he heard a sharp sound, then felt a vibration ripple through the plasma. As his head started down, he reached out and grasped two of the cross braces. He felt himself slowly somersault forward the first time, then again with more speed. The sphere vibrated a bit side to side as it lumbered down the newer section of the ramp, then settled down as it hit the older portion.

Inside, Vrasha's mind clinically compared the sensations of his current journey with those of the days he had spent in the center of a giant wheel his minions had spun faster and faster. He had accustomed himself to the motion of rolling forward until it no longer made him dizzy, and he felt pride swell in his breast at his own foresight. Aside from the thunderous vibrations shaking him, being in the sphere felt exactly like being in the wheel.

Suddenly the globe shifted ever so slightly, and the rotations started him whirling at an angle. The harness kept him suspended in the middle of the sphere, but the new direction of stress threatened to pull one crosspiece loose. Faster and faster he spun, and wood screamed in protest. He could even begin to feel the sphere shift and become misshapen.

Vrasha slid his right hand along the crosspiece to its joint with another brace and sank his claws into both pieces of wood. *I will not fail!* The globe slowed almost imperceptibly, and suddenly he felt much heavier. *I cannot fail!*

Just as suddenly as the sphere had turned on its axis, the rumbling roar of his ride down the ramp ended. In an instant he realized he was airborne.

A heartbeat later he hit the Chaos Wall.

A net of razors ripped him apart. Millions upon millions of chiggers gnawed on his flesh with their steel teeth. Boring worms made of fire burned tunnels through his bones, and ice-winged wasps flew through the holes to build their frozen nests where their larvae could feast on his marrow. Each hair in his pelt became an agate needle that pierced his skin from the inside out.

His brain boiled within his skull. His eyes saw colors that did not exist, and his ears heard those same colors as the death screams of creatures yet unborn. Unable to think, left only to sensing, dread swallowed him, terror crushed him, and hopelessness ground him into nothingness.

A bone-blasting impact jarred him partway out of the nihilistic darkness closing over his being. In one second he felt pummeled as a shock wave bashed him from all sides, and the pressure closed a tight fist on him. Then, in the next, the closeness vanished, and he knew a moment's freedom as the ball bounced up. He could tell, from its lightness and speed, that the first impact must have ruptured the skin and sprayed the liquid from it.

The sphere turned over lazily and hit hard again. The stressed cross braces snapped and stabbed through the upper part of his right arm. He screamed aloud and yet louder as the sphere took to the air again and ripped the wood from the wound. He pulled his legs up and hugged his arms in, then waited for the earth to batter him one more time.

His journeycraft slammed into the ground, and the lattice gave way. Splinters peppered him back and flank. The harness's straps snapped, and he pounded the ground a second after his broken vehicle, then lay stunned as it lazily rolled over and the hide collapsed on top of him.

The tingling weakness in his limbs distressed him at first. He remained very still and forced his mind clear. Slowly, in a deep voice that echoed within itself, even when whispering, he began to speak a spell. As he did so, a reddish gold aura surrounded him, and in seconds he had an accurate assessment of his wounds.

Aside from the hole torn in his right arm, he had not been damaged. Vrasha allowed himself a smile, and instantly banished the concern he felt over the draining effort required to sustain it. Flicking out the claws on his left hand, he sliced through the thongs binding him into the harness. Once he had freed himself from its confines, he slashed away the hides covering him and tore off the blindfold.

Kneeling amid the ruins of his vessel, he blinked

blood from his eyes and looked up. He saw constellations gleaming in a black sky that no other Chaos demon had ever seen. He instantly forgot the pain in his arm and found a new energy begin to course through him. Cradling his right arm against his side, he forced himself to his feet and stood, bloody, battered, but not broken, in a world that had forever been denied to his kind.

Vrasha stooped and recovered a section of wood no longer than his forearm. With his claws he carved in it the runes for the message "I Live," then hurled it long and high back through the Chaos Wall.

"I live." He breathed the words out like a talisman against all possible evil. "I live, and everyone in Wallfar will soon learn to live in fear."

1

Here we go again!

I snapped my head to the right, flinging sweat from my eyes. The dagger in my left hand rotated spasmodically in time with my heaving chest. I held my rapier steady and pointed at my brother's throat, but I saw no fear in his bullock brown eyes. Poised on the balls of my feet, I waited for him as the afternoon sunlight glinted from his sword.

C'mon, Dalt. I know you. You're bigger than me. You hate waiting. He licked his lips and screwed his face into a fierce, angry expression. Sweat dripped down his chest and arms, coating him as it did me. His right toe inched forward through the barnyard dust, presaging the attack I had expected all along. The point of his rapier dipped abruptly, aiming at my left thigh. He lunged.

I let my sword point drop, then I pivoted on my right foot and slid back a half step. This pulled my body out of line with his lunge, which was enough to defeat his attack. Dalt, seeing my move, started to recover and looked surprised when I brought my right arm up and carried his rapier with it. As the blade came up to the height of my shoulder, I locked our hilts and stepped forward, ducking beneath his arm.

At least, that is what I meant to do. I had intended to twist his sword free from his grip, then whip my sword back across his unprotected flank, but he locked his wrist and used his incredible strength to prevent my move. His right knee caught me behind my left leg, driving me to my knees, then I felt the cool caress of his dagger on the side of my neck.

"You're dead, lambkin." Exultant, Dalt threw back his head and laughed.

His laughter died abruptly as an older, taller, more slender version of him chuckled aloud and approached the two of us. "And Locke has just guaranteed you will never sire any children." Geoff pointed down to where my dagger, the blade lying flat against the underside of my forearm, required only the lifting of my arm before it gelded him. "I think the last laugh would be his."

"Laughter sounds hollow from the grave." Our grandfather shook his head and looked quite disappointed at me and my brother. "Dalt, you are taller than Lachlan and have nearly six inches in reach over him. You should never have let him get in that close to you. And you, Lachlan, when will you learn that you are too small to play your strength against a larger, stronger opponent?"

I started to protest. "But, I thought the sweat would loosen his grip. He would not expect it . . ."

"Dalt has been trained by me, as have you. Do you let your hands get sweaty enough to have a blade twisted from them?"

I looked down. "No, sir."

Audin nodded solemnly. "I know you have heard heroic tales about your father or your uncle or the Valiant Lancers and the things they have done, but they are dead! They thought the same sort of thing you did. For every one of them that used an unusual move to gain fame, many died. I have taught you to be better than that."

"Yes, sir." I stood and walked off the field of combat, my face burning.

The slight breeze cooled me and made Grandfather's wispy white hair float. "Dalt, you have won the fight with Lachlan. Now you will face Geoff. Let me see that you two have learned your lessons better than your younger brother."

I laid my sword on the bench beside the water trough, then followed it with my dagger and sweat-soaked gloves. Bending over slowly to stretch out the muscle Dalt had kneed, I grabbed the edges of the trough and dunked my head full into the water. The cool water washed away the dust on my face and cooled some of the embarrassment.

I felt a hand on my back and came up with water dripping down over me. "Yes, Grandfather?"

Audin's brown eyes regarded me carefully. "Let me guess why you tried what you did with Dalt. You read about Driscoll dueling with the 'giant' of Port Chaos."

I nodded sheepishly. "He'd hit the man in the fore-arm and the blood and sweat had loosened the man's grip on his blade. Driscoll twisted the blade free, then stabbed him clean through his armpit. It should have worked against Dalt. I am better than he is."

The older man sat down on the bench. "You are ranked as an Apprentice and Dalt is ranked as a Sworder. He defeated you."

I held back because we had discussed this situation before. My grandfather, being the only Bladesmaster in Stone Rapids—and having owned his own sword school until about a dozen years ago—was the final arbiter of our rankings. If he decided, and he had, that I was not ready to progress from Apprentice to Journeyman or Sworder, nothing I could do would convince him. *Especially failing at fancy tactics designed to shame your brother.*

"I am sorry, Grandfather, you are right." I looked up at him and gave him a hopeful smile. "I should not have tried to emulate my uncle, especially when a bard's tale is the source of my inspiration."

"Do not err too far on the other side, Locke." The old man returned my smile. "Yes, the giant's blood and sweat did make his sword too slippery to be gripped well, but that is not what defeated him. Driscoll, though a tall man himself, recognized his disadvantage and got inside the giant's guard. You accomplished the same with your dodge of Dalt's lunge. You could have had him, if you had not tried to impress me with your audacity. And think, which would you prefer being a living Apprentice who is cautious and victorious, or a dead Sworder who is sung of by bards?"

"The former, of course." I bowed my head and scraped mud from my chest with my left hand. I sat down beside Grandfather on the bench, perching on the edge so I would not put pressure on the muscle bruise Dalt had given me. Grandfather nodded at the other two so they could begin their combat. Though I knew who would win, something about how they moved and played against each other drew me in.

Dalt had Grandfather's powerfully built torso and thick legs. Making use of that strength, he favored attacks that beat the other fighter's blade aside or parries that numb a hand with their heaviness. More than once Dalt had used his size advantage to punish me in the process of defeating me. Even so, in doing that, he had forced me to learn how to avoid or counter exactly the sort of tactics he loved.

I pounded my right fist against my leg. I *had you, Dalt. I had you, then let you get one step closer to the prize.*

I knew Dalt would never be able to use those types of tactics with Geoff. The eldest of my brothers, Geoff is long and lean—just the sort of person that could be formed by adding me to Dalt and splitting us in half. He was quick enough that he could lunge at a candle and snuff it, then resheathe his blade before darkness fell, or so it seemed whenever I had to face him. He formally held the rank of Warrior, but I think that is only because he refused to go to Garikopolis and become a Bladesmaster like Grandfather.

As Geoff circled Dalt slowly, I wished I was as tall and slender as he was. I would have died to possess even a fraction of Geoff's fluidity. I knew, just from watching him back Dalt around the yard, that I would never be his equal in swordsmanship. I might have been able to outride him or beat him at chess, but in single combat he did not have an equal in the yard.

Geoff lunged, and somehow Dalt managed to wrestle Geoff's rapier up into the air. Dalt twisted his wrist and locked their blades together, then both of their daggers came up and trapped each other against the swords. Face-to-face, toe-to-toe, the two of them stared at each other for a second, then Dalt set himself to use his strength against Geoff.

Geoff, smiling, brought his forehead down into Dalt's face. I winced as I heard something crack. Dalt reeled away, covering his face with his hands. Blood leaked through his fingers as he dropped to his knees and hunched over. Sputtered curses sprayed blood over the ground in front of him.

Geoff let Dalt's blades fall to the ground, then properly saluted Grandfather. "Master Audin, I have vanquished my foe."

Audin stood and patted Geoff on the shoulder. Turning, the Bladesmaster fixed me with a stare that filled my guts with ice. "Dalt lost in the swimming race, and he has lost here. He has forfeited any chance at the prize. Geoff, your choice of trials will end our contest. What did you choose?"

I swallowed hard, knowing Geoff's choice would make no difference—he would win and get to go to Herakopolis. Instead of making the decision required by the communiqué our grandmother, Evadne, had sent all the way from the capital, Grandfather had decided his grandsons would have a contest consisting of three trials. Each of us selected one area of competition and wrote his choice down on a small piece of paper. Audin had restricted us from choosing that which we knew we were best at, then all the choices had been put in a pouch, and Audin had selected the trials at random. Defeats in two of the trials put a contestant out.

I still considered it incredible luck that my choice of trial had been chosen first. I knew I needed something that would let me beat Dalt and give me a chance to defeat Geoff. I selected a swimming race because Dalt hates to swim, and I can go at a pretty good pace. As it turned out, I beat Dalt going away and would have lost to Geoff, but his leg cramped up in the last part of the race. He waded ashore after disqualifying himself, which put me in the unlikely position of having won a contest.

Dalt, optimistically believing lightning would strike

and he would be able to beat Geoff, had selected swordfighting as his trial. I knew Audin would have forbidden Geoff to choose swordfighting as his contest, and suspected Dalt had been told he could not pick any test of strength. I had hoped Dalt would have been smart enough to stay away from Geoff's forte, but Dalt's ego often eclipsed his common sense.

I wonder what he chose? I just love being humiliated in new and novel ways. I toed a pebble out of the dust. *Of course, it is possible he will have made Dalt's mistake. No, not possible. Geoff is smarter than Dalt, so he wouldn't lunge to my strength.*

His sapphire eyes twinkling, Geoff smiled. "I selected chess."

"Chess?" I shook my head to clear my ears of any water they still had in them. "You chose chess?"

Geoff nodded, then met Audin's bemused stare calmly. "I assumed you would put us through our contests in rank order. As I am a Warrior, my contest would go first and Locke would destroy Dalt. I thought that would distract Dalt enough that he would be poor competition. As it turns out, by luck of the draw, Dalt fell to Locke in Locke's trial, and I obtained the desired result."

Audin accepted the explanation, but the tightness around his eyes told me that he did not believe it entirely. "It is a good thing that your leg recovered from its cramp before you had to fight Dalt."

Geoff's nostril's flared as he pulled his head up. "Bladesmaster Audin, if you truly believe I would deliberately set out to lose this contest, then you should disqualify me from the competition. Void my defeat of Dalt and let him play chess against Locke to determine who is the victor."

"You are definitely your mother's son." Audin smiled proudly. "You know Dalt would have no chance against him. If you cannot beat him, Locke and not you will escort your grandmother to the Emperor's Ball on Bear's Eve."

"I will do my best, Bladesmaster, as always." Geoff bowed and walked over to me while Audin crossed to Dalt and squatted down to take a look at his nose. "Come on, Locke. I will play the fly to your spider."

I shook my head. "This is one spider that knows the buzzing in his web could be a spiderhawk wasp just as easily as a fly."

"I could only hope." Geoff laughed as we both passed into the barn and over to the stall that had been remade into an armory. "This time, when we play, I want you to at least look at the board during the game. Do that for me, will you. Locke?"

I slid my rapier home in the bracket mounted on the wall. "You should have chosen 'self-effacement' as your contest, for you would have won handily with that."

The larger man dropped his dagger into the sheath hanging from a belt. "I did not, however, so now you have a chance at winning the prize Grandmother has offered us."

I smiled despite myself. Grandmother's message had said that she had been invited to attend the Emperor's Bear's Eve Ball and she had requested Audin to send one of her grandsons to act as her escort. While there would be celebrations throughout the Empire of Herak welcoming the new year, the Emperor's Ball was the largest and grandest party of them all. Though Grandfather had joked that Evadne had been invited just because she'd not yet had the good grace to die, we all knew she had to be someone of importance in the capital to be invited.

Suddenly fear made my mouth go sour. "Geoff, if I win, do you actually think he will let me go? I'm hardly the sort of person who should represent Cardew's family at such an important occasion."

Geoff clapped me on the shoulders. "What do you mean? You are more than fit to represent us. Grandfather has said it himself—he's worked us harder than he ever did our father or Driscoll when they were his pupils."

"But he had his own school back then, not just the three of us. Besides, he is always after me, berating me for failing when I do things the same as you or Dalt did at my age." My hands tightened down into fists as I folded my arms across my chest. "To hear him tell it, I'm incompetent enough to have doomed countless Imperial Legions in Chaos."

Geoff's hand snaked past my shoulder and grabbed me by the hank of my long, light brown hair. "You have to remember that he still wakes up with nightmares about his having failed Cardew and Driscoll. He has been tough on us because he does not want our blood on his hands. He's not had a moderating influence since Aunt Ethelin died, but I also think we have done better than even he dared dream. He would be proud to have any of us go to Herakopolis."

"How do you know?"

"He's letting the choice be made by this contest, isn't he?" Geoff arched a dark eyebrow. "He is letting us choose our own representative. If he were not happy with each of us, he would have made the choice himself."

"I think he thought you would win. You are more like father than Dalt or me. Even Dalt is large enough to command respect." I brought my left arm up and tensed my bicep into very modest muscle. "You have a hero's looks and skills, Dalt has a hero's strength, and I have, well, ah . . ."

"You have a hero's sense of reality. You have father's skill at training animals."

I shook my head. "Many heroes are lauded because their horses come when they whistle. Why, there must be a hundred bardic tales of such masterful feats."

"Blooded on first pass, but that's still a skill. Locke, you're already better at chess than our father ever was." Geoff cuffed me lightly on the back of the head. "Now do you want to have our game, or shall I claim victory by default?"

"Default? I'd sooner have to fight Dalt again." I led the way from the barn to the house and back into the little room Grandfather had set up as mine when my mother brought me to Stone Rapids from Herakopolis. A small room, the preponderance of books and scrolls and all manner of other treasure I had collected in my eighteen years barely gave me enough room for the tiny bed in the far corner. Geoff ducked his head beneath the wired-together skeleton of a bat hanging from the ceiling and removed a green toy wooden horse from a chair before seating himself.

"I can still remember when you dunked this thing in green paint." Geoff spun the wooden wheels connected by an axle running through the front hooves. "Mother and Aunt Ethelin were very angry when you pulled it through the house, leaving parallel tracks of green everywhere."

I shrugged and blushed. "At the time it seemed like a very sensible thing to do."

I took my place opposite him and moved the piles of books on the table from there to my rumpled bed. The newly cleared tabletop revealed an eight-by-eight, black-and-red checkerboard and a thin layer of dust where the books had not been.

"Chaos or Empire," I asked. Before he had a chance

to answer, I slid the drawer open and started pulling out the pieces.

"Empire, I guess. I need all the help I can get." Geoff started reaching for the red pieces and began setting them up on their appropriate squares. "The Emperor on his own color, right?"

"Yes. Fialchar, on the other hand, is always black." I passed the Emperor while I put the hooded and cloaked figurine clutching a knotted staff in one skeletal hand on his square. "The Queen of Darkness goes next to Lord Disaster, then his Generals, his Wizards, and his Cavalry. Chademon Pawns go up front."

I slid the movestone over onto his side of the board. "Chaos, of course, goes second, so the movestone is yours."

Geoff moved the Emperor's Pawn forward two spaces, then pushed the movestone to me. "You did a good job carving a new Emperor."

"Do you really think so?" Carved from cedar, the Emperor piece represented a tall, slender young man whose brow was encircled by a crown. "Thetys V has only been on the throne for four months, but I thought I should go ahead and make one for him." I glanced toward the book-covered desk. "I did save the Daclones figure, though."

"Nothing wrong with that, Locke."

"Are you certain? You know the rhyme Ethelin used to say:

> *Fire and silver*
> *Beat cold and night,*
> *But try to avoid evil's sight.*
> *When all is lost,*
> *Brave heart have you,*
> *And evil's thrall will then be through.*

I should have burned it so no one can use it to work evil on the Emperor."

Geoff shook his head. "I think the assassins saw to it that the old Emperor is beyond much evilworking. What I want to know is how you can remember all those little things Ethelin used to say?"

I blushed. "I think she used to say them to me a lot more than you. That one I used to repeat to myself every time I became scared of you or Dalt or Grandfather or the night."

"I see. I wonder if saying something like that would help me win this game?"

Geoff fell silent as we went through a quick series of moves that developed the game from the opening to the midgame. I saw Geoff's moves become more tentative as things went along and knew my drive to open up the Empress's side of the board would be successful. I watched Geoff react to feints and successfully pinned one of his Generals in place to protect the Empress from a Cavalry charge.

Geoff moved the pinned General to set up an attack on my other Cavalry piece. He hesitated, then slid the movestone over to me.

I frowned. "You can take that back if you want to. If not, you lose the Empress."

"Here I tell you to watch the board, which is what I should have been doing." The Warrior frowned, then shifted his expression to a sheepish grin. "Bad luck on my part."

"Bad luck? You?" I shook my head. "You don't have to throw the game, Geoff. Don't you want to go to the Bear's Eve Ball?"

Geoff sighed. "First off, I'm not throwing the game. I made a mistake. I don't see the board the way you do. I never have, never will. I actually *do* have to look at the board, and even then I don't see everything. But, to answer your other question: No, I don't particularly want to go to the capital."

My jaw dropped open. "You don't? Just think of what you would see and whom you would meet!" I started pointing at various red pieces on the board. "You could meet the Emperor or his mother Dejanna, or the Imperial Warlord, Garn Drustorn, and . . ."

Geoff held up his hand to cut me off. "And someone would offer me a chance to join a sword school, or I'd be drafted into a group of Chaos Riders, or I'd be handed some commission in an Imperial Company."

"Don't you want that?"

"May not be fitting for Cardew's son to say so, but, no, I do not want that. I want to stay here and learn as much as I can from Grandfather."

"But you already know everything he can teach you. In Herakopolis you could learn from a Grandmaster."

Geoff's face darkened. "But I could not learn how to reopen Audin's school and make it great again."

All of a sudden I felt closer to Geoff than I had ever been before, and my respect for him increased incredibly. Geoff actually remembered our father and had started his sword training in the school Audin had run here in Stone Rapids. Three years after I arrived from the capital, when I became five years old and was due to start training, Audin had closed his school to make his grandsons his only students.

I swallowed hard. "You've seen it in his eyes, too, haven't you?"

Geoff nodded solemnly. "He had always planned for Cardew and Driscoll to come back from their time with the Valiant Lancers to continue his sword school. When they died he decided to train us so we would never succumb to those things that killed them in Chaos.

Because he took no other students, his school has all but been forgotten, and it shouldn't be. Deep down I know he still dreams of having his school continue, and I want to make that dream come true."

He folded his arms across his chest. "You and I have an alliance, little brother. I will see to it that his dream of having his school reopen is realized. I leave it to you to fulfill his dream of having another of his pupils praised by the Emperor for service as a Chaos Rider. Is this bargain acceptable to you?"

"You're a good swordsman, Geoff, and you will be every bit as much of a hero as our father. I think the course you give yourself is more difficult than the one you give to me." I looked down at my hands. "I want you to do what will be best for you."

"In that case, Locke, you will execute the Empress and put me out of my misery in what, five moves?"

"Four. You missed the Wizard fork."

"Always my bane." Geoff reached over and toppled the Emperor. "Locke, go, see the capital. Go meet the Emperor, and even dance twice with each of his sisters—once for you and once for me. Then come back and tell me all about it."

"You will have no regrets if I go in your place?"

"I might, I just might." He reached out and tousled my hair. "But I'll live knowing you're off having the adventures that will inspire whole legions of students to come to Audin's school again."

2

I looked down from the promontory overlooking the Garik Road. Off in the distance I saw the dusty cloud that marked the approach of the caravan with which I would travel to the capital. All of a sudden my stomach turned itself inside out because I would be leaving home for the very first time. I pulled my sheepskin coat more tightly about me and looked over at Geoff and my grandfather.

"The caravan is coming." I swallowed hard. "Geoff, you can take my place if you want."

My older brother shook his head. "I'm a Garikman born and bred, Locke. I'm not the sort that should attend the Imperial Ball. You, being born in Herakopolis, are."

"I may not be Garik-born, but I am Garik-bred." I nodded to my grandfather. "I will make you proud. The Empire will have another of your students to remember."

The old man pulled me to him and enfolded me in a hug. "I am more proud of you than you could know,

Locke." He held me out at arm's length and touched the sword-and-dagger badge sewn on the left breast of my jacket. "You may only be an Apprentice in ranking, but there is much more to you. You know that. Be confident in yourself and your skills, but be aware that, like you, not everyone can be defined on the inside by the rank badges they wear on the outside."

"Thank you, Grandfather." I turned to Geoff and firmly grasped his forearm. "Two dances with each princess—one for you and one for me."

Geoff laughed, the early-morning chill turning his chuckle into steam. He reached inside his coat and pulled out what appeared, at first, to be an inlaid wooden box with a gold clasp on one side and hinges on the other. It rattled as he extended it to me. "I know it is early, but this is my Bear's Eve gift to you. Just so you won't forget us back here in Stone Rapids."

I took it and opened the narrow box. Inside I saw a chessboard with holes drilled in the middle of each of the squares. The rattling had come from thirty-two carefully carved chess pieces, half in red, the others black. Each had a small peg on the bottom that would fit in the holes, holding them in place. A small trough ground out at the end of each side provided a niche for the movestone.

"Geoff, this is wonderful! Now I can play while on the road, if anyone in the caravan plays."

"You will find plenty of players, I think." Geoff smiled openly. "Wiley, the woodwright, made it for me in return for my giving some basic fighting lessons to his sons. Grandfather has agreed to help me teach them. If they work well, we might even reopen the school."

"Might, Geoff, might." Grandfather frowned a bit. "I'm really getting too old to teach children."

My brother and I exchanged a smile, then I whistled

aloud for my horse. Stail's head came up, and the bay gelding trotted over to me. I slipped the chess set into my saddlebag, then swung up into the saddle. "I will come back in the spring, after the mountain passes have thawed, and tell you all about everything. And I'll have Bear's Eve gifts for all of you."

"Good-bye, Lachlan. Farewell." My grandfather lifted his hand and waved. Even though I felt his eyes upon me, it seemed to me that he was not seeing me at all.

Both he and Geoff watched as I took Stail down the switchback trail and joined up with the caravan. I paid the caravan master, a man named Haskell, the five gold Imperials my grandfather had given me for that purpose, and he told me to find a place in the train that suited me. I waved up at the two of them, and they waved back, then the caravan's dust cloud swallowed them.

Deep down inside I felt I had betrayed my family because I did not feel properly homesick. Over a week out from Stone Rapids and I'd not dreamed once about my home. I wanted to feel lonely and desolate, but the caravan was full of interesting people and stranger things that took my mind entirely off those I had left behind. It hardly felt appropriate for me to be happy and excited so much.

During the days I tended to spend most of my time riding beside the cumbersome wagons driven by merchants from Garikopolis. Laden with all sorts of wonderful things, from spices and crystal to delicately woven tapestries and shiny metalwork, they were bound for the capital in time for the frenzy of Bear's Eve gift purchases. Being a native of Garik province, I felt proud about the way my people's goods were cherished and coveted above and beyond those produced elsewhere in the Empire, but I restrained myself from believing all the stories the merchants told of past years in the capital.

At night, as the caravan settled down to prepare meals and let the draft beasts rest, I found myself drawn to the company of the various groups of guards who had hired on to protect the caravan. Some merchants had retained their own soldiers, while the caravan company itself had hired a large number of warriors to ward it. Because the private soldiers were paid better than and refused to take orders from the caravan guards, a certain amount of friction existed between the two camps. Because of my training I had more in common with the soldiers than normal folk, and the warriors tolerated me because I listened attentively to their stories.

As the caravan made camp in the Haunted Mountains, approximately a day's journey west of the City of Sorcerers, I watched several of the guards in the employ of Kasir the gold merchant fence with each other. Stripped to the waist and using blades sheathed with leather practice covers, the two men sparred on a narrow strip between two bonfires. Others, including some of the caravan's guards, watched the two men, offering applause, advice, and odds on victory as the battle wore on.

Having spent my entire life in the village of Stone Rapids, I had never realized how important rank insignia were taken in the outside world. When we rode into town for Bear's Eve, Grandfather always donned a sash that bore a badge marking him as a citizen of Garik and another proclaiming his rank as a Bladesmaster. The black triskele badge of Garik had been fastened to the sash with green thread, as it was his home province, while gold had been used to sew the Bladesmaster badge on. This let everyone know Audin made his living as a Bladesmaster and that he could take on students if he so desired, but only a stranger wouldn't know that anyway.

As was appropriate, we all wore sashes with our rank badges, too, but the people of Stone Rapids really paid scant notice. All of them could have worn a Garik badge as we had, but there seemed no purpose to it. Within our little community we knew each other, and many folks found the formality of rank badges unfriendly. Still, when two young men were vying for the hand of a girl, rank badges tended to proliferate like mosquitoes in a swamp.

Here, within the world of the caravan, rank counted for everything. I quickly bought and sewed a Garik badge to the front of my coat, just above the Apprentice swordsman badge. Because I wore a Garik triskele, those people from Herak naturally treated me as an inferior. This did not bother me overmuch both because of what my grandfather had told me before I left and because the triskele also won me instant company among the folks of Garik. My Apprentice badge, on the other hand, brought me no end of snide comments and piteous headshakes from Journeymen and Sworders employed by the merchants.

To watch this one particular fight, I worked myself into the circle of spectators between one of Kasir's guards and a caravan guard. Kasir's man wore the badge of a Sworder, which placed him a rank above either one of the Journeymen dueling on the strip and supposedly made him Dalt's equal in skill. The caravan guard, a tall, slender man wearing a black eye patch covering his left eye, bore the four-ax badge of an Axman, making him the equal of Kasir's man in level of skill. They had used gold thread to secure those badges to their belts, but I already knew they made their living through being guards. Both of them, according to their province badges, were from Garik, and both wore other badges, but I only glanced at them as I focused on the fight.

The man at the south end of the strip held his blade in an unconventional guard that left the forte high and the tip pointing down toward his foe's knee. His foe clearly did not like it, and I knew, from fencing with Geoff during one of his periods of experimentation, that particular guard was annoying if the person facing it was unimaginative. As the other man dropped his blade down in a weak attempt to imitate his enemy, the first man snapped his blade around and smacked it against his foe's thigh.

As the struck man yelped and limped backward, Kasir's man turned to the Axman. "Well, Roarke, do you still think Timon can be beaten? More to the point, does your gold think he can be beaten?"

I turned at looked at Roarke, unconsciously nodding my head in answer to the other man's question. Roarke cocked his left eyebrow above the patch and grinned with half his mouth. "It must be so, Ferris, because our little Apprentice here thinks he can be beaten."

Ferris, firelight clinging to and evaporating from his bald pate, frowned heavily. "What can this little one know? If your gold bets with him, it is only because it rides on the belt of a fool."

Roarke leaned over toward me. "What say you, little one? Can Timon be beaten?"

"Y-yes, sir," I stammered, not because of any fear that I might be wrong, but because of the good look I had gotten of Roarke's face. Three parallel scars started at the middle of his forehead and slashed down beneath the eye patch to reappear again to score his left cheek. His right eye, which I saw as predominantly blue, had hints of other lights glowing it in. That meant only one thing to me—Roarke had been in Chaos because *Chaosfire* had begun to burn in his eye.

Ferris spun me around roughly. "What would you know, child? You're merely an Apprentice."

I backed away from Ferris and instantly killed the desire to call him out into the fighting area. "I have seen a man using that guard be defeated." I chose my words carefully because I knew it would not be a good idea to mention I had actually scored a touch against Geoff once when he was using that guard. "If an attack comes low, that guard forces an outside parry. If the attacker can come up over the other man's wrist quickly enough, he gets a clear line into torso or throat."

Ferris's dark eyes narrowed. "You have seen this, have you? Then perhaps you would like to show us, *Apprentice*."

Roarke's hands descended on my shoulders like hunting falcons returning to their roost. "Ferris, leave it alone. As he is an Apprentice, he cannot challenge anyone without leave of his Bladesmaster. Likewise, because Timon is a Journeyman, he cannot challenge down. However, the boy has given you the key, so perhaps you can unlock Timon's guard yourself."

Roarke's appeal to Ferris's vanity worked to deflect the private guardsman. With careful yet insistent pressure on my shoulders, Roarke steered me away from the circle of warriors. I stumbled forward into the fragmented darkness of men's shadows. Behind me I heard Ferris voice a challenge to Timon, but Roarke's strong hand on the back of my neck stopped me from turning around to watch.

I tried to shrug off Roarke's hand. "Thank you, I think, Axman."

"Thanks are in order, Lachlan, because you'd have beaten Timon, and he's a nasty man to anger." The larger man released his grip on me. "However, if you're who they say you are, no thanks are necessary. This works toward squaring your blood with mine."

"What do you mean? And how do you know who I am?"

Roarke scratched at the corner of his covered eye. "Your kin rode with you to meet the caravan, remember? Audin is not unknown, and enough people have heard of his tragedy that the story has meandered through the caravan."

I felt myself blush. "People know, then, that I'm Cardew's son?"

Roarke nodded solemnly. "That they do. They've been saying you're a hero born, going to see the Emperor to become a General." He pointed off toward a fire at the camp's perimeter. "But I know from Haskell that you're bound for a visit to your grandmother. From what I have heard of her, that could be heroic duty in and of itself. Let's head to my fire, and I'll give you some supper to fortify you."

I nodded, then frowned. "What you said about squaring your blood with mine—you knew my father?"

The one-eyed man looked back over his left shoulder and nodded. "Eat first, then talk later. Eirene has cooking duty today, so it won't do to let her boil things down to mush."

All around us the caravan's people settled into what had become a normal routine. Nestled in a hollow between two sets of hills and with guards at various sentry points, we felt safe from attack by bandits. Despite the thick pine forest surrounding the campsite and the possibility that it harbored highwaymen, I had heard speculation that our caravan was far too large for any one bandit group to attack anyway. The likelihood of several groups banding together had been dismissed out of hand, but Haskell still posted guards on the hill-tops at night.

Mountain streams provided water for the caravan's needs, and Haskell supervised the digging of waste pits so no one would foul the streams. The forest itself sup-plied plenty of fuel for cookfires and a couple of intrepid hunters wandered off to see if they could bag something more fresh and tasty than salted meats and grain. Beyond that, little or no order had been imposed on the camp.

The small campsite Roarke led me to had obviously been used before by other caravans. A circle of fire-blackened stones surrounded the crackling fire. A tri-pod of iron rods reached their apex above it, and a blackened pot hung from it, just above the flickering tongues of flame. Something in the pot bubbled and steamed. Though I had no idea what it was, my stom-ach rumbled as I caught scent of it.

Roarke stepped over his saddle and into the fire-light. "Cruach, easy, boy." Roarke held out a hand to stop my approach. "I have a hound that travels with me. He doesn't take to strangers, so move slow and let him get used to you." He squatted down and clapped his hands twice. "Come on, Cruach. Meet Lachlan."

Out of the darkness bounded a huge hound with a broad, flat head and shaggy coat. In the mercurial light cast by the fire I thought the hound's coat shimmered silver, but the beast silhouetted himself against the fire too quickly for me to tell for certain. I did see, in the hound's shadowy head, two eyes full of *Chaosfire* and a mouth brimming with very big teeth.

In fact, I noticed the teeth about the same time I noticed that the animal was not slowing as it approached me. Before I could retreat, Cruach leaped up and dropped both forepaws on my shoulders. Unbalanced, I crashed backward and ended up with the hound pinning me to the ground. I felt the wiry hair of his chin against my throat and my nose was full of dog breath.

"Roarke," I squeaked, "some help here?"

The Axman laughed aloud and dropped on his butt, clutching his stomach. "Hold your hand out to him, easy, so he can sniff it."

"I think we are a bit past that stage, Roarke." I reached up with my left hand, willing to sacrifice it in case Cruach decided I was dinner. Roarke smiled and clapped his hands to call the beast off, but the hound ignored him. Cruach sniffed my face, then licked it with an incredibly soft tongue.

I got the impression I wasn't on the dog's menu.

I reached up and scratched Cruach behind his ears. As my fingers met stiff resistance on the beast's pelt, I looked over at Roarke. "His fur is steel!"

"True enough. Things like that happen in Chaos." Roarke reached over and pulled the dog off my chest. Cruach slid to the side and lay there beside me. He lifted his left forepaw and dropped it across my ribs.

Roarke shook his head. "You wouldn't have food on you—something he thinks is meant for him?"

"Sure, I have half a Tarris buffalo dressed and hidden here in my pocket."

"I wish that was true." The Axman straightened up and glanced in the stewpot. "Lentils, again."

"So your dog doesn't take to strangers, eh?" I crawled out from beneath the hound's paw and stood. Cruach came up on all fours, then leaned heavily against me. His shoulder came up to hand height on me, so I petted him. "Did you take Cruach into Chaos with you?"

Stirring the stew, he shook his head. "No, Cruach has been there a lot more than I ever have, as you can tell by the eyes and his pelt." Roarke smiled easily. "Cruach found me in Chaos and managed to help me home. Haven't been back in sixteen years or so."

I frowned. "Sixteen years? The Hamptons, in the next farm over, had hounds like Cruach here, and said they never live past ten or eleven years. That means Cruach is . . ."

"Different?" Roarke nodded quickly. "Things like that happen in Chaos."

"Lots odder things, as well." A black-haired woman whose long tresses were streaked with green walked into the circle of firelight. I noticed that the elbows and heels of her leather riding clothes had been capped with bony spurs that could be used in combat. *Chaosfire* totally filled her eyes, though even without it her slightly pointed ears and green hair would have marked her as someone who had spent a great deal of time in Chaos.

"Roarke, are you filling this youth's head with all sorts of romantic pictures of Chaos?" She gave me a quick, appraising glance that made me feel, momentarily, as if I were naked, then she shook her head. "He's only an Apprentice. Have mercy on him. Let him grow up before you tell him of Chaos."

"Lachlan is also Cardew's son, Eirene." Roarke rested his fists on his hips. "Chaos is bound to be in his blood."

Eirene arched an eyebrow above a black-opal eye. "So this is Cardew's get?" She tossed me one of the wooden bowls she was carrying. "Help yourself, Lachlan."

I caught the bowl deftly. "Thank you. I normally go by Locke, if it suits you." I waited for Roarke and Eirene to serve themselves, then took something less than either one of them had. Roarke gave me a wooden spoon, and I seated myself on the ground to eat. Cruach lay down beside me and put his head on my knee.

The lentil stew, flavored with bits of formerly dried beef, actually tasted fairly good. "Again, thank you. This is good."

Eirene smiled for a second, then narrowed her eyes. "So what are you doing on the road, Locke? Going off to win great battles in Chaos?"

Roarke frowned at the question, but I answered it without balking. "My grandmother wanted one of her grandsons to accompany her to the Bear's Eve Ball at the Imperial Palace."

"I am certain the balls have not been the same since your father and uncle stopped attending them." Eirene looked over at Roarke, and something passed between them, but I could not decipher it.

"You seem to have spent a long time in Chaos, Eirene." I set my half-finished stew down, taking care to keep it away from Cruach. "Did you know my father?"

"No, but his story is well enough known among Chaos Riders." She shrugged effortlessly, and I sensed some of her tension easing. "Your father led the Valiant Lancers into Chaos, and they did not come back. Your mother left the capital and returned to her father's home in Garik. She died, leaving you in the care of your grandfather." She shook her head. "It is best if Chaos Riders have no one left behind."

"How about you, Roarke? Did you know my father?"

Roarke hesitated for a second, then shook his head. "Same as Eirene—I know his story, but never met him."

"But you said you made payment on a debt when you pulled me away from Ferris. What were you talking about?"

Roarke glanced at Eirene, then smiled. "Out in Chaos many things are strange. There are places where time moves faster than it does here, sometimes very much faster. There are spots where you'd age to death and beyond, your bones being reduced to dust before they could hit the ground. You can tell them because they are big circles of white powder on otherwise normal ground. Your father ran into one of those spots and tricked a Chademon into it. I used his ruse to get myself out of a similarly difficult situation."

I accepted what Roarke told me as the truth, but I knew the Chaos Rider was holding something back. Roarke said he had not been in Chaos for sixteen years, which I believed was the truth. Unlike Eirene, Roarke only had the beginning of *Chaosfire* in his eye, so I guessed he had made only one or two expeditions in Chaos. Out there, somewhere, Roarke ran into something that made him never want to return beyond the wall. It followed, logically, that Roarke probably lost his eye at the same time. Given that sequence of events, I could easily understand his reluctance to talk much about Chaos.

Spooning more stew into my mouth, I noticed a rank badge I'd not seen before on Roarke's belt. Red on a black background, the Cavalry piece's silhouette marked Roarke as a Journeyman chess player. I smiled and swallowed quickly. "You play chess."

The Chaos Rider nodded. "Reached Journeyman rank two months ago on the previous trip to Herakopolis." He took a close look at my coat, then frowned when he saw no rank badge there for chess. "Do you play, or do you just want to learn?"

"I play, but never outside my family." I smiled. "If you want, we could play. I have a set."

Eirene groaned, and Cruach growled. Roarke looked sternly at both of them, then gave me the biggest smile I'd yet seen the man wear. "Set them up, Locke. I'll even give you the Empire to start."

3

"**C**heck." I smiled as I passed the board over to Roarke. The motion opened my coat to the cold wind, and I quickly pulled it closed against the mountain chill. "Sorry to trick you with that last gambit, but I had to offer it to you."

The Chaos Rider accepted the board and turned it around so he could view the game from behind his own lines. He rested the board on his left knee, which he had wrapped around the pommel of his saddle. The skin around his eyes tightened as he winced, then his steamy breath drifted up like smoke as he swore under his breath. "Chaos take you, Locke. You are a two-Cavalry player who has decided not to wear his badges just to vex me."

I reined Stail a bit back away from Roarke's horse as the mountain trail narrowed. "As I have told you, I've not been ranked. The village of Stone Rapids did not have a Master to test me."

Riding near the middle of the caravan, I looked back and saw half of it stretched out along the snowy switch-back trail leading up through the mountains to the City of Sorcerers. In just the half a day's climb from the forests to the alpine heights the weather had gotten cold. If the dark clouds coming up from the southwest made it into the mountains while still loaded with moisture from the ocean, we'd be buried in snow by dawn.

Trying to distract me during the game, Roarke had gone on about how this last snaky run would lead to the lip of the high mountain valley in which the sorcer-ers had built their citadel. Carved by centuries of wag-ons, horses, and other packbeasts, the trail had been ground into the granite rising above the last of the forests. Try as I might, while Roarke worked on his moves, I saw nothing to indicate we were really getting near the power source for the Ward Walls holding back Chaos.

To me, everything on the trip was new and utterly fascinating. Stone Rapids had been the largest human settlement I had ever seen, but the caravan itself had more people than the whole village *and* surrounding countryside. The geography around my grandfather's farm had been largely flat and very fertile, in direct con-trast to the rocky soil here in the foothills, or the gran-ite mountains where only lichen and scrub trees existed. The blue sky, which had been limitless at home, appeared smaller here, where the mountains sliced up into it.

And all that, I kept reminding myself, was normal. The things I had seen that had been touched by Chaos, like Cruach, were even more strange and intriguing. Despite Eirene's admonition about the fantasy of romance involving Chaos, I found myself drawn to hearing more about it. *Roarke said I had Chaos in my blood.* As I spent more time with Eirene, Roarke, and Cruach, I slowly realized that attending the Emperor's Ball, instead of being the adventure of a lifetime, could pale in comparison with actually going on an expedition into Chaos. Though I knew Chaos and the Bharashadi warrior Kothvir had killed my father, I found myself wanting to go beyond the wall.

The trail broadened again after we passed between two dolmen. I gently kicked Stail in the ribs, and the bay gelding responded by pulling up alongside Roarke. We rode two abreast for all of a minute, because Eirene and her mount worked their way back from the front of the caravan toward us. Stail liked the creature she sat astride no more than I, so I let Stail drift back in behind Roarke's mount.

Eirene's horse—at least I *thought* it had started life as a horse—had clearly spent a lot of time in Chaos. Instead of having a normal coat, a black-and-orange lizard-flesh covered the beast, though its mane and tail remained normal and black. Its eyes were full of *Chaosfire* and the two fangs protruding from either side of its muzzle gave it the look of a carnivore, which was what I assumed disturbed Stail. I had no idea what the creature ate and no real desire to find out, either.

It had taken me a day or two to figure it out, but the green in Eirene's hair and the points on her ears were not the only changes Chaos had wrought in her. When she smiled, especially in the daylight, I could see she had a set of fangs to rival those on her mount. I also gathered real quickly that the bony spurs on her elbows and heels were *not* part of her clothing.

When I asked Roarke to confirm my suspicions, he answered, "Things like that happen in Chaos." He also quickly added that Eirene was lucky because the changes Chaos created were not always symmetrical or easy to look at.

Eirene reined her mount in, stopping us. "Roarke, Haskell wants you to ride ahead and let the magickers know we're going to defile their valley again." She tapped his knee with her quirt. "Did you hear me?"

"That's what I've always liked about you, Eirene, your assumption I hear with my knee." Roarke looked up distractedly from the board. "I heard, and I obey. Locke, I resign, you win."

Eirene smiled. "Again?"

"Again and always." Roarke closed the hinged board and slipped the catch before he handed it back to me. "Next time."

I grinned like a wolf spotting a flock of sheep. "If you let me ride with you, we can play while the caravan catches up with us."

"Good idea." Roarke looked over at Eirene. "Keep an eye on Cruach. Ride on, Locke."

We reached the head of the caravan easily enough, and Haskell waved us on our way. The trail continued upward, but leveled off as it ran just below the mountain ridgeline. We rode along the shore of a lake fed by melting snow, and I saw ice already forming along the edges of the shore. Looking into the lake's murky green depths, I imagined I saw large *things* swimming about, and commented on them to Roarke.

"I doubt that, Locke. Hauntblood Lake supplies the water for the City of Sorcerers. Were there anything in it, it would have long ago been slain." He hesitated for a second, then grinned. "Then again, there just *might* be things in there, just to keep people from doing anything to the water supply."

"But why would anyone want to cause harm in the City of Sorcerers? They keep Chaos at bay."

"There are those who think Chaos should rule the land." Roarke coughed lightly into his hand. "The Empire has many enemies."

"But they are in Chaos, right?"

"Not all of them." Roarke reined his horse around a stone outcropping. "There are some people who think Chaos was preferable to life within the Wardlines."

I frowned heavily. "But that's insane. How could they hate the Empire? Life is good here."

"Is it?"

"Isn't it?"

Roarke nodded. "I think so, as do you, but not everyone agrees with us. The fact is that some people resent the order the Empire impresses on everything. They dislike the whole system of ranking, all the regulations and limitations. They're not creatures of Chaos per se, but their personalities are less than orderly."

The image of the whole Tugg brood back in Stone Rapids came to mind. "I've known people like that, true, but they didn't want Chaos to sweep over the world again."

"Of course not, but from their number are drawn those who do. There are not many of the virulent ones, but they can be quite dedicated to their cause. You must have heard of such things. Stone Rapids wasn't *that* small."

I shivered, and it wasn't just the cold. "The Church of Chaos Encroaching."

"Black Churchers." Roarke nodded slowly. "They are one group that believes Chaos should reign supreme. There are also other groups of renegade magickers who resent the hold the Grandmaster of Magicks has on magickal knowledge. While outwardly the Etheric brotherhood may disdain politics and interfering in the affairs of the Empire, they practice the manipulative art among themselves with great relish."

The last vestiges of my naive view of a world being united to oppose Chaos slowly evaporated. "You make things sound as if the Wardlines will collapse tomorrow."

A jet of steam shot out with Roarke's laugh. "Not at all, Locke. It's just that most folks overestimate the threat of Chaos, and underestimate the threat from within. It all balances to the level of terror we've grown used to, so you need not get all anxious about it. Still, the nice thing about Chaos is this: there you have a fairly good chance of knowing who your enemies are just by looking at them."

Rounding a bend, we entered a narrow pass through which the wind howled and a few flakes of snow swirled. I noticed the biting cold for all of a second or two, then slowly forgot about it. A hundred yards down the trail, halfway through the pass itself, I saw two gigantic granite statues. Winged humanoids both, the naked figures knelt on one knee and had their heads bowed. The one on the left, the bearded male figure, rested his hands on the hilt of a sword that had been driven into the ground. The female figure held a magick staff, and as we rode closer I could not see any chisel marks or weathering on either titanic carving.

"How old are these statues?"

Roarke shrugged. "Five centuries or so, I would guess. They date since the time of Chaos."

"They must have taken forever to carve out of the mountain." I craned my neck back to look up toward the woman's face. "She's bigger than the tallest tree around Stone Rapids."

"They're both big, and would have taken a long time to carve, but they were magicked into being." Roarke pointed to where the colossi joined the rocks behind them, then directed me to look up. In sharp contrast to the rough, craggy walls of the canyon, above us I saw a smooth chimney that looked eroded through the rock. "Some sorcerers caused the granite to run like water while others used their power to shape it into the statues you see. When the spell that liquefied the stone wore off, the statues solidified into the new shapes they had taken."

As we passed between the statues, Roarke rubbed at his missing eye, then spurred his horse forward. I matched Stail's gait to that of Roarke's stallion and followed the Chaos Rider through the rest of the pass. I felt a tingling all over my body as I rode between the two guardians and felt mildly uncomfortable. It seemed to me that the statues were watching me and studying me more closely than my grandfather had when I passed from Daggerman to Apprentice.

They marked the summit of the mountains, so the trail beyond them began to slope downward. It cut back and forth three times before opening out into a green valley. While riding through the latter half of the pass the feeling that I was being watched stayed with me, but I found it more easily explained as we got closer to the City of Sorcerers. I knew the narrow trail would prove an excellent ambush point for defenders higher up in the mountains, so I assumed sentries in hidden watching posts were keeping an eye on the both of us.

Roarke reined up as we entered the valley. A small blue river cascaded from the western end of the valley and splashed down into a pool on the valley floor approximately sixty feet below. From there it split the valley in half and provided water for the fields, which were, uncharacteristically for the time of year, green. From my vantage point I saw a few people in the fields, but no one seemed to be working at any particular task.

The road wound its way down into the valley and toward the east end split, where one part headed south toward Duaropolis and the main branch continued on to Herakopolis. Near the crossroads tents and pavilions marked the campsite of at least one other caravan. I could not tell if it was heading toward the capital or back toward Garik, but I assumed it had arrived earlier that day, as people still appeared to be erecting shelters for the night.

Coming around a granite finger, I got my first glimpse of the City of Sorcerers, and, with it, all other details of the valley dwindled to insignificance. Massive obsidian battlements encircled the city and gleamed brightly in the sunlight. One of eight towers sprouted from the top of the wall at each main point of the circle, and red pennants flew from the tops of them. By squinting and carefully counting archers' ports, I figured each tower to be four stories high, yet the towers were but a third of the height of the walls upon which they stood.

Yet taller than those towers, a single spire rose from the center of the city. Its gentle spiral fluting made the blackish purple tower look more like a horn grown up out of the ground than any construct made by the hand of man. At its pinnacle something glittered and sparkled like a captive star, its light starting at bright shades of white and yellow, then shifting through green and red to blue and purple. The light show seemed familiar, but it took me a moment to recall where I had seen it before. When it came to me, it did so with crystal clarity—I had seen it in Eirene's *Chaosfire* eyes.

As we rode closer my eyes confirmed what I already knew in my soul. The citadel's walls showed no seams where block had been fitted to block. Their smooth exterior was unmarked by signs of construction or siege. "They did this all with their magick, too, did they not?"

Roarke nodded his head respectfully. "They built their city in a manner similar to that they used to create the pass guardians. Bear in mind, however, obsidian is not a stone you find in these mountains. It came all the way from Kea, and the city itself appeared almost overnight."

I rode in awed silence the rest of the way toward the city. As its heights soared above me, I kept trying to think of ways to describe it to Geoff when I returned home. I knew it would take a Songsmaster to adequately paint a word picture of the majesty and the sheer power of the monument to themselves the sorcerers had created. If this was indeed the source of the power that kept the Ward Walls in place, I did not fear their coming down anytime soon.

The two of us rode up to the main gate, and, following Roarke's example, I dismounted. As we turned our horses over to a pair of young men, an armored guardsman left a doorway built into the siege wall itself and marched over to greet us.

"Back already, Roarke? I thought you would stay with Haskell in Garik this winter."

"Haskell decided to winter in Herak." Roarke shrugged, pulled off his mittens, and blew on his hands. "A gaggle of merchants decided to make the run for Bear's Eve before the snow closes the passes and offered Haskell enough money to make it worth my while. Besides, Aneurin, I wanted to see if you made Captain as you were bragging you would."

The redheaded warrior hooked a finger through his ceremonial sash and displayed a badge proudly. It showed three squares of white arrayed in an arrow pattern within a circle on a background of red. "Made Captain right after you left. How many people are in the caravan?"

"Fifty and two hundred, with one hundred wagons." Roarke looked back out toward an expanse of field a bit west of the area occupied by the other caravan. "This company is fairly self-contained and not too disruptive. A metals merchant has some simpleton sellswords attending him. If some of your fighters so desire, they can earn some money wagering on duels. If you put us on Southfield, we will not be any problem."

"Good. I will dispatch a man to clear the way between the Guardians for you." Aneurin looked back toward the gate. "Do you want to see Zavendir?"

Roarke nodded. "As always. I know the way."

"Let these two pass," Aneurin shouted to the guards near the doorway. "Good luck, Roarke. He granted me a two-Pawn advantage and still had me in thirty moves."

Roarke answered Aneurin's grin with a wry smile, then turned and led me on into the City of Sorcerers. The tall tunnel leading through the wall looked to be a good forty feet long to me, and at least half that in height. At the entrance, all but hidden in a dark cut near the ceiling, I saw a raised portcullis that I assumed would block the way if an invading army ever tried to enter the city. Overhead, in disturbingly neat rows, I saw two sets of archers' ports on either side of the tunnel, and a line of murderholes drilled at the apex of the tunnel's arch. I had no doubt that breaching the portcullis would be the rough equivalent of committing suicide for the warriors foolish enough to attempt it.

At the far end we passed through a small human-sized doorway cut in the left of two stout oaken doors. Inside I noticed that a wooden bar as wide as my own chest held the doors shut. I also noticed some heavy blocks against which other wooden braces could be placed to help hold the doors shut.

Within the shadow of the walls I saw a smaller, seamless wall grown up out of the native granite. Tiny houses, shops, and stalls lined the double-wide street between the two walls. While I found the scene utterly normal to the eye, my ears thought they had been frozen clean off. I saw people shopping in the bazaar, but heard none of the excited shouts or haggling that would have filled the streets on market day in Stone Rapids. Instead the lot of them—buyers and sellers both—gesticulated wildly and with such a definite purpose to their motions that I wondered if they weren't all moontouched.

"Roarke," I whispered, "why is everyone so quiet?"

The Chaos Rider smiled broadly and replied in a normal but subdued voice. "This is the City of Sorcerers, my friend. Working great magicks—and even training in lesser ones—requires concentration. Those who live just outside the city have developed a unique method of communication to provide the solitude needed for the magickers to do their work."

I blinked away my surprise. "What about inside the city itself?"

Roarke shrugged. "Only magickal adepts are allowed inside the city, so only they know what happens there." To forestall any further questions, he raised a finger to his lips, then led me through the streets toward the west. About a tenth of the way around the circle of the city, Roarke ducked into an arched doorway leading back into the obsidian wall. I followed close behind as he mounted a set of stairs in the right wall and climbed up three flights to a circular landing. It had a silver diamond set three feet from the floor on the westernmost point of the circle. When I joined him on the landing, Roarke pressed his right hand to the device.

I felt an invisible force ripple over me as a split appeared in the seamless rock. It bisected the diamond top to bottom. As the split widened in front of me, I glanced backward and saw the passage back to the stairs narrowing. I thought, at first, that the sides of the circle might be shifting around on some hidden mechanism, but when I looked at where the floor joined the wall, I couldn't see a seam. Furthermore, I saw the patterns in the rock shifting as if I were looking at them under running water. As the wall eclipsed the stairs, and the silver diamond re-formed itself there on the other side, I suddenly realized I'd just seen a practical demonstration of the magick that created the City of Sorcerers.

Roarke slapped me on the back. "These magickers greatly enjoy knowing their power impresses people. Try to act surprised."

I choked back a laugh. "Act? Perhaps when my heart stops beating like a war drum."

Roarke escorted me into a fair-sized room furnished with a small table, four chairs, a sideboard, and two sleeping pallets. The table had a chessboard on it, with the pieces already set up. The Emperor's Pawn had already been advanced two rows. The sideboard had a platter of bread and cheese on it, as well as a pewter pitcher and two goblets. Until I looked at the food, and my mouth began to water, I did not realize how hungry I was.

Off to my right, a large circular section of the siege wall's interior lightened toward transparency, granting us a view of the City of Sorcerers. Roarke ran his fingers along a rectangular strip of silver set beside the window, with each stroke making it more clear. "Here, Locke, this is about the best vantage point outsiders get on the city."

I did my best to keep my teeth clenched so my jaw would not gape open. The window looking out showed us to be on a higher level than the interior wall, though I felt fairly certain the stairs we had climbed had not been *that* long. *More magick, no doubt.*

The City of Sorcerers looked, to me, like a huge wheel that had as its hub the tall, black tower swirling up from its heart. From my position I detected multiple architectural styles, each conforming to the boundaries that looked to comprise one-eighth of the city itself. I vaguely recalled someone in the caravan having mentioned eight different schools of magick, so I assume each section of the city was home to one of the schools.

"It is a very strange place." Roarke pointed toward a sector where the buildings had a spartan simplicity about them. "That is where mages learn spells of a martial nature. At night you can see flashes of light and glowing balls exploding as they practice their spell casting."

I tried to focus my attention on another section of the city, but found that the outlines of the buildings kept shifting. At times they mirrored the city sectors on either side, then they faded or changed colors. "What goes on there?"

"Concealment magicks. That is the specialty of my brother, Zavendir, isn't it, Zav?"

I spun as the magicker's image wavered into view. He sat in the chair behind the Imperial board position. "I should have known better than to try to fool you, Roarke." He saluted the Chaos Rider with an upraised cup of wine. "What gave me away?"

Roarke pointed to the sideboard. "Three chairs, but only two cups and a line of liquid running down the front of the pitcher. Furthermore, you have drenched yourself with some perfume that I could not help but noticing."

Zavendir shrugged. "When I heard there were two of you I hoped one was that delightful creature Eirene."

"Liar. If you thought she was going to be here, you would have only had one pallet in this room so you could offer her more hospitable accommodations in your home."

"You know me too well, brother."

I looked from Roarke to Zavendir and noted a similarity to their noses that could mean they were kin. In fact they looked more alike than Dalt and I did. "Wait, Roarke, how did you notice all that with the wine?"

"How? I trained myself to be observant. Being observant is what will keep you alive in Chaos."

"Then why haven't you been back?"

Zavendir answered for the Chaos Rider. "There are times you can observe too much."

I blushed. "Forgive me."

"Curiosity is nothing to forgive, Locke, provided it does not get out of hand." Roarke moved from the window and, pressing a hand to the middle of my back, directed me toward the chair opposite the mage. "Now my curiosity prompts me to discover how you will fare against a Master rank player."

Zavendir looked at the badges on my coat, then glanced up his brother. "He is not even a Pawn. What is this?"

"Consider it 'discovered check.'" He gave my shoulder a squeeze. "Go ahead, Lachlan. Show him there's magick that can be worked on the board, too."

4

"Ouch!" I sucked at my needle-stuck finger.

Eirene glanced over and gave me a grin full of pointed teeth. "I have seen fewer holes in a dead Chademon."

I grumbled and shrugged, then showed her the front of my jacket. "You can see I am ranked only in sword-fighting and, now, chess. A seamster I am not."

"Nor likely to become one if you keep trying to attach that badge to your finger." Roarke gave the bubbling stewpot one final stir, then stood, his knees creaking as he did so. "This has got the last of the spice Zavendir gave me a week ago, so you had best enjoy it."

I filled my wooden bowl, then went back and leaned against Cruach to eat the steaming rice-and-lentil gruel. In the time since I had met Roarke and Eirene, the Chaos Riders had all but adopted me. I combined my supplies with theirs and had even taken a turn cooking—though both of them decided after that I need not share in *those* duties. To compensate I assigned myself the job of finding firewood and fetching water when we needed it, which meant Roarke and Eirene usually had a fire waiting for them when they finished their work of helping to settle the camp down.

During the days I rode mostly with Roarke as an outrider or a scout. While the rolling hills that led down to the sea plains of Herak were not exactly full of danger, to me they could have been in the very midst of Chaos itself. Roarke did not talk overmuch, but he did take time to point out things of interest and help to expand my meager knowledge of woodcraft and geography.

Eirene remained cordial, too, but aloof, which bothered me a bit at first. I thought, initially, she was just being polite in covering her dislike for me. Later I got a chance to contrast her behavior around others with the way she treated me, and discovered she gave me a lot more latitude in asking questions and doing things my own way than she did other caravan guards. I decided that the caution which had kept her alive in Chaos and her comment about how Chaos Riders ought not to have people to leave behind meant she didn't let people get close to her. I gave her plenty of room to be herself, and our relationship thawed a bit.

Fairly often Roarke or other members of the caravan's guards used me as a messenger between them and Haskell or someone else in the group. In this way I got to know Haskell, the burly, swarthy caravan master, and the man praised my ability to repeat messages and make reports in a clear, concise, and exact manner. Haskell even hinted that a position with the caravan could be mine if I wanted to hire on for the return trip in the spring.

The winter wind hissing through the bare branches of the trees overhead reminded me a bit of Stone

Rapids. I surprised myself when I realized I was actually weighing the good points and bad of staying with the caravan and never returning home. While I knew I would miss Geoff and Dalt and Grandfather, something inside felt hollow when I realized that I felt no great desire to return to Stone Rapids. Traveling with the caravan and talking with Roarke had opened up a world that I had glimpsed in books, and had kindled a desire in me to see faraway places. Stone Rapids had nothing to offer that could rival the Imperial capital and Chaos.

Sadly I discovered that I had already begun to change. In the City of Sorcerers I had actually *beaten* a chess Master! In just over a week I would be a guest at the Imperial Palace, attending the Bear's Eve Ball. I could not imagine anyone from Stone Rapids having done what I had done and would do, then returning to the village to live contentedly. This realization both thrilled me and shamed me.

I ran my hand over the Novice patch Zavendir had awarded me. Looking up, I asked Roarke a question. "Do you think Zavendir was upset that I beat him?"

"How can you ask that?" Roarke frowned and set his bowl down. "You played him in three games. He beat you the first time, you beat him the second, and you drew the third game. Upset? He was thrilled someone was able to offer him more of a challenge than I do. What makes you ask?"

I dipped a finger into my gruel, then held it out for Cruach to lick clean. "I wondered because Zavendir made me a Novice, but I had beaten him . . ."

"I see your confusion." Roarke picked his bowl up. "Zavendir could make you a Novice, which jumped you past the rank of Pawn, but no more. While he is ranked as a Master, he only wears white thread in it. Because it is an avocation with him and he is not paid to be a

Chessmaster, he cannot confer upon you more than two ranks. He has, however, given me the name of a Gold-thread Chessmaster in Herak who, after a few games, could assign you to your proper rank."

"I understand now, I think." I smiled sheepishly. "Growing up in a very small village, I had little experience with ranking and testing. My grandfather only let me test up to the rank of Apprentice, obviously, and we had no one ranked in chess at all."

"Ranking protocols can be strange." Roarke scratched at the corner of his left eye. "Given that I started with the ax late in life, I will never progress above this rank. Don't have a pedigree for my training, you see."

Eirene pointed her wooden spoon at him. "Not that patches or ranking mean much in Chaos. There it's just the edge on your weapon and your ability to keep wielding it that matters."

My grandfather's admonition to trust myself instead of patches again rang in my ears. As the caravan moved on and got closer and closer to Herakopolis, I found myself considering who and what I was. I knew I was a better swordsman and a better chess player than my patches indicated, but was that really important? To many people, because my father had been elevated to the rank of legend, nothing I could do would be sufficient to please them. I wondered if I would be accepted in the capital for being who I was, or would I be damned for the differences between who my father had been and what I had grown up to be?

Part of me braced for such a disaster. I hoped everything in the capital would be wonderful, but my nervousness at meeting the grandmother I could not remember started to gnaw away at me. In Stone Rapids I had heard enough stories about this person or that having met my father, that I dreaded hearing the same from people who had known him when he had become a hero. As we reached the plains outside the capital, and my time to leave the caravan behind drew near, my reluctance to do so grew.

I eagerly devoured anything and everything Roarke told me about Chaos and his years spent as a caravan guard. I devoted a lot of time listening to stories told around the campfires in the caravan. In the process I discovered that many of the books I had read in Stone Rapids were hopelessly out-of-date, which helped increase my anxiety. Whereas I had studied particularly hard so I wouldn't appear to be a lackwit from Garik, I found all my knowledge appropriate for the time when my father first traveled to the capital almost twoscore years before.

Then, all of a sudden, it occurred to me that my father might well have had the same concerns and fears I did when he rode to the capital at my age. Though I harbored no illusions that I was in any way my father, I knew the capital had not killed him when he arrived. I decided to assume that, were I true to myself, I could avoid embarrassment. Moreover, if anyone decided to fit me with a bumpkin badge, they would be more the fools for it than I.

After supper I wandered down to the nearby stream to draw a bucket of water for washing up. A chill breeze nipped at my nose and ears, so I walked with my shoulders hunched against the cold and my eyes looking down at the twisting trail. In the twilight rocks and roots made the trek dangerous—if not to life and limb, certainly to one's self-respect, as taking a tumble would undoubtedly make news faster in the camp than one's return.

I made it to the stream uneventfully, dunked my bucket into the water, and turned to make my way back to the camp when I saw her standing at the foot of the path. I nodded to her respectfully. "Evening, Miss . . ."

Her icy blue eyes narrowed. "Who are you?"

I must have looked like a fish that had just jumped from the stream and landed on the bank, because I stared at her gape-mouthed. That question didn't stump me, of course, but her tone of voice surprised me completely. She demanded an answer of me, but an undertone of fear colored her words.

The fear almost seemed appropriate for her because at first glance she could easily be taken for a timid thing. Small and fine-boned, she seemed almost child-like. Her flesh had a translucency that didn't reveal the bones beneath it, but suggested she would shatter like porcelain if hit. Her large eyes contributed to the image of helplessness.

The fire in them also worked against it. Her brilliantly red hair covered her shoulders and framed a face that was pretty now, but clearly would become beautiful as she grew into womanhood. There was no real mistaking her for a child, yet it was also hard to describe her as a woman. She was caught in that in-between stage of adolescence—a stage from which I was slowly emerging myself—so I felt a vague kinship with her.

I closed my mouth, then opened it again to answer her. "My name is Lachlan. I come from Garik province, from Stone Rapids."

She shook her head vehemently, allowing her straight hair to lash back and forth against her pale throat. "No, that's not it. That's not what you are called in my dreams."

I raised an eyebrow. "Your dreams?" I'd never had anyone say I'd been in their dreams before.

"My dreams, yes." She frowned. Glancing down at the ground, she touched two fingers of her left hand to her left temple. "I see things. In dreams and in visions, I see them. I have seen you as a warrior—older, fatter somewhat. You fight demons in Chaos."

"These things you see, are they of the past or of the future?"

She shrugged her slender shoulders weakly, as if the green woolen cloak she wore had been woven of Cruach's fur. "Some is past, much is future, but I cannot distinguish which is which in some cases. With you I cannot tell."

As much as I would have liked to believe she was seeing visions of me as a Chaos Rider, from the description I knew she was seeing my father. "They are visions of the past. That's my father you see."

"No, no, don't be silly." Her eyes flicked up toward me, sending a jolt through me. "Don't you think I would know what I see?"

"But you just said . . ."

"You don't understand!" She spun on her heel and stalked off back toward camp.

I started after her, then realized I'd forgotten the bucket. I went back for it and hurried along as fast as I could, but I couldn't catch up with her. Somewhat bewildered, I returned to our campsite and sat myself down next to Roarke. "Something weird just happened."

"Oh?" Roarke slid to the left as Cruach lay down between us. "What was that?"

"Down at the stream I met this girl. I think she joined us at the City of Sorcerers—I mean I think I've caught glimpses of her a couple of times since then. Small, red hair . . ."

Roarke nodded and scratched the dog behind an ear. "You met Xoayya. She did join us at the City of Sorcerers. They were sending her home."

"Really? Why?"

"She's a wild talent, a feral mage." Roarke gave me a half smile. "Among warriors the equivalent would be a natural-born fighter. If you take a scrapper like that and give him some training, he usually turns out pretty well."

I nodded. "But with magick the problem is not one that is so easy to train, right?"

"Exactly." The Axman snapped a small stick in half and tossed it into our fire. "Haskell said Xoayya's mother died when she was young. Her father was a fairly wealthy merchant who married into another merchant family. His bride was on her second marriage, too, and had two daughters who were slightly older than Xoayya."

"And they treated her badly . . ."

"No, they actually doted on her and spoiled her. Xoayya was sheltered because they thought her very frail. When she started reporting she had visions, they thought her a bit insane and did what they could to cover up her little stories. Her father died somewhere along the line and it wasn't until her mother's mother intervened that anyone realized she was very talented in the way of Clairvoyant magick. By that time, though, the girl was untrainable and not much of a fan of discipline and hard work."

I frowned. "I don't understand that. I mean, I lost both of my parents, and yet I'm not afraid of hard work."

"No, but you were trained to it from early on. She wasn't." Roarke shrugged. "There's also some hint that, at least in the case of her father, she foresaw how he died and feels she might have been able to prevent his death."

"Could she have?"

"You have multiple questions wrapped up there together, Locke. First you have to figure out if what she saw was accurate, or just a dream. When spells are invoked to look into the future, as I understand it, there is no solid way of telling if the vision is true or not. Clairvoyance is supposed to work best when the time factor is minimized."

Roarke held up a hand. "In addition to that question, you have a more important one to look at. It is this: is the future seen the only possible future?"

I shook my head. "I don't understand."

"Let's suppose you decide to get up now and go fetch more water. Or let's suppose you change your mind and sit back down. Now what if what had been foreseen was along the time line that required you to get up and get water now? Since you didn't do that, does that future no longer exist?"

"Ahhh, I see." I nodded. "Or, is the fact that it's been seen something that compels me to do everything that needs to be done to make that future come true."

"Right. Are we creatures of free will, or is our future determined for us and we just become players in a production for which we don't have a script?"

I closed my eyes and rubbed at them for a moment. "I opt for free will, but aren't there prophecies and the like that predict the future?"

"Sure there are, but take a good look at them. Oracles that make such pronouncements always do so in vague terms. Your father, it was said, was destined to kill the Chademon Kothvir, but no method was specified. If your father had run him through or served him bad oysters, either method would have fulfilled the prophecy. Lots of room for free will there."

"Fascinating."

"Free will versus determinism is one of those discussions that can make long rides much shorter." Roarke clapped me on the shoulder. "So, what did she say to you?"

"She wanted to know who I was and why I'd invaded her dreams. She saw me fighting in Chaos." I shrugged. "Sounds like she saw my father, but she didn't like that suggestion. She marched off in a huff."

"Wild talents are like that. They don't have the control over their ability. With Clairvoyants it's especially hard because they can never be sure what they are thinking. For all you know she'll see her meeting with you as a vision and never be able to sort truth from dreams." Roarke smiled. "She's a cute one, though. Having her dream of you can't be all bad."

"Not my type."

"You grew up on a farm with your two brothers and your grandfather. When did you have time to determine you have a type?"

I started to explain about all the Bear's Eve celebrations I'd attended, but I stopped. "No matter what I say, you're going to make me feel foolish, right?"

"Gotta get back at you somehow for beating me so often in chess, don't I?"

Riding ahead of the caravan through a snow-dusted meadow on the last day, I caught up with Roarke. "The night we met you said you knew stories of my father."

Roarke's lean body swayed with the motion of his horse's walk. "I did, didn't I?"

"How did my father die in Chaos?"

"I don't know what happened to your father." Roarke exhaled a plume of steam. "I *heard* he went on an expedition and never came back, but then again I heard he's buried with your mother back in Stone Rapids. When Chaos is linked to a legend you can never tell truth from fiction."

I felt my mouth go dry. "Was my father a good Chaos Rider?"

Roarke smiled easily. "That he was. Whereas other men would just use muscle against the Chademons, Cardew foxed them. He said, I'm told, fighting in Chaos was like a big chess game. He had mapped out many of the areas where time flows differently, figured out what the difference was, and was able to use that map to his advantage."

My face brightened. "How did he determine what the time-rate difference was?"

The Chaos Rider arched his back and rotated his shoulders to loosen them. "Cardew was a thinker, he was. He took two twelve-foot-long planks and lashed hourglasses between them at the far ends of the boards. When he found a boundary he would insert one hourglass beyond it, then invert the whole contraption. By looking at how much sand was left in one when the other ran out, he was able to calculate the difference."

"That *was* smart!" I smiled proudly. "He could use fast zones to speed healing for lightly wounded people and slow zones to secure his flanks."

"Like father, like son." Roarke winked his right eye at me. "That is very much the sort of thing he did. One time he had a man who had been mortally wounded. He placed him in a very slow zone, then sent riders all the way back to Port Chaos to fetch a magicker who could spell the man back to health."

"But you don't know what happened to him—my father, I mean?"

Roarke shook his head. "I don't know. Cardew and the leader of the Black Shadows, Kothvir, had quite a rivalry. Kothvir even forged a sword with a likeness of your father etched into the blade. Mark of being a dangerous man, that is, to have a *vindictxvara* made to deal with you. And Kothvir stopped being a force among the *Bharashadi* at the same time your father disappeared, so perhaps Cardew got him after all."

I had heard a similar thing in the past, but it felt good to have a Chaos Rider say it instead of a bard. "You said there were pockets of Chaos in which time moved very slowly, correct?"

"Yes."

"So it is possible that my father and my uncle are still alive and trapped in one of those zones, or that they have been wounded and exiled themselves to one of them?"

The hopeful note in my voice seemed to make Roarke wince. "It is possible, Locke, but not entirely likely. I would rather bet that the sun and moons will collide than on your kin still being alive, I'm sorry to say."

"But it could be true." My eyes narrowed. "You said it yourself, 'things like that happen in Chaos.'"

"So I did, Locke, but I didn't say they happened all that often." Roarke shook his head. "Anyone expecting to find a miracle in Chaos better be damned lucky, or prepared for a big disappointment."

Cresting the hill on Herakopolis's western edge, I saw a city that exceeded even Roarke's glowing descriptions of it. Some of the larger estates in the outlying district had seriously impressed me, and I had embarrassed myself by refusing to believe that one or more of them were *not* the Emperor's property. That individuals would have amassed enough money to own one building that itself was larger than my grandfather's homestead quickly redefined my concept of personal wealth.

The capital started me redefining my concept of reality. Stretched out in a vast demilune around Herak Bay, the city consisted, for the most part, of whitewashed buildings with red tile roofs. Gaudily colored clothes flapped in the sea breeze from lines strung between many of the buildings, setting whole portions of the city in motion. A seawall and breakwater split the azure bay from the deeper ocean, while huge walls rimmed the city itself to protect from landward assaults.

The Imperial Palace dominated the top of the highest hillock in the city. A monstrously large building, each of the eight wings had been built by artisans from the different provinces. They worked with native materials from their homelands and created in the palace a simulacrum of the Empire as a whole. Appropriate provincial flags flew from the towers that capped each wing, while the white triskele flag of the Empire flew above the heart of the palace itself.

Northeast of it I saw a strange collection of buildings, each with a different architectural style, yet all arrayed around a central green. "Is that the Imperial University?"

"You see, the book you read about the capital was not all that antiquated." Roarke glanced back along the road at the distant line of the caravan, then looked at the city again. "And there, to the north, is the Imperial Theatre. It is the stepped circular building with all those pillars. The one in white marble."

"I see it. And that must be the Street of the Gods." I pointed to a double rank of tall buildings with towers topped by stars and moons and animals. "And, obviously, that's the waterfront."

"Correct." Roarke again looked back at the caravan, then frowned. "Listen, Locke, I have to ride back to the caravan and get the papers we have to present at the gate. You should ride ahead to your grandmother's house. Do you know how to find it?"

"If the streets have not been changed in the last forty years." I laughed. "I ride past the Church of the Sunbird for two streets. I go east and then north along Butcher's Row. She lives in the fourth house on the right as you go up the hill."

Roarke nodded with pride. "Spoken like you've lived in the capital for ages."

"Thank you for your friendship on this trip. Will you, if you have time, come see me?" I asked quietly. "Will you bring Cruach?"

"The hound will probably hunt you out on his own, the way you feed him." Roarke gave me a reassuring smile. "After Bear's Eve, I will find you. Unless they decide to sail you back to Stone Rapids, I think Haskell will have work for you with his first caravan heading west again."

"If you don't, I'll hunt you down at the Umbra." I grinned as he looked a bit surprised at my naming a tavern that catered to Chaos Riders. "See, I remembered everything you told me about Herakopolis."

"Sharp lad, but I don't recall mentioning the Umbra."

"You must have; I know I didn't read about it." I shrugged. "Bye, Roarke. Say good-bye to Eirene for me. Have a happy Bear's Eve."

"And you, lad. Try not to step on any princess's toes when you're dancing in polite company."

"I won't, promise." I tugged gently on Stail's reins and started toward the capital of the Empire. I joined the trickle of other folks entering the city, and the guardsman leaning against the wall barely gave me notice. By keeping an eye on the Sunbird Church's tallest spire, I managed to negotiate the narrow, cobblestone streets of the city's oldest section. The Street of the Gods proved to be a wide boulevard that I crossed easily.

I turned where I had been told to turn and located Butcher's Row by seeing a bloody stream washing down the gutter. Heading up the hill, I counted houses once, then frowned and counted them again. *Grandfather told me it was the fourth house, but it can't be. That one is so . . . so* big!

Audin had always spoken of my father's mother in decidedly neutral terms, though he regularly expressed his disbelief at a woman of Garik finding happiness in Herakopolis. I knew very well the story of this girl from Stone Rapids marrying a merchant from the Imperial capital, but I had always assumed, from the way Grandfather told the story, that Evadne's husband, before he died, owned a bazaar stall and sold copper pots.

Somewhat stunned by the size of the three-story building, I dismounted and just let Stail's reins drop to the ground. Clearly this house belonged to someone more important than a bazaar barker's widow. The wall around it hid the ground floor from sight, but trees and ivy vines overhanging it from the inside told me the house had a nice garden. I heard the tinkling of water landing in a pool, so that meant they had a fountain as well. The windows themselves were fitted with glass—much akin to the home of Stone Rapids's Lord Mayor—but the blue and gold brocade drapes I saw in them were a lot finer than the Mayor had managed.

Even the stories Aunt Ethelin had told of this house had underestimated its grandeur. I turned around and counted one final time. It was the fourth house, but I couldn't get rid of a sense of dread as I reached out and pulled the clapper cord for the bell beside the gate. It rang loud and strong, like an alarm bell, and I almost ran away because I just knew I had to be in the wrong place.

I probably would have run, but seconds after the bell's echoes died, I heard a door open and close. I saw an old man accompanied by two hounds a bit smaller than Cruach come trudging up the crushed-stone carriageway toward the wrought-iron gate. I smiled at the man, but nothing short of a hive's worth of honey could have sweetened the sour look on his face.

The man grabbed two of the gate's iron bars. "And who would you be?"

"I am Lachlan. I have traveled from Stone Rapids to see my grandmother, Evadne, and accompany her to the Emperor's Ball." I stood up straight and wished I'd brushed the trail dust from my boots. "She sent for me."

"Did she now?" The man scratched at a scraggly beard. "And who was it who sent you?"

I frowned. "My grandfather, Audin, Bladesmaster of Stone Rapids. He arranged a contest to choose from among my brothers and me for the honor of answering her request."

The badges the man wore sewn to his sleeve marked him as a native of Herak and Evadne's gardener. "So you're claiming to be one of Cardew's sons, or are you Driscoll's whelp?"

"Cardew, sir." I answered him fairly, only realizing at the last that he was baiting me.

"Fifth one this week. Just because she has a good heart, every orphan claims to be Cardew or Driscoll's bastard." The man backed away from the gate and waved me off. "Begone with you, or I'll set the dogs on you. Bear's Eve is still a week off, so you'll not be bedeviling my mistress for seasonal beggings today." He turned and wandered back toward the house.

Angry and embarrassed, I yanked the clapper cord once, hard, and the sound stopped the man cold. "Herakman, I will remain here and pull this cord once every ten heartbeats if you do not tell your mistress I am here. I am Lachlan, and I am here at her request."

"Away, beggar, away! I'll not be bothering her over the likes of you." He turned his back on me and muttered to his hounds as he headed back to the house.

Mad enough to spit fire, I turned and whistled for Stail. The gelding trotted up to me, and I pulled myself into the saddle. Turning the horse around to take one last look at the house before I rode out to rejoin the caravan, I saw the man hurrying back toward the gate. The dogs both had run to the gate before him, and I took no joy in their eyeing me with their tails wagging.

I assumed he was running to get his dogs, but he held up his hands. "Wait, wait, young Master."

I hardly felt the desire, but I kept my voice seasonably cordial. "What is it, Goodman?"

"I'd know that whistle anywhere, I would, and the hounds did, too. That's from Audin to your father to you." The old man squinted at me. "Sure as the sun rises in the east, you're Cardew's son."

He unlatched the gate and swung it wide open. "Welcome to Herakopolis, Master Lachlan. I trust you will enjoy your stay."

5

The man bade me dismount, which I did, and he took up the reins of my horse. "I will be putting your horse in the charge of the stableboy, Master Lachlan." He gave me a wink, and the twinkle in his eye told me that by benefit of my blood, I had passed muster with him. Still, the formality in his address of me made me feel uneasy.

"Call me Locke; everyone does." One of his hounds brought its head up under my right hand, so I scratched it behind the right ear.

The man gave me a half nod of his gray-capped head, but then shook his head in full denial. "Might be the way it is out in the wilds of Garik, Master Lachlan, but not here in the capital of the Empire. We knows the proper ways to talk and all. Your kindness is appreciated, but your grandmother is a grand lady in this city, and I'll not do her disrespect by calling you familiar-like."

"Thank you," I hesitated, not knowing the man's name.

"Nob, sir, just Nob." He smiled infectiously. "Andrew is the stableboy, and my grandsons help him out. James, he sees to the house—'cept where me wife, Rose, holds sway. Been with your grandmother for years and years, we all have, save my grandsons."

I pulled my saddlebags from the bay and looped them over my right shoulder. "Then you would have known my father?"

"Met him on numerous occasions, sir. To these old, tired eyes you look his spitting image, too, Master Lachlan." Nob looked me up and down, head to toe, and nodded proudly. "Was him what taught me chess. I ne'er did get ranked, and he always beat me, but he said as how I was getting better."

"If I want a game, I will find you."

"That would be nice, sir. You'll whip me good, of that I am certain, but I can show you a few things I've learned since your father, well, since the last time I played him."

I clapped Nob on the shoulder and gave him a nod. "I will look forward to that." I let him lead Stail off toward the stables in the back and headed directly toward the secondary entrance to the mansion. Part of me realized I probably should have gone to the front door and made a proper entrance, but the house felt too familiar for me to go through such formality.

I kicked the steps twice to knock the dust from my boots, then upped the latch and walked into the kitchen. Immediately the sweet scent of pies and bread baking in the ovens hit me. I shut the door quickly against the cold and luxuriated in the warmth being put out by the ovens.

Without looking up, the older woman kneading

dough at the table in the center of the kitchen jerked her head toward the water pump behind her. "Nob, you worthless lout, I told you not to dawdle. I need some water, and I'm not of a mind to pump it meself."

I let my saddlebags slide to the stone floor. "Nob is taking care of my horse. I will draw your water."

At the sound of my voice her head came up, and her jaw slackened. An apple-cheeked woman with hair as iron gray as Nob's, she stared at me with gray eyes as steady as stone. "It's you! Forgive me, my lord. We were expecting you, but . . ."

I held up my hands. "Nothing to be forgiven. I am Lachlan." I crossed the room in three long strides and scooped up the wooden water bucket. I hung it by the rope handle on the little hook beneath the pump's spout. "Rose, your baking smells wonderful."

"Oh, Master Lachlan, I didn't mean for you to get the water. Let me."

I brushed her suggestion aside with a wave of my right hand. "Nonsense, good woman, I will pump your water. After a month fetching it from cold mountain streams and lugging it back to camp, I had begun to think a pump was but a faery tale."

She wiped her hands on her apron and reached for the bucket. "I will handle it from here, Master Lachlan."

I pulled it from the hook and held it out of her reach. "Where do you want it?"

She pointed to the table, and I lifted it to the spot she indicated, even though I knew that would not be its final destination. The way she and Nob deferred to me made me feel uncomfortable, but it also made me feel proud. I did not feel I was better than they were by any stretch of the imagination, but I took their attitude, as Nob had explained, as a reflection of their love for my grandmother. I could also have imagined my father playing such games with them when he lived here.

A gaunt man in quite fine clothing appeared in the doorway to the kitchen. His tunic and breeches were not of homespun, and the latter had been fitted with buttons to draw them tight at the knees. He wore white hose and freshly polished black shoes with a big silver buckle on them. His waistcoat and breeches were the same color as his shoes, the buttons on them being silver as well, while his shirt was white.

I knew he was James, and I sensed instantly that he knew me better than I knew myself. It was an uneasy feeling, but one that drained away almost immediately. "James, how good to see you ag . . . I mean, to meet you. I have heard of you from the stories my aunt Ethelin told of her visit here."

The man bowed toward me, and a single strand of his thinning hair drooped down over his forehead. "Master Lachlan, how pleased we are that you have come to visit us." He glanced over at my saddlebags as he straightened up. "I will see to it that your things are taken up to your room. You will have the suite your father used. Your grandmother is . . ."

I smiled. "She is in her solar." Without waiting for his confirmation of my conclusion, I stepped beyond the pump and mounted the servants' stairs. I climbed to the top floor, then exited the stairwell and turned right. I marched down the hallway toward the back of the house.

I can recall my grandfather Audin noting what an extravagant waste of money he thought the solar was. With the house aligned on a north–south axis, my grandmother had hired artisans to build a glass wall and ceiling to enclose a veranda. From there, Aunt Ethelin had said, one could see the palace and the theatre beyond it. Audin thought it just showed how Evadne had grown soft since she moved to the capital.

I paused in the doorway and cleared my throat. "Grandmother, I have arrived."

She looked older than I had ever imagined. Still a tall woman, age had sapped her of her physical vitality. Her legs lay hidden by a blanket, and the chair in which she sat helped make her look small. Her parchment flesh barely covered the fine bones of her hands and face. A book lay open in her lap, and it seemed to me that even turning a page would be an effort for her.

Then her head came up and I saw fire in her blue eyes. That fire touched something deep inside of me. Under its influence, my imagination had no problem peeling back the years and layering her youth back upon her. Gold flooded back through her white hair and her full figure hid her skeleton in a most seductive manner. Her gestures were delicate yet forceful and her laughter like wine for the ears.

Her lower lip quivered. "It is you, isn't it? Cardew, you have returned to me."

I choked down the lump that swelled in my throat and crossed the room. Kneeling at her feet, I took her chilly hands in mine. "I am Lachlan, Grandmother. I am Cardew's son."

She blinked away a single tear, then smiled at me. Slipping one hand from between mine, she patted my hands lightly. "I know that, child. I am merely an old woman waking from resting her eyes." She took hold of my hands and tugged me upward. "Don't kneel here, Lachlan, let me look at you."

I stood, and as she bade with a hand motion, I turned slowly so she could survey me. When I came back around I saw her smiling. "I meet with your approval?"

She nodded once. "You are leaner than your father was when he came to Herakopolis—Audin has worked you hard. Poor man always thought your father's loss in Chaos was because he had not made Cardew more proficient a swordsman."

I grinned. "He said you would say that. He told me to point out to you that I am only ranked as an Apprentice."

"So you are, as was your father." Her bright eyes narrowed. "Likewise you are, with good reason, dusty and dirty, which makes you very much like your father. You can read?"

I nodded proudly. "I have read every book that Audin had, and those my father owned at least twice. I have also read every book you sent me." I looked out toward the city. "Things have changed since many of those books were written, but they have still given me a general sense of the Empire."

"Have you read your father's journals?"

"No. Audin would not let me see them, but he did put all of us in the habit of keeping one."

"Good." She looked beyond me toward the doorway. "Where is James?"

"I believe he is taking my kit to my room." I smiled. "He told me where you were, and I came up here."

"Without a guide?" She arched an eyebrow at me.

I grinned sheepishly. "This is a room meant to catch the sun. It had to be up on the top floor, and it had to be at the north end so it would have sun all day." My mind raced as I outlined to her the logical manner in which I had managed to locate the room, but I knew something was wrong. While the explanation I gave her was perfectly true and valid, I realized I had consciously thought of none of it until questioned. In heading to this room, I had just gone where I knew the solar to be.

"Besides, Aunt Ethelin was much taken with it on her visit, and often said how grand it was."

"You are quick, Lachlan, and you have a strong memory. That is good." I heard the rustle of cloth behind me and started to turn as my grandmother said, "Yes, Marija, what is it?"

Given that James, Rose, and Nob had been with my grandmother forever, I fully expected another elderly servant to be waiting in the doorway. For that reason I was surprised to see as young a woman as was Marija standing there. Ringlets of black hair hid the shoulders of the blue dress she wore. Had the framing of the door not showed me she was just slightly shorter than I am myself, I would have thought her tall because she had the same sort of statuesque beauty my grandmother had once known.

The impish light in her hazel eyes told me the effect she had had on me pleased her, then she looked beyond me to my grandmother. "Mistress Evadne, it is time for your afternoon tonic."

My grandmother held up her hands. "Seeing Lachlan has been enough of a tonic for me, my dear. I feel as though I do not need it."

Marija walked over to the sideboard and pulled a small bottle from behind a built-in door. "That may well be, Mistress, but I am sure Master Lachlan would agree that taking your medicine is the best way to ensure you remain healthy." She filled a small silver tumbler with a greenish liquid and added some water to it from a pitcher. "You would not want to fall asleep and splash facefirst into your soup tonight, would you?"

"That would be a sight, would it not?" Even though my grandmother clearly did not like taking the draft, she accepted it from Marija and drank it in one long swallow. She winced and shivered. "That may be keeping my heart beating, but there are times I wonder if just slipping away in my sleep would not be easier."

I saw Marija covertly glance at the cup to see if it was empty, then she smiled. "Perhaps easier, Mistress, but not nearly as exciting. If you were dead, you could not see your grandson."

"A grandson who should, actually, be cleaning the road grime off himself. Please, excuse me." I bowed to both women, then headed straight for the door. I turned before I exited the room, however, and grinned at Marija. "I enjoyed meeting you. I am glad someone is seeing to it that Grandmother is around for her grandsons to visit."

"My pleasure, on both counts, Master Lachlan."

I left the solar and headed toward the front of the house. I took the wide stairway down to the second floor and, not surprisingly, saw James heading in my direction. He paused at a doorway halfway down the main hallway, and I assumed it led to the suite I had been given. "I apologize for bolting like that, James."

The elderly servant shook his head. "Your father, your uncle, Master Driscoll, and even your cousin, Master Christoforos, have made me accustomed to your family's penchant for being impulsive. Mistress Evadne claims you all have it directly from her."

"I cannot dispute her claim, James." I entered the suite of rooms and stopped barely a stride and a half inside the anteroom. A chill ran over me, as if I had dug up some ancient tomb and stepped into a treasury. The room felt that long unused and, in many ways, just that sacred.

The walls had been painted a goldenrod color that felt richer and warmer than a plain yellow. Even so, I could barely see the color because of the vast number of things hanging on the walls. Directly across from me, between two windows, a pair of crossed greatswords hung beneath a battered breastplate and helm. Below them stood a small table with two chairs and an oil-wick lamp that James lit with a taper.

On the wall to my left, swords and daggers had been arranged in a spiral pattern that covered the entire expanse of wall. To the right, against the wall that was split by a doorway leading to my bedchamber, two full sets of armor mounted on mannequins flanked the door. Behind them hung two tapestries depicting battle scenes that I had to imagine, from the purple-and-red border, had taken place in Chaos. Turning around, I saw the room's interior wall had been festooned with axes, bows, quivers full of arrows, and several shields that had clearly seen plenty of action in battle. Several standing racks of swords lined the base of the wall, reminding me of a similar display at home in Stone Rapids.

James smiled as he saw the surprised look on my face. "Yes, Master Lachlan, this is how your father deco-rated this room. Each one of these items was his, or was taken as spoils of battles he waged in Chaos. We do not use this room much, which accounts for the musty air."

I drifted toward the wall with swords and daggers. Two of the knives had wickedly barbed blades and the ghostly image of a man on them. "Vindictxvara. It is true, then, what Roarke told me about Chaos—that Chademons make weapons with the image of their ene-mies on them. Were these made to kill my father?"

"Master Cardew said the artisans should have been better, and their chosen medium larger, had they truly wanted to get him."

I reached out to touch one of them, then shivered and let my hand drop away. Roarke had said Kothvir had forged a sword with my father's image on it. *Did the demon hear of my father's boast and accommodate him, or did he just consider my father that much greater a threat?*

James led the way to the bedroom. "This is where you will be sleeping, Master Lachlan."

The bedroom had also been painted in the goldenrod hue, but here it was far more visible and made the room seem larger than it really was. The large bed, set with headboard against the house's front wall, took up most of the space. To the right of the doorway stood a chest of drawers and beyond it a small table with pitcher and bowl on it. To the left, built into the wall facing the bed, I saw shelves lined with books. I turned to face them and slowly started reading the titles to myself.

The servant squinted at me, then walked over to a drape-shrouded window beyond the table and pitcher. "You are more slender than your father was at your age. I believe we have some of his clothing still here that will fit you, at least until we can have proper clothing made for you." His nostrils flared slightly. "I took the liberty of sorting out your clothing from your saddlebags and had most of it burned."

"It wasn't *that* dirty." I had, after all, washed most things two weeks earlier in the City of Sorcerers. *I guess they are very particular here in the capital.* "I told my grandmother that I needed to bathe."

"Nob has drawn water for a bath down in the kitchen and, by now, should even have the water heated enough so you will not freeze to death. While you are down there I will select proper attire for you." He looked at my scuffed riding boots. "Leave those here with me, and I will have Nob polish them. We cannot have you going about in them this evening."

I frowned. "I can appreciate my clothing being road-worn and perhaps not as stylish as might be found in the Empire, but I hardly think it improper. Is there something going on that I do not know about?"

James smiled broadly. "My dear boy, this is the first day of the final week of the year. Tonight begins a series of parties and celebrations that will culminate in the Emperor's Bear's Eve Ball."

"I know. That is why I am here."

"Yes, well, what you do not know is that tonight your grandmother is hosting a party for many important people, including the Emperor's Warlord." He opened his hands as if to say everything else was obvious.

"And you cannot have me looking the country bumpkin."

"You understand me perfectly, Master Lachlan."

"Then I put myself in your hands."

The old servant smiled. "Good. Leave your boots and go boil yourself. After that we will make a gentleman out of you."

6

Standing there in front of the mirror hung on the back of the door, wearing clothes made for my father, I finally began to see what others had told me for as long as I could remember. In a way, when I held my head high and turned it to the right a bit, I did look like him, but only just barely. James stood behind me and I smiled when I saw his reflection nod solemnly. If it were a jury trial, I would have been convicted.

In reality, my confusion was not that odd. My father had been lost in Chaos when I was still just a wee babe. I never saw him, so my impressions of what he looked like came from a legion of diverse sources. Some, like the stone statue that was part of the monument for my mother, were made by people who had actually known Cardew. Others, from anonymous wood carvings to a bronze statue in miniature, were made by artisans who were working from stories and their own imaginations.

Forever and ever my image of Cardew had come from the statue of him that watched over my mother's grave. Literally larger than life, his eyes had the steady gaze of a hawk, and the beard tracing his jawline did not soften the angularity of his face at all. Heavy of chest and thighs, he stood poised, watching and waiting for my mother to join him, though I had always imagined him waiting for his sons to ride into battle at his side.

Unlike my brothers, I often found myself thinking of our father as Cardew the hero, not my father. For a while I felt like an outsider because of that, then I told Geoff about how I felt. As per usual he laughed away my concerns and explained it to me very succinctly. Because I did not remember our father, my total experience of him had come in the stories told by villagers and Aunt Ethelin. No one, in telling stories of Cardew, stressed his family life—other than to say he loved his wife. The stories in which he lived were grand tales of magick and battles and Chaos.

"You have to remember, Locke," Geoff told me, "any hero would pale in comparison to the stories told about him. All you have to remember about our father is that he was real and he loved us. If he lived in our memory in that way, I think he would be happy."

I had no doubt my brother was right in his assessment—and he'd been eight at the time of our father's disappearance, so he did have strong memories of him. Even so, Geoff's assurances did little to lighten the burden we inherited from Cardew. We were the sons of a *hero*, and from the first my grandfather seemed intent on training us to accept that mantle.

But *am I a suitable candidate to do that*?

James coughed lightly. "The tunic and trousers are suitable, if a touch large. Here, try on this jacket."

James might have felt the clothes were appropriate, but I found them somewhat annoying. The black trousers came all the way up to cover me nearly to my breastbone and were held up by suspenders. Of course, to be stylish, a slender leather belt with a silver clasp held them tight around my waist. The tunic had been made of a nearly iridescent green silk that I liked very much, but James had forced me to button it tightly to my throat—which was the only point at which the clothes were actually not too large. A piece of starched stiff black fabric slid beneath the collar and crossed in front, to be pinned in place with a silver stickpin. Its only virtue, as nearly as I could see, was that the stickpin had been fitted with a piece of triangular malachite that matched my tunic.

The black jacket James held out for me fitted, more or less. The sleeves ended at my elbows and had three raven's feathers dangling down along my forearms. The jacket itself stopped at my waist and was held loosely closed in the front by a silver chain looped between two buttons. As I tugged the sleeves of my tunic down to a comfortable length, James fastened the front, then backed away and smiled. "Yes, excellent."

"The canvas thanks the artist." I gave him a grin, then worked my arms forward and back to test the range of motion the jacket gave me. It tightened across the shoulders when I crossed my forearms, and I could have split it down the back, but I refrained from over-stressing it. I did not exactly feel comfortable in the clothes I had been given, but I knew there were other, far more torturous garments hidden in the closet, so I saw no reason in taking chances.

As I worked my arms around I balled my fists. I felt an odd sensation in my right ring finger. For a second or two I experienced a strange sense of loss or incompleteness. It was as if a weight I expected to feel on that hand had gone missing.

"A ring, James." I frowned as the sensation drained out of my hand. "Dressed up like this, I feel as though I should have a ring or something."

James looked at me with a blank stare. "Master Cardew was not much given to wearing jewelry, Master Lachlan."

"But I thought my grandfather, mother, and aunt all traveled here to Herakopolis for a ceremony in which Emperor Daclones made him a Knight of the Empire. Someone, Aunt Ethelin most likely, told me that Cardew wore a ring to mark that occasion."

The elderly servant shrugged his shoulders. "I recall the ring, but I am unaware of what became of it. I could try to find you something suitable, though I'm not certain where at this hour."

I shook my head. "No matter. My father's ring would be Geoff's by birthright anyway, and I've never worn rings either, so I'm not sure why I even thought of it." The image staring back at me from the mirror melded with that of my father's statue, and I saw the ring the sculptor had added to his hand. *That must be it.*

"As you will, sir." James looked me up and down. "Will there be anything else?"

Backing away from the mirror, I swung the door open and looked out into the weapons chamber. "Are you certain this belt will support one of these daggers?"

"Why would it be necessary for it to do that, Master Lachlan?" James shook his head. "Unlike your month on the trail, you are not required to provide your own tableware for this evening's festivities. And, despite what you might have heard about the politics here in the capital, it is quite unlikely a fight will break out this evening."

I laughed lightly at the image of some of the cara-vaners being invited to the sort of party that required my attire. "It is not that, James. It is just that I do not have a sash with my rank badges sewn on it, so I thought wearing a dagger would be sufficient to let people know I am ranked in that discipline."

James rolled his eyes skyward. "What must they teach you in the provinces?"

"Huh?"

"Master Lachlan, as the party is being held in the home of your grandmother, you are one of the hosts. As such, your rank badges have been sewn on to a ban-ner that will hang in the entryway. For the parties you will attend later in the week we will see to it that you have been provided with suitable rank insignia to sat-isfy social convention."

I bowed my head to him. "I see my social success is well warded in your hands. To you I commend it, then."

"It will be my pleasure to serve you in that capacity as long as I am able, sir." James waved me toward the door. "Your guests await."

Out in the provinces we handled the Bear's Eve cele-bration a bit differently than they did in the capital—and probably any other real city—of the Empire. In Stone Rapids everyone brought food according to a list created by a cabal of elderly widows. No one was ever asked to bring more than they could afford, and what-ever someone was selected to bring was something of which they could be proud. Being as how Bear's Eve falls in the middle of the winter, many items were put up after the harvest and served to make folks mindful of the past year.

Our celebration lasts only one night, the actual eve

of the month of the Bear. We build a big old roaring fire in the town hall and everyone comes in their best clothing. People have generally exchanged gifts within their families before coming to the celebration, but presents are given to neighbors at the big town gathering, and a special show is made of things exchanged between people who have grown distant or hostile during the preceding year.

After all, as everyone knows, it is an ill omen to go into a new year bearing anyone malice. The giving of gifts makes it easier to dismiss past wrongs, and it also adds a bit of brightness to the long, dark nights of winter. The food and drink and singing and dancing all bring to mind the warmer, happier times of the year, again making winter much more bearable.

In the capital the parties start up to a week before the actual holiday. Whereas Stone Rapids held the party in the town hall, my grandmother just used the ballroom in her house—which looked to me to be much larger than Stone Rapids's town hall anyway. A row of tables formed an island laden with victuals while smaller, round tables near the corners of the room bore polished goblets of silver and pitchers full of wine.

The guests, who began arriving an hour or two after sundown, all seemed in a festive mood and genuinely happy to be attending. They were met at the door by one of Nob's four grandsons. He relieved them of their cloaks and coats and also accepted from them whatever gift they had brought for my grandmother. Usually the gifts were small and offered out of social convention, but those brought by close friends instead of social acquaintances were more substantial and handled with extreme care.

James then led the guests to the receiving line and introduced them to my grandmother. He kept his voice just loud enough so that I could hear the name, for which I was very grateful. I found myself able to remember names for as long as it took the guests to work their way down from where my grandmother was seated in a big chair, past Marija, to me. Once they had passed beyond me to other family friends and, finally, the Imperial Warlord, I forgot them entirely and prepared myself for the next person.

In the background, however, Nob's other three grandsons were very busy. When James would announce a guest, they would sort through a whole roomful of small wooden boxes wrapped with bright ribbons. Finding the box that matched the person, they would put the box on the table at the end of the line. As a result, when the guests finished their introductions, they would find a Bear's Eve gift waiting for them.

Many of the men I met that evening told me they had known my father or had ridden with him. They grasped my forearm with a strong grip, just as my grandfather had taught all of us, and I returned the gesture solemnly. Most of the women allowed me to kiss their hands, with the notable exceptions of those who were the closest to my grandmother in age and acquaintance. They hugged me and gave me light kisses on my cheeks. They often whispered to me that it had been a long time since they had seen my grandmother as happy as she seemed with me in the capital.

This I took to be very polite lying on their parts. Then, attempting to justify whatever my grandmother felt for me, I made the social error of introducing Marija to people. It seemed only right to me, as there she was standing behind and beside my grandmother's chair, but apparently such things are not done. She was, after all, a servant in the household, but most people were polite and wished her the joy of the season. Finally James corrected me, and I blushed, but Marija's warm smile took the sting out of my embarrassment.

Of all the guests, I knew only one and was quite surprised to see her. The evergreen gown Xoayya wore set off her red hair. The tight bodice and low cut of the neckline emphasized her breasts. She clearly was not a child, but she still lacked the full self-assurance of some of the other girls her age whom I had already met. The conservative application of cosmetics brought a bit more color to her face and flesh, as well as more emphasis to her large blue eyes.

I kissed her hand. "I had not expected to see you here, Mistress Xoayya."

Something halfway between surprise and distraction flickered through her eyes to greet my use of her name. "My grandmother is good friends with your grandmother, Master Lachlan. We have met before?"

I hesitated, then nodded. "On the trail, coming into Herakopolis from the City of Sorcerers."

"I do recall that, I think." She graced me with a smile. "Perhaps you will dance with me later?"

"I hadn't thought. . . ."

"Oh, you will." Her voice carried with it an assurance I'd not heard from her before.

"But . . ." I started to offer a protest, but she freed her hand from mine and moved further along the line. I glanced over at Marija and saw her hiding a giggle behind her hand, but she didn't share her amusement before another guest demanded my attention.

About halfway through the guest arrivals a most extraordinary thing happened. The door opened and a tall young man whipped his cape at Nob's grandson Carl. Beneath it he wore a military uniform, but hardly the sort of dressy version I had seen parade past me so far in the evening. Despite the Warlord himself being dressed in clothing that looked more utilitarian than formal, the brash young man's arrival started an alarm bell tolling in my head.

At least a head taller than me, his brown hair, eyes, and something else intangible reminded me of my brother Dalt. Still the look of intensity on his face and his long, stringy moustache made him far more alive and animated than I'd ever seen Dalt even at the best of times. Whereas my brother seemed to revel in brooding, this man clearly approached life with a fire that would take lots and lots of dousing before it would go out.

As he cut around the line of people waiting for James to announce them, I thought him a local soldier who had decided to attend uninvited. I started to move and intercept him, but the odd grin on Carl's face and the way James held the other guests back kept me from doing anything rash. I was glad I had not acted when I saw the happiness in my grandmother's eyes when the soldier dropped to one knee in front of her.

"Forgive me for coming without warning."

She held his face in her two hands. "There are no unwelcome guests on Bear's Eve, not that you would ever be unwelcome here." She stroked his hair and tugged at it playfully where it extended over his collar in the back. "I was hoping you would be here."

Grandmother looked over at me and beckoned me forward. "Lachlan, meet your cousin, Christoforos."

The man stood again and towered over me. "Kit. Welcome, Lachlan."

"Locke." I took his arm and grasped it firmly just below the elbow. "Best of the season to you."

"And you."

As we broke our grip, James directed Kit to take up a

place next to me in the receiving line. Kit nodded his acquiescence, then shivered. "I should have waited for another hour and escaped this duty."

I must have looked stricken. "Another hour?"

He threw me a wink. "Likely not that long." He let his voice get a bit louder and added, "Of course, were I standing next to Marija, I would find the time would pass much, much too swiftly."

Marija gave him a smile in return that was all cat to his being a mouse. "Swiftly for you perhaps, Master Christoforos."

Kit clutched a hand to his chest. "You wound me."

"You will recover, I think, my lord." Marija smiled at me, and added, "He has all the other times."

The resumption of guest flow put an end to their banter. One old soldier tapped Kit's company badge and noted that he, too, had belonged to the Emperor's Horse Guards. "I had heard they were up on the Menal/Chaos border for their winter tour."

"We still are, but the capital still wants reports coming in and has orders coming out, so I am here in service to the Emperor." Kit gave the man a salute and thanked him for attending the party. "I will be certain to tell Colonel Grimands I met you."

So sharply removed from his easy exchange with Marija was his reaction to the soldier that I knew instantly Kit had lied to the man. I waited for the soldier to become absorbed in his conversation with the Warlord, then, with a smile plastered on my face, I whispered, "You were not sent back to the capital as a messenger, were you?"

Kit's smile eroded at the corners for a heartbeat, then he glanced down at me. "Military secrets are not the stuff of idle party chatter, Locke." He glanced around the room, then back at me again. "Would it be paranoia or just common sense to imagine at least one person here knows someone who might be a member of the Black Church?"

I shrugged. "For all I know, everyone here might be . . ." As he slowly started to nod, I let my voice trail off. "Blooded on first thrust."

Kit laughed aloud. "It's been a long time since I've heard that little saying. I saw your lips moving, but I heard Audin's voice. How . . . amusing."

The tone I heard in Kit's voice concerning Audin irritated me, but no verbal riposte came to me, so I remained silent. I went back to introducing myself to countless people whom I promptly forgot. Finally, as the last couple moved through the line, I stamped some feeling back into my feet and turned to speak to Kit, but he'd vanished. I looked back to talk with Marija, but she had gone to get the wheeled wicker chair Grandmother used to get around, and Grandmother was engaged in conversation with two of her dowager friends.

I felt abandoned for a moment, then my stomach rumbled. As a host of the party it struck me I should certainly see that the food was fit for consumption, so I headed for the nearest table. Unfortunately for me, sitting in a half-opened shell of some sort, on a bed of ice, I saw reddish white things that looked like the tail end of some very fleshy insects. People seemed to be enjoying them with great relish, but I was new to seafood, and it looked as if one had to be at least an Apprentice in some culinary discipline to be able to even get at the meat.

"Eating a *tsoerit* is worth the effort."

I turned and found Xoayya stand beside me. "I've never seen one before. I wouldn't know how to start—and I'm not certain it would appeal to me."

"It should, really. *Tsoerits* are remarkable creatures. They never stop growing. When their carapace becomes too confining, they slip from it and grow another. In one life they endure multiple rebirths." She smiled and focused distantly. "Perhaps an allegory for our lives."

I shook my head. "I don't think I understand your point."

"No?" She pointed to where my family's rank banners were displayed in the foyer. "Those banners define us, and even confine us, much as the *tsoerit's* shell defines and confines him. That says what you are, and if your ranks and disciplines are not correct or high enough, you are barred from some things. As we change, as we learn more and become better at what we do, we shed those old ranks and banners and become defined by new symbols."

"That life moves in stages is obvious, Mistress. People move through infancy, childhood, adolescence, adulthood, and then old age."

"Don't forget death."

"I don't think of death as a life stage. It ends life altogether."

"But that ending becomes a new beginning as our souls are clothed with new flesh, and we are sent back to live again."

I nodded. "Of course, and in that way, I guess, death is a stage of life. What I'm saying is that your observation is obvious."

That brought a smile to her face. "Is it? For moving through all these stages of life, what is the *tsoerit's* purpose?"

"Purpose?" I shook my head. "I don't know? To propagate?"

"For some, perhaps." She pointed a delicate finger at the chilling *tsoerit* carcasses. "For these their purpose was to be eaten. From the moment they were born, they were destined to be here, now, sating hunger."

"But perhaps that's not true."

"But they are here, aren't they?"

I recognized the fact that we were arguing free will and fate. While I didn't think a *tsoerit* had enough brainpower to really have free will, I couldn't imagine the sole purpose for these creatures being to fill up a hole in some mage's future vision of this party. "You're using a circular argument here. You're saying that because they *are* here, they were destined to be here."

"And you don't believe that?"

"No."

"Then why are *you* here?" She opened her arms. "Aren't you here because you are destined to be here?"

I shook my head. "I don't think so. I'm here because I beat my brothers out for the honor of being here."

"Is that the only reason?"

"I don't know." I shrugged. "I know of no other reason for my being here."

"You will find one." Again she spoke with an iron certainty in her voice that I found rather spooky. The fact that she was looking right through me at the time didn't help matters much either.

"And what would that reason be?"

Xoayya laughed lightly. "I don't know, I just know there is one. The problem of being cursed with second sight is that I do not see everything or even *most* things. I get glimpses."

"Such as?"

"Such as my grandmother needing me." Xoayya laid a hand lightly on my shoulder. "There is much for you to learn, Locke, and learn you shall. Then we will dance." She laughed lightly, then vanished into the crowd.

Now feeling confused as well as abandoned, I reminded myself that I had a duty as the host of the party. In keeping with it, I began to look around for our guest of honor, the Imperial Warlord. Even with him being as tall as he was, I had no luck in spotting his head above those of the crowd. I started making my way through the press of people to find another vantage point from which to look for him, but when I did so, I still could not find him. I did, however, see Kit wandering out of the ballroom and deeper into the house.

Probably off to find some more suitable clothing. Utterly at a loss, I decided to look for James, to have him tell me what to do. I made it as far as the hallway outside the ballroom, but I couldn't even see one of Nob's grandsons, much less James. I stopped for a moment and scratched my head, then I heard the sound of footsteps from the floor above. The noise ceased, and I frowned.

Whoever or whatever was upstairs, it had just entered my suite.

I ran to the nearest set of stairs and sprinted up them two at a time. Something clicked inside my head, and I started to think in the tactical patterns my grandfather had beaten into me with repeated lessons. One step into the room and I could easily free one of the swords from the rack just inside the door. I smiled because as soon as that bit of strategy occurred to me, I knew Cardew had placed the weapons on the right side of the doorway with a mind to their utility as well as display.

Whoever was in my room had lit the lamp on the table across from the door and had left the door ajar. I pushed it open with my left hand and, with my right hand, twisted a rapier free of the rack. "I don't know who you are, but it is a poor thing to rob your hostess at a Bear's Eve celebration." Shutting the door behind me to prevent their escape, I leveled the blade at the two men looking at the spiral of daggers on the left hand wall.

Whatever else I had planned to say evaporated from my mind. Their faces half-hidden in shadows cast by the lamp, Kit and Garn Drustorn regarded me with a look that dismissed my threat. In his hands Kit held a dagger that even I could tell, in the weak lamplight, had not been made in the Empire.

"It might be rude, as we've just met, but I will kill you, cousin, in a heartbeat, unless you can satisfy my curiosity." I centered the rapier's point on his chest. "You've not just ridden in from Chaos, so what is a *Bharashadi* dagger doing in the possession of one of the Emperor's scouts and where, on this side of the Ward Walls, did you find it?"

7

"How and where I got it is information undoubtedly worth killing for." Kit shifted his shoulders rather uneasily. "Despite your threat, the answers to those questions are not the sort of thing to be discussed with someone in the capital for nothing more than the Bear's Eve Ball." He looked to the Warlord for confirmation of his assessment.

Drustorn stood taller even than Kit, and, while they probably weighed the same, I had the feeling that the wiry man would beat Kit easily in any sort of fight they could have. *Chaosfire* filled his eyes fuller than it had Eirene's, but I saw no other indication of the changes commonly wrought on a man by Chaos. Of course I knew the stories about Garn Drustorn and his famed Chaos Raiders, but my experience with the things said about my father had been enough to make me wary of believing everything I had heard.

"It is my feeling, in this case, no harm will come if Locke is allowed to hear what you have to tell me." While older than Kit by nearly a dozen years, but not even twice my age, Drustorn's voice had a calm strength that made me feel good and, apparently, vanquished Kit's reluctance to talk. "Locke, please put the sword up. After you tell me what you know, Lieutenant Christoforos, I will want to hear how Locke knew that dagger was manufactured by the *Bharashadi*."

Kit sat down in one of the chairs, and Drustorn waved me to the other one after I locked the door. He remained standing and folded his arms across his chest. "Lieutenant?"

"Approximately three weeks ago I was leading a small patrol in Menal to check on some ruins that had once been in Chaos, but have been part of the Empire since the province was liberated. There had been reports of some Church of Chaos Encroaching activity in the area. We all knew that those reports were false, since the Black Church tends to be active near the borders, not in the middle of farmland."

The Warlord nodded. "Superstitions die very hard, I know. So you rode out to check and had a magicker with you."

"An Aelven woman of Warder rank, yes sir. We found the ruin and checked it thoroughly but found nothing. Taci, the Warder, used a spell that she described as being akin to a sieve. Because Chaos magick has a certain taint to it, she said its residual effects could be detected by her spell. She even put enough energy into the spell to let me see it as a cerulean ball that flattened out into a glowing cobweb. It grew and spread out with its anchor at the ruin, then faded.

"She reported she had found nothing, so we made camp that night at the ruin. It was already snowing in the plains, and wolf packs were coming down from the mountains to hunt. We decided braving whatever ghosts the locals had seen was preferable to freezing to death or being overrun by wolves. The ruins provided enough shelter for ourselves and our mounts, and the well meant we had fresh water."

"I know I would have chosen to stay there, too," I commented. In Kit's description I could hear the whistling of the wind and the howls of wolves coming across a snowy plain under the bone white light of a full Lovers' Moon. I smiled as I imagined being alone on those plains with only Cruach as a companion, and I knew instinctively it would be the wolves that would be fearing us and not the other way around.

"Shows you're not entirely without sense, Locke." Kit turned the dagger over in his hands and concentrated on it. "That night Taci awoke with a start and cried out. Even by the time I got to her she had not fully become aware of where she was. My lord, it was as if she were in shock, or so I thought. I had my people bank up the fire, and we made her some *vusopeh* tea. We had to force her to drink it, but once she got some into her, it started to bring her around.

"Once I made sure she had not been hurt somehow, I asked her what happened. She was not certain. She said her hands were numb, much the way they feel after you accidentally hit something very solid with a sword. Obviously she'd not done that while sleeping, so we assumed the cause of her shock might be magickal."

The Warlord nodded. "A rather logical conclusion."

"Yes, sir. Taci considered whether or not she'd been attacked by an enemy, but rejected that idea since she'd suffered no real harm. In thinking about everything she decided her shock had something to do with the spell she had woven earlier in the evening. Because she had put the extra strength into it to enable me to see it take effect, the spell had remained active over a much greater range. Just how far, she said, she could not be certain. What had shocked her, however, was the sheer virulence and power of the Chaos magick spell she had detected. Unprepared for it, it had addled her."

I narrowed my eyes. "So there were Chaos Encroachers in the area."

"That's what I thought at first, Locke, but Taci said what she had felt was nothing like their magick. She pointed her hand out in the direction in which the Chaos magick had been sensed, and I had several of my patrol make an arrow out of building stones pointing straight out in that direction. Then Taci and I rode about a third of a league to the west and she cast another of her detection spells. This time she refined it so it would only search in a ninety-degree arc. It went out invisibly this time, and within a minute she had a new direction for the magick.

"I marked everything down on my chart of the area and was able to determine that whatever she had felt looked to be four leagues off to the south, just entering the forests. As that area of Menal is not heavily populated, I was very reluctant to tangle with anything that powerful in the middle of the night because we were only a scouting patrol with a single magicker. I forced everyone to get some sleep so we could be alert the next day, when we did go after it. In light of what we found, I don't know if this was the correct tactic to choose."

Garn Drustorn shook his head. "You're here now, reporting this information. That's far more valuable than our learning about the problem you encountered after you'd gone missing for a week and another patrol found your corpses."

"That was my feeling, too, sir, but the risk might have been worth it." Kit sighed heavily. "Taci knew from her spell that we'd located the nexus point of the casting, and I knew it from what I saw. The snow, which was running about knee-deep thereabouts, had been melted down to the ground in a triangular pattern about ten feet on a side. All around there, throughout this small clearing in the forest, lay dead wolves. Some of them had been flash-burned with all their fur singed off, while others looked as if they had been roasted for hours on a spit."

The Warlord frowned. "With no cooking pit in sight."

"No, sir." Kit's face hardened as he continued his story. "Being out there in Menal, I have no love for wolves, but this pack died hard, very hard. We couldn't tell if they got a piece of what they attacked, but they'd been dogging its steps for the better part of a day. They surprised their prey because that spot wasn't particularly defensible—though with magick it turned out fine.

"From there we started tracking the thing, and I think I saw it once. It surprised us by trying to cut back on its own trail. It came in toward our camp from downwind one evening, and the horses let us know they were upset. We chased out after it, and I think I got an arrow into it—left shoulder. I can't be certain—it was running, at night, and fair distant. I saw a blood track, though."

My jaw dropped. "You hit it at night at something beyond point-blank range? How big was it?"

"Man-sized, more or less." Kit glanced sidelong at the Warlord, then nodded. "The thing looked pretty much like the picture-book illustrations of a lion, from the time before Chaos came. It had a mane and a long tail with a bushy brush of hair at the end. The mane seemed to trace down the spine, but it was difficult to tell because the whole thing was black, excepting, perhaps, its eyes. I saw glints of gold in its eyes, but that could be as much my imagination or reflections of firelight as it is fact."

"I think you saw gold eyes all right. You realize, Lieutenant, your description is consistent with that of a Bharashadi Chademon." Drustorn held his right hand out, and Kit gave him the slender, barbed blade. "You said you saw blood."

"Yes, sir. On more than one occasion. Where I got my arrow into it I saw blood in the snow, and it looked dark purple. Hansen, one of my people, said he'd seen blood that color from a Chapanther that had been killed over in Tarris. Later we saw some more from where a bear had fought with the creature. The bear had been killed, and its hide had been stripped off. Apparently the creature had appropriated the bear's lair for shelter."

"It killed a bear?" I shook my head. "Did it use magick?"

"No. Taci sensed no residual magickal power, and the marks on the bear's carcass indicated it had been killed by dagger and claw."

I blinked. "If it was the size of a man and did that, it must be very strong."

Drustorn nodded. "Chaos demons are often quite powerful."

Kit winced. "True, but could this have been a Chaos demon?"

Kit's question focused me on the problem with which he and the Warlord wrestled. Everyone knew that creatures born in Chaos could not penetrate the Ward Walls and live. It just could not be done without resulting in their death. We all knew it. We had been given that as the one fundamental tenet of our lives in the Empire. It was a fact that no one disputed.

Another fact not in dispute was that an incredible number of Chaotic creatures had been released into the Empire when the provinces of Menal and Tarris were incorporated into it. The activation of the Ward Stations that created those new provinces pushed the Ward Walls out instantly, trapping an incredible number of creatures nurtured by Chaos within the new province. While many creatures had been slain in the century since Tarris's birth, some of the Chaos beasts had established a stable population and were breeding true even in my father's time, or so his books reported.

None of those creatures, at least as nearly as I knew, were capable of using magick. Clearly the thing Kit had chased was a magick user, but it was also possible that any magick it used was an inherent power, not a spell. While a spell might mimic a dragon's ability to breathe fire, a dragon's breath is not a spell, for example. Even as I offered that idea as a possible explanation, I knew it did not truly cover the facts available.

"Where did you find the dagger?" I asked. "You said a dagger was used on the bear's corpse, but do you know if it was this one? Could someone else have inflicted those wounds with a knife afterward?"

"In other words, how do I know the creature carried this dagger?"

"Right."

"Good question." Kit gave me an appreciative nod. "We didn't see tracks from anyone else around the bear's body, so I assume the wounds were inflicted by the creature. The kill was fresh, but I didn't have the dagger to match against the wounds, so I don't know if this was the one used on the bear."

The Warlord nodded. "Not an easy thing to determine at the best of times."

"No, sir, though Taci said some magickers could have used a spell to do the job. As for the dagger itself, well, who was carrying it is still something of a mystery. We tracked the creature further south and two days later, at a cabin in the forest, found more evidence of its passage.

"It had snowed during the early morning just lightly enough to dust the whole area. We found a dead man lying facedown beneath this thin blanket of snow, so we assume he died in the night. When I rolled him over I found the knife stuck in his chest. There were plenty of signs of a struggle in the area, but no more purple blood. I cannot tell if he was stabbed, or just knocked down to where he fell on the knife himself."

"And the man had a history of being a Chaos Rider, correct, Lieutenant? That way you could not be certain if the dagger was something he had brought back from Chaos himself, or something the creature left behind."

"That is the mystery, Warlord." Kit sighed heavily. "The creature ran upright, and it ran on all fours. It did some very intelligent things to elude us, and it did some very stupid things to put us back on the track. Aside from changes made to put us on a false trail or to make travel easier, it always angled south." Kit plucked at his service tunic. "We tracked it to within a league of the capital here before we lost it."

The implications of what Kit had related made me swallow hard as I considered them. I saw three possible solutions to his problem. The first was that some sort of strange Chaos creature—one that had not been seen in Tarris or Menal before—had wandered from its normal range and found itself being hounded south. The second, which was really a variation of the first, was that a small band of Chademons had managed to anticipate the annexation of Tarris and had hidden themselves in the province when it was reclaimed. They stayed quiet and only now decided to make trouble. It was even possible that Chademons born within the Ward Walls would be able to pass freely through them as anything else born on this side could do.

While that second conclusion was quite nasty in and of itself, it paled by comparison to the third. That one, quite simply, was impossible by everything I knew of the Ward Walls, but I realized that was painfully little. Simply stated, a Chaos demon, apparently of the Black Shadows tribe, had managed to pass through the Ward Walls. Of course, the most terrifying thing about that was that if one could do it, others could as well. This was, then, the worst-case scenario, and I thought it would be foolish not to give it some weight, no matter that I knew that it was impossible.

I shivered. "Could a Chaos demon have made it through the Ward Walls?"

"Not possible." Kit crossed his arms over his chest. "Even Audin should have taught you that such a thing is impossible."

The Warlord smiled. "I think impossible is too strong a word to use here, Lieutenant. Impossible really means that no one has found a means for doing something up to this point in time. As powerful as the Ward Walls are, they are just magick. Whenever a spell is worked, a counterspell can destroy it. The Ward Walls are strong because of the number of Warders we have maintaining them, and because of the complexity of the weaving. That does not mean they cannot be breached."

Kit's face darkened. "How?"

"I'm not a Warder, Lieutenant, so I don't know if I

can give you a full answer to that question." Drustorn shook his head. "As an example, though, we know there were many magickal items of great power lost when Chaos overswept the world, and only a fraction of them have been recovered. There are undoubtedly also countless sorcerers' strongholds that were likewise subsumed, and we have no idea of what or even who might lurk in them. Of the most powerful of wizards— the Twelve who formed the Seal of Reality—nothing has been heard since the time of the Shattering, so this might be their doing."

I frowned. "But if magick was used to breach the Ward Walls, wouldn't someone have felt the taint of the magick? If Kit's friend Taci has a spell that allows her to detect such things, I can't imagine that the sorcerers tasked with maintaining the walls wouldn't use a similar spell to monitor assaults against the walls."

"That's a good point, Locke, but it could have been non-Chaos magick that created the hole."

I nodded to the Warlord. "Or it might not have been magick at all."

"Meaning?"

I shrugged my shoulders. "Perhaps there is something in Chaos that absorbs magick the way a bandage absorbs blood. If it soaked off enough strength from the walls, something might be able to make it through from the other side."

My cousin shook his head. "I don't think I like that idea."

"Nor do I, but we are speculating well beyond anything we can support with the evidence you have brought us, Lieutenant. What we do know from it is that a fairly lethal creature of Chaotic origin is close to Herakopolis. This is not something that can be taken lightly."

The Warlord looked toward me, then flipped the dagger around and extended the hilt in my direction. "So tell me, Lachlan, how did you recognize this as being of *Bharashadi* manufacture?"

I accepted the weapon and tested it for weight and balance point as I had been instructed by Audin. The heavy hilt felt good in my hand, and I had no fear of it twisting in my grip. The cross hilt felt solid enough to be used for parrying, and a line of stars twisted along its edge for decoration. The wide blade had been crafted with a long, slender diamond in cross section to strengthen it down the center. A third of the way down on the lower edge, and halfway back on the upper a wicked hook had been cut down and into the blade. The knife, when thrust in and rotated even slightly, would pull and slice on retraction, making the wound virtually untreatable without magick.

Staring at the knife I tried to answer Drustorn's question. "I am not certain, sir. I know that Audin, my grandfather and Bladesmaster, mentioned the Black Shadows frequently as I grew up. The stories of Cardew likewise emphasized his hatred for Kothvir, their leader. As I saw this dagger closely resembled those on the wall, I must have assumed it was of *Bharashadi* origin. It was a snap judgment, made in haste. Was I wrong?"

"I suspect if I asked either of you to name Chademon tribes you'd start with the Black Shadows, so even a guess would have brought that answer. In this case you were correct." Drustorn walked over to the wall and pulled the other two *Bharashadi* daggers from the wall. "You are aware these are special?"

Kit and I both nodded. "They are *vindictxvara*—my uncle Cardew brought them back from Chaos."

"Right," I added. "They both have images of my father on them. They were meant to kill him."

"True enough, but there is something more here. The shape of the cross hilts and the way the star pattern is worked along the edges indicate these knives were fashioned for a Chademon who was a member of Kothvir's brood."

I looked down at the blade I held and saw the pattern of stars repeated. "It's the same with this one. Perhaps the man Kit found murdered had ridden with the Valiant Lancers on an expedition with our fathers. He could have gotten it then."

"That's likely the answer, Locke." The Warlord's eyes narrowed. "If it isn't, however, the magnitude of our problem has grown. On the off chance we are dealing with a Chaos demon who has actually found a way to breach the Ward Walls, its pedigree means it is far more dangerous than we might otherwise dare to believe."

8

I looked up at the Warlord. "Is it true that Kothvir killed my father?"

Drustorn, seeming more shadow than man in the lamp's dim light, shrugged. "I do not know for certain, but he tried many times to kill Cardew." He returned the daggers to their brackets on the wall. "His attempts were not very successful, but his intent remained constant. I've heard it said Kothvir forged a *vindictxvara* with which he intended finally to kill Cardew."

"Do you know why Kothvir hated Cardew so?" In growing up I had heard many stories to explain their animosity, from bawdy ballads to absurd metaphysics. None of them satisfied me—hatred that deep and unrelenting had to be born out of something more than some clever slight or trick.

Drustorn laughed for the first time in my company, and I found I liked the warm, rich sound. "Mind you, I did not learn this until well after your father had disappeared, but it seems to fit to me. The Sunbird knows Cardew gave Kothvir plenty of reasons to want him dead. The Valiant Lancers were a formidable group of Chaos Riders, and they took special delight in attacking the *Bharashadi*. Wherever Kothvir went to pursue his dream of conquering all of Chaos—and subsequently destroying the Empire—your fathers and their troops arrived to harry and attack him."

I frowned. "The Chaos demons war amongst themselves?"

"Of course. They have little more love for each other than they have for us. Chaos is a very difficult place to live, so expanding into a neighbor's territory and taking his resources makes life that much easier. There are battles between Chaos demons all the time, and this is the key to what angered Kothvir."

The Warlord pressed his hands together. "Somehow Cardew managed to engineer a truce with Fialchar that kept Lord Disaster from attacking your father's troops while they were on campaign in Chaos. Kothvir's dream of uniting all the Chademons included destroying Lord Disaster, so this truce served Fialchar as well as it served your father. Kothvir knew he would never succeed in his own plans until your father was eliminated, and years of frustration made him bitter and furious."

"Does Lord Disaster rule Chaos?"

"No, Locke, though I suspect he would have a different answer for that question. He certainly considers it his realm." Kit drummed his fingers on the side table. "Politics in Chaos is only slightly more organized than it is here in the Empire. Lord Disaster has, however, reserved the right to destroy the Empire, and he tends to act to thwart the ambitions of anyone who would rob him of his claim."

"Well put, Lieutenant." Drustorn moved back into the lamp's circle of light. "Fialchar probably would rule Chaos, but attending to all the little details of such a realm would bore him. The fact that the Ward Walls preserve the Empire from Chaos is his focus. Anything he can do to crush the Empire is his goal, and he has enough power to take serious steps in that direction."

I shivered, then blushed. "I'm sorry, but Fialchar is someone I learned to fear as a child."

"Many mothers frighten their children with him, but that's because they do not realize how potentially dangerous he is." Drustorn smiled. "From what I understand—and I was very young when Cardew and Driscoll led the Valiant Lancers—Cardew's truce with Fialchar kept Lord Disaster's plotting to a minimum. Those were good days in the Empire."

I nodded. "On the road Roarke, one of the caravan guards, mentioned a prophecy about my father and Kothuir. What was that?"

"There is a great Chademon book of prophecy, known as the *Chronicles of Farscry*. In it was foretold Kothvir's killing at Cardew's hands. I don't know the exact details of the prophecy, primarily because we only know of the *Chronicles* from relatively unreliable sources. At least this is the explanation that I was given by the Lord of Shadows when I inquired about the matter."

As Garn Drustorn was the master of all the Imperial Armies and Navies, so the Lord of Shadows oversaw the action of all spies, counterspies and constabularies in the Empire. Something in the way the Warlord made his statement told me that bit of information had probably come from a Black Churcher, and undoubtedly had been verified by magick or torture.

Drustorn looked at Kit. "Lieutenant, I commend you and your people for chasing after this thing. I will expect a full written report by tomorrow, and I will want the dagger turned over to some of the court Mages for analysis."

"Yes, my lord." Kit stood and gave Drustorn a salute that he returned crisply. Kit accepted the knife from my hands. "I will keep the knife in my room here tonight, then I will give it to the Mages tomorrow."

"Very good." The man looked at me, and I shivered under his opalescent stare. "I am impressed with your quick thinking in confronting us here, and your analysis of the situation, Lachlan. From what I have heard of your father, you would make him proud."

That put a smile on my face. "Thank you, sir."

"Now, I would suggest we return to the ballroom. If anyone asks, I think we can say I inquired about seeing the collection of weapons your father had accumulated while in Chaos, if that seems believable?" Both Kit and I nodded in agreement, so the Warlord smiled. "Excellent. Shall we go?"

Kit went to his room both to hide the dagger and change into some more festive clothing. I kept trying to think of something really intelligent to say to Garn Drustorn, but I felt there was little or nothing a villager from Garik could offer that would interest the Imperial Warlord. As my grandfather had often reminded me, 'tis better to be silent and thought a fool than to speak and remove all doubt, so I said nothing as we marched back downstairs to the party.

At the entrance to the ballroom, the Warlord clasped my forearm. "You have been most kind in showing me the weapons your father collected in Chaos. I apologize for taking you away from your guests for such selfish reasons."

"You are most welcome, sir. My father would be proud of your interest in his handiwork." I smiled up at him and tried to keep my face open and honest, despite our conspiracy. I looked about to see if anyone was watching us or listening closely, but no one seemed to take any interest in us at all.

Drustorn nodded, broke his grip, then vanished into the crowd. Part of me wanted to follow him just so others could see us together and know he saw me as something more than a provincial youth, but doing just that was what everyone would expect from a provincial youth. To earn the trust he had already displayed in me, I had to tamp down the elation I felt and carry on as if nothing special at all were going on.

That was not easily done. Upstairs I had seen evidence of an event that was potentially shattering for every man, woman, and child in the Empire. As surely as we believed the sun would rise in the morning we believed the Ward Walls could hold back Chaos. Without that assurance no one would ever feel safe. There could be no peace of mind because an attack could come at any time, day or night, winter or summer. In that one moment when vigilance flagged, everyone would know they had doomed themselves.

I recalled nights back on the farm, nights I would recite the rhyme against evil my aunt had taught me. On those nights I was afraid of shrieking winds and moon-born shadows dancing across walls. I was afraid of phantoms and eventually outgrew such night terrors. If I had known the Ward Walls could be circumvented, however, I would have always been on edge, ever fearful, and that would have worn me down to nothing.

But, I reminded myself, *there is no proof the Ward Walls have failed. Until we have such proof, even suggesting such a thing would cause such turmoil that people would panic.*

I realized that one possible explanation for what Kit saw was an elaborate charade staged by the Black Churchers to make someone believe the Ward Walls had fallen. The resulting panic would serve their cause well. They could convince people to join them and avoid retribution when the Chaos demons destroyed the Empire. They might even become strong enough to overthrow the Emperor and deliver the Empire to Kothvir's brood without a fight.

I decided the chances of that happening were probably slender, but I decided to tell Kit about my idea so he could include it in his report. I almost headed back up to Kit's room at that moment to tell him, but changed my mind when I realized that leaving again might be viewed suspiciously. Attempting to appear as if nothing at all out of the ordinary were happening around me, I smiled and made my way back into the grand ballroom.

A quartet of musicians with stringed instruments had begun playing in the northeast corner of the room. From the direction they faced, and the way some of the spectators kept looking toward the opposite side of the room, I assumed I would find my grandmother seated there. The couples dancing in the middle of the floor would have cut off her view of the musicians, but I had no doubt that James would have arranged some way for Grandmother to communicate her desires for music to the players.

As stealthfully as I imagined Kit tracking through the snow after the Chaos creature, I cut through the crowd and made my way in the general direction of my grandmother. I found Evadne surrounded by her friends. They were laughing to themselves and pointing out individuals in the crowd who, I assumed, had committed some hideous social error. To me everyone seemed horridly overdressed—myself most emphatically included —and I was sure the conversations had more exaggeration in them than claims made in a bazaar on market day.

Back near the wall, hovering close enough if needed, I saw Marija. She smiled, and, needing little more encouragement than that, I walked over to her. "The musicians are good, are they not?"

"That they are, Master Lachlan." She watched the dancers for a moment, her brown eyes flicking after their movements, then she sharpened her gaze and turned it on me. "So, Master Lachlan, why are you not on the floor, giving some poor girl the thrill of a lifetime?"

I blinked my eyes once, then frowned. "First of all, I am Locke. Lachlan is a name that gets used when someone is inclined to be formal, or I am being disciplined."

"Well then, Master Locke, why aren't you dancing?" Her voice took on a playful tone. "You seemed quite taken with Xoayya earlier. I heard you promise her a dance."

"Me, taken with Xoayya? No." I shook my head. "Besides, she told me I was going to dance with her, I didn't ask her to dance. I don't intend to dance with anyone."

"And break the hearts of all the girls you met tonight?"

I looked around to see if she was speaking to someone else, but I was the only person around. "I do not have a clue as to what you are talking about. I'm not breaking anyone's heart."

"Oh, you'd be surprised?" Her grin became wolfish. "You're still not getting this, are you?"

"Not even close. Is this some sort of Herak joke?"

"No, but I thought it obvious enough that even a Garikman could get it." Marija sighed wistfully. "Mistress Evadne is quite wealthy, and both of her sons were quite famous before they were lost in Chaos. Her grandsons, the two I have met anyway, are most hand-some and would be quite a catch for any of the poorer noble houses of the Empire. Any of the young women to whom you were introduced this evening would love to have you ask them to dance. Their parents would be overjoyed with the idea."

I looked at the women on or surrounding the floor. I did remember quite a few young women being intro-duced to me in the receiving line, but I had forgotten their names as quickly as the echoes of them faded from my ears. While many of the girls were very pretty, and wore wonderful gowns that accentuated their beauty, I found something missing.

None of them, save Marija, laughed the way the girls did back home during our Bear's Eve celebration. There didn't seem to be any true joy behind their smiles. The setting and the way they appeared and acted seemed artificial to me. They might as well all have been wear-ing masks to hide Chademon faces.

"Not for me, I'm afraid." I shrugged. "Back home . . ."

Marija looked surprised for a moment. "You have a woman back in Garik?" I heard a bit of amusement in Marija's question. "Oh, hearts are crumbling already, and along with them the dreams of more than one des-titute parent."

"No, it's not that." I frowned at her. "Besides, I have two older brothers, and there is Kit, who can mend those hearts and rebuild those dreams."

Marija smiled and winked at me. "Ah, I see now, Master Lachlan. Foist these minor nobles off on your brothers and Kit. Brilliant. And then you, at the Bear's

Eve Ball, will charm one of the Emperor's sisters. Which will it be, Nassia or Eriat?"

"Only your wit exceeds your beauty, Marija." I folded my arms across my chest and shook my head. "A princess for me? Ha!"

Marija cocked an eyebrow at me. "You're a bit young to be setting your cap for the widowed Empress."

I shook my head and didn't want to say anything more, but I realized silence wasn't going to work for me. I grimaced. "The thing of it is, you see, I do not know how to dance."

"You cannot dance?" It was Marija's turn to be surprised. "But, even in Garik, you must dance on Bear's Eve. You *must*, it is tradition."

"Oh, yes, I can do that, but it is different here." I pointed off toward the musicians. "They are real musicians, not Ferran Tugg from the Hollows and his brother Burton with their fiddles. And the dances—bits and pieces of them look familiar, but the music is different. I would look as out of place out there as a frog."

Whatever she was going to say died as her face closed up. I turned to follow her line of sight, and I saw Kit swooping toward us like a stooping hawk. "Ah, Marija, there you are." He held his hand out to her. "Come with me, Ugly Duckling, and I will make you a swan on the dance floor."

"I a swan, and you my swain?" Marija shook her head. "I would have loved to, Master Christoforos, but"—she grabbed my hand—"your cousin has already asked me to dance."

The surprise on my face registered clearly in Kit's eyes, but he just smiled and acknowledged Marija's trumping of his play. He turned from us and found another young woman to invite onto the dance floor. Marija started after him, pulling on my hand, but I held my ground. "I told you I would look like a frog out there."

She came forward and kissed me lightly on the lips. "I am not a princess, so that will not make you a prince, but I think it should be enough to make a dancer out of a frog. Come with me, watch Kit, and just listen to the music. Let yourself go—this *is* a celebration, after all."

Marija was right in that under her tutelage I acquitted myself acceptably out on the dance floor. Of course, when compared to Kit's flawless grace out there, my efforts closely resembled those of a scarecrow rooted in a field, but I enjoyed myself. After a few dances, Marija finally relented and let Kit lead her out into the swirling mass of people. While they looked exquisite together, I gathered from the expressions on their faces that they continued their verbal sparring throughout their dances.

Watching them would have been entertaining in and of itself, but Xoayya descended upon me in a rustling hurry and demanded I fulfill my promise to dance with her. Having no choice—but not really resenting the lack of one either—I led her out onto the dance floor. The musicians began a slow dance that required the two of us to move as one, and Xoayya proved a very capable and fluid partner.

As could be expected, holding her close, with my hand pressed to the middle of her back, I learned more about her—things I had not expected. Despite her petite body, she had a fair amount of strength in her arms and back. She moved in perfect time with the music and anticipated our turns flawlessly. That latter point could easily have been explained by her clairvoyant skill, but she seemed sharper and more focused as we moved together.

She smiled wonderfully. "I love dancing. I just let the music fill me and carry me away."

I nodded. "You do seem different out here."

The joy in her eyes dimmed for a half second. "I can concentrate on the music, and that seems to hold some of the visions at bay."

"I don't think I understand."

We twirled around and flashed past Kit and Marija before she explained. "In the City of Sorcerers they tried to teach me to clear my mind to let the visions come, but that's not my problem. They come no matter what I do—often when I'm sleeping because my mind is less occupied then."

I gave her a quick smile. "That makes sense. You can't hear a whisper amid shouting."

"Yes, but whispers seem to fill my mind, except, that is, when music or something else occupies me. When listening to music I possess my own mind." She smiled bravely, but fatigue eroded the edges of the smile. "Was I mean to you when we met on the trail?"

I pulled my head back. "Mean? No. Perhaps abrupt, but not mean."

"Good. I don't want to be mean, and I can be. I'm so used to getting my way that I'm utterly unthinking at times."

"And having snippets of other people's lives parading themselves through your mind cannot be easy on you."

"No, it is very confusing. And frightening."

The music ended for that dance. Holding her hand, I pulled back and bowed to her. I was going to let her go, but she tightened her grip on my hand. "One more dance, please, Locke? Help me be myself for a bit longer."

"It would be my pleasure, Xoayya, but dancing with

me is not the only way to accomplish that goal." I pulled her close again as the musicians began to play. "It strikes me that you can use music or other things to keep the visions under control."

"Now I don't understand you."

"No surprise there, since I don't really know what I'm talking about. However, I'm wondering about what they told you in the City of Sorcerers. If the visions come when the mind is clear, and if they don't while your mind is occupied, perhaps you need to occupy your mind on purpose." I smiled carefully. "In Garik we have a tune best known as 'the birthday song.' There's one verse for each year of a person's life, and if you like the person, you only sing the last verse. If you want to have fun with them, you sing them all."

Xoayya nodded slowly. "We have that here in Herak, too." She hummed a bit of the tune. "I hate the song because I can never get it out of my head."

"Exactly."

Her smile blossomed fully. "It would work, I think, though that tune is more torture than the visions."

"Agreed, but there are other tunes, or you could do sums and products in your head, or memorize poems."

"That's a lot of work."

"Isn't possessing your own mind worth it?"

"That it is." As the music stopped, she stood on her tiptoes and kissed me on the cheek. "I think, Master Locke, you've just given me the greatest Bear's Eve gift ever. I will find a way to repay you."

"If this makes you happy into the next year and beyond, I will have been more than repaid." I kissed her hand and surrendered her to Kit.

Marija looked over at me with a smile on her face. "So dancing with her wasn't as difficult as you feared, was it?"

"Not at all, Marija, not at all." I winked at her. "Of course, we were nothing compared to Kit and you."

"Ha!" Marija nodded toward my cousin and Xoayya. "He'll enjoy having danced with her because she's much lighter on her feet than I was on *his*."

The party itself continued late into the evening, with Kit and me having to assume full host duties when Marija took Grandmother to her chambers for the night. Fortunately for me, because I was still exhausted from the trip to the capital, most of the guests started filtering out after Grandmother left. Those who remained tended to be people more Kit's age, and I felt justified in leaving them to him as fatigue ground me down to nothing.

Though I dropped off to sleep the second my head hit the down pillows, slivers of Kit's report to the Warlord haunted my dreams. I had no trouble at all visualizing a sable-coated lion-man stalking through the streets of Herakopolis. I saw his bushy black mane, long and luxurious, hiding his face like the shadow of a hooded cloak. Light from somewhere lit his face for a half second, showing me eyes that were nothing but cold, gold orbs. He flicked one hand out, and a reddish backlight washed through his eyes, then I heard a distant scream.

I sat bolt upright in bed. I knew what I had seen was a dream; it had to be a dream. Yet, even as I comprehended the differences between it and reality, I also discovered a nugget of truth hidden in it. The Black Shadow I had seen wore his mane full, not cropped in the manner of *Bharashadi* warriors. That meant it was a sorcerer.

Deep down inside I had no doubt that Kit had chased a Chademon sorcerer halfway across the Empire. Ignoring for the moment the disturbing portent of the Chademon having somehow gotten through the Ward Walls, I wondered why he had made his perilous journey. He appeared no more suited to wandering around in the Empire than I, as a virgin traveler in Chaos, would be to adventuring in his homeland. Most people would have assumed the Chademon would have come here to wreak havoc and spill blood, but this creature had been smarter than that. While his inexperience might have led him to make the mistakes that let Kit track him, his attempts at evasion and his desire to remain hidden marked his intelligence.

After all, had he been the cause of the destruction Kit described in the clearing with the dead wolves, what would have stopped him from using that sort of magick against Kit's patrol? The only answer I could come up with was that the Chademon wanted to avoid another display of power that would make him easy to pinpoint. That meant he had a purpose in having come across the wall, and that his mission had not yet been fulfilled.

I knew there could easily be a thousand answers to the question of why he had come into the Empire, and the Warlord's caution about his possibly being of Kothvir's brood made me doubly wary. Still I knew the majority of people who braved Chaos did so for one of three reasons: greed, adventure, or revenge.

From what I had heard of Chaos, I would have imagined living there would be adventure enough for any Chademon. As far as revenge went, I knew Chademons created weapons with the image of their enemies on them, but I had not heard of them being mindlessly obsessed with pursuing their enemies. In at least two tales concerning my father I knew of Kothvir leaving him alone as Cardew went after the Storm demons and the Devils in Motley.

Stories of riches lost when Chaos swept over the world abound and become embellished during each retelling. Still, some expeditions were mounted into Chaos to recover items of power or great antiquity. Even in Stone Rapids I had heard rumors of covert missions into Chaos made at the direction of the Grandmaster of Magicks in the City of Sorcerers. Could it be that this Chademon had braved the dangers of the Empire to get back something he needed?

If he had, what could it be? I lay back down in my bed and forced myself to close my eyes. If he was powerful enough to break through the Wardlines and had come for something specific, could anything be reasonably expected to stop him?

9

I returned to sleep, and, when I awoke again, the lees of my dreams made waking very difficult. Under normal circumstances, including the necessity of early travel with the caravan, I rose before the sun and felt as alert as a cat whose tail has just been stepped on. This morning, however, the sun had beaten me up by at least an hour, and it would have been easier to claw my way out of quicksand than to escape that bed.

The lingering impressions of my dream proved frustrating. Part of me felt they were right and true, yet I knew I had no proof of anything. All of a sudden I had a disturbing window on Xoayya's difficulties in dealing with her gift—and she knew it was a gift and had some validity. I had no such assurances.

Conclusions that had seemed irrefutable in the middle of the night began to collapse in the light of day. I had believed my identification of the Chademon as a

Black Shadow sorcerer because of how it wore its mane to be confirmation of its existence. The fact was that I'd known about the difference between *Bharashadi* warriors and sorcerers since I was a child. Because there was a good chance the creature had used magick, endowing it with the proper grooming was nothing less than I would have expected in my dreams.

As with the discussion the night before, we had a handful of maybes. Raising an alarm because of my dream or the bit of Kit's tale would be sheer folly. While Kit would undoubtedly humor me if I told him of my dream, it really had no value. If he were to include it in his report, he'd deserve the criticism that would come from his superiors. Decisions had to be made based on facts, not the wild imaginings of a provincial's dreams.

I considered possibly seeking out Xoayya and consulting her about the veracity of my dream, but I rejected that course of action. She had trouble enough determining what was true and predictive from what was not. Telling her enough to let her evaluate my dream would betray confidences. Worse yet, if Chademon images invaded her dreams because of me, she might raise an alarm and cause the panic all of us knew we had to avoid.

I dressed quickly in blue woolen pants and a thick, wool tunic with a plaid green-and-black pattern to it. Pulling on my boots, which Nob had succeeded in making look almost straight from the cobbler, I headed out of my suite and down to the warm kitchen.

Rose stood stirring a black pot of thick porridge as it hung over a fire. Nob stood beside her with an empty bowl, and she kept him at bay with stern looks. When she turned to face me and smiled, Nob dipped a finger through the porridge and plopped it into his mouth. He winked at me, and I smiled as Rose greeted me. "Top of the morning to you, Master Lachlan."

"And to you, Rose. Nob, these boots are perfect. What do I owe you?"

The grizzled old man shook his head. "You owe me naught, Master Lachlan. My pleasure it is to do that for you. If you're of a mind for a game, later . . ."

I gave him a big nod. "That I would like, Nob."

"It'll be a long day worn short before you've time to play, Nob." Rose brandished her wooden spoon at him. "You've yet to finish painting the coach for Bear's Eve, then you and Carl will be out delivering the Mistress's gifts for Bear's Eve."

She turned back to face me. "Don't you be letting this old fool tie up all your time. He has more than enough excuses not to work around here. You're young, and you're in the capital for the first time. You'll be wanting to see much of it. Now if you go into the dining room, I'll bring you your breakfast presently."

I walked over to a cupboard and pulled a wooden bowl from it. "Please, just give me some porridge and a spoon, and I will be fine." Rose looked a touch disappointed, but I squeezed her shoulder with my right hand to reassure her. "At my grandfather's home I usually do the breakfast cooking, so I feel spoiled already. Were I to go to a special room to eat, I would be afraid to eat. Wouldn't know what to do."

"Seems to me I heard you say that about dancing, Master Lachlan. Even so, you proved quite adept on the dance floor."

I turned toward Marija and struck a high guard with my spoon. "True enough, but on the dance floor I had an able teacher, and I was not required to use implements like a knife or spoon."

Rose filled my bowl with porridge, then poured a little milk from a crock on it. She looked over at Marija. "Would you like your breakfast now, child?"

Dark curls covered her shoulders as she shook her head. "Not yet. I will have it after I return and take Mistress Evadne's tray up to her." Though already dressed for the cold in a woolen tunic and a long plaid woolen jumper, she reach for a thick black cloak hanging from a peg across from the hearth.

I hastily swallowed the first steaming spoonful of porridge and wiped a droplet of milk from my lower lip. "You are going out?"

"Aye, Master Lachlan. I am bound for the apothecary to get more of your grandmother's tonic. As she wants to attend several of the celebrations leading up to the Emperor's Ball, we will be using a bit more of it than usual."

"I see."

Rose looked up at her husband. "Nob will walk with you, Miss Marija. Do his bones good to get them moving."

Nob frowned, and I rescued him. "Actually, if you don't mind, Nob, I would be happy to walk with Marija. It would give me a chance to see the capital. That is, if you don't mind, Marija."

"Why, Master Lachlan, I would be delighted to show you Herakopolis."

"Good." I looked for a place to set my bowl down but, seeing my distress, Nob plucked it from my hand.

"Be glad to help you with that, I would, m'lord."

Rose did not look overly happy. "Nob, you're a worthless old goat. At least fetch Master Lachlan a cloak."

"Don't get up, Nob. I forgot something up in my rooms anyway. I will go." I darted from the kitchen and took the steps two at a time. Inside my suite I passed to the interior room. In the closet I saw a number of cloaks and selected one of dark evergreen with a hood. I fastened it about my throat with the silver clasp, then started back toward the kitchen.

I am not quite certain what made me think of it, but it struck me, as I passed through the middle of my sitting room, that to go unarmed into the capital was just the sort of mistake a joskin from the country would make. I pulled off the belt with my dagger and took stock of the swords racked beside the door.

Being a Garikman, and one raised by a Blades-master, I recognized the various different types of blades there and thought I saw a pattern to how they had been stored. All the way on the left, the furthest from the door, were the heavy, curved blades of sabres and scimitars. Those blades were well suited to crushing and slashing attacks, best if used from horseback in thick-melee battling. While I had not been trained with them formally, being only an Apprentice, I had listened well as Audin had instructed my brothers.

In the middle came the heavier but straight-bladed weapons. Broadswords, longsword and greatswords, their grips varying from short for the smaller blades up to thick and long enough to wrap two hands around them for the heaviest. Although best suited to crushing blows, especially against foes in heavy armor, their thrusting points did make them appropriate for limited amounts of dueling.

Nearest the door, however, I found the swords most suited to me and to the city. With slender blades of well-tempered steel, the rapiers varied in length from three to five feet. I knew, being as small as I was, that the shorter blade would make me overly vulnerable to anyone with a longer reach. While the tallest of the blades might more than make up for that advantage in a foe, I knew the long blade would be too clumsy for me to best a skilled enemy.

I reached for a swept-hilted sword of medium length and slid it from its scabbard. The sword felt perfect in my hand and hissed through the air as I flipped it around in a couple of experimental cuts. The balance put sufficient weight in my hand to let me control the blade with ease, yet left enough heft in the blade itself so a slash could carry through a light leather jerkin.

This was the weapon for me. As I slid the leather scabbard back onto it, watching the blade fill it like bones filling an empty snakeskin, a shiver ran down my spine. The sword I had chosen was the one I had used the night before. It was the one nearest the door, and I realized it had been placed there deliberately to come to hand easily.

Apparently my father truly did possess the foresight all the tales had credited to him.

I slid my belt through the loops on the scabbard's harness and refastened it around my waist. The blade hung perfectly at my left hip, and I practiced a quick flip of the cloak back from my left shoulder so I could draw the sword with my right hand. My hand fell to the hilt as easily as breathing, and I smiled. No country bumpkin was I to be accosted by city ruffians.

By the time I returned to the kitchen Nob had finished my bowl of porridge, but Rose had just started in on him for wanting "his" bowl as well. Marija and I quickly headed out of doors to avoid the domestic tiff, though I gathered it was more a game than a true fight, and mentioned that to Marija.

"Ah, you noticed. Yes, they love each other, but seem to get a great deal of enjoyment out of battling like that. Rose rules with an iron fist in the house, but she defers to Nob for anything outside those four walls."

"Not unlike your little matches with Kit."

Marija's eyes flashed as her head jerked around. "Master Christoforos and I are not in love, Master Lachlan."

"Locke, please, or I start calling you Missy Marija." Steaming breath trailed from my mouth as we left my grandmother's courtyard and stepped into the street. "Were your antics with Kit measured against the yard-stick of Rose and Nob, I'd have to judge you a couple bound by long years."

"It might seem that, but our fighting is more the teasing of brothers and sisters, I think. I do not know that for certain, however. Do you not engage in verbal sparring with your brothers?"

I smiled, remembering them, then shook my head. "Not that often. Dalt is not a man of many words, and Geoff is quick enough that I would be the loser in any battle of wits with him. I take it, though, from what you said, you have known Kit for a long time, and you have no siblings. How long have you known Kit?"

She turned her face from me and looked farther up the road. "Since before I can remember, actually. I have lived in your grandmother's house for just shy twenty years. I was even there when you first came to the house."

"But you would have been . . ."

"A wee babe. That is true; I was." She smiled slightly. "My father, Seoirse, was a lieutenant to your father. He had served in the Valiant Lancers and proved himself intelligent and resourceful. Cardew, Driscoll, and my father got on famously. In fact, your father and uncle all but adopted my father as the younger brother they never had. And when I came along, well, my mother often told me of the wonderful celebration thrown by your father for my naming."

I smiled at the laughter in her voice. "The party last night doubtless paled in comparison."

"As my mother told it, even the Emperor's Ball would seem but a drink hoisted between friends compared to this feast. At one point your father looked at me and said I was the most beautiful baby he'd ever seen. He added that if his wife chanced to die before he did, he'd seek me out and make me his new bride." She glanced down at the ground. "My mother, may the gods safekeep her soul, was very proud of that."

"I learned earlier this morning my father possessed foresight, but now I must think of him as being as clairvoyant as Xoayya."

Marija nodded as we passed onto Butcher's Row. She kept toward the center of the street to avoid the iced-over puddles. I followed closely to catch her if she slipped, but she negotiated the iciest part without trouble, then crossed to a wooden boardwalk on the east side of the street.

The majority of the buildings in this particular section of the city had been built of wood. Given the differences in architectural style between these buildings and my grandmother's house, I decided they were much newer than my grandmother's. I assumed these double-story boxes had been put up to replace buildings destroyed by some calamity or other. The buildings felt alien to me, as if they did not really belong here.

As I walked at Marija's side, a feeling of dread cored a hole through my stomach. "Seoirse accompanied my father and uncle on their last expedition into Chaos, did he not?"

She nodded mutely. "My mother was crushed when the Valiant Lancers did not return. We were left in utter poverty. Your grandmother tried to take us in, but my mother refused to accept charity. Your grandmother countered by hiring her to be a live-in nurse for Christoforos, as his mother had died of childbed fever when bearing him three years earlier."

"So you were raised together?" I had to shout my question as a dray wagon clattered past us, and stray curs barked at the horses.

"Fought like cats and dogs. We refined our battling into the civilized form you have seen because my mother thought it disrespectful for me to fight with Kit." Marija smiled as an embarrassed blush added yet more color to her rosy cheeks. "I think she hoped Kit and I would fall in love and marry someday."

"Why didn't you?"

"What, and ruin a perfectly workable friendship? Despite what you have seen, Kit and I are able to confide in each other, and woe be to anyone who chooses to attack one of us because he will find us side by side in any fight." I started laughing, and her hot-eyed stare spitted me like a rabbit on a spear. "What is it?"

"Nothing, really, but I think you know exactly what it is to have a brother. Dalt and I do not get along at all, but I remember when some of the cooper's boys decided they wanted to beat someone up, and I was their target. They'd surrounded me and had taken turns seeing who could punch me the hardest when Dalt waded into them all fists and feet and fire in his eyes. Thrashed the lot of them."

A smile softened her face. "You are very lucky to have Dalt for a brother."

"That was what I was thinking at the moment, but

then he gave me a cuff or two for having been stupid enough to have been trapped in that situation."

Butcher's Row went slightly up a hill, then curved to the right, where it became Jewelpath Road. Here, likewise, the buildings were made up mostly of wood, but they all started from a solid first story of stone, so they felt more familiar to me. Marija stopped at one tiny place with a high stone arch over a narrow doorway. A mortar and pestle hung from the keystone, making it easily identified as an apothecary.

We squeezed in past two old women swaddled in enough cloth to make both of them as thick as trolls. I heard snatches of gossip pass between them, but as I heard no names I recognized, I let their droning voices drift into the background. Not only did I not have a real taste for gossip, but the shop itself held more than enough to keep my attention occupied for a lifetime.

The walls on either side rose up two full stories and had built into them countless wooden drawers. Ladders fitted to a cast-iron track at the top and bottom of the wall rolled along to provide access to the upper drawers. Hanging down from the blocky support beams bridging the space beneath the arched roof, dried plants, bones, and one or two arcane devices I did not recognize filled the room's middle reaches. Down on the floor level, aside from three casks of pickled vegetables along the far wall, a display of two standing chests—each of which brimmed with enough drawers to make it a simulacrum of the walls—took up all the floor space excepting a narrow pathway toward a counter in the corner.

"Good morning to you, m'lady Marija," the thickset man behind the counter happily greeted her. "You would be wanting more of Lady Evadne's tonic, I would guess."

"Correct, Goodman Birger." Marija turned toward me. "I would also like to introduce to you Master Lachlan, one of Lady Evadne's grandsons from Garik."

The apothecary offered me his meaty right arm, and I grasped it firmly. "Pleased to make your acquaintance, Goodman. Please called me Locke."

"And you, Master Locke." His smile forced his cheeks to widen his face enough to partially eclipse his ears. "I will have more of that tonic for you in a moment or two."

I had seen, from the rank badge sewn on the breast of his yellow tunic that he was a Chemist. This meant he was the rough equivalent of my grandfather's being a Bladesmaster. As he moved from drawer to drawer, he pulled out pinches of this, or great hunks of that. He piled each ingredient on a white marble table beside a mortar and pestle made of some gray stone I did not recognize.

"I have seen my grandmother take this tonic, and it does seem to enliven her, but I was wondering what is wrong with her?"

The florid-faced man's smile lessened a bit. "She has the disease that will be the death of us all, save those who go as your father did." He shook his head. "She is old, and her heart is not quite as strong as it once was. This tonic eases some pains, reduces some swellings, and makes it easier for her heart to do its job."

I frowned. "If her heart is the problem, could not a magicker use his art to make her heart strong again?"

Birger turned from the mixing table and planted both of his hands on the counter. The look he gave me was serious, yet I sensed no anger in him. Instead he reminded me of Audin preparing to lecture me on some point of swordsmanship I had clearly misunderstood.

"Magick, my boy, has its limitations. So does your understanding of it—unless, of course, you've spent time studying it and are hiding your rank badges."

I shook my head and noticed, to my mortification, that Marija seemed amused by my being lectured.

"Now if you were cut in a fight and you went to a magicker and he spelled your wound shut, you'd think yourself healed, wouldn't you? Of course you would, but you would be wrong. The first thing you have to learn about magick is that almost anything done by magick can be undone by it—and there are times the undoing magick carries only a fraction of the power of the spell it undoes. When you have a wound spelled well, what the magick does is to knit you back together long enough for your body to repair itself. Yes, it might even speed the healing process, but if dispelled, you'd be in the same fix you were in before the first spell was cast."

"Less any healing my body had done?"

"Smart lad. Now, in your grandmother's case, there just is no cure for aging. There is no way for the body to heal itself. To be certain, spells might work to do the things this elixir will do, but this combination of herbs and things works in a manner too complex for spells to mimic easily."

He went back to the mixing table and carefully added the ingredients to his mortar. He splashed in some water, then mumbled something as he picked up his pestle and pressed it down into the mix. Grinding and stirring, he blended the tonic's parts into a smooth syrup that he repeatedly diluted with more and more water.

As he worked I saw the grayish mortar shift color. It brightened slightly as if the elixir was leaching color from it. I knew instantly that he was using magick to create the tonic, but I did nothing to interrupt him as he continued mixing and talking to himself. When he finally tapped the pestle clean on the edge of the mortar and reached for a bottle and funnel, I asked another question.

"You said magick would not help my grandmother, yet you used magick to create her medicine. How is that, especially given that you are not ranked in the ways of magick?"

"I am not skilled in the ways of magick, but the Sorcerer who created this mortar and pestle was. By speaking precise instructions over it, I am able to condense the work of weeks into a few minutes. This tonic, for example, would require long steeping and repeated distillations to produce without magick. And to answer the question in your mind, no, dispelling the magick now would not return this to its component parts. At best a spell cast during the mixing could stop the brewing in the middle, but what was crushed would remain crushed and what was wet would still be sopping."

The Chemist poured the tonic into the bottle and stoppered it with a bit of cork. "There you go, Miss Marija."

Marija took the bottle and placed a gold Imperial on the counter, but Birger waved it off. "No, I'll not be hearing of Lady Evadne paying for this batch. Tell her it is my Bear's Eve gift to her." Marija frowned, but Birger perched his fists on his wide hips and clearly would brook no argument.

"Then the warmth of the season be upon you and yours, Goodman Birger."

"Likewise, m'lady." Birger looked past me toward the two women by the door. "Triona, leave off gossiping like a fishwife and meet Master Locke, Lady Evadne's grandson."

The woman nearest me turned and snarled at Birger. "We are not gossiping, husband mine, but discussing what happened down in Old Town. You remember how it was said the baker there, Bald Ugo, was a member of the Black Church?" Triona thrust her face forward in a challenge to Birger, but being between them, I felt uneasy.

"Unproved tripe, lies spread by Jurik because Ugo had more customers."

"Well then, how come is it, that this morning the Emperor's constabulary forced its way into the shop when it had not opened for two days and began to stink bad? When they went in, or so it is told, they found a trapdoor leading down to a hidden cellar. There they found Black Church things, and Ugo's whole family dead."

"Dead?" I heard myself ask quietly.

Triona nodded, her dark eyes glittering like stars. "Worse than dead, Master Locke. Carved up. Carved up by something horrid that opened them like a fisherman gutting his catch. And, mind you, lad, it ate most of what it caught, too."

10

Despite the festive nature of the season, the news of the murders in Old Town was a topic of fascination for most folks in the capital. Throughout the rest of the week I heard the story repeated and embellished to the point where a whole congregation of Black Churchers had died when they summoned Fialchar from his sanctum in Chaos, and he was displeased with their efforts. The manner of death of Bald Ugo and his family also varied, from the bodies being desiccated into parchment skeletons to their having been reduced to puddles of boneless flesh that begged to die.

In very short order the whole incident became wrapped in a fabric of fantasy that could have made me think it all a fable. If Triona's version of it had not painted an image into which I could slip the person of a *Bharashadi* sorcerer, I would have refused to believe any of it, I think. Kit, who heard his own versions of the story, did not comment on it overmuch, but told me enough to keep my wild speculations alive.

Despite the story's seeming confirmation of my dream, I stuck with my decision to keep it to myself. Kit and his people had chased the creature back toward the city and, apparently, were involved in a search for signs of it within the capital, so they didn't need the distraction. Moreover, Kit already knew it could use magick, and he had seen enough evidence of what it could do to link Bald Ugo's death with it if facts warranted that linkage. What I had to offer was a bad dream that clothed itself in bits and pieces of stories I had heard as a child.

I could not imagine the Warlord not already working on the worst-case scenario—namely that the creature was a sorcerer with a mission to perform in the capital. Try as I might to spy out clues to what was being done, I saw no signs of extra preparedness or caution. Then again, not having been in Herakopolis before, I had no way of judging if any special precautions had been taken or not.

The holiday season in the capital lasted longer than it did in Stone Rapids and seemed more powerful. Whereas in the village where I had spent my entire life to this point we would prepare gifts for our kin and close friends in anticipation of the single Bear's Eve celebration, here parties appeared to be as much a part of the season as snow and ice. As the days shortened and the night grew toward the longest it could possibly be, the festive atmosphere became frenzied, and I found myself quite caught up in it.

James took me to a tailor the afternoon of the day Marija and I ventured out. In that shop I was measured every which way and that, then shown countless fabrics from all corners of the Empire. Because the invitation for the Emperor's Ball had specified white and silver as the dominant colors, with an accent color allowed for each person, the patterns and weaves and fabrics themselves became important to create the proper social image.

The tailor steered me away from anything heavy with a sniffed, "They do have fireplaces in the palace, m'lord." We settled on a tunic of silver silk with a quilted cotton jacket and cotton pants that I could tuck into the top of my boots. The tailor suggested I choose a green ribbon for my accent color to match my eyes and that I have it run up the sleeves and down the legs of my suit.

I agreed with the choice of color, but I asked for the ribbon to be cut into strips that could be hung like fringes from the underside of my jacket arms and along the back of the yoke. In Stone Rapids no one had the money or the time to prepare clothing solely for use on Bear's Eve, so we made things more festive by sewing on ribbons in that manner.

The tailor mumbled a remark that ended with the word, "quaint." He seemed to have no problem with the gold Imperials James gave him for doing the job. James then took me to a cobbler's, where we purchased a pair of boots in white leather. I protested that my brown boots were fine, but James pointed out that the color was wrong for the ball, and that put an end to the argument.

The rest of the week became something of a blur. I attended parties every evening with my grandmother and Marija. I met more people than I had even imagined existed in the world, and many of them had daughters or nieces or sisters to whom I was also introduced. I would just as soon have remained in Marija's company, but her status as a servant kept her segregated from the revelers. What had been acceptable behavior at my grandmother's party would have been scandalous at these other celebrations.

Because of the parties, the very nature of the Empire impressed itself upon me as never before. While Herakopolis was larger and more grand than any city I had ever visited, it was in the homes of the people we called upon that this point was made most emphatically. We attended celebrations in houses that dwarfed my grandmother's house. While I had thought *tsoerits* to be exotic, at other parties I found them as common as chicken eggs. I tasted fruits I never knew existed before, drank wines of all different flavors and colors, and was enticed into trying all sorts of other things against my better judgment.

Xoayya attended most of the parties I did and, in Marija's absence, took it upon herself to introduce me to the various treasures the capital had to offer. She seemed to know where things came from, where they had been purchased, and trivial little facts about our hosts that amounted to gossip, but that I suspected were garnered through visions.

"I want to thank you, Locke, for your suggestion about the song." She regarded me over a crystal goblet of a blue wine that was only slightly darker than her eyes. "It is effective."

I smiled. "You're only getting visions when you want them now?"

"No." She glanced down. "Inconsequential things appear to be sifted out. What does get through appears to be stronger and more intense."

"Is that good or bad?"

"I don't know." When she looked up I read fear in her

eyes. "I had a vision—a dream—that concerns us." She pressed a hand against the breast of my jacket. "It wasn't sexual—at least I don't think it was—but it *was* very strong. There was a connection between us and another creature."

I did my best to keep my voice even. "What sort of creature?"

"Something dark and decidedly evil." She lowered her voice. "You heard of the slaughter, didn't you? Whatever did that is what is linking us. It has something to do with our destinies. Through that thing we will find out why we are here."

"How do you know this?" I frowned. "I know it comes from a vision, but you're placing a lot of weight on it. Have you seen what happens to us or . . . ?"

"I do not know what happens to us, nor have I seen anything that would tell me what will happen. I know something will happen, though, because I feel now as I did before my father died. Some visions, the worthless ones, fly past my notice like an overheard comment or something seen from the window of a speeding carriage. Their brevity is a mark of their intensity and importance."

She set her wineglass down on a sideboard, then pressed her hands together. "The feeling I have of the linking is very strong. It's like the ocean's undertow. We're being pulled along, and we can't escape it. Our destinies are wrapped up in the destiny of this thing."

I slowly shook my head. "I'm not doubting anything you've said, Xoayya, really, I'm not."

Anger creased her brow. "What you've just said indicates you don't believe me."

"Not true. I believe you're reporting everything you've experienced accurately and completely." I shrugged. "I'm just not sure I find the argument about destiny very compelling. We don't even know what did the murders, much less that it's some dark creature linking us."

She clutched my right forearm in both her hands. "You do know the creature I'm speaking about, though. Don't deny that."

I coughed lightly behind my left hand. "Xoayya, I've had a dream, but it's cobbled together out of stories and rumors. It felt real to me, but I know it was just a dream."

"How do you know that?"

I hesitated, then shrugged my shoulders. "I just do."

A frosty tone entered her voice. "I see." Her blue eyes narrowed. "What if I could prove to you that your dream was real?"

"How can you do that?"

Xoayya looked left and right to see if anyone was watching us before she answered me. "The reason my grandmother knew to come rescue me is because she is a powerful clairvoyant herself. Not many people know this—I doubt even your grandmother does. My grandmother gave up magick when she met and married my grandfather, so those who know her secret outside our household are few. She could convince you that what you dreamed was real."

"You want me to speak with her?"

"More than that, I want you to sit with her and have her divine your future. She will be able to tell you things about yourself that no one but you could know."

I shook my head. "Not interested."

"You will be."

"I don't think so."

Xoayya smiled confidently. "Oh, you *will* meet with her. I have seen it."

"Perhaps." I reached down and freed her right hand

from my wrist. "Have you also foreseen my asking you to dance right now?"

Her smile grew. "I did see that you would try to deflect me."

"Did I succeed?"

"We'll see."

I did, but only temporarily. As it was, that was enough because my grandmother tired somewhat quickly at many of the parties, requiring us to make our departure rather early in the evening. Returning home, I was able to meet Nob for an occasional game of chess and still get enough sleep so I could rise early and put myself through the regimen of exercises Audin had forced on me for as long as I could remember.

Part of me would have been happy to forget the training and discipline with which my grandfather had made me greet each day of my life. Being out and on my own for the first time, I wanted to rebel to show that I was better than he imagined and that I did not need his exercises. After all, here I was in the capital while he was stuck back in Stone Rapids. What could he know that would benefit me here?

The truth was, though, that the capital was so alien to me that I needed an anchor. Waking before the sun slipped over the horizon, I forced myself out of a warm bed and into the weapons chamber. There, the cool air puckering my flesh, I paced myself through stretches and sit-ups, push-ups and balancing myself on my hands. Choosing the rapier I had worn, I took myself through various guards and worked up a sweat fencing against shadows.

One morning, as I recovered from a lunge that had spit a foe, I heard my door open and solitary applause. I spun and saw Kit leaning against the jamb. "Audin's training has taken root deeply in you, Locke."

I wiped my forehead against my left forearm. "It has, indeed. You speak as if you disapprove." I pointed the rapier at the rank badge of five arrows shaped into a pentagram that he wore. "What would you know of him or his methods? You clearly studied beneath another because Audin would not touch a bow if his life depended upon it."

Kit smiled like a fox. "You Garikmen are fools for letting a foe get as close as needed to finish him with a sword."

"And you Herakmen are cowards for not daring to feel your foe's breath on your face when you kill him." I sheathed the rapier. "I do not think provincial insults suit us, cousin. We can do much better."

The lanky scout laughed lightly. "No need for insults at all, Locke, for I am not your enemy. To answer your question, like my father before me, I was sent off to Garik to train beneath Audin. I endured a month of his harsh treatment—during which time I did not so much as finger even a dagger—then I decided I wanted nothing to do with him or his skills. I ran away and convinced a caravaner that I had been kidnapped. I told him that if he returned me to Herakopolis, my grandmother would pay him a vast reward."

I frowned as a distant memory started to bubble up through my consciousness. "So, you are the student who chose to flee. You were used many a time to frighten me into compliance. I had heard you were devoured by wolves or killed by bandits or frozen to death in the wilderness. Whatever skill I seemed not to be able to master was somehow linked to the doom that had befallen you."

"Better that, then, than to be scourged with our fathers' deaths in Chaos. Audin asked me if I wanted to end up like my father. So much so, in fact, that I decided I did not want to be like him at all. That included being trained by a man who obviously had failed to keep my father safe with his training. I decided to find myself a Bowmaster to let me kill my enemies at a vast distance."

I smiled. "And I would bet that you did not touch a bow for a month or more under his instruction."

Kit shook his head. "In fact, you are quite wrong. Herluf took me out to the gallery he had prepared and shot a single arrow into a target at fifty paces. He then gave me a piece of string and pointed me toward the forest behind his cottage. 'Go, boy, and build yourself a bow. Come back with it and three arrows.'"

He crossed the room and seated himself in one of the chairs. "I did as I was told and came back with a wretched piece of wood and three reeds. Herluf invited me to shoot, and even if the arrows had flown straight, they would have gone nowhere near the mark. My Bowmaster turned to me and said, 'Now you know you know nothing. When I am finished with you, you will know everything.'"

"Did he give you a new bow?"

"No. I worked with my little toy for over a year. I kept it with me at all times and got so I felt strange without it in my left hand. Herluf again sent me out into the woods to get a piece of wood for a bow and, this time, I made a better selection, but it was still not good enough. Finally, the third time he sent me out, I stopped and asked him his advice on my selection. At that point my true education began."

I slipped the rapier off and returned it to the rack. "And now you are a scout, just like your father."

Kit nodded with resignation. "It must be in the blood, like father, like son."

Like father, like son. That is a tall order for you, Lachlan.

My cousin must have read my mind. "I shouldn't worry if I were you, Locke. Filling our fathers' boots may be difficult, but they had two decades to build their legends. We should get at least half that to create ours."

I felt uneasy about taking money from James for buying Bear's Eve gifts, but he said my grandmother insisted, and after a quick stroll through the bazaar down near the docks I knew I could afford nothing with the money I had left over from my journey. As it was I found myself selecting things offered by merchants from Garik over bits of finery sold by folks from other parts of the Empire. The prices asked were high, but I managed to haggle them down to an area where I found them scandalous, not utterly outrageous.

I bought my grandmother a knitted shawl of good Garik wool that I knew would keep her warm. For Marija I bought a scarf with blue and red flowers on a background of green and for Kit chose a belt buckle of onyx and coral with an arrow motif. I got Rose a hairbrush and James a small book of poetry that, somehow, struck me as quite appropriate for him. For Nob I found a hardwood dowel that I planned to carve into a likeness of the Emperor to update his chess set. Lastly I found some red cloth and blue ribbon to wrap my gifts.

Upon returning to the house, I wrapped my presents and set them on a shelf to await presentation the next day. James had already laid out my clothes for the ball, and I dressed quickly. The silk tunic felt cold on my bare flesh, but I warmed it quickly enough. The jacket and pants fit perfectly, and I was pleased at how the ribbon fringe looked, though I did note that the tailor had run ribbons down the sleeves and pants in addition to hanging them the way I had desired.

I pulled on my new boots and could feel where they would rub against my feet at heel and across the top of the foot, but I decided I could endure the discomfort for at least one night. I fitted my dagger sheath to the belt and strapped it on, then pulled the slender blade from my weapons belt and slid it home in the costume sheath. I knew being allowed to wear a ceremonial dagger in the presence of the Emperor was an honor, but walking out of my suite without my father's rapier made me feel uneasy.

I met Kit downstairs in the foyer and marveled at his uniform. His silver jacket and pantaloons were regulation military, as was the white tunic with stiff collar he wore beneath it. As his accent color he had chosen black, which manifested itself in his knee-high boots and the thick black ribbon that circled his neck and was pinned in place by a pearl at his throat. A silver cloak and tall, white woolen hat completed his uniform and made him look every bit a dashing hero of the cavalry.

"I can see, Kit, why you believe it will only take ten years for you to become as much of a legend as your father. You already have the poise and the heroic profile."

He smiled and looked back down the hallway. "I must at least *attempt* to look suitable for escorting the two most beautiful women in the capital."

Walking slowly, but with stately grace, our grandmother made her way down the hall with only a walking stick to aid her. Her silver gown emphasized her slender height, yet managed to disguise the frailty of her age. Patterned with circles and triangles and other geometric figures, it also had worked into it her rank insignia. A white blouse rose up to cover her to the throat, but its floppy collar and cuffs showed beneath the main body of the dress itself. Her white hair had been gathered back tight against the nape of her neck and had been bound with a clip of silver and what looked to me to be sapphires. The blue stones likewise made up the buttons on her blouse, and one set in a ring of silver encircled the third finger of her left hand.

Behind her came Marija, and she took my breath away. The low-cut gown she wore appeared white enough to have been the preferred garb of a ghostly bride. The bodice hugged her body tightly, and its stiff-boned front extended down past her waist. Her gown flared out from there to flow to the ground along with the two ends of the simple silver chain she wore around her waist like a belt. Bits of silver braid and silver satin ribbons decorated her gown to complete it and bring it into compliance with the directive issued with the invitation.

Her accent color manifested itself in both the tiger's-eye pendant she wore against her bosom and the matching earrings. She wore her black hair in a complicated braid that kept it bound against the back of her head so her earrings would not be hidden. The golden brown light glinting from them matched the hazel glow in her eyes. She smiled as she took pleasure in the effect her appearance had on the both of us.

Kit turned and offered Grandmother his arm, while he pointed me toward the cloakroom. I found a gray woolen cloak for Grandmother, along with a thick pair of mittens and a similar set of outerwear for Marija. I helped both of them don their winter gear, then helped Kit guide Grandmother out the door James held open, to the coach which Nob had at the ready by the front.

We helped Grandmother into the coach, and Marija joined her, spreading out a blanket to cover both of their legs. Carl brought Stail over along with a black stallion that greeted Kit with a frosty snort. I swung myself up into the saddle, then the two of us followed the coach out the gate and toward the palace.

The Imperial Palace occupied the highest hill in the capital. Magical light lit it as if it were noon on a cloudless day, making it impossible to miss. While each of the eight wings had been built by artisans from different parts of the Empire, the eerie, pale blue witchlight made each wing all of a thing with the rest of them, unifying the palace as the Emperor unified the nation.

This is not to make it sound as if the rest of the city were black. Bonfires burned at crossroads, and lanterns glowed from windows. People filled the streets more than usual for an hour past dusk on a cold evening. As we rode through the city I heard and returned greetings and best wishes offered by strangers. For this one night, bound together by highest hopes for the coming new year, all the various people in the city forgot provincial differences and petty squabbles. While I had seen that and thought it wonderful in Stone Rapids, here, in this sprawling metropolis at the heart of the Empire, I found it unbelievable.

Nob brought the coach through the gate and right up to the front steps, while Kit and I dismounted near a crowd of men pressed into duty as stable hands. Some of them were from Kit's own company and chided him about his dress, but he dismissed them with a mocking high-handed wave that set them to laughing. Walking away from them, we reached the red carpet running down the steps and climbed them right behind Grandmother and Marija.

As we reached the doorway of the palace, Grandmother spoke to a military officer just inside the door. He consulted a list, then smiled at her. He also looked over at two other officers standing back away from the door, then glanced at me.

"Lachlan of Stone Rapids?" one asked.

"Aye." I removed my cloak and draped it over my arm. "I am Lachlan."

"You will come with us."

Grandmother and Kit both looked surprised by the command. Kit interposed himself between me and the guardsman. "What is this, Sergeant?"

"Begging your pardon, Lieutenant, but this is none of your business." The heavyset fellow planted his fists on his hips in a wordless challenge. "I've been ordered to bring Lachlan of Stone Rapids to the Emperor when he arrives, and Bear's Eve or not, no sorry scout will keep me from doing what I have been told to do."

11

K it politely bowed his head and stepped out of my way. He took my cloak from me, then handed it to the servant who had taken the wraps from Grandmother and Marija. As they headed off toward the northern wing of the palace, the sergeant and the private he led fell into step before and behind me. Losing sight of my companions as they turned round a bend in the corridor, I followed my guides across the rotunda and deeper into the palace.

The rotunda, with its high dome and checkerboard flooring of black and white marble, gave way to an arched corridor. Massive granite pillars upheld the roof and defined the edges of circular alcoves. Each of the alcoves held a statue of a previous Emperor or Empress. All were chiseled from stone and made far larger than life, just like the statue of my father. Though I felt dwarfed to insignificance while walking between them, I felt a curious sense of satisfaction in imagining my father as being of similar stature to them.

The sergeant led me on through the palace, seemingly picking corridors at random. It would be too much to say that each was more grand than the last, especially when we had started in a hall containing statues of all the august people. The fact was, though, that each corridor was magnificent. Deep down I knew there was no reason why the Imperial Palace would not be furnished with the best the Empire had to offer, but actually seeing those treasures in such abundance was nothing short of staggering.

Ivory, gold, jewels, and silver adorned all manner of chairs and couches. I saw one miniature tree sculpted from gold with branches laden with snowflakes, each one carved from a razor-thin slice of a pearl. I saw cups carved whole from opals and a battle mask fashioned after a *Bharashadi* warrior, done in jet and gold. Armor and weapons made from precious metals and decorated with fine filigree work haunted alcoves and warded doorways.

And the murals, they were everywhere and fantastic. Walls and ceilings alike had been covered with them. Scenes of history, both ancient and recent, appeared all over. Some I recognized—like the Lost Prince, Jhesti, pulling on Lord Disaster's beard—but the rest baffled me. In Stone Rapids I had learned that Herakopolis was the center of the Empire, but here, in the palace, it was proved to me in no uncertain terms.

My grandfather would have been furious with me because I failed to watch my backtrail and look for signs that could fix my position within my mind. Had the soldiers suddenly disappeared, I could have stumbled about forever—and would have deserved to die for my carelessness. That grisly thought couldn't make me concentrate, primarily because so beautiful was the labyrinth that when I finally expired it would not have been from boredom.

I suspect another reason I did not concentrate on anything other than the works of art and the wonderful architecture was that I did not want to begin gnawing on the central problem I faced. Why would the Emperor want to see me? I was no one, from a little village in far Garik. In my journey to the capital I had seen much, but I had done nothing to draw the attention of a guard at the city gate, much less of the Emperor himself.

The sergeant brought me to a room large enough to encompass the entirety of my grandfather's home. "Wait here. Don't break anything."

I frowned at him. "I'm not a barbarian. I'm from Garik."

"You're visiting from Garik, so don't break anything. The Emperor will see you when he wants to see you." He and his aide left and shut the doors behind them with a solid clump.

I felt too overwhelmed to do anything but gawk at the room. Off to my right I saw another set of gold-leafed doors I assumed led to the Emperor. The room's walls, which benefited from the double-high ceiling, had been covered with more murals depicting epic battles against Chaos demons right after the Seal of Reality was shattered. Directly across from the doors through which I had entered, the two windows set in the wall broke the mural there into a triptych depicting a campaign against Chaos demons who appeared to be wreathed in flames yet unconsumed by them.

The furnishings in the room looked solid and hardly in keeping with the splendor of the palace, yet appropriate for a room decorated with these martial paintings. The table and chairs were stout and unupholstered, though they did look more refined than something pounded together by a farmer from scraps of lumber. Two smaller tables bracketed a long bench that ran beneath the windows, and two tall wardrobes flanked the doors leading deeper into the palace.

The table in the center of the room had a small wooden box on it. In contrast to its surroundings, the box seemed almost delicate. The Emperor's triskele crest had been inlaid in mother-of-pearl on the top, and I saw no latch holding the lid shut. Even so, I was not tempted to open it.

I wasn't going to have anyone think a Garikman didn't know his manners.

The doors leading to the Emperor opened toward me. I instantly dropped to one knee and bowed my head. I saw Garn Drustorn walk through the doors, then he turned and smiled as the Emperor followed him into the room. The Warlord glanced at me. "Highness, it is my pleasure to present to you Lachlan, the son of Cardew."

"Rise, Lachlan."

I did as the Emperor commanded. As my head came up I did my best to conceal my surprise at the Emperor's appearance. Though he stood taller than me by a fist-width, we shared the same lean physique. His black hair and brown eyes could have made him Marija's brother. Clean-limbed, and with the flush of health upon him, he clearly was barely older than I was. It was this apparent youthfulness that surprised me.

Of course I had known his age, as did everyone in the Empire who had drawn a waking breath since Daclones's death, but it had never truly struck me what it meant. His being the Emperor had added years to him in my mind, and even though I had carved a chess piece of him and tried to make it accurate, I was working mostly from imagination and his profile on a silver Provincial. I'd aged him at least ten years.

I suddenly realized that until this moment I thought of him more in terms of a statue or symbol than as a man.

"I am at your service, Your Imperial Majesty," I mumbled. I heard my nervousness echo within my voice, and I glanced down at the floor as a blush rose on my cheeks. "I am honored to meet you."

"The honor is mine, Lachlan."

"No, Highness, I am no one, but you are the Emperor."

"I am the Emperor because my father was the Emperor." The young man smiled effortlessly. "To be revered for an accident of birth is rather ridiculous."

I shrugged uneasily. "It could seem that way, Highness, but being your father's son brings with it burdens. Accepting them is something that's worthy of respect, and respect it I do."

Thetys nodded at the Warlord. "Your report of him was accurate, Garn."

"He and his cousin both are polite and intelligent—as were their fathers."

"So I understand." The Emperor looked at me, then pointed to the box on the table. "Lachlan, open that box and take out of it what you find within."

Thankful for something to do other than try to think of ways to live up to the Warlord's assessment of me, I crossed to the table and gently pried off the top of the box. Setting it aside, I saw a silver ring nestled in folds of black satin. A dark line of tarnish ran around each edge of the band and helped define the shield-shaped crest on the ring itself. The second I pulled the ring from the box and the light fell full upon the symbols on it, I recognized the crest as that of the Emperor's

Valiant Lancers, the company my father had led into Chaos.

I turned to face the Emperor. "It's a ring, sire." I blushed as I realized he knew that already. "It's old."

"That it is." Thetys clasped his hands behind his back. "My father gave that ring to your father over a score years ago. It is my pleasure to present it to you so it once again can be borne by its rightful owner. Put it on."

I hesitated. "Forgive me, Highness, but if your father gave this ring to my father, then it is not for me to wear. I have two brothers, both of them older than I. First to Geoff, then to Dalt it would pass before it became mine."

The Emperor let a grin twist the corners of his mouth. "Indulge me, Lachlan, for this night. It is my desire that one of Cardew's blood wear that ring to greet the new year. When you return to Stone Rapids you may pass it on to your brothers if you wish, but for this evening the ring will belong to you. Is this acceptable?"

"Well, Geoff would get it first, and I think he'd not mind if I wore it in his stead tonight." I slipped the ring onto the third finger of my right hand. The metal's cold touch sank straight into the bone, but the weight of the silver felt good. While the ring was a bit too big for my finger, its heft seemed right and proper on my hand. The ring filled the phantom absence I had felt on the first day in Herakopolis.

"In the memory of my father, I accept your gift. I can't thank you enough for it, Highness." I clutched my left hand over it and felt a cold chill run down my spine. For the first time in my life I had something unique that had belonged to my father in my hands, and it felt right. Here was something that had been very special to him, and it was being shared with me—not handed down from Geoff to Dalt and then on to me. It felt as if I had a direct connection to my father, and the intensity of the link shocked me.

I looked up and met the Emperor's steady gaze. "I hope, someday, I can serve you in the same way my father served your father and earned this ring."

"I have no doubt, Lachlan, you will be of such service to me." He folded his arms and cocked his head as he looked at me. "The Valiant Lancers died in Chaos with your father. Mayhap we will rebuild them around you, your brothers, and your cousin."

I smiled. "Geoff is both wise and a skillful fighter. My brother Dalt is not much less of a fighter than Geoff. Kit is every bit the scout his father was."

"Good. We will take only the best for the Valiant Lancers, I think." The Emperor looked over at his Warlord. "Garn, please take Lachlan to the ballroom." He turned back to me. "I would join you now, but tradition and ceremony must be observed if the new year is to be welcomed without calamity. You understand."

"Yes, sire." I bowed my head and refrained from mentioning how disastrous the harvest was the year Ferran Tugg refused to play the music for the Ceremonial Dance because he knew his brother Burton would ask Runa from Three Elms to join him in it. Ferran had been lovestalking her all fall and winter and was afraid Burton would win her that night. Grandfather said he'd never seen a drought that dry, or locusts that thick in his whole entire life.

The Emperor retreated to the other room, and the Warlord led me back through the palatial maze toward the ballroom. "I trust you are enjoying your time in Herakopolis, Lachlan?"

"Yes, sir." I wanted to ask him about Bald Ugo's

murder, but didn't since I wasn't sure that was the sort of omen I wanted to mark the coming of the new year. "I've seen a lot of things and eaten a lot of things I never even knew existed."

"There is much new and unusual in and around the capital at the time. Much of it is just rumor, you understand. You can trust very little of it, but ferreting out the truth is something that is an ongoing task." The opalescent light in his eyes seemed to flare for a moment. "The truth is elusive, but we'll nail it down soon enough."

I thought I knew what he was saying without saying it, but I couldn't be certain. "I'm not given to gossip, sir, so I've kept my own council in matters I can't explain."

"I expected nothing else. If I learn something I can share with you, I will."

"Thank you, sir." I smiled because of the secret we shared and felt not a little relieved that I didn't know that much more about it.

"Here you are, Lachlan. Please, enjoy yourself at the ball." The Warlord pointed toward a short corridor that ended in open, double-wide doors. I took my leave of him with a nod and joined the other people heading into the ballroom. Even though I had wandered through a large portion of the palace already, I was not prepared for what I saw when I entered the ballroom.

If the room where I met the Emperor had been large enough to hold my grandfather's house, the Imperial Ballroom could have encompassed the whole village of Stone Rapids. I entered through a doorway in the southwest corner of the room. This put me at the head of a sweeping staircase that curved around to the north and east. Aside from the pillars supporting the ceiling, the eastern wall of the room had been made solely of glass. Down at the ground level I saw doors likewise made of glass panels that led out into snow-dusted gardens. Beyond them I saw the lights of the city and the scintillating gleam of moonlight on the ocean.

Huge tapestries with fabled scenes covered the other walls. The staircase on which I found myself had a twin in the northwest corner of the room, though at its head I saw no doorway. Up there, on the landing, musicians gathered, and I heard their varied instruments linked by the discordant strains born as they were tuned.

A third staircase, this one straight yet broader than the other two, led directly down from a dais in the center of the west wall. Two bronze doors were built flush into the wall, and the Emperor's triskele crest stood in bold relief on each. On the dais in front of them had been placed one large chair and four smaller ones. From there the Emperor and his family would have a clear view of all the festivities.

People crowded the white marble floor, but did not fully obscure the Imperial crest worked in black stone in the center of the dance floor. I saw, lined up against the north and south walls, tables laden with enough food and drink to feed the whole city for a week. Crystalline chandeliers burning with sorcerous light provided the illumination for the ball, and their reflections on the eastern wall emblazoned new constellations on the night sky beyond.

From my vantage point I managed to see Kit quite clearly and, seated beyond the circle of young women and fellow officers he had attracted, my grandmother and Marija. Descending to the dance floor, I made my way to them easily and held my right hand out. "Look, look what the Emperor gave me."

Grandmother took my hand in her icy grip. "They have returned to you the ring." She smiled for a second, her lips quivering a bit, then she pulled my hand to her and gently kissed the silver ring. "Cardew braved horrors to win this honor, but he gladly accepted the responsibility it represented. Never forget it, and never betray it."

"Never." I nodded solemnly. "I will never dishonor my father." I bent down and kissed my grandmother on her forehead.

She patted my cheek with a leathery hand. "No mother could have ever desired a better son."

The ring of steel-shod wood on stone cut through the whisper-choked air and brought everyone around to look toward the dais on the west wall. The bronze doors had been opened, and a liveried minister stood beside them. Again he brought his staff of office down and sent a metallic peal echoing through the room. "His Supreme Majesty, Emperor Thetys V and his mother, the Empress Dejanna."

Her right hand resting lightly on his left arm, the Emperor and Empress walked through the doors and to the thrones on the dais. Thetys wore a padded silver doublet over a blue tunic. White breeches, hose, and slippers completed his outfit. Instead of a crown he wore a simple circlet set with a sapphire in the middle, and it struck me that he had dressed as if he and my grandmother had collaborated on their choice of clothing.

His mother, who was a small woman, wore a traditional gown of silver-and-white satin with a roll fastened around her hips and hidden by her overgown. It made her waist look positively miniscule. She had chosen purple as her accent color and displayed it in the amethyst necklace and coronet she wore. She let her son's arm go when they reached the thrones and moved to the seat on his left hand.

A third time the Chamberlain's staff struck the ground. "Imperial Prince Lan and the Princesses Nassia and Eriat," he announced.

Prince Lan stood closer to my height than he did his brother's, and showed the stocky build my father was supposed to have had. His clothing resembled that of his brother, though his tunic was a shade lighter than his brother's. He wore no crown and smiled as he led his two sisters onto the dais.

Though Nassia and Eriat were identical twins, they had done what they could to differentiate themselves. Nassia, on Lan's right arm, wore her black hair at shoulder length, like her mother. She had chosen a gown of primarily white satin and had trimmed it with silver and green. Eriat, by contrast, had trimmed a silver gown with red and white ribbons. That adornment extended to the ribbons she had woven through her long raven hair.

They were pretty enough to make me think I might dance with each three times: once for Geoff and twice for me.

With his family in place, the Emperor stepped forward. "I welcome you all here and thank you for kindly accepting the invitation to join my family and me on this festive night. This is the first Bear's Eve celebration of my reign, and it is my fondest wish that this will be a ball no one will ever forget."

He cast a glance back at the Chamberlain, who had announced him, then smiled at his audience. "My advisors have urged me to make a speech of some length to outline my plans for the coming year, but I think, as my gift to you, I will refrain. I trust, in return, as your gift to me, you will thoroughly enjoy yourselves."

Thetys extended his left hand to his mother and guided her down the steps to the dance floor. Up in the corner the musicians began playing the opening chords of the Ceremonial Dance. Keeping his back to the throne, he led his mother around to face him, and all the women in the audience moved to form a rustling circle around the dance floor.

I looked to help my grandmother up, but she waved me off and gently pushed Marija toward the circle, letting her perform as her surrogate. Grandmother smiled at me warmly. "You dance with Marija, Lachlan. Dance for yourselves and dance for me."

The men present, save those who were unsteady like my grandmother, formed another circle around the ladies. I noticed that Garn Drustorn stood across from Duchess Nallia of Jask while her husband, the Grand Duke, sat in the corner and rubbed his left leg. Kit chose as his partner a strikingly petite woman who, if I read her rank insignia correctly, was a Priestess within the Church of Pleasure. I lined up opposite Marija and grinned like an idiot.

The Chamberlain hammered the floor with his staff. In unison with the other men in the room, I bowed deeply to my partner. When the Chamberlain again signaled with a staff strike, I straightened up and she curtsied to me. As she and the other women recovered themselves, he raised his staff for the final blow that would start the dance.

"Let the celebration commence!" he shouted as he brought his staff down.

If it made any sound at all when it hit the floor, I did not hear it. Thunder exploded in the center of the floor amid a flash of midnight tinged with blood. I felt the sound as much as I heard it, and the shock wave knocked Marija forward into my arms. I caught her deftly and swung her around to place my body between her and the thing congealing in the center of the Imperial crest.

Shadow rolled off it like malignant fog. At first it appeared to be no taller than a dwarf and built much like a tree stump, but then it grew up out of the floor. The chandelier swinging above it cast its shadow long and tall all around the circle, and I felt a burning sensation when the darkness touched me. The air smelled bitter, and the stink of fear sweat filled the room.

When it had grown to my height, which took no time but seemed like forever, it unfolded itself and stood tall enough to tower over even the statues I had seen elsewhere in the palace. Wearing a hooded robe that looked more mildew and moss than any fabric I could name, the creature stared straight at the Emperor. His hood slipped back to reveal a piebald patchwork of silver-and-ivory flesh stretched thinly over its skull.

"Forgive the manner of my arrival," it buzzed in a cicada voice, "but I could not bring myself to miss this, the first and *last* Bear's Eve Ball over which you shall preside!"

12

The Emperor shielded his mother from the monstrosity, and I did the same for Marija. "How is it possible . . . ?" Though his flesh had paled, no fear invaded Thetys's stance, nor did I hear any undermining his words. "Leave here, you are not welcome."

"Come, come, now, Emperor mine. This is a night of charity and good intentions." The humanesque creature shook his head ruefully. "If you do not purge yourself of your hatred, this coming year of the Griffin will be horrible indeed."

"How appropriate it is you show yourself now, in the end of the year of the Scorpion, exactly where one would expect to find the sting."

The creature's metallic flesh squealed as lips parted in a feral smile. "Word games are unworthy of you, Imperial Majesty. Save your venom to spew upon another. I have for you a gift."

The Emperor waved aside any offering from the gaunt embodiment of corruption. "My invitations specified my guests were to bring no gifts."

"But as I was not invited, I am not bound by your social contract." The creature threw back its head in an attitude of laughter, but what issued from its throat was the crackling wet sound of maggots chewing corpse-flesh. "What I give you, boy-lord, is a year. I will return here in a year's time, and you will hand your crown to me."

Thetys folded his arms across his chest. "There, you have given me your gift, now you will leave."

The flesh tightened around the creature's eyes. "What a poor host you are, Thetys the Last. You would send me hence without so much as a dance? Unthinkable you should do that, and I will not permit it. I will not have you be thought so ill-mannered."

The creature raised his arms above his head, and the sleeves of his robe slipped down to his shoulders. The left arm appeared perfectly formed except in one sense. It looked to be composed of something very dark green, yet transparent. The way the light from the chandeliers wavered as it passed through the arm made me mindful of how the world shifts when viewed from beneath the surface of a lake.

The other arm should have been mouldering in a tomb. Blackened flesh hung from it in tatters, letting me see the reddish brown of muscles and the yellow-ivory of aged bone. Insects scampered up and down it like ants on a tree branch. A dark, viscous fluid dripped from it at the elbow, yet evaporated before reaching the floor.

He opened both his hands and shouted a word I could not understand. It came out all hisses and clicks and gave me the same sick feeling inside as when I had heard Dalt's leg break two years ago. Shadows swirled in from every corner of the room and clotted into a staff of onyx with a smoky quartz globe on one end.

He looked toward the musicians and cackled, "You will play for me so I may dance."

The musicians, to a man, set their instruments down.

Moving his right hand down to the staff's midpoint, the uninvited spun the staff once and the globe began to glow. He snapped it around to point at the musicians, and the globe flared with a scarlet light. I saw that light reflected in their eyes, then one man raked bloody furrows across his face with his fingernails. Others fainted, and one man stumbled blindly forward to trip and dash his brains out as he fell down the stairs.

Wrapped in a red-gold aura, their instruments floated up from where they had been abandoned and hovered in the air. Slowly and faintly they began playing a song of clashing chords and screeching notes. The music pricked at my ears as if each note were an invisible thorn, or silent stinging insects.

The monster closed his eyes for a moment and let his staff sway in time with the tune, then he nodded. "Clearly a song of this complexity would have been beyond your people. This is another gift I give you."

He loosened his grip on the staff and let the globe fall toward the ground. When his corpse-hand reached its tail, his fist closed and whirled the staff around in an all-encompassing gesture. With its first pass I felt a weariness wash over me. With the second my muscles tightened as if they were strings, and he was tuning me. The third pass, and they tensed yet again, knotting my hands and curling my toes inward. At the globe's last orbit my every muscle locked rigid and my spine arched backward like a bow strung taut.

Marija reached out to touch me, but where her fingers fell even lightly they sent lightning bolts of agony shooting throughout my body. I gasped sharply against the pain and saw the horror in her eyes. I forced myself to try to speak, but could barely croak out a whisper. Funneling my pain into my voice, I managed one strangled word.

"Run."

Before she could heed me, the sorcerer gestured fluidly with his left hand. Dozens and dozens of slender golden threads floated from his fingers and touched each woman in the center of her forehead. I saw Marija's dark eyes glaze over. Her head slumped forward, and I fought against the power holding me so I might catch her and prevent her from falling to the floor.

She did not fall. The monster's left hand grasped the threads like so many reins, then his staff again started swinging in time with the hostile melodies warring about the room. Marija's head came up as the silver-fleshed guest jerked the threads, and a pulse of red power played along the line and to her brain.

In unison with the other women, Marija began to move to the floor and dance around in time with the music. At first the women stepped lightly and formally as they unconsciously observed the proper forms for the Ceremonial Dance. Their faces remained blank, and though many of them were physically pleasing, their lack of animation robbed them of any beauty.

The music's tempo increased, and with it I heard my heartbeat also quicken. I could follow a line of stringed-instrument melody for a moment or two, then a horn would cut through it and lead me off on a brassy trail of notes. Woodwinds would steal me away from that course, then abandon me again to the strings. All the while the percussion instruments hammered out a message I did not willfully understand, but I felt its growing effect on my body.

The pain wracking me ceased as other emotions flooded through me. My muscles slackened slightly, bringing with the change a sense of relief that the music sought to pervert into gratitude for the monster's mercy. I caught myself and held back from that trap, but I still found myself beguiled into a sense of camaraderie with this strange being in the center of the floor. The women danced for him, but he shared them with me.

By his power, they danced for *us*.

And, oh how they danced. As the pace increased in the dance, so did the wanton grace of their motions. Slender hands caressed lovingly long throats and then slowly inched downward. Full breasts strained against silks and satins while the women pulled fabric taut across flat bellies. Fingers tangled in skirts and raised them to expose deliciously long legs sheathed in the finest hose. Women tossed their heads from side to side, shaking out combs and clasps to free their hair in displays of unthinking abandonment.

I found lust rising in me. My desire for any one woman was eclipsed as the next pirouetted through my narrow cone of vision. Tall women, fat women, old women, and young girls—children really—all frisked past, one supplanting the next as the embodiment of my carnal need. Only the rictus of the monster's magick held me back, and yet, curiously, I did not resent it because the music assured me that the anticipation would heighten the consummation.

A new melody wove through the demonic concerto

and injected a note of caution into my thoughts. The range of my vision expanded, and I saw the lustful expressions on the faces of all the other men. I knew in an instant that they wanted the women I had chosen to be my mates on this night. A bloody haze filled my sight, and my fingers itched to surround the throat of the first man I could get my hands on.

It mattered not at all that the first man I saw was Kit.

Fury nibbled away at the spell the creature had spun. My hands closed into fists, and I felt the warm weight of the ring on my finger. *Yes, the ring. If I hit him with the ring, I am certain to leave a scar. An impression of the crest!*

I looked up and fingered the ring. Its heft and the fact that it felt right being on my finger gave me a moment of introspection. It freed me from Fialchar's influence and let sanity return to my mind. *No, no. Kit is not your enemy—the monster is! Fight him.*

I struggled against the magick that still held me. My fists convulsed in the hopes that their freedom would spread to the rest of my body. When nothing happened I snarled and willed myself to break free, but it was no use. Whatever he had done was too powerful for me. While I might have escaped the mental madness, his evil still held my body in thrall.

Suddenly I remembered the rhyme against evil I had learned so long ago and concentrated on it. *If ever there was a time it was meant to be recited, now is it!* Deliberately and slowly, I pronounced each word. I forced my lips to form each letter carefully, so that even if my lungs failed to provide me enough air to speak, the words would exist.

"Fire and silver beat cold and night, but try to avoid evil's sight." Heat washed over me in a wave as if I had been given refuge in the arms of my aunt or my mother.

My arms bent at the elbows so I could return the embrace, and my toes uncurled.

"When all is lost, brave heart have you," I barked out as my spine returned to my control. I could feel my legs and instantly spread my feet into a fighting stance. "And evil's thrall will then be through!"

With the last word of the charm, Fialchar's control over me vanished. I lunged forward and caught Marija up by the waist in my left arm. My right hand wrapped itself around the magickal thread and, despite the searing pain, I yanked sharply downward. The golden line parted around the ring and writhed like a wounded snake, severing other lines with its thrashing. Marija went limp in my arms, and other women spun to the floor as they were released from the creature's power.

The music stopped so abruptly that only the clatter of the instruments striking the ground told me I'd not gone deaf. All around the room men staggered, all slump-shouldered, with limbs trembling uncontrollably. Most of them sank slowly to their knees, leaving Lord Disaster towering over all of them.

The creature turned slowly in my direction, though his robe gave me no hint of what he might have used for legs. As he came around, and I saw his face in more than profile, my admiration for the Emperor grew. The thing's gangrenous stare was enough to rot a man from the inside out.

"How dare . . ." he began in anger, then his mouth snapped shut. He furrowed his brows, and I recoiled, as if his stare had physically struck me. "How is it that you are here, now? This is impossible!"

He turned back toward where the Emperor knelt over his mother. "Little tricks will not save you or your throne. It will be mine, and you will give it to me. I have played for you a tune, and in a year I will collect your Empire as payment for it."

He raised his staff in both hands above his head, then drove the point down into the floor. The resulting thunder crack knocked me down, but I twisted and managed to catch Marija on top of me. By the time I sat up again, all I saw was a fast-dissipating column of greasy black smoke and a smallish green flame burning in the center of the Imperial crest.

Kit dropped to one knee and slid Marija to the floor beside me. "Is she hurt?"

"I don't think so, just unconscious." I stared at the green fire. "I never expected anything like that tonight."

Kit shivered. "A memorable but inauspicious way to start the year." He chewed his lower lip a second. "I am not certain, and I do not know how he got here, but I think that was Fialchar—Lord Disaster."

"No question about it." I shook my head. "That was him."

"How do you know?"

I shrugged. "Who else could it have been?"

Kit hesitated for a moment, then nodded. "You have a point there—it must have been him. And if he can walk in the Empire . . ."

I finished it for him. "Even a year's warning won't be enough to let us stop him."

13

Marija's hazel eyes fluttered open and became normal again as the pupils contracted. She looked at me, started to say something, then blushed and looked away. She raised a hand over her mouth to stifle a sob.

I took her other hand and held it tightly in my own hands. "What you went through, what *we* went through, was horrible. What we were thinking, what was going on inside of us was not our doing. Fialchar did it."

Marija swallowed hard. "You can't know . . ."

I nodded and kept my voice low. "I don't want to even imagine because I know what he made me think—about you and about everyone else. I was ready to kill Kit . . ."

"And I was ready to kill Locke." Kit gave her just a hint of a smile. "Corruption was able to tempt us here, but that tempting means nothing if we don't give in. No matter what you thought or saw, it counts for nothing unless you choose to act upon it."

Marija closed her eyes for a moment. "What you say, Master Christoforos, makes sense, but how do I get those thoughts out of my head?"

I gave her hand a pat. "Find new thoughts to replace them. That's what I'm doing." I winked at Kit. "Right now I think revenge fantasies will fill my mind up."

"My head is fair full to bursting with them."

Marija nodded and opened her eyes again. "You're right, and I have work to do."

Kit and I eased her up into a sitting position. "How do you feel, Marija?"

"I'll be f-fine, Locke." She managed a weak smile. "Please, get me to my feet."

Kit and I stood, then complied with her wishes. She dutifully rearranged her skirts, then looked over at where my grandmother had been sitting. None of us could see her because of the other people milling about, but Marija immediately dove into the crowd, heading toward where she had last seen Evadne. I started to follow, but Kit held me back. "A moment, Locke."

"What?"

"You and I had both assumed the killing of the baker and his family was because of the thing I saw in the wilderness, but I recall you have said something about a 'summoning.' What was that?"

I frowned and closed my eyes as I tried to remember. "Triona, the apothecary's wife, said something about a creature from Chaos having been summoned." I reopened my eyes and looked hard at Kit. "Do you think Fialchar made it into the Empire through that summoning? Could that magick have gone undetected? And if those people had summoned him, why would he kill them?"

Kit shrugged. "What if they were killed as part of the

summoning? We have no proof they died *after* any summoning. Concerning the detectability of the magick, that I know nothing about."

"Then what was it that you were chasing?"

Before Kit could answer my question, Garn Drustorn cut through the crowd and found us. "The Emperor would like to speak with you, Lachlan. You should come, too, Lieutenant. He will value your counsel in this as well."

We threaded our way through the crowd and made as directly as possible for the thrones and the doors beyond them. Being as small as I am, I had a hard time seeing much more than Kit's back, though two people with the flowered badge of the Healing Magick discipline did pass right by me as they ran to the musicians' aid.

When I reached the stairs I did venture a look back at the dance floor in a vain attempt to see Marija and my grandmother. The confusion on the floor looked so inappropriate. Some people were prostrate, while other folks were kneeling and softly sobbing in the arms of other victims. All of their postures and the way they moved and sounded was appropriate for the sort of catastrophe they had endured, but the gaiety of their clothing mocked them. It made them all look like actors in some grand theatrical presentation of a tragedy.

The sheer misery caused by Fialchar's intervention underscored how truly dangerous an enemy he was. His arrival and what he had done were almost casual, yet the effects were gross and profound. He had taken people gathered to celebrate one of the most momentous nights of the year and reduced them to a wretched, pain-ridden, crying mob—all for his pleasure.

That casual disregard for the consequences of his actions should not have surprised me, given what I knew of him. Fialchar had long ago sparked a debate within the magickal community about the feasibility of creating a magickal item that encompassed in it the fabric of reality. The sorcerous brotherhood split down the middle on the subject. Fialchar convinced a dozen of his brethren who believed the task could be accomplished to go ahead and do it in secret, just to prove to the others that it could be done.

They did, and proudly displayed their handiwork at a convocation of sorcerers. The Twelve stood by their creation, immeasurably proud of what they had done. Their labor had taken a dozen years, but they had finally succeeded. They had created the Seal of Reality.

Then, at that convocation, Fialchar joined them and shattered the seal. Chaos immediately exploded and washed over the Empire. Sorcerers throughout the Empire immediately erected Ward Walls to hold Chaos at bay, but even after centuries the amount of the original Empire they had recovered from Chaos was tiny.

Fialchar, before or since, never did explain why he had shattered the Seal of Reality. There are those who maintain that doing such was always his plan, hence his instigation of the discussion that resulted in the seal's creation. While I was willing to accept that explanation, after seeing him in action it struck me that he might have destroyed the seal on a whim.

Another casual gesture with hideous results.

Kit and I followed the Warlord through the doors, and I heard them clang shut behind us. Over by a door across the room I saw Thetys and recognized his brother Lan from seeing him announced to the gathering. The Emperor hastily returned Kit's salute, then bade us follow him deeper into the palace. "Forgive me wanting to talk as we go, but we have a problem that is somewhat larger than Fialchar's being in the Empire."

My eyes grew wide at that statement. "What could be worse than the sorcerer who destroyed the Seal of Reality being in the Empire?"

Lan answered me while his brother inserted a key in a small hole in a wall mural. "You saw the staff Fialchar had with him? You felt its power?"

"Yes." I nodded.

"That was the Staff of Emeterio, one of the dozen sorcerers who helped create the Seal of Reality in the first place. When Fialchar shattered the seal, the dozen sorcerers he had tricked into creating it were overwhelmed by the flood of Chaos." Lan grew pensive as he explained. "We had long assumed they were all killed and their tools destroyed at that time, but stories keep cropping up to suggest that one or more of them or their artifacts continued to exist in one form or another after Chaos."

The Emperor pulled back on the key, and a portion of mural swung away to reveal a dark passage. Lan preceded me into the narrow, rough-stone tunnel and cautioned me about the stairs as we started spiraling down through the palace. Flat discs on the ceiling of the passage supplied us light, but I noticed the illuminated area approximated the half-moon crescent the Lovers' Moon showed tonight. I kept my balance by letting my fingers touch each wall, and that was by no means difficult. Were I given to the fear of enclosed spaces that torments Dalt, I would have gone utterly mad in the dusty dry wormhole.

From behind me I heard the Emperor's voice. "Fialchar knows that we possess the one item powerful enough to destroy and be destroyed by the Staff of Emeterio. That is the Fistfire Sceptre, and we keep it in a vault here in the palace. There are enough magickal wards on the vault to prevent him, I hope, from appearing in it the same way he disturbed the ball."

We stopped at a wide landing. The tunnel continued on to the right, but Lan didn't go very far down it. He stopped beneath one of the moon lights, dropped to one knee, and started counting bricks up and over to the left. Once he found the one he wanted he passed a hand over it, and I saw a faint glow outline the brick. Looking up at his brother, he shook his head.

The Emperor smiled uneasily. "Some of my predecessors found having access to the Imperial Treasury without the benefit of the Minister of the Exchequer knowing anything about it rather useful. This entrance, my brother has just indicated, has not been disturbed tonight."

Lan nodded. "Nothing to worry about right now."

The Warlord frowned. "I know others are going to enter the vault through the main doors, once they get the wards out of the way, but I think we should check on the interior before they get to it."

"I agree." I opened my hands. "If Fialchar decides to come back, a little rhyme isn't going to stop him. If the Fistfire Sceptre would do that, I think having it in hand is a good idea. As he could come back at any moment, the sooner we have it available, the better."

Thetys nodded. "That's some of the wiser counsel I've had in a while." The Emperor's dark eyes narrowed. "The reason I asked for you to come with us here, Lachlan, is because you managed to break Fialchar's spell, and he seemed displeased to see you—as I hope he will be now. How did you counter his magick?"

I shrugged. "I don't honestly know. The rhyme I mentioned earlier was one I learned as a child. 'Fire and silver/beat cold and night,/but try to avoid evil's sight. When all is lost,/brave heart have you,/and evil's thrall will then be through!' It was for banishing night terrors."

"Let us hope it has lost none of the potency it showed earlier." The Emperor drew a curved dagger from his belt, and the rest of us armed ourselves with our daggers. "Do you know why Lord Disaster said what he said to you?"

"No, sire." I shook my head and found myself flicking my thumb against the band of the silver ring. I brought my hand up. "Perhaps he recognized this ring, or whatever impressions my father had left on it. Whatever the explanation, I am glad it disturbed him."

Lan looked to his brother. "Ready?"

"Yes."

Lan pressed his hand to the brick he'd found earlier and mumbled a spell. A portion of the wall faded to black, then evaporated like a shadow doused with light. Chests of golden coins that had been stacked against the wall toppled into the corridor in a flood of ringing metal. Torchlight from the vault's interior flashed from yet more coins and burned in the jewels encrusting crowns and swords and hundreds of other treasures. In the rectangular room I saw more valuables than I had ever dreamed existed. In any of the smaller chests I knew I'd have found enough gold to keep me comfortable for even an abnormally long life.

In fact, even the smallest chest the thieves were hauling toward the hole in the far wall would have satisfied me for two lifetimes.

The appearance of a dozen human thieves in the Imperial Treasury surprised us as much as our arrival doubtlessly surprised them. The falling chests of gold had buried one man and bowled another over, while most of the rest stopped in the act of lugging loot toward their egress. Dropped chests crashed to the floor, spilling their contents in sparkling circles from the point of impact. Two robbers sprinted for the hole, while the others drew their knives when they saw we were alone.

Kit and Garn Drustorn rushed forward into the fight while I knelt and grabbed up a gold Imperial coin. Clutching it in the curve of my index finger, I brought my right arm back. Keeping my hand parallel to my waist, I whipped the coin forward. The Imperial sliced through the dim air and smashed one of the thieves square in the face. His head snapped back, and he lost his footing on the gold carpet. As he went down an ornamental suit of armor toppled over on top of him.

A thief swaddled in dark clothes and reeking of the sewers lunged at me with a hooked dagger. I blocked his strike by parrying his forearm wide with my left hand. Closing my hand on his wrist, I brought his arm up high and, with my dagger blade extending down away from my right thumb, stabbed through his right armpit. Bright arterial blood spurted out as I withdrew the blade and backhanded him across the face.

As he reeled away, I flipped my dagger around so the blade poked out of my fist on the thumb side. The next thief rushed me, seemingly intent on bowling me over. He thrust his right hand forward, trying to stab me in the stomach, but I stepped to the left and let his attack slide past my belly. I tangled my left hand in his wet hair and yanked back, then slashed my dagger across his throat.

He gurgled and thrashed as he hit the floor, but I did not notice his death throes because of what I saw further in the room. Something moved, something I had seen from the first but had dismissed as unreal, or at best as the golden glints from a masterpiece hidden within a shadow. As it split itself off from the darkness where it had been hidden, I recognized the black mane and the tufted tail. The malevolent glow in his eyes touched me, filling me with an arctic chill.

As our eyes met I sensed nothing to indicate he recognized me, but the creature clearly saw he had an audience. He lifted his left hand and brandished a yard-long sceptre made of gold. Rubies and emeralds alternated to form a band around the wrist of the metal hand at the top of the rod. Above, the golden hand clutched an absolutely perfect black pearl as large as an apple.

With his treasure in hand the *Bharashadi* sorcerer bared his gray needle teeth in a soundless challenge, then leaped to the hole and disappeared.

I have heard other fighters describe their feeling when urgency or anxiety or frustration overwhelmed them. They speak of "snapping" as if something inside them breaks and allows them to plunge headfirst into a desperate fight. Often they use that term to describe what must have happened inside the head of a madman before he made a suicidal charge.

For me there was no snapping. I just knew that allowing that Chademon to escape with his prize would be a disaster that no magick could repair. Two thieves stood between me and the hole in the wall; they were obstacles that *had to be* overcome. I didn't see them as men or fellow citizens of the Empire, but as the sort of foe that, as I grew up, my grandfather had drilled me to deal with in daily exercises.

I moved through them by reflex, without conscious thought. Their moves and my reactions to them had been pounded into me for so long and so thoroughly that my body took over. I did not see the fight as a disinterested observer, but like a general watching the flow of battle, evaluating tactics and anticipating what needed next to be done.

Sliding step forward and twist to the right. Let the thief's lunge pass between my left arm and my body, then clamp my arm down on his forearm. Jam my dagger up through the bottom of his chin. Ignore the feel of his scraggly beard and the blood trickling from his mouth. Swing his body around and use it to block his comrade.

My hand opened, releasing my dagger. The dead man spun away, undercutting his partner at the knees. That man stumbled forward as my right knee came up to flatten his nose. He groaned loudly, then flopped to the ground, all boneless. A quick kick to the temple kept him down, opening the way to the hole in the wall.

I bolted for it, trying to peer into the darkness at what awaited me there. Realizing I was unarmed, I plucked a jeweled Dwarven shortsword from a scabbard half-buried in treasure. Longer and heavier than my dagger, it was the perfect weapon for the sort of chop and thrust butchery I anticipated beyond the hole.

The stink filling the treasury left no doubt that the hole led to the sewers. I had visions of a dank tunnel with catwalks on either side of a flowing ribbon of water, for that's how one of my father's books described the marvels of the capital's sewer system. Clearly the sewers beneath the palace would handle wastewater and storm-water drainage, but I had never given much thought to what the palace's being on a hill would portend for the sewers. Nor did I take into account the effect of the winter and the cold weather on the dank tunnels.

The first thing I hit on the other side of the treasury wall was ice. My right leg slipped forward and out in front of me as I flew across the sewer tunnel and collided with the far wall. I rebounded, filling the air with shattered icicles that had previously hung from an arch.

I tried to get my feet under me, but the smooth ice coating the far catwalk made that impossible. With both feet flailing and flying up toward the top of the tunnel, I landed on my back in the sewer channel.

If ice is slick, wet ice is yet slicker, and being on a wet icy slope in the dark with enemies lurking about is not where I had envisioned being to greet the new year. The cold soaked straight through to my bones faster than a tax collector appears after a windfall. Having been momentarily stunned by my fall, I could do nothing to stop my slide down the sewer channel. I tightened my grip on the Dwarven sword but abandoned any hope I could use it to stop my descent.

I brought my heels down, but as they touched the ice, they immediately kicked up a cloud of stinging ice needles that prickled my face before melting. My right heel remained down a half second longer than the other and started me spinning around to the left. My left shoulder crunched into the edge of the stone channel, and I started back in the other direction. Quick application of my right heel to the ice straightened me back out at the cost of another ice-scourge across my face.

I raced along swiftly as the sewers arced through a gentle curve toward the sea. I knew I was descending, and fairly rapidly, but I could only guess at how close I was to the level of the sewer tunnels running through the rest of the capital. As it was I braced myself a good three heartbeats before I actually splashed into a sluggish river topped with floating chunks of ice.

I went under the water like a rock tossed from a cliff, but I found solid footing as my momentum died and shot to the surface. I whipped my head around to clear my eyes and yelped aloud at the aching cold of the water. My shout echoed up and down the main tunnel and shocked those waiting there enough to give me a chance against them.

My slide had actually carried me beyond the two thieves who had fled the treasury when we entered. They stood like twin sentinels on either side of the flow, with a torch in one hand and a knife in the other. Being groin-deep in an ice-river did nothing to make them swift or sure as they struck, while I had enough fear in me to inspire whole Imperial Legions.

I spun to my right, turgid water being churned by my thighs, and chopped through the flank of the man nearest me. The Dwarven blade bit through him as if it actually enjoyed the frigid surroundings. It popped free of his rib cage and dropped him into the water. His torch sizzled out and I dove forward.

I did not like going under the water again, but I preferred that to the prospect of getting a poke in the back with a torch. I rolled to my back and came up again as the other thief stalked toward me. He brought the torch around for another swipe at me and, in doing so, let his dagger hand fall to his side.

I blocked the torch with a solid chop, then whipped the blade free and twisted it through a slash at his midsection. He jumped back away from that cut, but being waist-deep in water meant he didn't get far enough away to avoid my backhanded return slash. The shortsword caught him over the right ear. His leather cap stopped the blade from splitting his scalp, but I heard bone crack and saw the man's eyes roll up in his head. He half grunted a surprised sigh, then sat back down in the water. He sank slowly, bobbing like a piece of ice, then vanished, leaving only bubbles to mark his grave.

Before his left hand went under, I freed the torch from it and spun to face further down the tunnel. There, trying to flee from the torch's weak circle of light, I saw the Chademon. I held the torch high to get a good look at him.

From his dripping mane I knew he had preceded me down the channel, but his long legs had taken him well away from where the palace tunnel played out. Even so, the distance between us could not hide the misery in his expression. He was no more comfortable in the frigid water than I was, and I wasn't hundreds of leagues from my home, lurking in the darkness beneath an enemy stronghold.

I started after him. "I can't let you get away, *Bharashadi!*"

The Chademon glanced fearfully over his shoulder at me, then turned to face me. As he did this I realized I was very much alone. The Chademon seemed to come to the same conclusion because his head came up bravely, his gold eyes narrowed, and his lips peeled back in a feral grin.

I was in serious trouble.

With the same casual, contemptuous motion I saw in my dream, the Chademon flicked a gesture toward me with his free hand. An incendiary red spark leaped from his fingers and shot at me like the coin I had thrown earlier. His spell started small, but it grew quickly, allowing its increasing brilliance to fill the tunnel. The spell became a scarlet triangle of light with a circular hole in the middle sizzling in toward me. I felt its intense heat from the moment he sent it spinning toward me and knew nothing my grandfather had drilled into me was of much help in this situation.

I did the only thing it occurred to me to do. I parried the spell with my shortsword.

The blade shattered as if it were glass. The triangle, slightly diminished, whirled on through my forearm, turning my sleeve into a torch. I screamed as it burned into my right shoulder. Nerveless fingers dropped the sword hilt, but I never heard it splash into the water because black agonies swallowed my consciousness whole.

14

I sputtered and snorted back to consciousness the second after the freezing sewer water forced its way up my nose. Struggling my way back to the surface succeeded in dousing the torch and left me in utter darkness. Echoes of my thrashing about drowned out any noise the Chademon made escaping.

If he is escaping.

I crouched up to my neck in the water in case the Chademon was lurking around to finish me off. Floating chunks of ice bumped into me, and I spun this way and that in reaction to them. Because of the darkness, I had no way to detect any sign of the Chademon. I kept facing in what I hoped, but had no way of knowing, was the direction in which I had last seen him.

I steeled myself to submerge if I saw another flash of red. Trying to stay hidden seemed like a good idea, but I realized the cold would finish me off a lot faster than the Chademon would. If he wanted to find me, all he had to do was listen for the chattering of my teeth. Deciding that what I needed to warm me up was another of his spells, I rose to my feet and got my torso up and out of the sewage.

My right arm hung limp at my side and felt numb, except where someone had poured molten iron into my marrow. I gently probed the wound on my wrist with the fingers of my left hand, but the cold had completely numbed them. Even so, as I moved them over my arm and jacket, I could feel them catch and tug in the holes the spell had burned in the jacket. From the weight at my right elbow and the way the cold cut through my upper arm, I had to assume my garment had been similarly burned through at the shoulder, allowing the soaking sleeve to catch at my elbow.

In the darkness, with sewer water still in my nostrils and my body rapidly losing all feeling, I knew I was not going to last long. It did not matter that I could not see my wounds. I knew that my arm had not fallen completely off, but it might as well have for all the use it seemed to be. I could have easily been bleeding, but I had no way of telling, which scared me. I realized that my survival now depended more upon my ability to find warmth and help than it did on anything I could do alone.

Trying to be as quiet as possible, I waded back through the icy water toward where I heard the stream from the palace flowing in. I climbed out of the channel and onto a narrow walkway. I wanted to rest against it, but that would have meant leaning on my right shoulder, which I didn't think was a good idea. Setting one foot before the other, I worked my way up on the stairway serving as catwalk along the palace tunnel. I quickly learned that every dozen steps I had to duck my head to avoid the arches with which the tunnel had been strengthened at those points. Having icicles rain down upon my shoulders was a torment I could do without.

I focused myself on one thing: walking. It was both surprising and terrifying to realize how difficult such a simple and vital task had become. I had no way to judge how far up I had gone or had yet to go, but I knew I would see the hole in the treasury wall when I reached my goal. The possibility that the Emperor had immediately summoned a sorcerer to seal it again did occur to me, but I couldn't see Thetys doing that without first sending rescuers out for me. I clung to that hope because if he had magickally repaired the wall, I was dead, and dying struck me as the last thing I wanted to do to greet the new year.

Four arches from the hole I met Kit and the Warlord on their way down. "Is that you, Locke?"

"Y-yes, my lord."

Drustorn shouted back up the tunnel. "We have him!"

The expression on Kit's face when I entered the circle of light cast by the torch he carried told me I looked as bad as I felt or worse. It seemed that the light from his torch increased the burning sensation in my arm. The resultant pain caused my fingers to jerk and twitch, which let me know I'd not lost use of them, and let me feel the weight of the ring again.

"Locke! What did you run into down there?"

"The thing that killed your wolves. A Chademon. Here. In Herakopolis." I reached up with my left hand, batted away icicles, and steadied myself on an arch. "It stole something. It got away. I'm sorry." My knees buckled.

The Warlord caught me with surprising ease and looped my left arm over his shoulders. "Easy, Locke, easy. No reason to be sorry. We have troops scouring the city, and the squads have magickers with them. We will find him." He glanced at Kit. "Head back up and get a litter and some bearers."

"Yes, sir." Kit winked at me. "Be back in a heartbeat."

I tried to return the wink, but my eyelids didn't seem to want to work right. "Thanks."

Garn Drustorn brought his right arm around my back and got a good grip on the waistband of my pants over by my right hip. "Let me take some of your weight. It's not too far now."

"Sorry about the wet." I frowned as we started forward, and the Warlord ducked the arch. "Would have gotten the demon but for the other two thieves. They slowed me down."

"Not thieves, Locke, but Black Churchers. Three or four are still alive." He grunted as I slipped, and he held me up. "Surprisingly enough, even one of yours lived."

I wanted to ask him what he meant by that remark, but I had no chance before we arrived at the hole and stepped through into the treasury. The Emperor and his brother looked at me with a hint of terror in their eyes, and I knew it came from more than just my appearance. The second I focused on the scene and was able to sort out what the flickering shadows gave me in tantalizing glimpses, I understood both the Warlord's comment and their incredulous stares.

The three men I had killed lay sprawled out in most unnatural positions. The first lay on his side with his left hand jammed in his right armpit, but the torchlight washed gold into the wet slickness on his right flank. The second man had fallen backward over a chest. His arms flung wide and his head lolling toward the ground accentuated the dark slice through his throat. The third man had ended up on his belly, with his head cranked back abnormally far as it rested on the hilt of the dagger protruding like a steel beard from his chin.

My mouth went dry. *Oh, Grandfather, look what you did. You trained me to be a swordsman, but I have become a butcher.*

As I looked at the dead men, two parts of me started to battle. I had been raised on heroic tales of my father, my uncle, and others who had won fame by defeating the enemies of the Empire. Storytellers were able to paint gorgeous and glowing accounts of epic battles with their poems and songs, yet none of them carried with them the dark side of having killed. I had, with one casual cut, reduced a person from being human to being a lump of meat. The fact that any one of these men might have had friends and lovers and children and family to mourn him meant little in comparison with the transmogrification I had caused to happen.

By the same token I knew that I had only consigned their souls to the Deathbird. There they would be beaten clean by the hammer Purifier until the Sunbird would again bring them to the world. I had not so much ended their lives as I had started them on a journey that would avail them of a better fate. What I had done was not a tragedy at all, but a continuation of life.

Pain pulsed in from my arm, and I realized that both views were weights on the ends of a balance pole. I sought the fulcrum upon which the pole rested and saw that the latter view made life worthless, while the former made it so sacred that death could be seen as preferable to action that might prevent the deaths of others. Pacifism for the sake of pacifism in the face of tyranny became the utmost in selfishness and arrogance, which made it just as evil as inciting or committing wanton slaughter.

These men had embarked on a mission that quite probably would bring horror and death to the Empire.

They had attacked me, and I had defended myself. Members of the Church of Chaos Encroaching, they willfully plotted against the Empire and had been placed under a ban that would kill them if they were caught. I had every moral, legal, and ethical reason to kill them. I still did not like what I had done, and felt pleased that it made me uneasy, but I also knew there were times that conflicts could be solved by no other method.

To my right the massive bronze doors to the treasury had been opened, letting light from the marbled hall outside flood the room. The Chamberlain stood guard at the doorway, a dark frown marking his displeasure at the scene he surveyed. Squads of soldiers entered the vault beneath his baleful gaze and escorted the wounded Black Churchers away to the palace dungeons.

Another group of soldiers came in with a litter and set it down next to me. I started to wave them off, but my right arm barely moved at all, and, for the first time, the growing pain made me dizzy. The Warlord eased me down onto the white canvas, and his image split into two.

Then my head hit the canvas and blackness again shrouded my sight.

I came back to consciousness with the tingle of a spell rippling over me. An old man, with bald pate and craggy wrinkles on his face, slowly straightened up, then smiled at the Emperor. "He's back with us, Majesty, as I said he would be."

"I did not doubt you, Sava, but merely wondered at how long Locke's return would take." Good-natured sarcasm underscored Thetys's words.

"Haste is not the handmaiden of efficacy, Highness."

"Nor is sloth, Sava."

Their verbal sparring gave me a moment or two to collect myself. I was not cold, and, in fact, the roaring blaze in the fireplace to my left was making me feel downright hot. I twisted around and pulled myself up into a sitting position on the daybed, then tried out a smile. It seemed to work, as did the rest of my body, including my gauze-wrapped right arm—a vast improvement over the state of affairs I last remembered.

The Emperor gave me a warm smile. "I was worried when you collapsed in the treasury. Sava says you will recover fully."

I looked over at the old man and saw he wore the rank badge of a full Mage, as well as the badges of the Healing and Construction schools of magick. "Thank you for your work." I smiled and flexed the fingers of my right hand. "I feel no pain."

"Which does not mean you are healed yet." Sava clasped his hands together tightly. "You were very lucky, young man."

"You would not say that had you been the one down in the sewers, Master Sava."

"Ah, but knowing what I know of magick, Master Lachlan, I would." The Mage lifted the lower-sleeve portion of my jacket from a spindly-legged table. "If there is a luckier man in the capital today, more than one gambler will be bankrupt before tomorrow."

The sleeve, as I had guessed down in the sewers, had been burned away, but I had not been prepared for the scorched brown of the unburned portions. The spell that hit me had been incredibly hot because it had managed to scorch fabric that had been sopping wet. I moved my right arm around gingerly and didn't even want to think about what it must have looked like before Sava worked his magick.

"It was bad, yes?"

"Suckling pigs on a spit have been less roasted." A wry grin twisted the old man's lips. "The spell used on you was quite powerful and should have burned right through you. I am not sufficiently versed in combat magick, and certainly not in any varieties used by the Black Church, but I would guess your foe used an energy focus. What did you see?"

I sensed from Sava's use of the term "Black Church" that he had not been told the thing I had been chasing was a Chademon. I decided the Emperor had determined the man did not need to know everything, and I respected Thetys's wishes on that score. "He gestured at me with his right hand. I saw a spark, then it grew into a red triangle about a foot on each side. It spun through the air at me. I parried it with a shortsword, but the blade fragmented. The spell then hit me. It did feel hot as it came toward me and burned when it hit."

The Mage nodded slowly. "As I thought. He focused the energy of his magick down into a physical manifestation: the triangle. That was his mistake. The sword, which was cold from the water, and your clothing, soaked in cold water, bled off enough of the heat energy to mute its effects on you. The fact that you were able to parry it suggests it was hastily cast and not as strong as it should have been. You are luckier yet that he was lazy."

I reached up and touched the gauze wrapped around my shoulder. "What have you done to me? I assume your magick is the reason I feel no more pain."

"True. The burns were serious but treatable. There was blistering, and the burns were all deep enough to weep, but you had very little charred tissue to clean away." Sava rubbed his jaw. "I used one spell to sterilize and cleanse the wound, then another to numb it. I also did something to speed up healing and lessen the chances of a scar. You will have to change the bandages on the wound and pack it with salve to finish the healing process. In two weeks your arm should be back to normal."

I gave Sava a big smile. "Again, you have my thanks."

"And you are most welcome, Master Lachlan. One caution, however."

"Yes?"

"Do not fall into the trap of thinking yourself invulnerable to magick because you survived this attack. By rights you should not have survived at all." The old man's voice turned hard, and I heard bitterness in it. "The person you faced did an inexact casting down there. With a second or two more taken in his spellwork, he could have focused the spell on you, foregoing the triangle. He would have roasted you from the inside out, and the last thing you would ever have done was vomit fire. This is not a horse that threw you or a dueler who drew first blood. He should have killed you outright, and might well do that if you meet again."

I met his intense gaze. "I hear what you say, and I will heed your advice. Perhaps you would have done better to leave me my pain to remind me of the wisdom in your words."

He shook his head. "I have been assured you are wise enough that such action was not needed." He bowed to me and to the Emperor, then took his leave from the small sitting room that had become a temporary infirmary.

The Emperor drew a chair across the line of firelight coruscating off the white marble floor and seated himself opposite me. "Lieutenant Christoforos said you told him you saw a Chademon down in the sewers. The Warlord and the lieutenant were too distracted to see what you saw, and I must confess I saw little beyond the Black Churchers. My brother said he saw something dark dart through the hole, but he only saw it at the last. Are you sure what you told your cousin is the truth?"

I nodded solemnly and pulled the sheet up to mid-chest with my left hand. "As certain as I am that you are the Emperor, that is how certain I am that I saw a Chademon. A *Bharashadi* sorcerer, in fact. You have my word on this."

"I do not doubt you, Locke, I merely want to determine how massive a disaster we have here. It had the Fistfire Sceptre?"

"It's missing from the treasury?" I shook my head. "An obvious question, which you wouldn't have asked if you had found it in there. Was it a sceptre made of gold, with a black pearl clutched in a fist at one end?"

Thetys nodded mutely.

"That was it, then." I slammed my left fist into the daybed. "I should have known and found a way to stop him."

"You did what you could—which was all anyone could have done." Thetys leaned forward, and the fire-light winked from the sapphire in his coronet as he rested his elbows on his knees. His eyes focused elsewhere as he quickly assessed what I had told him and determined the extent of what it meant.

I knew the very concept of a Chaos creature possessing an item that could stop Fialchar terrified me as much as the idea of someone's slipping the leash on a vicious dog and sending it after children. I realized that I defined this threat as one directed against my grandmother and Marija and others I knew and loved. For the

Emperor, the threat was one that could destroy a nation that looked to him for leadership and security.

That is a burden that would crush me utterly and completely.

Finally the Emperor looked up at me. "This is not an auspicious way to begin a new year, is it?"

"No, Highness."

"Well, sitting here is going to make it no better. Garn and Christoforos have found the sorceress who detected the Chaos magick out in Menal. They are with her in the sewers to determine if the spell used against you was cast by the same creature they found in Menal. My brother is gathering those advisors I can trust with the enormity of this problem. We will have a council of war to determine what we can and must do to resolve this situation. You and your cousin, because of your parts in this, will join us."

I shook my head. "Majesty, Christoforos is a good choice because he's smart and has practical experience. I'm just a Garikman who will be as lost in your councils as I've been in Herakopolis."

"I appreciate your modesty, Locke, but what I need now is your intelligence. Garn has told me how you deduced the origin of the *vindictxvara* your cousin found, and your conviction that you saw a Chaos demon in the sewers has not wavered even though we all know that is impossible." Thetys looked at the door through which Sava had exited the room. "The reason he thinks you were attacked by a Black Churcher is because he would never accept the idea that a Chademon has penetrated the Ward Walls. That kind of unwillingness to explore such possibilities will hamper us, so having someone whose mind is not cluttered with preconceived notions will not be a burden."

"I appreciate that, Highness, but . . ."

"Do not even begin to imagine refusing to help me,

Locke. I charge you with the duty of making us prove our assumptions as we discuss things. I don't mean you should assume no facts are true, but our conclusions need to be supported. If we cannot prove what we believe, any plans we make to deal with things will be fruitless." He nodded once. "This all means, of course, that we have a lot of work to do and much to introduce you to."

He stood slowly and scratched at his throat. "I have seen to it that your grandmother and her attendant have found their way home without incident. Both are well and have been assured that you and Christoforos are doing my bidding. If you feel up to it, I would like to show you a project started before my father's reign. It will, I assure you, be very important, and I would like your thoughts on it."

I pulled the sheet closed around my body and swung my legs over the edge of the daybed. "As you have noted, I am yours to command, Highness."

"Excellent. Follow me."

Thetys led me from the small room, and immediately the palace floor started sending a chill back into my body through my bare feet. The Emperor dispatched a servant to find me suitable clothing while we headed off into the palace wing that had been built by Garik's greatest artisans. It might have been my imagination, but this Garik wing of the palace seemed friendlier and less hostile to me.

We descended one broad set of stairs, then turned the corner into a dark corridor and came to a metal gate not unlike the lattice door inside the treasury vault. The Emperor pressed his hand to it and muttered a couple of words. I saw him shiver for a second, then the door swung back revealing some very steep steps leading down.

"Is that lock a *leechspell*? "

Thetys nodded. "It is more difficult to open than conventional locks and were a spy to use the incorrect trigger-phrase, the result would be quite horrible."

What little I did know about magick did include information about *leechspells*. Each spell cast requires energy, and apparently all living creatures possess what it takes to empower magick. Only magickers, however, take the time and have the discipline to be able to work magick. A *leechspell* provides a compromise whereby someone unschooled in magick can activate a device that has been enchanted.

Like the mortar and pestle Birger had used to create my grandmother's tonic, the lock had a *leechspell* set to drain enough strength from the Emperor to unlock the door. Given the caution he had mentioned against spies, I assumed that the *leechspell* was fairly complex in that if the wrong word was used, it could take energy from the spy and use it to trigger a spell that would kill him. The result was determined by the trigger-phrase used by the person touching the lock.

"I would have thought the treasury would have had such dire spells to keep thieves out."

"Yes, your thoughts run parallel to mine." The Emperor shook his head. "Spells designed to defeat thieves are changed on a regular basis so no thief can be certain to command the proper counterspells. The Mage who last cast those spells on the treasury appears to have been induced to reveal which spells he cast, enabling the thieves to dispel them. We do not know if he was a Black Churcher—he appears to be missing."

A shiver ran down my spine. If Black Churchers could infiltrate the palace staff, well, the very idea of that having happened would have been impossible for me to entertain before the events of that evening had unfolded. The threat to the Empire presented by the Black Church had always seemed minor, but now it took on far larger proportions in my mind.

In silence we descended the dark stairwell, then walked through a narrow corridor that was similarly unlit. I felt the Emperor's hand in the middle of my chest and stopped. He muttered another word, and a portion of the wall swung inward. Red light from the other side washed over him, then he beckoned me forward.

I stepped out onto a wooden catwalk approximately twenty feet above the floor of the room below. Moondiscs, similar to those in the passage leading down to the treasury, covered the ceiling and walls and provided the room's light. Each of the discs was full and red, which meant they were linked to the phases of the Assassins' moon.

Below me, filling the entirety of the cavernous room, I saw a crazy-quilt landscape that had belts of glacial ice cutting through bone-dry desert or thick jungle. I saw countless ruins, all in miniature, perched atop rugged mountains or nestled in box canyons. I heard the tinkle of water and saw, there in the distance, a dark, flat body dotted with strange islands.

Suspended from the ceiling by thin wires I even saw an uprooted castle floating in the air. Flags with strange symbols dotted the landscape. Row upon row of tiny figures surrounded those flags, and a set of them nearest the edge were painted black and stood beneath a golden-orb flag.

In an instant I knew what it *had* to be, but I could not believe it. "This . . . this is a topographical miniature of Chaos, isn't it, Highness?"

"It is, Locke. Your father and your uncle came to my

grandfather with the plan for creating it, and every expedition we have sent into Chaos has come back with more information to refine and expand it. We have plotted the zones of variable time, and we know the boundaries for each tribe of Chaos demons. Everything is exacting and to scale, which has enabled commanders like your father to successfully wage war beyond the Ward Walls."

I pointed to the floating fortress. "And what is that?"

"That, Locke, is Castel Payne." He leaned forward on the catwalk railing. "That is where Lord Disaster lives and where we will have to go to destroy him."

15

D own on the room's floor a closer look at the display made it even more incredible. The sculptors had created a very realistic and painstakingly exact simulacrum. Even though I had never been in Chaos, it was not hard to make that assessment of the model. Parts of it mirrored geographical and terrain features I had seen on the trip to the capital. Since they looked very lifelike to me, I had to assume the rest of the model was equally accurate and, as such, quite an achievement.

A sorcerer ranked as a Warder both in Construction and Clairvoyant magicks greeted the Emperor as we studied the nearest edge of the model. "Highness, I am honored to see you as always, though I regret the circumstances necessitating this particular meeting." A man of middle age, his hairline had begun to recede, and his red hair had generally thinned. "I have prepared the scrying room for the meeting. The others your brother gathered are already here."

"Excellent, Warder Illtyd."

I watched the magicker pull a small, flat, hexagonal slice of clear quartz crystal from a pocket in the folds of his blue velvet robe. He gently flicked it toward the model, and I expected it to land hard, gouging up terrain and scattering the small *Bharashadi* figures. To my surprise it hovered an inch above the surface and, because it had landed in the area of hillside, even tipped a bit to remain parallel to the ground.

Illtyd waggled his fingers at the disc and it became parallel with the floor again. "When I have more time to complete the design, I will create a spell that will bind the control, flight, and sympathetic spells all into one. That way I will not have to recast each as it wears out."

His comment meant nothing to me, but I smiled politely as if it had. He started toward the doorway beneath the stairs we had descended. The Emperor followed him, and I trailed behind. I frowned because I knew I should have asked the Warder what the piece of quartz had been for. For better or worse I was engaged in very serious business, and in the battle between being polite and informed, the latter side should win each time.

I decided to ask the Warder to explain about the quartz, but that question changed as we entered the room. A ring of chairs cast long shadows like spokes from the hub of the room out to the walls. Centermost I saw the largest quartz crystal I had ever seen—it literally linked floor to ceiling as if it were a pillar holding up the palace. It had been cut in a hexagonal shape that had to have been at least a yard wide at each face. It provided the illumination in the room, but that was not its primary purpose.

What surprised me—and changed the question I intended to ask the Warder—was that the crystalline column displayed a view of the model landscape. All of the terrain features appeared to be in life scale. By staring into the crystal I was staring into the vista I would have seen had I been standing at that spot in Chaos itself.

Illtyd smiled as I looked at him with amazement on my face. "Warder, the small piece of quartz is linked with this stone?"

He nodded solemnly. "The disc was cut from the same piece, in fact, which makes linking them much easier, as the Law of Contagion would suggest, of course. As commanded, the disc will move over the landscape, and what it sees will be presented here."

I shook my head. "Incredible. The only thing better would be to place these discs in Chaos so we could see what is actually happening there."

"The problem with that idea, Master Lachlan, is twofold," commented one of the other individuals in the room. I looked past the crystal and recognized Grand Duke Ijegron of Jask from earlier that evening. "When we tried to use this sort of magick previously, the Ward Walls interfered with the images. They appeared as insubstantial as heat mirages, which makes them less than useful. In addition, the magick needed to make them work over such a great distance competed with that needed to maintain the walls themselves. To gain an accurate vision of what was happening beyond the Ward Walls we had to damage the walls themselves."

I shook my head. "Not a good thing at all."

"Succinctly put." The older man smiled easily. "Most importantly, though, the linked crystals allow anyone who has obtained one of the pair to be able to see what transpired around the other. I recall being in this very room and finding myself face-to-muzzle with Kothvir himself."

A reptilian Baron from the island of Shar rested a hand on Ijegron's shoulder. "Yesss, that was the greatest danger of posting these magickal windows in Chaos. What were magickally insurrmountable problems fell victim to logic and hard work. Your father saw the sssimple sssolution to them. He chose to sssend scouts into Chaosss to perform sssurveys that allowed usss to create the model you sssee through the column here."

The Baron let his forked tongue slither out of his mouth and snap back in again. I had to stop myself from staring, but I had never before seen a Reptiad. I knew, from things I had read, that these lizard-men had been discovered in Chaos when an effort to reclaim some of the islands was made. At first they were believed to be Chaos creatures because of their scaly gray-green flesh and the fact that they only had three fingers and a thumb, but that thinking soon changed. Aelves and Dwarves pointed out that the islanders had clearly been warped by Chaos to better survive in their inhospitable homes the same way Chaos had adapted some folks into Dwarves to live beneath the mountains or other folks into Aelves to let them thrive in the Imperial Forests.

"Baron Sali'uz has the right of it." The Dwarven Duke Kozor Goll of Besdan came around the edge of the crystal and hooked fingers in his broad leather belt. "Your father even had me with him on one expedition because he wanted to explore a complex of caverns out in Chaos. We measured those caves so precisely I still know them better than I do my own fortress."

The Dwarf did not surprise me because I had met more of his kind in Stone Rapids. Two Dwarven prospectors worked the area near the village and came in to trade for supplies from time to time. Like them, the Duke stood nearly two feet shorter than I and his dark brown eyes looked to be mostly pupil. Gray streaked his brown hair and full beard, but I found I could no more think of him as old than I could consider rocks old. I mean, I knew rocks were old, of course, but the ravages of age had a less obvious effect on the Dwarven Duke than Grand Duke Ijegron.

The Emperor waved the nobles to the chairs, and they seated themselves on either side of Grand Duke Ijegron. "Please, my lords, let us begin. As my brother has told you, more than the appearance of Fialchar has disturbed us this night. When we went to recover the Fistfire Sceptre from the Imperial Treasury, to use in case of Fialchar's return, we discovered a robbery in progress. We were able to drive them off, killing several and capturing others. The perpetrators appear to be members of the Black Church, but among them there was another. This thief got away with the Fistfire Sceptre, which is a dire thing in and of itself. Worse yet, the thief has been identified as a B*harashadi* sorcerer."

Ijegron blanched. "A Black Shadow *here*? That's impossible."

Thetys shook his head and nodded toward me. "Locke saw him and engaged him in combat. He is confident of his identification, and I believe him."

Baron Sali'uz's dark flesh began to approach the ivory shade of his throat. "Lachlan hasss never ssseen a Black Sshadow before. Could he have been misstaken?"

I shrugged. "This B*harashadi* fit all the descriptions of Black Shadows I've ever heard. The possibility that I'm wrong always exists, of course, but if it wasn't a Black Shadow, I've got no idea what it was."

"If Cardew's son saw a Black Shadow, I am willing to accept that identification." Kozor Goll tugged at his beard. "It is not a good thing that the sceptre has been stolen, or that the Black Shadows are doing Lord Disaster's bidding. An alliance on their parts is very frightening."

Thetys shrugged eloquently. "Unfortunately that is the situation. While Fialchar distracted us at the ball, his agents worked to steal the Fistfire Sceptre. He reveals to us the great artifact from before the Shattering while its bane—the Sceptre—is taken from us."

The company in which I found myself cowed me, but I knew I would be useless if I could not grasp the subjects about which they talked. At the risk of being censured, I had to ask for clarification on certain things. "Forgive me, Highness, my lords, but you speak of the Fistfire Sceptre and the Staff of Emeterio as if they were . . ." I wracked my brain for an apt analogy and finally found it. ". . . as if they were to each other what my father and Kothvir were supposed to be."

The Emperor nodded. "Warder Illtyd, perhaps you can explain it."

The magicker addressed his explanation to everyone in the room, though he focused most of his attention on me. "Those two things are linked in a manner similar to how the disc and this quartz are linked. They come from the same basic material. You see, in the realm of magick, to obtain a device of great power, or to create a powerful spell, it is possible to imbue the item with restrictions. For example, if I create a spell that will create a roaring bonfire, it will require an expenditure of energy from me that I might ill afford. If, on the other hand, I limit the size of the blaze, or I make the spell only applicable during a certain season or make the fire only last for an hour, I have sculpted it in such a way that it will not require so much power to create."

I concentrated hard to understand what he was

telling me. In chess, if I limited myself to using only my Cavalry or my Wizards, I could cut down on the amount of time I needed to think about any move. This would limit my strategies and weaken my play, but if I were under time constraints for a game, it would greatly increase my ability to win.

I thought about Sava having told me about the *Bharashadi* spell cast at me. "This is akin to the Chademon that attacked me having limited his spell by making it have a physical focus. Because of that, the coldness of my swords and the water helped counteract the spell. In that case his spell was hurt by the constraints put upon it."

Illtyd smiled appreciatively. "Precisely, Master Lachlan. In the case of the staff, Emeterio wanted to create an item of vast power. The method he chose was to form an alliance with another Sorcerer, Quirc, who was of an entirely juxtaposed and antagonistic philosophical standing. The two of them agreed that both would create magickal talismans, one knowing the other's item would be able to destroy his. This created a balance of power between them that extended to the items they created. In the ritual that they cowrote and concelebrated, they performed what we call a *desecration*. From the pool of materials they both had contributed, they drew light from dark, in from out, and up from down. The material in the staff and the sceptre were divided by magick into forms that would destroy each other and negate each other's work."

Desecrate and create at the same time. I shivered. "And now both halves of that *desecreation* are in the hands of Fialchar?"

"Provided we cannot stop the *Bharashadi* from reaching Chaos." I turned around as Garn Drustorn entered the room. He took a chair next to the Dwarven Duke. "We found the Warder Taci, and she confirmed that whatever cast the spell down in the sewers was what Lieutenant Christoforos and his patrol chased across Menal. With Locke's identification of it as a *Bharashadi* sorcerer, we have to acknowledge the Chaos demons have found a way to breach the Ward Walls."

The Warder frowned. "An easier explanation is that a family of Black Shadows has been living in the Empire since or even before the formation of Tarris."

"And remained undetected, especially while being schooled in Chaos magick?" The Grand Duke shook his head. "As much as I believe it is impossible for the Ward Walls to be breached, your alternative strains credulity even more, I think."

"I think, my friends, I like neither of those alternatives—though the former is something of an academic point." The Emperor held his hands up to forestall any argument. "After all, Lord Disaster showed he was capable of appearing here, in the capital, at will. If he can do it, other creatures of Chaos should be able to do so as well."

"Highness, I hasten to point out that Fialchar was born before the Shattering. While the wave of Chaos may have changed him, it would not have made him subject to the ban of anything born in Chaos being unable to pass through the walls." Illtyd opened his hands helplessly. "I would prefer to think my explanation most likely, as horrible or difficult as that is to contemplate. The only real problem with that idea is the one the Grand Duke raised. The Chaos taint to the magick that Taci detected could not have been so strong *if* the creature wielding it were not born in Chaos. If a creature born within the Empire were able to become that powerful in Chaos magick, there are gaps in the spells used to safeguard the Empire that must be checked for and plugged immediately."

"Perhaps," offered the Reptiad Baron, "Lord Disaster teleported the sorcerer Lachlan reported over as a test of the staff's power."

Ijegron leaned forward in his chair, resting his elbows on his knees. "That idea is based on an assumption with which I am uncomfortable."

I frowned. "You don't think Fialchar and the Black Shadow sorcerer were working together?"

"We have no proof of any alliance being formed between them at all. The appearance of a Black Shadow sorcerer in the palace at the same time as Lord Disaster invited himself to the ball might suggest collusion, but using coincidence to suggest causality is a fallacy all of us should have long since outgrown."

The Imperial Warlord nodded. "That's a very good point."

Ijegron smiled. "Thank you, Garn. Lord Disaster's appearance, I feel, was clearly put in here to show off his new toy. He knows we possess the Fistfire Sceptre, and his possession of the Staff of Emeterio clearly neutralizes the sceptre as a threat against him. If it was to be stolen, would he come and reveal his possession of the Staff of Emeterio to us before he knew the deed had been done? He may be old and may have been changed by Chaos, but he is not stupid."

Duke Goll nodded in agreement. "I apologize for jumping to conclusions. As I recall, the history of Fialchar and the *Bharashadi* has never been one of friendship. I believe Cardew even convinced Fialchar to refrain from attacking the Valiant Lancers when they launched expeditions against the Black Shadows. Perhaps the Black Shadows learned of Fialchar's recovery of the staff and decided they needed to risk the theft of the Fistfire Sceptre to counterbalance it."

I shook my head. "Again, forgive me, but we have a link being forged where none is warranted. Warder Illtyd has said the Fistfire Sceptre is an item of great power all by itself. If it is comparable to the display of power put on by Lord Disaster during the ball, it must be capable of unbelievable things. We have seen it as the antidote to anything Lord Disaster may do with the Staff of Emeterio, but how would the Bharashadi see it? To what use could a Bharashadi sorcerer put it?"

The Emperor paled. In one voice with the Warlord he whispered, "The Necroleum."

"What?"

Thetys drew in a deep breath and exhaled it slowly while color returned to his face. "How much do you really know about Chaos demons, Lachlan?"

I blushed. "Each moment I'm finding out I know less and less."

That brought the hint of a smile to the Emperor's face and brief chuckles from the others. "It's time you learned more. The Chademons all have special abilities which, it is said, they obtained from their patron deities. The Storm demons, for example, are able to warp local weather to their own desires and can bring lightning and thunder or freezing rains down upon their foes. Flame demons burn with an unquenchable fire that does not consume them. The catalog of known tribes and abilities is huge and as bizarre as you might expect of anything originating in Chaos."

"I'd heard something like that from my grandfather, but nothing about the Black Shadows." I nodded. "I take it this Necroleum is connected with the Bharashadi power?"

Thetys shrugged stiffly. "What we know of it is rumor

only and treacherously unreliable at that. Some information came from a report of something a fevered Chaos Rider said though other Rider's efforts have lent a lot of weight to the report."

The Emperor seated himself in a chair and bade me sit as well. "The Bharashadi covenant with their god has strict limits, much akin to those you have discussed concerning spells. When a Black Shadow falls in combat, if it is at all possible, he is brought to a hidden place called the Necroleum. There a whole caste of funereal attendants deal with him. If he has been cut up, they sew him back together. If bones have been broken, they are set as best as possible. If limbs have been hacked off, they are reattached. If, at the end of this processing, his body is complete, he is placed in the deepest caverns of the Necroleum to await resurrection."

I shivered. The very idea of some stinking hole in the ground stuffed full of mouldering Bharashadi corpses in various states of repair made my flesh crawl. The idea that they could be resurrected didn't help at all with that feeling. "The bodies must be whole for resurrection?"

"As we understand it, yes." The Emperor nodded solemnly. "If one of our soldiers took a scalp, for example, that Bharashadi would be incomplete and find himself outside the covenant with his god."

"Unless the scalp could be returned to him?" I asked.

"I believe so." Thetys rubbed the palms of his hands one against the other. "Through a ritual specified by the god, using any of a number of items safely hidden beyond the Ward Walls, the complete Bharashadi warriors can be recalled from death."

The Warlord nodded his head in accordance with the Emperor's words. "Given the rate of reproduction and death rates of the B*harashadi*, it is estimated they would have over one hundred thousand warriors waiting to be recalled. The B*harashadi* are fierce in combat because they know they will be revivified some day. They believe their rank in the new society they will form will be determined by how bravely they acquitted themselves when they died. The greatest of their leaders will become their supreme commander, and the leading contender for that spot right now would be Kothvir."

A *hundred thousand Black Shadows, all being led by my father's mortal enemy*! I stared at the Warlord. "And you believe the Fistfire Sceptre is sufficient to help trigger this resurrection?"

"That *and* possibly enough to bring a portion of the Ward Walls down to let them invade the Empire." Garn Drustorn looked at the assembled nobles. "We will, of course, assemble a host and move to oppose the B*harashadi* in Chaos. If we are lucky, we will be able to entice other Chademon tribes likewise to attack the Black Shadows."

Grand Duke Ijegron's chair creaked as he sat back. "I would hope we had more than luck to count on in enlisting other Chademon tribes to our cause."

Kozor Goll shook his head. "Though opposing the Black Shadows might be in their best interest, the power to bring down the Ward Walls might be enough to allow Kothvir to forge them into one force that will sweep down over us. I think we can only count on ourselves, which is why taking the battle to Chaos will be important."

"Wait a minute." I held up my hands and looked at the quartz column displaying a vision of Chaos. "Raising an army sufficient to defend the Empire will take time, especially during the winter. You have the model. Why not use it to plan a quick raid on the

Necroleum and destroy it before this B*harashadi* sorcerer can resurrect the demons?"

The Emperor gave me a wan smile. "Would that the action were so easy as the words. The major problem is that no one knows where the Necroleum is located."

I pointed at the crystal. "Yes, the model might not show us where it is, but it can identify where it is not. That limits the search area. Through a process of elimination, we can finally locate it and go after it."

"Agreed, which is what we will have to do, but that is the easiest part of this whole operation." Thetys sat forward in his chair. "Remember, Lord Disaster possesses the one item capable of destroying the sceptre."

"True, but as much as Lord Disaster hates the Empire and wants to destroy it, I am certain he will not want the B*harashadi* usurping his prerogatives in conquering it." I opened my hands. "It may be hopeless, and it may be a fool's errand, but it is worth the try."

"I agree, Lachlan, that it is." The Emperor's head came up. "That is the reason your cousin is out gathering his patrol. Within a week you and he, and whomever you choose to accompany you, will go into Chaos to get the Staff of Emeterio, find the Necroleum, and destroy it."

16

Hard on the heels of the Emperor's stunning announcement came word that the servant the Emperor had dispatched to find me some clothing had succeeded in his task. The Journeyman magicker who passed that information to Illtyd was charged with the duty of leading me from the viewing room to a place where I could dress myself in private. I trailed after him out to the head of the stairs leading down, and he gave me directions to follow from there.

I think it was a good thing for me to be sent from the room after I had been given that mission because I needed time alone to think about it. My absence also made it easier for any of the others in the room to question the Emperor about the wisdom of his choice. I could not imagine Imperial advisors worthy of the title not questioning the Emperor's thinking in this matter.

After all, I certainly was.

All my life I had grown up with heroic tales of my father and his brother. I had also always measured myself against Geoff and Dalt, and found myself physically lacking in comparison with them. Both of them fit the heroic mold better than I, but in me was the desperate fear I would never have the chance to prove myself an apt heir to our father. At home I was always a little brother, but in the capital I was a man. Here, with this quest being thrust upon me I knew, if nothing else, that I would get the chance to succeed.

But the question truly was one of how great *was* the chance for success? The Emperor had to send someone after the B*harashadi* sorcerer, and choosing a small, select group of individuals to do just that would minimize the attention that would be attracted if, say, a whole battalion of lancers were to be put into the field. In addition, regular army troops would be needed to fill the host that would oppose the Black Shadows. Wasting a full unit in this foolsquest was not a good idea.

My mouth dried out a bit as I realized my companions and I were decidedly expendable. If we succeeded, we would be lauded and feted. If we did not, the Black Shadows would resurrect their warriors, which meant the lot of us would be forgotten in the annals of the war that would follow. Our expedition was one the Emperor could not afford to prevent, and one that he could easily afford to gamble.

The Valiant Lancers had started out as a small group, then grown to the size of a company and later a full regiment. I had no doubt many of my father's early expeditions were similar in nature to the one I was facing. The bards would have had me believe my father laughed at odds and faced every challenge with a defiant roar and confident smile.

The prospect of failure was making my stomach turn sour. *But fail is not what I want or intend to do.* While my father would have been realistic about the mission, I didn't think he would have let doubts or the chances of failure poison his effort. I resolved I'd not do that either—for the sake of my companions and my father's reputation.

I allowed myself no illusions about the nature of the mission. Kit and I would need capable people with us. We would need some who knew Chaos well and were formidable fighters. We would have to be self-contained, as foraging in Chaos would be chancy at best, and could be downright dangerous if we ate something poisonous. Stealth and secrecy would be keys to our survival, while quick thinking and no small amount of luck would prove vital for our success.

By the time I finished dressing in clothing of forest green cut along military lines, Thetys appeared and nodded his approval of the way I looked. "Good, that suits you better than bedclothes. How does your arm feel?"

"Fine, Highness. A bit sore getting it into the tunic, but other than that it does not hurt much. It does itch, though."

"You have my sympathy." He held out to me a small casket about twice the size of the box which had held my father's ring. I took it and found it quite heavy. "These are Imperial Medallions. I have given you five of them and another five have been given to your cousin. You will give one each to the people who are to accompany you into Chaos. The medallions will tell my armorers that these people are part of your expedition, and they will be outfitted as appropriate for this foray into Chaos."

I opened the box and pulled out one of the bronze

discs. The Imperial triskele crest decorated one face and the obverse showed a Ward Tower on the frontier with Chaos. The disc felt substantial and strong, as if symbolic of the Imperial support it represented. The cool metal felt good in the palm of my hand.

"I understand, sire, but do you not want to approve my choices?" I frowned and pressed my lips flat together. "This is a mission of utmost importance, yet you entrust it to me and my cousin as if we were our fathers. I am honored that you trust me and you trust Christoforos. Kit, he knows people here and knows whom to choose to accompany him into Chaos, but I know no one here. How can you trust me to choose companions wisely if I'm not certain I can do that?"

The Emperor looked at me long and hard. I saw a dozen different emotions flicker across his face, but ultimately he smiled. "You are, of course, correct in that I am placing a great deal of trust in you, but I have no choice. If your mission succeeds, we will have no threat to the Empire from the Bharashadi. If it does not, I lose a dozen people and get to anticipate an invasion from Chaos that could easily destroy us all. Make no mistake about it, while I pray your mission will be successful, I actually believe I may well be sending you off to die in pursuit of an unattainable goal."

I nodded. "Thank you, Highness, for confiding your thoughts in me."

"Sending people off to die is not, nor ever should be, easy." His dark eyes narrowed. "Of course, you'd already assessed your chances of success in this matter, so what I had to say came as no surprise."

"Not really."

"I hate to say this, given the circumstances, but that is a good thing." He pointed to my right hand. "When I awarded you that ring you said you hoped you would be able to do something to earn that honor. I had hoped that you would as well, but I never thought it would be with anything this dangerous or this soon. And, yes, I would very much like to exercise a veto over your choice of companions, but I cannot do that."

"But, Highness, no one would refuse you if you asked them to join us."

"Of this I am well aware, and that is very much at the core of the problem. I have been told that when going into Chaos—where I have never been—a cadre must be chosen for their ability and the trust they have in one another. I believe—I *have to believe*—you and Christoforos will make the correct choices of those who will accompany you. And those people will have to know that their chances of coming back alive are hair-thin and dry-rot-weak."

I nodded calmly. "And will have to choose to go with us despite the poor odds, for their own reasons, not out of any feeling that they had to go because you have suggested they go."

"Precisely." A wry grin twisted across the Emperor's lips. "Despite the fact that I have given you and your cousin no such freedom to refuse."

I laughed lightly. "We'll be like Jhesti the Lost Prince. We'll have to beard Lord Disaster in his own den, get from him his newfound staff, then defeat the whole of the *Bharashadi*, including those killed over the past five centuries. The stuff of legends, just like the Lost Prince. How could any sane person resist?"

"The tally of sane folk willing to accompany you will not be great, Lachlan." The Emperor shook his head slowly. "In fact, given the nature of the assignment, I would think you would want to recruit from a group that has already shown itself mentally unstable."

"Yes, sire, the Chaos Riders." I smiled and remembered my promise to find Roarke. "If I may have your leave, I think I will begin my recruiting drive at the Umbra."

From things I had read and heard I knew polite society considered the waterfront area of the capital an enclave of Chaos because of its relative lawlessness. Even in the wee hours of the first day of the Bear things remained rather wild. Wandering in drunken knots, sailors on liberty from ships filled the streets. More often than not, when these little groups managed to collide with each other fistfights broke out, but being pounded into a bloody pulp didn't seem to spoil anyone's fun.

Despite the clear abandon with which the denizens of the waterfront greeted the new year, the riotous action stopped toward the south end. There the zone reserved for Chaos Riders began, and even the blind drunk seemed to shun it. Dodging roiling brawls got easier as I headed into that section of the city, and the preternatural quiet in the area made it easy to understand why Chaos Riders call it the Asylum.

The nature of the denizens made it simple to see why most others call it Quarantine.

Much of the waterfront area, which is largely the older part of the city, is not paved with stones. Consequently, the snow, being churned to mush by wagons and hooves, left the streets muddy. At night, as the temperature dropped and the traffic slowed, the mud froze, leaving the Asylum's streets a chilly catalog of the odd creatures that had wandered through it. I saw more than one track of an animal that, because of the depth of the print, had to weigh as much as a horse, yet the splayed-foot spoor suggested it was something else entirely.

Like the rest of Old Town, the Asylum's buildings were largely made of wood, though a fair number had been built out of sod or stone. A few had signs in front proclaiming them to be businesses, but most were just dark. The streets ran this way and that, splitting and becoming far narrower paths the deeper I went into that section of the city.

Though I felt as foolish as someone walking through a graveyard in the wee hours of the morning, I could not feel afraid here. I knew I would see people and things I had never seen before, if Roarke and Eirene were in any way typical of Chaos Riders. While those people would be queer and terrifying, they had braved Chaos. I could do nothing but respect that, especially if I meant to recruit people for the Emperor's mission here.

Deep in the Asylum, back hidden amid a labyrinth of streets, I found the Umbra. My feet seemed to know the path as if I had been there a million times before. I descended the rickety wooden steps to enter the tavern as easily as I would walk into my grandmother's house. I pulled aside the thick hide covering the doorway and stood alone on a compact landing. A stairway led down on my right, and another headed up a half level straight ahead. I looked down, and between the steps I could see more stairs that descended at least one more level below the street.

Drifting clouds of smoke diffused the yellow light from the thick candles burning atop tables and in wax-encrusted wall brackets. The murk made it difficult to see very far into the place at all, but the people I did spot seemed to come in all sorts of lumps and bumps and colors—easily from all the races of the Empire and every province. A muted buzz punctuated by an occasional shout reverberated from each level, and the thick stench reminded me of a stable that had not been mucked out in far too long.

A huge creature peered down at me from the upper level. I guessed he was a man, though his head sat lopsided on his neck, as if someone had tried to twist his head around so his ears would be top and bottom on it. His eyes, which I thought were set perilously close to each other, glowed with *Chaosfire*. His left hand he kept hidden in his vest, while the other grabbed the stair railing. "What would you be wanting, hatchling? You've ne'er left the nest, so you're not the sort we want here. Be gone."

I smiled politely at the man-thing. "I have come to. . ."

"Deaf, are you?" He took one step down toward me, and I saw that his left knee appeared not to move in the normal way. "There are other places you can go to gawk, boy. Leave 'neath your own power, or I'll throw you out." He came another step closer, and his left knee definitely bent backward when he moved. "Go on, out!"

Off to my right a silvery behemoth leaped from the lower level to the landing and imposed himself between me and the man-thing. A low growl rumbled from Cruach's throat, then he barked once, sharply, at the man. The hound lifted his broad head beneath my left hand, and I scratched him behind his right ear.

The man-thing dexter-slashed a toothy smile across the lower half of his face. "So you know Roarke, do you? You'll find him down there. Whatever your business, be quick about it."

"Thank you, sir. Best of the new year to you, sir."

He snarled in response to my greeting, but retreated quickly enough as Cruach's ears came forward, and the hound swung his head around to look up the stairs. I patted Cruach heartily on his right shoulder, then scratched under his chin. "And the best of the new year to you, too, Cruach. Now, where's Roarke?"

Cruach, being an intelligent hound, and having heard his master's name more than once, turned and trotted down the steps to the first level below the street. He looked back to see I was following him, then trotted on deeper into the room. Despite plunging directly into a sea of round tables distributed in an utterly random pattern, Cruach's tall silver back remained in sight like a ghost ship sailing through an archipelago.

I followed his course as best I could, though various individuals shifted their benches to make my progress difficult. I heard the words "hatchling" and "virgin" muttered more than once, and from a host of throats barely suited to mouthing human speech. Many of the Chaos Riders appeared to be little more than misshapen figures hidden by thick cloaks, and fairly often I saw two or more *Chaosfire*-filled eyes staring out at me from hoods. The words and glances and actions told me I was not wanted here, and that most of them wanted nothing more than to have me break and run.

Virgin I might be in the ways of Chaos, but being intimidated by hostility was a habit of which my brother Dalt had long ago broken me. I kept my head high and worked my way through the crowd as best I could. I avoided touching people when possible, and politely slipped past the impromptu barricades raised to impede me.

Without too much delay I found my way back to a distant table where Roarke sat with his typical grin plastered on his face. "Welcome to the Umbra, Locke." He sat back in his chair, his motions obviously lubricated by whatever lurked beneath the froth in his tankard. "You came to Herakopolis to attend the Emperor's Ball. By the look of your clothes either you missed it, or my invite misstated the requisite color scheme."

"A little of both, actually, I think." I lowered myself onto a bench, then nodded to Eirene as she sat down across from me. "Joyous new year to you, Eirene."

"And you, Locke." She set a tankard down in front of me, then took a sip from its twin. "So, is it true what they say happened at the ball tonight?"

I wrapped my hands around the steaming tankard and tried to suppress a shiver. "It depends up on what they say happened. It certainly *was* a Bear's Eve Ball I will never forget." The drink smelled like hot spiced cider, but I sipped it carefully in case it was something else entirely.

Roarke laughed easily. "The way the word filtered down here, Lord Disaster and a horde of *Bharashadi* lighted in the midst of the ball and slew the lot of nobles there. Said they burned the palace, too, but I have some doubt about that as I can't see the glow from here."

I leaned forward and lowered my voice. "Fialchar did show up, and he had the Staff of Emeterio with him."

Eirene tucked a green-streaked lock of hair behind one of her pointed ears. "The Staff of Emeterio? I don't think I know of it."

Roarke waved her to silence. "It's a trinket of some power, but that's not the whole of the story, is it, Locke?"

"No, not by half." I kept my voice quiet. "At the same time a *Bharashadi* sorcerer and some Black Churchers managed to steal the Fistfire Sceptre from the Imperial Treasury Vault below the palace."

Eirene's expression closed up, and she sipped at her

cider to mask her face. Roarke frowned as if willing himself to clearheadedness. "Locke, that can't be. No *Bharashadi* sorcerer could be inside the Ward Walls."

I unbuttoned the cuff of my tunic and pulled the sleeve back to show them my bandage. "He used a spell to try to kill me, and by luck alone I survived. I saw him, Roarke. Sure, I've only seen Black Shadows in my dreams, but this one matched every description of them I've heard."

"First time I've heard the word dream used to describe seeing Black Shadows in your sleep." Eirene shook her head. "Sensible folks call them nightmares."

I nodded. "You have the right of it, Eirene. I fear I will see this one in many a nightmare." I pulled the Imperial Medallions from the pouch on my belt and placed one each in front of them. "The Emperor believes the Black Shadows will use the sceptre to stage an invasion of the Empire. He wants an expedition to go into Chaos to stop the invasion, or delay things enough for the Warlord to field an army that can stop them."

Eirene stared at the coin as if it was a snake coiled to strike at her. "An Imperial expedition? How many of us are there?"

I winced. "Twelve, counting my cousin and me. He's a scout with the Emperor's Horse Guards. He will have his patrol, and I am to recruit five people to go with us. We can have thirteen with Cruach."

Roarke raised a finger. "Not a good idea to be mentioning thirteen as the number in your little venture, Locke. Fialchar was the thirteenth person involved with the Seal of Reality, and he shattered it, so thirteen is not seen as very auspicious."

"Sorry."

"Superstition isn't what's bothering me." Eirene

pushed the medallion back in my direction. "A dozen people going into Chaos to put a stop to a Bharashadi invasion? Locke, in the event someone has hidden this information from you, that is exactly the sort of mission that got your father killed, and the Valiant Lancers numbered a dozen dozen." Eirene glanced over at Roarke. "As for him, even drunk he would not go back into Chaos. It cost him too much last time."

I looked over at Roarke, dreading his confirmation of Eirene's statement. He looked shocked and had paled considerably. Cruach forced his head between Roarke's right hand and his body, but the man just let his arm dangle by the beast's flank. "Roarke?"

He swallowed hard. "It's about the Necroleum, isn't it?"

"Yes. How do you know about it?"

He shook his head. "I know because I know."

I watched him carefully. The Emperor had said they had learned of the Necroleum from the fevered ravings of a Chaos Rider. I wondered for a moment if that rider had been Roarke. "If you know of the Necroleum, you know how important this is. With the Fistfire Sceptre it's possible to raise all the Bharashadi from the dead. If that gets done . . ."

"I have a grasp of the general scenario, Locke." Roarke picked up the medallion I'd set before him and spun it around between forefinger and thumb. "Been a long time since I've had one of these in my hand." His fist closed over it. "I'm in."

Eirene drew back away from him. "Roarke, are you crazy? You said you would never go back."

"No, Eirene, I said I'd only go back if the objective was worth going blind for. If the Bharashadi get the Fistfire Sceptre to the Necroleum, *everyone* will become Chaos Riders. I reckon this is the quest that I've been waiting for." He pushed her medallion back toward her. "Come on, Eirene, you're too pretty to want to live till old age will take you, and too damned spiteful to die in the Empire."

She picked the medallion up and hefted it in her right hand. "I'll go, Roarke, but only so I know the truth behind the bragging you'll be doing when we return. If we return."

The one-eyed Chaos Rider beamed at her. "That's the spirit, Eirene."

I grabbed Roarke's right wrist. "The Emperor wants us to convince Lord Disaster to let us use the Staff of Emeterio to stop the *Bharashadi* from raising their dead."

Eirene coughed down some cider. "And there's to be only a dozen of us?"

Roarke wrinkled his nose. "Thetys is more cautious than his father. Daclones would only have sent ten— maybe eight if he knew Cruach was coming. How many more of those medallions do you have, Locke?"

"Three." I held my hand out, and he plucked two of them from my palm.

"Keep the last because we'll want someone from the Church of the Sunbird, and they always jump at the chance to please the Emperor. We might even get two."

"That would be a big help."

"Indeed. And now to find bigger help." Roarke stood and hooked his index and little fingers between his lips. He let go with a powerful whistle that made me cover my ears and wrung a yowl from Cruach. The Umbra's din dropped to silence, and, except for a lunatic cackle rising and falling from below us, it remained quiet.

Roarke flipped one of the medallions in the air and casually caught it. He looked up and smiled when he found himself to be the center of attention. "I've news for all that's likely to mark the rest of the year, so listen good. Seems the Emperor had a visit this night from Lord Ugly himself. Disrupted the ball, Fialchar did, and was right impolite to the lords and ladies there. Thetys wants a delegation of us to go and explain to Fialchar proper conduct at an Imperial Ball."

Roarke smiled slyly and let shouted gibes slide past without reply. "The difficult part of this mission is that the Emperor has also angered the *Bharashadi*, and they're likely to make our passage less than comfortable. Not to worry too much, though, because this here is Lachlan, Cardew's son. His cousin, Driscoll's son, is with the Emperor's Horse Guards and will be bringing his patrol, too. I would deal with this alone, mind you, but there's always firewood that needs chopping and the occasional Chademon that wants for killing."

Laughter and more biting comments ripped through the crowd. The unfocused hostility I felt before had slackened with Roarke's identifying me. A couple of people nodded in my direction, and I heard my father's name bandied about in whispers and croaks. I wasn't openly accepted because of my heritage, but it brought me to neutral in the minds of many, and the change made me grin.

Roarke flipped one of the two medallions at a huge figure seated three tables away. A hand moved swiftly to catch the metal disc, and I heard a sound like that of a coin striking stone. The Chaos Rider stood slowly but could not straighten up all the way without hitting his head on the ceiling. Instantly I saw he was a Reptiad like Baron Sali'uz, but the light glinted off his scaly hide as if his flesh was made of mica.

"Nagrendra, I want you with me. Can you think of a better way to start a year?"

"If it calls you to Chaos, Roarke, it will be quite an adventure." The Reptiad nodded slowly. "I will pay my respects to Lord Disaster and see if Jhesti left him any beard."

Roarke tossed the other medallion out toward one person, but another shot from a chair and pulled it down. The intended target grabbed the interloper's wrist, but the interloper pulled his hand free, then jerked his elbow back into the face of Roarke's target. I heard a sharp crack, then a moan and the sound of a body sliding to the floor.

Roarke frowned as the man who caught the medallion walked toward us. He held the disc like a talisman out in front of him. *Chaosfire* filled his eyes and looked out at me from the eye sockets of the wolf-skull that formed his cowl.

"I am Tyrchon." He slapped the medallion down on the table and looked straight at me. "I asked your father to let me accompany him on what was his last mission. He told me I was too young to die." The man folded well-muscled arms across a broadly built chest. "I believe I have aged enough since then." He half growled his words and attracted Cruach's attention.

As he spoke I found it easy to imagine him much younger and brasher. I could see my father smiling at his offer, but sending him away because his foray was too dangerous for so young and inexperienced a fighter. Tyrchon had missed his chance with my father, and thought himself fortunate enough to have a second opportunity with me.

I looked over at Roarke. "What do you think?"

He shrugged. "The Emperor gave the medallions to you, not me."

Tyrchon looked at Roarke. "I have been on many expeditions to Chaos. I have spent much time there. I have slain many Chademons: *Bharashadi*, *Tsvortu*, *Drasacor*, *Hobmotli*. I have found much in Chaos and brought it back."

Roarke yawned. "Aside from Locke here, there's no one in this place who couldn't say the same for himself."

Tyrchon nodded slowly. "Well said. With me along, though, we will not be surprised by the enemy. They may hide, but not from me."

Eirene looked up at him. "That's a tall claim. Prove it."

"Gladly." Tyrchon raised his hands to encompass everyone in the room. "Ask any of them what they have seen of me in Chaos."

Roarke looked around the room. "Can anyone verify his claims?"

Dead silence answered the question.

I frowned and placed my hand over the medallion. "It would seem, Tyrchon, your claims go unsubstantiated."

Roarke smiled and tapped me on the shoulder. "Don't be so hasty, Locke."

"But no one was able to back him up."

"Right, which means he travels in Chaos alone."

Eirene nodded. "And to do that you have to be very good or you get very dead."

Tyrchon folded his arms across his chest. "And I'm not dead."

I held the medallion up to Tyrchon. "Let's see to it you stay that way. I would be honored if you would join us."

I swear the ears on his cowl twitched as he took the coin from my hand. "I will settle my affairs and meet you tomorrow."

He turned away and I noticed the wolfskin did not

move freely. I stared after him, then turned to Roarke. "That cloak, that cowl. Are they *part* of him?"

"Things like that happen in Chaos, Locke." He gave me a broad smile. "Be careful what you decide to wear, because you could be wearing it for a *long* time."

17

Jhesti the Lost Prince. Gavin Madhand. Scarlet Elk. Mira Vilewolf. My father. My uncle. The list of Imperial heroes was long, and their exploits were impressive. I had always dreamed of joining that august company, but never did I imagine I would be given an opportunity to do so quite this soon in my life. I had secretly hungered for the day when Cardew would be remembered as my father instead of me always being described as his son, but had anyone suggested I would participate in an expedition going into Chaos before I'd reached a full score years, I would have considered them insane.

And I was insane for going, but that seemed appropriate because this whole business was insane. A Chaos demon in the capital, Lord Disaster disrupting the Bear's Eve Ball—none of it made sense. In fact, it violated the tenets of reality as far as I was concerned. *Can I be insane if the measuring stick for reality and sanity has been this badly broken?*

As I returned to my grandmother's home I got to watch the sun rise from the ocean and send the first rosy rays out to paint the thin clouds. *That* certainly seemed normal enough, but I suspected that would be my only brush with normalcy over the next week. I clung to it, using it as an omen that not everything had changed, and that we might be able to put things right again.

If we couldn't, the red in the clouds would be from the burning of Imperial cities by Black Shadow invaders.

The presence of a Chaos demon in the capital was known only to a few very trusted individuals, and I trusted Eirene and Roarke as much as the Emperor trusted me. We all assumed that the *Bharashadi* had either left the capital immediately after his theft had been discovered, or that he was still in the city hiding with members of the Black Church. To announce this to everyone, however, would have started a panic that quite probably would have resulted in riots and vigilante slayings of anyone even remotely suspected of being a Black Churcher, so attempts to uncover his location had to be made carefully.

Lord Disaster's coincidental visit gave the Emperor the excuse to lock the city up tight. He started, using a rumor that Lord Disaster had not really appeared at the ball, but that it had been some renegade magicker trained in Chaos as his apprentice. The visitation had been part of a plan, heralds reported, to demoralize the Empire. The Emperor announced his intention to find the culprits and make them pay.

Immediate and harsh security measures were put in place. The city gates were closed, and people were let in and out only after strict searches by soldiers and sorcerers in the Imperial service. Heavily armed patrols headed out from the capital to comb the surrounding area for the demon and to set up a cordon he would have a difficult time negotiating. All shipping was blockaded, and orders were given to sink any ship that did not allow itself to be boarded and searched.

As my head hit the pillow, I said a silent prayer that the patrols would find and destroy the *Bharashadi* sorcerer before he reached Chaos. That would make everything so much easier, even if it meant I would have to wait to become a hero. Given the nature of our mission, having to develop the virtue of patience was something I found infinitely preferable to dying in Chaos.

James entered my room and awakened me just past midday. An Imperial messenger had arrived and conveyed to me an invitation to visit with the Emperor within the hour. I washed quickly and dressed myself in the clothes the Emperor had lent me the previous night. I was all set to head out immediately when I realized I'd not seen my grandmother since before Lord Disaster appeared and that I wanted to make certain the previous night's excitement had not taken its toll on her health.

I headed up to the solar and found her dozing there as I had on the day of my arrival. She sat there, bathed in sunbeams, with a blanket covering her legs. Needlework lay in her lap, and a faint smile twisted the corners of her mouth.

I started into the room to wake her gently, then stopped. She looked so pleased and content that I chose not to disturb her. She had watched her sons march off into combat many times, and on the last of these they had not returned. Now their sons, her grandsons, were going to be sent on a mission similar to the one that had killed her sons. To wake her up and inform her of that news would be unforgivable, so I backed slowly out of the doorway.

Better she rejoices in my having won favor with the Emperor than she worries about what I must do for him.

My retreat from the solar took me all the way down to the kitchen. I grabbed three hot biscuits from Rose and gave her a peck on the cheek by way of a thank-you. I looked around for Marija to see how she had recovered from the ball but could not find her. Outside Nob told me she had gone off to the market, and that he had sent Carl along to watch after her. I thanked him and tossed the heel of one biscuit to Striapach, the taller of the two wolfhound bitches he had on lead.

In the street I headed as straight as possible for the palace. I had been surprised at how my stomach hitched when Nob told me his grandson was escorting Marija to market. I knew I liked her, but this involuntary reaction suggested I liked her a lot more than I realized. As nearly as I could remember, I'd never actually felt *jealous* about anyone before—not that being jealous is something to brag about.

Too much seemed to be happening too quickly. Any *one* of the things happening to me would have been enough to make the trip to the capital an adventure. I had met the Emperor. I had confronted Fialchar. I had found a girl I liked. I had been given an Imperial mission to travel into Chaos.

In one short trip I'd done what others took a whole career to accomplish. For all the excitement, though, meeting Marija seemed somehow more important than all the other things. That realization certainly gave me something to think about, but the mission for which I had been chosen did not give me much time to do that thinking.

At the palace I was immediately ushered to the map room. It came as no surprise to find Kit, the Warlord, the Emperor, and Warder Illtyd already present. A table over near the opening to the viewing room had a crust of bread on it, along with a wine pitcher, some fruit, cheese, and several half-filled goblets.

"Good morning, Locke," Kit greeted me. Kit looked as if he had not gotten that much sleep, yet he looked less haggard than Thetys or Garn Drustorn.

"Morning, Kit. Grandmother seems fine after last night." I lowered my voice. "Is there any news?"

"Some." Kit brushed some bread crumbs from his tunic. "We attempted to use spells to locate the Fistfire Sceptre, but they didn't work."

"Why not?" I glanced at Warder Illtyd. "Wouldn't that powerful an item be easy to pinpoint with magick?"

"Under normal circumstances, yes, but it appears our thief is not wholly stupid." The Warder wiped sleep-sand from the corner of his eye. "We believe the thief broke the sceptre down into its component parts. He can't use it in that state, but if he is as powerful as you and your cousin indicate, he would not need it until he reaches the Ward Walls and wants to cross over to Chaos."

I frowned. "Forgive me for being so slow, but magick confuses me. Why would his having broken the sceptre down into various parts make it difficult to detect?"

The sorcerer smiled. "Your question is a difficult one to answer. What is it that makes a chair a chair?"

I hesitated for a moment, sensing a trick. "It has four legs, a seat, and a back."

"But if it only has three legs, in a triangle configuration so it still stood, would it still be a chair?"

"I guess so."

"But you could tell the difference between it and a three-legged stool?"

"Yes."

"Why?"

"Well . . ." My frown deepened. "It has an inherent chairness about it, I guess."

The Warder nodded. "Exactly. So it is with everything, from rocks to people and magickal items. That inherent quality of being whatever it is helps identify that person or item as far as magick is concerned. When the sceptre is dismantled, whatever that quality is, it undergoes reduction until we can't identify it anymore. If and when the Chademon reassembles the sceptre, we'll know it, but until then we have no chance of detecting it."

"I see, I think." I shrugged and let the matter drop as another sorcerer called Illtyd aside to deal with some problem. A number of other individuals moved around the room, placing standards with color-coded flags on the miniature landscape to mark out zones. The vast majority of spaces were encompassed in a boundary of white flags.

The Warlord nodded to me. "Just before you arrived, Warder Illtyd explained that the information about the various areas of Chaos correspond roughly to the color of the flags outlining them. The darker the flag, the more recent and solid the information."

"White means we know little or nothing?"

"Not exactly, Locke." Illtyd, who had returned, frowned and pointed to the miniature with his right hand. "All of the geographical features you see depicted here have been painstakingly reproduced from survey reports. The level of that information is very good, but noting the layout of stones on a plain tells us nothing about what might live beneath the stones. We know what the mountains look like, but we have little or no idea about what might be inside of them."

Kit leaned over and squinted at one detail of the map. "We can and should make some assumptions if we want to locate this Necroleum. The first, I think, is that it must be in territory held by the Bharashadi. I cannot imagine, if it is so important to them, they would not protect it very well."

Thetys nodded in agreement. "I doubt other Chademons would allow it to exist given what the presence of thousands of Bharashadi warriors would mean to the balance of power in Chaos. I think we can limit our search to Bharashadi territory."

That assumption, it struck me, still left a great deal of Chaos for its location. "I think we can also assume that it is in a very defensible area. I would doubt it is located in ruins or anything else that we might know about from books or maps written and drawn before the invasion." I pointed to a white-flagged area of labyrinthine canyons and river valleys. "I would bet it is in there somewhere."

Illtyd pointed us toward the small room used the day before to explain the situation to the nobles. "That is as good a place as any to start, I suppose. I will have my aides bring us the survey reports, maps, and journals from any expeditions in that area. Let us hope we find some clue that will help you in your expedition."

We pored over volumes of material for the next six hours. The material we used was incredibly varied in reliability and presentation. A lot of it seemed based on talks with Chaos Riders after their return from expeditions. Hyperbole characterized many accounts, but they also contained a wealth of information. I pored over the ones I'd been given, drinking in details and facts that I hoped would help me in Chaos.

Despite the hours we put in, we only covered a quarter of the area we had decided to explore. I discovered many things that astounded and amazed me, but I learned little I could consider useful to the task at hand. Reading about legendary creatures like the Emerald Stallion or of spotting Castel Payne aloft were interesting, but really had little bearing on our task. What might have been a promising trail in one set of documents was proved to be false by another. While gaining a very good feel for the area, the only thing that time did for me was clarify the enormity and impossibility of our mission.

Illtyd put several of his aides to work compiling a definitive gazetteer of the valleys and canyons we read about. One woman combined all of the maps and sketches we came across into a composite view of the region that included demarcations for variable time zones, safe watering holes, old ruins in which we might take shelter, and known ambush sites. Each site was given a number which corresponded to an entry in the gazetteer, and we were assured we would be given multiple copies of each to study and use during the mission.

As the day wore on into midafternoon, I was granted leave to go and meet Roarke at the Temple of the Sunbird. The Emperor approved of his suggestion to get a member of the Church to go with us, so I took that as a good sign. I left the palace and made my way to the Temple district, finding Roarke rather easily on the broad steps of the Sunbird temple.

"There you are, Locke." The one-eyed man smiled and greeted me with a slap on the shoulder. "I spoke with one of the Priests earlier, and I think we will be given help."

"Good." I looked around and frowned. "Where's Cruach?"

Roarke laughed lightly. "I went to your grand-mother's home to bring you with me earlier. You were gone, so I left Cruach with Nob. I will get him later. Come on."

The mammoth granite temple reminded me more of a fortress than a place of worship. It had pillars holding up a frieze depicting the Sunbird in battle with the Demons of Night, but the austerity of the rest of the structure mocked the ostentation of the other temples on the street. The dark tunnel that led through the guarded gate had murderholes cut in the top of it, and when the iron doors were closed and barred at either end, an army could have been held captive. Nowhere in the tunnel did I see grand murals or tapestries giving glory to the Sunbird or the accomplishments of the Sunbird believers.

"Rather a forbidding place, is it not?"

Roarke shrugged. "The Sunbirders spend most of their gold on weapons and training, which will be money well spent given what we need on our expedition."

The far end of the tunnel opened onto a massive courtyard that was split down the middle by an elevated walkway linking front to back. All around the exterior a broad marble avenue a good ten feet above the central training ground allowed people to move from one part of the temple to another without disturbing the Novices, Brothers, and Sisters being put through their paces by Teachers and Priests.

The walkway bridging the entrance to the Inner Sanctum arched up over the practice field and gave me a bird's-eye view of how members of the Sunbird Church were trained. Cadres of a dozen put themselves through a host of physical-conditioning drills and weapon-skills exercises. All in all, what I saw reminded me of my grandfather's training regime, though easier.

Roarke pointed toward some of the rooms accessible from the exterior walkway. "The Church, in addition to being a training ground, has developed knowledge that is very good in helping to rehabilitate warriors who have been wounded. They also take care of old warriors and have a division of their brethren devoted to recording histories."

At the far end of the bridge a man waited for us. He smiled at Roarke and acknowledged me with a nod. "I am Valarius. I will conduct you to the Bishop." I could tell from a rank badge with seven small, equilateral triangles in a circle on it that he was a Priest. "If you will follow me."

Valarius led us back into a much more grandly appointed area of the temple. Here I saw the murals and statuary I would have expected in a temple, though these were far more martial in nature than I had seen in other places of worship. Whereas another temple might have a dozen little alcove-shrines in the corridors, each one with a statue reflecting another aspect of the god or goddess being worshiped, the Sunbird temple had these filled with tributes to heroes. Some were beautifully executed statues, while others contained suits of armor and weapons. By that standard the antechamber of my suite could have been a Sunbird shrine, but here the weapons and armor seemed more suited to contemplation than actual use.

Valarius brought us to a small, enclosed arenalike area built down into the floor. I recognized it as similar to the type of area used to judge duels or tests to determine if a student had sufficient knowledge to pass from one rank to another. I had never been in such a place before, but my grandfather had described it in exquisite detail on a number of occasions—generally using it as an illustration of where I did not want to be when I again made whatever stupid mistake he had previously corrected me for.

"Gentlemen," Valarius said as he pointed to the person on the arena floor, "this is Bishop Osane."

The Bishop to whom Valarius led us did not at all fit my idea of a holy man. That probably stemmed, initially, from his being a holy *woman* and her being relatively young. I had been expecting a man with a long beard and wrinkles deep enough to draft a ship, and instead I found a tall, powerfully built woman working her way through a series of fighting stances and parries with blinding speed. She had to be of Champion rank in skill with the hand-and-a-half sword she used.

Clad in boots, a loincloth, and a padded leather tunic, Osane swung the blade through a cut that would have bisected anything less stout than an ox, then laid the sword on a stand. She wiped her forehead on the back of her right sleeve. She had tied her light brown hair with a cloth at the back of her neck, and the light from oil lamps flickered gold highlights into it. In her eyes I detected a hint of *Chaosfire*, but barely enough to mark her a veteran of more than one campaign beyond the wall.

"Thank you, Valarius." Osane slowly walked up the steps to the level on which we stood. She watched me closely, and I felt uneasy under her steady gaze. I felt as if I were being studied by a predator.

She shifted her gaze from me to Roarke. "From what you related to Valarius, and what he has passed on to me, this expedition you are planning into Chaos is purest folly. A dozen individuals are to convince Lord Fialchar to hand over the Staff of Emeterio? I know there must be more to it than that, but I cannot imagine how the truth could be any better than the fiction."

"True enough, Holiness." Roarke glanced at me. "I told Lachlan that the Church of the Sunbird would have no interest in this and would not participate. Still, he's an optimistic youth . . ."

My eyes grew wide with surprise, betraying Roarke's deception. Somehow I got the feeling he had not fooled the Bishop, who had expected me to be taken by surprise. I shook my head, and she smiled openly.

"Oh, I know of you, Roarke, and I know this is all your doing." Osane narrowed her silver eyes. "I know enough of you to know that anything that would have you going back into Chaos must be something special. This forced me to evaluate the unknown and decide if it would be in our best interest to aid you."

I kept a smile from my face as the Bishop made her comment. The Church of the Sunbird had pushed the Ward Walls out to reclaim Tarris from Chaos nearly a century back, despite an Imperial prohibition against such action. That released many Chaos creatures into the Empire, and the Church of the Sunbird had been doing its best to make amends since that time. If she felt the Church's participation in our mission would help rebuild the Church's reputation, she would give us help.

Our mission, if we succeeded, would certainly go a long way toward redeeming the Church's reputation. It certainly would not hurt the career of the Church member who went along with us. The Church of the Sunbird considered fighting against Chaos a sacred duty, and a mission like this, if not divinely inspired, certainly could be seen as divinely mandated.

Osane closed her eyes for a second and mumbled a prayer. "I have discussed this matter with my superiors.

It is clear this enterprise is very important, and we should encourage its success."

Roarke nodded. "That was our reasoning behind approaching the Church to have someone to come along with us."

"I am glad you approve of our thoughts, Roarke." Her eyes opened again. "It has been decided. I will join your group."

Roarke looked stunned. "You, Holiness?"

"Is there something wrong with that?" Osane watched Roarke carefully. "Did you think we could entrust the mission to someone who has less training or ability?"

"Ah, no, just, I, ah," Roarke shrugged. "I would not have thought the Church would risk so valuable a member of the clergy on so chancy an expedition."

She smiled easily, clearly pleased she had confounded Roarke. "Suffice it to say, Roarke, I am more at home in Chaos than I am here. My restlessness disturbs some of my superiors. By mutual consent we have decided I would represent the Church in this matter."

"I see." Roarke offered her his arm, and she grasped it firmly. "We are pleased to have you with us, Bishop Osane. Locke, give her the medallion."

I handed it to her, and she hefted it in her right hand. "I will see to it the Emperor gets more than he pays for."

Outside the temple, I stopped Roarke. "What did she mean when she said she was more at home in Chaos than she was here?"

The Chaos Rider shrugged. "Many of us who have been out of the womb feel ill at ease here. Apparently she is one who does."

"But she has next to no *Chaosfire* in her eyes. How often could she have been there?"

Roarke smiled. "Far more than I have, Locke. The

lack of *Chaosfire* has more to do with protection from her deity than it does any lack of experience in Chaos. Aside from Nagrendra, she probably has more time in Chaos than anyone in our company."

"But if the Sunbird can prevent her from being warped by Chaos, I mean if he has that much power over Chaos, why doesn't he sweep it away?"

"Locke, have you ever captured a fly and tossed it into a spider's web?"

I nodded. "Sure."

"Why?"

"I wanted to see what would happen." I folded my arms across my chest and looked down, embarrassed by the cruelty of that sort of thing. "It was something to do—I was a child."

"Locke"—the one-eyed man patted me on top of the head—"the gods get bored, too, and who's to say they're all that grown-up anyway?"

18

Roarke and I parted company as he headed to the Umbra and I started back toward the palace. The addition of Bishop Osane to our group buoyed my feelings about the mission. I knew our chances for survival were still slim, and chances for success even more slender, but now I felt they were sufficient that magickal augmentation wasn't necessary to see them.

The fact that I wasn't more terrified about the trip surprised me. I knew that my ignorance of the realities of Chaos was insulating me from fear. Likewise, the sheer urgency of the mission and the need for its success made acknowledging fear counterproductive. I couldn't afford to be afraid, so I wasn't. As much as that state of affairs seemed to work well at the moment, I wasn't looking forward to dealing with what the future would bring.

Focusing on all I had to deal with in studying the

Chaos model, I came around a corner and slammed full on into a woman, knocking her down. I immediately bent down to help her back up and found I knew her. "Xoayya, this is a surprise."

She let me pull her to her feet. "It was at that."

I smiled. "You mean you didn't see us meeting here?"

"Oh, I did, but I did not see far enough to see our collision." She let the green velvet cloak close around her, then lifted the fur-trimmed hood up to hide her coppery hair. "I have to speak with you. I have to ask you something."

"Ask away."

She looked up at me with an intensity to her stare that almost made me recoil. "You must take me with you into Chaos."

"What?" Her demand stunned me. I couldn't even begin to guess how she could have heard of the expedition—I didn't see her as someone frequenting the Umbra, or associating with those who did. Beyond that, I couldn't see her surviving for a moment in Chaos. "Not possible, Xoayya."

"Don't say that, Locke." She reached out and clutched my right arm with both hands. "I have to go. It is my destiny."

Her grip hurt. "I can't take you with me. The party is set—all of the Imperial Medallions have been given out."

Xoayya shook her head. "I know that, Locke. I have *seen* you give them out. Roarke and Eirene will go, as well as Nagrendra and Tyrchon and this Sunbird Bishop. The medallion you gave them only entitles them to draw provisions and equipment from Imperial stores. I will pay for my own passage."

"This will be a combat mission, Xoayya, not a garden

tour." I tore my arm from her grasp to show her how weak she really was. "We will be fighting for our lives."

"I know."

"Then you know you have no place there with us."

Her blue eyes slitted. "What I *know*, Locke, is that you will have need of me. No, I cannot fight like a soldier, but I am *not* without other uses. I know some healing magicks, and if you are fighting, I think you will find those skills useful."

I shook my head. "The trade-off comes from the need to protect you from attack. You can't go with us."

She glanced down, and the tone of her voice shifted from demanding to a plea. "But I *must* go. It is my destiny."

I raised an eyebrow. "You have *seen* yourself with us?"

She hesitated, and I sensed a battle within her as to whether to lie to me or not. "No, I have not seen it, but it has been seen. Visions about myself, about important things, are always slow in coming, or woven in analogy so I cannot figure them out clearly."

"But you knew we would meet here."

She shook her head. "No, I knew you would be passing through the area around the palace, and this is the most direct route from the Temple of the Sunbird."

"So you don't know that going to Chaos or meeting me here is really part of your destiny, do you?"

"It is, Locke, it truly is."

"You say that, but you're not convincing me of it."

She again grabbed my arm, but more gently this time. "I *can* prove it to you."

"How?"

"Come with me to my grandmother's house." Xoayya's face brightened as confidence filled her voice. "She first recognized my talent and has been my mentor. She is the one who has seen me in Chaos, along with you and Kit. She will convince you that I must go with you."

I wanted to say no and continue to reject her request. In her mind, because she believed in the immutable veracity of visions, the fact that she had been seen in Chaos meant she had to be allowed to go along. I had no such belief in visions, so for me what she and her grandmother had seen could have been nothing more than dreams born of rumors. The fact that she knew about Bishop Osane long enough before I did to be waiting for me did add weight to the truth of at least some of her visions, but that weight was truly underwhelming.

What tipped my decision in favor of meeting her grandmother was my hope that I could reason with the old woman and use her influence to keep Xoayya in the Empire. It didn't take any talent to see that our expedition would be hard on Xoayya and could very easily kill her. While I did feel responsible for everyone going on the expedition, and didn't want to see any of them injured or killed, the fact was that they had all made informed decisions about their travel into Chaos. Xoayya was basing hers on visions that could have been the product of indigestion, which is not a good reason to go out and put your life in jeopardy.

I nodded. "Lead on."

Xoayya took my hand in hers and conducted me through Herakopolis. We left the Palace hill district and traveled away from where my grandmother lived. We skirted the open market, cutting around to the north to remain in the more affluent areas of the city. Once in Eastern hill district, we climbed up a steep street to a narrow home crowded between others of a similar design. They probably had as much square footage as my grandmother's house, but they got it out of adding additional stories.

Xoayya let me in through the cast-iron gate, then around to a set of steps leading down to a basement. The steps cut beneath the wide stairs leading to the building's main entrance. In most houses she would have been bringing me to the servants quarters, but what little I knew of her grandmother left me no doubt she owned the entire building.

As Xoayya led me into the dim, musty basement I was struck by the similarity to the suite of rooms I used at my grandmother's house. At first glance the resemblance was difficult to see, but I went more by feel than any objective evidence. In some ways the basement was the antithesis of my father's room. It was cluttered and unorganized, dark and smelling of mildew and dust. Like my father's rooms, I doubted this place had changed much in the past two decades, though time had managed to decay every-thing in it.

What struck me as similar to my father's rooms was the vast collection of artifacts and specimens that could have come from no place other than Chaos. The snarling faces of Chapanthers—some with full racks of stag antlers—haunted darker corners of the rooms, while their pelts carpeted the floor. More than one Chaos creature had been stuffed and mounted as if in mid-attack. The displays were impressive enough to provide a foundation for the fear I had earlier ignored.

They also strengthened my resolve that Xoayya should not be allowed to travel with us to Chaos. A rearing skunk-bear held its white paws wide, ready to crush and rend Xoayya, while a flare-hawk in mid-stoop flashed talons toward her. The innocent dropping of her hood and unfastening of her cloak while at the center of this disastrous tableau reinforced her unsuitability for our expedition.

Moving further into the room, past a sable lion that looked enough like a Bharashadi to scare me, I saw Xoayya's grandmother seated at a table. She wore a robe of white and had gathered her white hair into a tight coil at the back of her head. That added to the severe aspect of her visage—an effect heightened since all the light on her face came from the melon-sized crystal ball resting in the center of the table.

I vaguely recalled having met her at my grandmother's home. I bowed in her direction. "Greetings, Madam Jasra."

"And to you, Lachlan." She beckoned me forward. "I know why you have come."

"Good." I could not suppress a smile. "Perhaps you know how our discussion will end as well."

"Oh, I think I do indeed, and that ending begins with you draining the mocking tone from your voice."

That stung. "I apologize. I did not intend to mock you."

The old woman smiled ever so slightly. "If you choose to believe that, so be it." She looked over at Xoayya. "Though our discussions will concern you, you are not to be part of them. Go prepare our guest some tea and biscuits. I will let you know when it is time to serve them."

"Yes, Grandmother." Xoayya bowed her head and wandered off toward a doorway I assumed led to stairs.

Jasra turned her attention back to me. "Before we begin, I wish to thank you for suggesting to Xoayya that she could use music to discipline her thoughts. You have done what I and others could not do. What you have done will be of great benefit to her and to you."

I nodded and sat across from her. "I am glad I was

able to help her. She is very special, and seeing her in pain is not something I want."

"Which is why you do not want her to accompany you into Chaos."

"No good will come of her joining us."

Jasra stared at me intently, her chaos-filled eyes dark and narrowed. "You are correct: no good will come from her travel into Chaos with you, but that does not obviate the need for her to go."

My jaw dropped. "You agree that she will come to harm there, and you still want her to go? What kind of grandmother are you?"

"One who will not stand in the way of destiny." Her chin came up. "The same sort of grandmother as Evadne is, since she will gainsay neither of her grandsons their expedition into Chaos."

"No, no, there is a world of difference between Kit and I going and Xoayya joining us. Kit and I are trained in combat, which will help guarantee our ability to deal with Chaos. Physically we're stronger, too. This journey will be hard even before we reach Chaos. I traveled with Xoayya from the City of Sorcerers to Herakopolis, and she's not ready for this sort of journey."

With her elbows resting on the table, Jasra brought her hands together, fingertip to fingertip. This cast lines of shadow across her face, deepening the darkness around her eyes. "I know, she knows, this will be an arduous journey, full of privation and danger. She also knows, as do I, that she must make this journey."

"Not with me."

"Ah, but she does, Locke." Jasra tapped the crystal ball with her forefingers. "I have seen it; therefore, I already know she will be there. I know you will acquiesce."

I pressed my hands flat against the table. "No. I

don't believe that just because you have seen something it necessarily must be true. I believe we each
make decisions that affect our futures. If that is not
true, if life is all a set piece just unscrolling itself
through time, then there is no purpose to life."

"Perhaps life is just a grand entertainment for the
gods."

"If it is, then the gods would be bored by it." I
recalled Roarke's earlier remark about the gods and
built on it. "I don't believe they would find a story they
knew the ending of very entertaining."

"Ah, so a ballad heard for the second or third time
has no value to you?"

"That's not an argument that is on point here.
Listening to the same ballad over and over again
allows one a sense of familiarity and to recall memories of other times that ballad was heard." I tapped the
table with a finger. "Moreover, your suggestion that all
events are governed by destiny means the gods would
be locked into their actions as well. If they are not, then
they could do things to reshape the destiny of others.
And if the gods can do that, it is impossible to say
others cannot do the same."

"An interesting argument. One I have heard before,
of course, but interesting nonetheless." She held her
left hand out to me. "Give me your hand."

I started to, then hesitated. "Why?"

"I thought I would tell you something of your own
destiny."

I withdrew my hand. "No thanks."

She arched an eyebrow at me. "You are about to
mount a dangerous expedition into Chaos, and you'd
not like a hint of what will happen to you?"

"To what purpose? If you see disaster, and your pre-
destination argument is true, then I can do nothing but

ride into it despite your warning." I shook my head. "If, on the other hand, I can do something to change the future, and I do change it, your foretelling will be invalid. This means that I can never trust your vision, so knowing what you think will happen and my search to find correspondences between it and what I see in Chaos will distract me. Distractions I don't need."

Jasra slowly nodded. "Let us follow your reasoning to its logical conclusion, then. If your argument is true, there should be multiple futures for each one of us out there. The future we end up living through is determined by a myriad of choices, some major and some minor. Visions I have, visions Xoayya has, would be picking and choosing from among those futures. Depending upon what you do, our visions will be proved true or false."

"Exactly."

"And you would concede, I suspect, many of those futures only differ in minor details. The difference between your wearing a red shirt and a blue shirt, for example, would be minor within the scope of your whole expedition."

I sensed a trap there, but the logic of her comment was fairly clear. "You are suggesting that events and futures may vary, but tend to be channeled in general directions, along specific courses?"

"And those courses are selected by major or significant decisions, yes." Jasra again steepled her fingers. "You would concede this point?"

"If you concede that there are multiple futures, certainly."

"And I, as a seer, should be able to see scenes from those multiple futures."

I nodded slowly. "And Xoayya's accompanying me into Chaos is just one of a multitude of futures for her."

The intensity of Jasra's expression softened some-what—not with joy at having gotten her point across, but by a wave of regret or pain that washed away some of her expression's power. "This is what concerns me, Lachlan, and something I have not told Xoayya. Though your argument is interesting—and despite my not find-ing it compelling—it is something to which I cling at times like this. I would love to believe there are multi-ple futures for all of us, and I would even admit, at times, I have caught glimpses of alternate futures for people. They are dim and distant, as if their probability or lack thereof determines the strength of vision they project."

She glanced down at her hands, then folded them together and pressed them over her heart. "For Xoayya I see only one future. I see her in Chaos, and I know she is seeking you out. Aside from that, there is *nothing*."

Her voice broke on the last word. "Nothing?" I felt a chill run through me. "You're telling me that Xoayya has no other future than to go into Chaos? If she doesn't go, she will die?"

"How would you interpret a lack of any other future?"

I glanced down at the crystal ball and sought inspi-ration in its depths. Somehow it had been possible for me to accept the fact that the expedition might result in the deaths of myself and my companions. There seemed a justice there in that we were risking much, but the reward was great, and we would be the masters of our own fate. What we did on the expedition would shape our future. That sense of control suggested that we could win, and that suggestion was enough to make the problem manageable.

With Xoayya the situation was worse because her death would be passive. By making a decision to exclude her I would be killing her. She had no way to influence what was going to happen, no way to fight against her fate, since the decision was out of her hands. By leaving her behind I would kill her.

I realized that her grandmother had managed to make her case using her view of destiny and mine of free will. It was not hard to believe that a decision could put someone in a position where they died—that was the entire argument for free will since the chance of getting out of that same situation was present as well. Unless I wanted to reject out of hand *any* veracity to Clairvoyance—and doing so would have been stupid since that was one of the major concentrations of mag- ickal study in the Empire—I had to believe Xoayya would die if she did not come along with us.

I looked up and met Jasra's steady stare. "What do you see if I agree to let her go with us?"

"A blizzard of images of which I can make no sense." The old woman rested her folded hands on the table. "If you are right, there are legions of futures for her await- ing decisions she will make. If I am right, then someone wiser and more powerful than I must interpret what I have seen. I just take heart in the fact that she will live."

"That *is* something."

Jasra reached out and grabbed my right wrist. "Understand this, Lachlan, her destiny is entwined with yours. I've not seen you as lovers, and usually as friends, but your lives were not brought together by accident."

I gently twisted my arm free of her hand. "I will do all I can to look after her in Chaos. You know that."

She again reached for my hand, but held herself back. "I would tell you much about yourself—not for you, but so you could safeguard my Xoayya. I will not, however, out of respect for your wishes."

"Thank you. I have enough to worry about that I

don't need to know futures that might not come to pass."

She smiled. "Thirty years ago your father made the same comment to me when I offered to look into his future for him. It is good to know the son has the same strengths as the father. In this business I would rather trust in your strength than that of visions."

19

Over the next four days I spent an appreciable amount of time at the palace studying the reconstruction of Chaos. I pored over reports and charts and journals, constantly checking what they said against other accounts and the model in the larger room. I worked very hard and even spent one night sleeping there as opposed to going all the way back to my grandmother's house on a particularly snowy evening.

In working that hard on the geography of Chaos I half expected to see my eyes filled with *Chaosfire*. I got so I knew the hills and valleys better than I knew my grandfather's farm and Stone Rapids. I found myself dreaming about grand expeditions into the land beyond the Ward Walls, and, when I wakened, I found my dreams described the terrain and conditions perfectly. In less than a week I felt I had learned enough about Chaos that, if forced to, I could navigate through it without maps and stand a good chance of coming home again.

The Emperor joined us when the affairs of state did not call for him actually to run the nation. Our discussions varied greatly, though all remained centered on the expedition to destroy the Necroleum. Once we had made our choices of people to join the mission, Thetys reviewed and approved the rosters.

"I think you and Kit have chosen wisely, though I am intrigued by your inclusion of this Xoayya in the group, Locke."

"I know she doesn't seem much of a likely choice, Highness, but there are a variety of reasons why I think she should come along. First and foremost she is clairvoyant, which means she can warn us of potential dangers. While I have no doubt Kit's scouts and Tyrchon can and will spot trouble, Xoayya gives us an added edge in that area."

The Emperor gave me a wry smile. "I am glad you have more trust in your visionary than I do in mine. None that I know of *saw* Lord Disaster's appearance at my ball."

"I agree, Highness, that their predictions must be used carefully, but Xoayya also has some magickal training in the area of Healing. This will clearly be a mission where there will be no lack of need for such skills." I glanced down. "I have other reasons for wanting her along. Please don't ask me to explain. . . ."

Thetys frowned. "You're not lovers, are you?"

"You think I would be taking someone I care for into Chaos?"

"No, no I don't think that, Locke, but I had to ask." He looked from me to Kit and back again. "This is not going to be an easy mission, so the thought of seeing to your own comfort has to have occurred to you both. I have heard many tales of grand expeditions into Chaos where nobles have brought mistresses and musicians, cooks and tailors with them so life might continue in some semblance of normality for them."

Kit shook his head. "Those stories get a lot of play in the more distant Imperial outposts, Highness, though I'm not certain how true they are. Regardless, Locke has reasons for wanting Xoayya along. She wants to go, which is the important point, and having an extra person along can't hurt."

The Emperor frowned. "Meaning?"

Kit stiffened. "Meaning no disrespect, Highness, but it would come as no surprise to me if it was known you gave out medallions so a dozen people could be outfitted for an expedition. Having another person along who is not accounted for in those reports is a good thing. It gives us an advantage over our enemies, and for that I am very grateful."

I nodded silent thanks to Kit. When I'd told him that Xoayya was coming along with us, he was dead set against her inclusion in the group. He pressed me hard for an explanation, and I gave him all the logical reasons I could think of. They didn't satisfy him, so I finally confided that if she didn't come along, she would die. He said that was the best reason he'd heard and agreed to have her join us.

The Emperor caught my nod, then smiled. "There are other reasons at play here—don't bother to deny them. My father, and his father before him, never knew exactly what your fathers were planning on their trips into Chaos, but they still trusted them. This matter of trust seems to be tradition between our families, and I see no reason to break it."

⌘   ⌘   ⌘

Four days into the effort the Emperor returned to bring Kit and me news of an attempt to run the blockade of the harbor. "Several small, fast boats, going out in the teeth of a storm in the middle of the night tried to get through. We sank two and others turned back, but some may have gotten through. We have to assume the Chademon is no longer in the capital."

Kit rubbed sleep from his eyes. "Another week and we could have the site pinpointed."

I shook my head. "I do not believe we have that much time." I hesitated, then brought up something that had been bothering me. "In all the studying we have done here, on a project you say my father started thirty or forty years ago, I have yet to see one report in his hand. Why?"

Illtyd looked to the Warlord, but the Emperor answered me. "That is my doing. I assumed, perhaps hastily and incorrectly, that you might give your father's reports more weight than they otherwise warrant. Garn has been handling them, so the information has been available to you, but you have been spared the distraction of knowing your father produced it."

I heard his words and had no reason to imagine he was lying to me, but I did not trust what he said completely. "I understand what you did, but I think it may have proved counterproductive, Highness." I looked over at the Warlord. "I think my father's accounts may hold the key to locating the Necroleum."

Drustorn's opalescent stare met mine openly. "How so?"

"If my father believed the *Chronicles of Farscry* when it said he was to slay Kothvir, and if he had heard rumors of the Necroleum, it would make sense he would want to locate it. In doing that he could make sure Kothvir would remain dead." I pointed to the crystal in the middle of the room. "Show me where my father's last expedition went."

Illtyd shook his head nervously. "I cannot. We have no record of that expedition because there were no survivors."

"Then show me where my father died."

The magicker again protested. "I do not know where that was."

I held up my right hand and flicked the silver ring with my thumb. "Then show me where this was found, for surely . . ." I started to say the ring would not have been far from my father's body, but I realized it could have been stolen and passed through a dozen Chademon tribes to prove he was dead.

The Emperor nodded, and Illtyd sent the magick lens whisking over the artificial landscape. It hovered over the reconstruction of an old manor house nestled within a maze of canyons. "An expedition of Chaos Riders found it here when they slit open a creature they planned to make their dinner. They found the ring in its belly. Where the rodent got it, I do not know."

I stared at the huge quartz hexagon. "Move back to the east, yes, there, now move north, slowly." At my request, the sorcerer sent his crystal swooping down into a valley. It started through a narrow, serpentine crack in the red rock, then had to turn sideways to work its way in deeper.

"You can stop now." I looked over at Kit and felt a shiver run through my body. "This is where our fathers died."

"What?" Kit stared at me, disbelieving. "You can't know that. Their bodies were never recovered. No one survived that expedition."

"I know that, but it doesn't matter. I can feel it." I

pointed at the tiny crack in the rock. "This is where we will find the Necroleum and the Fistfire Sceptre."

The sorcerer fixed me with a curious stare. "You base this judgment on a feeling?"

I twisted the ring on my finger. "That's right. I wish I had something more solid to work on, but that's it. The Bharashadi were a menace then, a menace our fathers did all they could to eliminate. I have to assume their last and most dangerous mission would have been to destroy the Necroleum, which means this area has got to contain it."

"There is a great deal of logic to his reasoning." The Warlord folded his arms across his chest. "I can see this area as the focus for my invasion of Chaos if they do not succeed in destroying the Necroleum."

I turned from Illtyd to the Emperor. "Given that someone may have run the blockade, I think we must head into Chaos immediately. We have to reach Castel Payne and get the Staff of Emeterio before we can stop the Bharashadi. If we are lucky, in fact, the sceptre has not yet left Herakopolis. What are the chances the thief will just ship into Chaos and go overland through Chaos?"

The Warlord smiled wryly. "As much as we would like to stop the Bharashadi, the hatred borne for them by other Chaos demon tribes is pretty virulent. Travel through the territory of other Chaos demon tribes will not be easy for our thief. I would guess he will make landfall still within the Empire and travel on this side of the Ward Walls until he reaches the area where the Black Shadows' territory touches the walls. I should also note that the thief most certainly will not be traveling alone."

"He had accomplices in the vault, so I agree with that assessment." I walked over to the same wall chart the Warlord was looking at. "That means they would probably land here in Menal and go straight up the Wardline. If we head out immediately and make for the boundary between the B*harashadi* and T*svortu* lands, we could cut them off before they slip through. This will also put us near Gorecrag, from which we should be able to see where Castel Payne is floating."

Kit nodded. "It is a plan."

I smiled. "Will your people be ready to follow it by tomorrow morning?"

"All will be present and accounted for." Kit stifled a yawn. "They have all drawn their supplies for the expedition. I think I will go get mine, then attempt to catch up on my sleep." He thumped one of the gazetteers Illtyd's people had created. "I know I will review this in my sleep."

"I'll go get ready, too. We will meet tomorrow, just before noon." I clasped the Warlord's forearm. "I hope, the next time I see you, it will be to report we will not need the army you will raise to defend the Empire."

I returned to my grandmother's home in midafternoon and told James I would be leaving the next morning for Chaos. Since the night of the ball he had been anticipating this notification, but I think he had expected more time when I told him. He immediately headed off to take care of errands, telling me, "Master Lachlan, do not fear. It may been years since I prepared your father for an expedition, but I remember what must be done quite well."

Earlier in the week I had drawn what supplies I thought I would need from the Imperial Armory. For me that came down to a suit of strip-scale armor, greaves, bracers, gloves, helmet, and face mask. I knew my grandfather would have chosen armor somewhat more substantial, like ring-joined plate, but the strip-scale was light and for someone as small as I am, to sacrifice any speed was a mistake. In heavier armor I might have been able to absorb more damage, but I thought hitting was decidedly preferable to being hit.

I think it was part of James's plan to have Nob invite me to play him in a game of chess to kill the time until dinner. Nob grumbled about how he'd not have a good opponent at chess until I came back and said he was happy that Cruach would not be around to bother his bitches. He called me by my father's name twice during the game, and I could easily imagine him having similarly distracted my father before expeditions.

I very much appreciated his effort, and fully abandoned myself to it. As excited as I was about going, I could see the waiting would be excruciatingly painful if I had nothing else to do. Anticipation and dread mixed together to threaten me with moody flip-flops that would have driven me crazy.

More importantly, though, I found myself reflecting upon the unspoken covenant between citizens of the Empire and those who protect them from Chaos. The vast majority of citizens could no more imagine leaving the womb than they could imagine committing suicide. For many of them the two things were one and the same. They were content to let others shoulder the responsibility of dealing with Chaos and we were content to accept that responsibility.

In return, however, they had a duty to make our sacrifice worth it. It was up to them to see to it that the Empire was worth preserving. Their part of the bargain was to do all the things that we found ourselves willing to fight to save. If they did not, we would find Chaos on either side of the Wardlines and have no reason to fight to save the land of our birth.

I think this is the reason the Black Churchers are seen as so perverse. They believe that men found their true potential under the influence of Chaos and, as a result, hailed Chaos Riders for what they became, even though that praise blasphemed against what Chaos Riders actually did. The fact that Black Churchers might actually work to bring Chaos back over the world again made them a group to be feared—and explained why they were outlawed and killed when found.

By telling me about his dogs and playing chess with me, Nob gave me a perfect view of normal life in the Empire. That normality was what I would give up by becoming a Chaos Rider. Despite having been weaned and raised on stories of heroes, I could envy Nob, his sons, and grandsons who had unremarkable lives. They married, they had children, and they formed the foundation of the Empire.

Without them, there would be nothing for which to fight.

We ended up playing two games, Nob and I. I nearly daydreamed myself into defeat during the first one. He'd place the movestone on my side of the board, then point it out to me when I didn't do anything. He started setting it down a little less gently each time until he finally came close to upsetting the pieces with a miniature earthquake.

"You are just like your father, you are! I beat him because he didn't think to concentrate on me."

I laughed and forced myself to focus on the game. Sixteen moves later I got Nob, but that game had been much closer than most. Nob immediately demanded another game and took Chaos. He pushed his pieces through a set of motions that I supposed to be some guild defense or other. It quickly developed the center of the board, but put Nob at a disadvantage because he lived and died on Wizard forks. This strategy put Generals to great use in long diagonal pins and skewers.

I concentrated my attack Emperor-side and overwhelmed him. I picked off a General by pushing Pawns forward, then bringing my Wizards up to force some exchanges. After one bad exchange, in which I moved pieces almost impulsively, I ended up a General to the better and cracked his defense. He saw the inevitable and, as Rose called us to dinner, tipped Fialchar on his face.

I could only hope that would be an omen for our expedition.

Dinner was a curious affair. Rose had prepared a dish that included things I could not recognize and dared not ask about. I did recognize potatoes and bits of meat, but exactly which creature they came from I couldn't be entirely certain because of the spicy red gravy covering everything. I gathered the stew had been put together out of bits and pieces of things that were meant to fortify me both physically and spiritually for the ordeal of going into Chaos. From what little Grandmother said about the food, I assumed this was traditional fare for those heading off for Chaos, but had been seldom served after my father and uncle were lost.

Rose seemed mildly distressed that Kit was not there to eat the meal, but then she decided that just meant there was more for me. I thanked her, ate as much as I wanted and then some, and made a mental note to get back at Kit later. It was not that it tasted particularly bad, but it just tasted different, and the texture of some parts just didn't feel right for chewing.

Grandmother, Marija, and I were the only ones eating together, though a place had been set for Kit. Grandmother did not say much, and her palpable anxiety snuffed any conversation after only a few exchanges. I knew she was trying to be brave and to hide her fear, but she failed, and that made her sad and started us on a downward emotional spiral.

Marija wasn't much better a dinner companion that evening, either. Her clear concern for my grandmother distracted her, but something else seemed wrong as well. She apologized several times when I asked her to pass me the salt or butter, as if she felt she should have somehow anticipated my request. She also solicited my opinions on a variety of subjects, then confessed that her thoughts in the matter paralleled my own.

After dinner my grandmother asked Marija to bring her tonic to the solar as she wanted to watch the stars for a while before going to bed. I gave her time to get up there and settled, then I went up to have a talk with her. As I stood in the doorway, Marija smiled at me, then slipped past to leave the two of us alone.

Grandmother looked incredibly small and tired in her big chair. In the time I had spent in the capital I had never seen her look so frail and weak. The blanket hid her legs, and, if not for the flicker of her eyes watching the stars, I might have thought her dead. "Your father used to come here and talk with me before he went off on his adventures, you know."

"I did not." The melancholy tone in her voice threatened to crush my heart, so I gave her a brave smile. "I will be coming back. I will not die in Chaos."

"Child, do not make promises you cannot keep." I

heard betrayal in her voice, but I sensed it was addressed more to the gods than my father. "Your father told me the same thing before he left so long ago. He had always told me that, but one time he was wrong."

I looked down at the rug. "I know I am hardly suited to the task the Emperor has given me, but I will go do it, and I will come back."

Evadne raised her head and shook it wearily. "Lachlan, you will do what you have to do. If you return, and I hope for that with all my heart and soul, you will be welcomed as was your father when he came back to me."

"Then start planning the biggest celebration this city has ever seen." I backed the fire in my voice with a broad smile. "I will be back. You have my solemn word on it."

"Please, Lachlan, make me no promises. I will not have you hesitate in taking action because you have said you would come back. What you go to do, as your father did before you, is more important than breaking a vow to an old woman. Your father understood that, and I love him no less for it."

She looked at me and smiled gently. "Were you a bit chubbier you would be the very image of your father when he first went into Chaos. Audin has worked you hard—harder than he ever worked your father, I think— and has prepared you for what you will find in Chaos. Were he to see you now, Cardew would be proud of what you have become."

I pulled the ring the Emperor had given me from my finger and held it out to her. "I know my father wanted to come back to you, but he could not. Here, this was his. He would want you to have it."

She refused my gift. "Your father always thought of that ring as a luck charm. I trust whatever bad luck it had has long since been used up. He offered it to me on the night before he left that last time, and I refused it. My memories of him, and my memories of you, will be enough. Go now, get some sleep. I have ever sent my warriors to Chaos well rested and alert."

At her request I left her and went to my rooms, but sleep was the furthest thing from my mind. I had decided from the beginning to take my father's rapier with me, but Roarke had pointed out that fancy dueling was not really part of the Chademon war doctrine. After questioning him I determined that most of our fighting would be done from horseback and that a good, stout blade capable of cutting and crushing would be best.

The rack of swords in my suite provided me with more than an ample supply of choices. I opted away from the curved swords because I felt uncomfortable with a blade that did not have two edges. I knew they could be superior in cavalry combat to a regular straight sword, but the second edge of a straight sword gave me another tool with which to fight.

I immediately ruled out the crossed greatswords on the wall because they were taller than I was. If I could have lifted either one of them, they would be incredible in combat, but even drawing one would be an impossibility for me. I needed a blade that I could manage; otherwise, all the potential damage it could do would just remain *potential*. That caution eliminated a number of other large swords in the room, and the lack of sufficient weight invalidated most of the dueling blades. From the remaining middle ground I selected a longsword that was four feet in length and nearly a hand-width wide at the cross hilt. I could fit both hands on the grip, yet the blade had been well enough balanced that I could use it with one hand if I so desired. I found the draw easy from my hip and decided I could even wear the sword strapped across my back if I thought it necessary.

I fastened it across my back just to test my theory, since I couldn't afford to be wrong about it in combat. In one smooth motion I drew the blade from the scabbard on my back and snapped it around into a guard position. As I did so, Marija slipped through my partially open door and the blade swung into line with her throat. She jumped back, and I lowered the blade immediately. "Forgive me, Marija."

She looked at me with wide eyes, reaching back to the wall to support herself. Color rose to her cheeks as her right hand rose to cover her throat. She blinked several times, then began breathing again.

"No, forgive me, Master Lachlan. I saw the light through the doorway and thought you must still be awake." Color slowly returned to normal in her cheeks. "Your grandmother is asleep, but she made me promise I would wake her to see you go. Are you still leaving just after dawn?"

I slipped the scabbard off and rehomed the blade. "Bright and early."

"Very good." She smiled and turned to leave.

"Wait, Marija."

"Yes."

"I, ah, wanted to thank you for taking such good care of my grandmother." I hitched for a second, then continued. "I am sorry I have to be going away after only having been here for so short a time."

Marija nodded. "Your grandmother loves you very much. She sees your father in you. She knows you will be the hero he was and only wishes a better life for you."

"I will miss her." I looked into Marija's dark eyes. "And I will miss you as well, very much."

"Please, Master Lachlan, don't say that." She blushed and looked down.

"Why not?" I leaned the sword against the table and folded my arms across my chest. "You are intelligent and witty, possessed of beauty and poise. I have enjoyed my time here the most when spent with you, and I have had damned little of that. You intrigue me, and I like you. I *will* miss you."

"You should not say that because I am not the sort of woman for you." She shook her head, but still would not meet my eyes. "You are destined for great things, and I am happy for you, but that means there are better matches for you. Your grandmother has wealth, and, upon her death, which will not be that long in coming, I fear, it will devolve to you and your brothers and your cousin. Already fathers and mothers plot how to have one of their daughters become your bride."

"But what if that is not what I want?"

"That still does not mean you want me." She smiled at me, then sighed. "There is so much about me that you do not know . . ."

I frowned. "What is there to know that I do not? I know you care for my grandmother far better than any of her blood kin. I know you are skilled as a healer." I laughed. "And even you told me that my father vowed to marry you if his wife died before he did, so I know he approves of you! What more could I want to know?"

She slowly exhaled. "Perhaps that I saw what losing my father to Chaos did to my mother. She told me again and again never to love a Chaos Rider because, someday, Chaos will kill him."

"I see." I rubbed my right hand across my chin. "Perhaps you need to ask yourself if your mother would have warned you off dray masters were your father run over by a cart?"

"That, Locke, has been something I have considered quite a bit of late." Her dark eyes sparkled. "Fare thee well, Master Lachlan. Were I going to fall in love with a Chaos Rider, I should think he would be very much like you."

20

We were a fine company, I thought. I smiled as we all joined up together twenty miles north of Herakopolis. Horses stamped their hooves and blew out steam, perhaps wondering why the lot of us had stopped beneath an open winter sky on a road cutting through vast snow plains. I saw, rather clearly, that some of our members wondered the same thing, and I could sense almost immediate tension between the Chaos Riders and the soldiers under Kit's command.

Roarke and Eirene had come for me at my grandmother's house before the sun's disc had fully cleared the horizon. Rose made them wait as she packed small loaves of bread into a sack, then started adding other things like apples and small sachets of spices that, she explained, could be used to make food on the road more edible. Roarke paid her close attention, while Eirene appeared to be very anxious to be on the road again.

Nob brought Stail out for me, and with him he had another horse. Nob and Carl loaded the packhorse down with the food Rose had provided, a satchel with my armor, another with spare clothes and a bedroll. Roarke eyed the supplies piled on Ablach, then shook his head. "What, no valet?"

I winked at him. "That's why you're here, isn't it?" I swung up into the saddle, then looked up and saw my grandmother standing at one of the windows. I waved, and she raised her hand in response.

"She wants you to be careful, Locke." I looked down as Marija, clutching a thick shawl around her shoulders, came out to see me off.

"And how about you?"

"Very careful." She reached out and touched my right leg. "I am not my mother. If you tell me you are coming back, I will believe you."

I leaned over and kissed her on the lips. "I am not my father. I will return."

Roarke, leading a packhorse more fully laden than Ablach, started out the gate. Cruach fell in trotting beside him. Eirene watched the load swaying on the packhorse's back, leading me to believe she had her baggage on it as well, and left the courtyard next. I brought up the rear and turned in the saddle to wave one last time to the people I was leaving behind. My grandmother was no longer visible in the window, but Nob, Rose, and Marija all sent me off with hearty waves.

On the way through the city we met up with Xoayya. She rode a gray gelding and led two other horses. Both of them had been laden with supplies and clothes, but neither of them was carrying a significant load, primarily because Xoayya brought with her no weapons or armor.

"Good morning, Locke." She gave me a smile that was positively radiant. "And best of the morning to you, Roarke and Eirene."

"Glad to see you so eager to be started, Mistress Xoayya." Roarke winked at Eirene. "I bet you girls will find plenty to talk about on the road."

The *Chaosfire* flared in Eirene's eyes. "Don't go making this a long trip, Roarke."

Xoayya shrugged her shoulders. "I'm sure we'll get along fine, especially after Eirene tightens that cinch strap when we reach our rendezvous with the others."

Eirene shifted uneasily in the saddle, and Roarke laughed aloud. "It's not me who will make this a long trip for you, Eirene."

"It's not going to get any shorter if we just sit here," I growled. "The others will be waiting."

We left the city through Northgate. The guards there gave us a fairly thorough searching, but passed us on our way when they found nothing out of the ordinary. From there we headed north on the road, and within three miles Osane caught up with us. Not long after that Tyrchon and Nagrendra likewise joined us and made my half of the company complete.

Osane rode a white charger that was the largest horse I had ever seen before Nagrendra rode up. The Sunbird Bishop wore glittering mail that had been washed in gold, and over that a surcoat of white with a golden sunburst over her heart. Along her left sleeve she wore the rank badges for the weapons she knew how to use, and in them I saw she was more than capable of holding her own with just about any weapon I could think of. Her hand-and-a-half sword hung from a saddle-scabbard at her horse's left shoulder while a bow and saddle quiver sat opposite it.

Nagrendra's huge brown draft horse had white stockings of long fur on each leg. Broad of chest and very tall, it galloped along with enough spirit that I knew anyone smaller than the Reptiad would have a hard time controlling it. The horse wore an armored head-plate with a long, twisting horn on the forehead, and I had no doubt that beast was just waiting for a chance to use it.

Nagrendra, clad in a thick woolen cloak of forest green, barely looked as if he belonged with our company. He had no weapons hanging from his saddle and apparently wore no armor. I would have thought him foolish except I knew he was a sorcerer, and that meant he was not at all defenseless.

Tyrchon's appearance was even more unnerving in the daylight than it was in the Umbra. I had no doubt that above his upper lip his head had fully melded with the wolf-skull he wore. The nostrils on the head quivered when he scented something, and one glance at Cruach likewise sniffing the air told me that was what Tyrchon was doing. The ears pricked up when he heard something, and the flesh around the wolf's-head eyes tightened when he squinted.

He wore a coat of mail over a leather jerkin along with bracers, greaves, and mailed gloves. A large sword hung from his saddle, but while riding he bore a long spear with a razor-edged, leaf-shaped head and a short crosspiece. I also noticed a number of daggers hidden at various places on his body, like the tops of his boots and his upper arms.

He rode a dark brown gelding and had another lighter-colored horse on a lead behind him. That horse carried two distinct sets of satchels, leading me to believe that like Eirene and Roarke, Tyrchon and Nagrendra both used it to carry their gear. Both of the horses had *Chaosfire* in their eyes, as did all the rest being ridden by our group, save my two horses, those belonging to Xoayya, and the creature Nagrendra rode.

Roarke commented on this when the Reptiad fell in beside him. "I thought you had another mount you used for expeditions."

The mage nodded. "Seilide. On my last expedition into Chaos she answered the call of the Emerald Horse. I lost her to him and was very sorry to see her go. It was a *long* walk back to a border camp. This is Nathair. I trust he will be able to resist the call."

"The call?" I asked.

"You must have heard of the Emerald Horse, Locke. He is a legendary stallion in Chaos," Roarke explained. "I've ne'er seen him, but he leads a great herd of horses abandoned by Chaos Riders in Chaos. There are times he 'summons' other horses to join his herd. The more a horse has been changed by Chaos, the greater is its likelihood of answering the call, or so it seems. Most of our horses are fairly normal, so that should not cause problems, but he's been a terror to many expeditions in the last decade or so. I heard of an expedition sent out to kill him, but it failed when most of their mounts joined him."

Xoayya ran fingers back through her red hair. "I know Chaos is horrible and dangerous, but there are aspects to it that are very romantic and thrilling. I should like to see the Emerald Horse."

Eirene scowled at Xoayya's comment and patted the snake-scaled neck of her mount. "The Emerald Horse is one of those dangerous things in Chaos, Xoayya. I've never heard of him appearing at a time other than one that's very dangerous for Chaos Riders. If he's a romantic figure, it's only from the Chaos demon point of view."

Xoayya frowned. "So cynical."

"No, still alive." Eirene showed her a flash of fangs. "The second you think something in Chaos can't or won't kill you, you'll be wrong and pay the consequences for being wrong."

We had deliberately planned to leave the capital in small groups and meet on the road to lessen suspicion on the part of anyone watching on behalf of the Black Church. Roarke thought my caution unnecessary, as the patrols roaming around the city were bound to occupy the time of most spies. I think the other Chaos Riders, as well as Osane, found my precautions a bit much, but they appreciated my having thought ahead about a way to decrease the trouble in which we might find ourselves.

Kit had brought his patrol out of the capital very early in the morning, well before dawn, so they were waiting for us. They looked very much like the other soldiers I had seen in the capital except that they wore the lighter strip-scale armor like that I had chosen. The five warriors all had swords in a saddle-scabbard and carried a bow and quiver as well. The golden-haired Aelf carried a baton that could easily have served as a club in combat, but I assumed she used it for casting spells.

They had their gear on six packhorses and had brought with them a whole string of remounts for us to use. The soldiers, most of whom were Kit's age or younger, seemed rather impatient with us and clearly did not like the looks of my group. On the other hand my people seemed unimpressed with the soldiers. Only one of them, a grizzled sergeant, had any hint of *Chaosfire* in his eyes, and the rest just looked like youths who had joined the Imperial Army because they thought the cut of the uniforms stylish.

Kit and I exchanged amused glances. I knew the people he had chosen were those he trusted, and I could say the same of my people. He and I had discussed the possibility of rivalry between our two groups and had resolved to ease the tension as quickly as possible. Before we could do anything, though, Roarke spurred his horse forward and offered Kit his arm.

"Lieutenant, I'm Roarke. Looks like you outrank anyone else here, so I'll defer to you. If you find yourself wanting some advice here or on the other side, any of us will be glad to help you out."

Kit took his arm firmly, then turned to introduce his people. The Aelven sorceress was Taci, and I remembered hearing of her from Kit's story my first night in Herakopolis. Aleix was the sergeant, Hansen and Urien the two remaining men, and Donla the lone female warrior in the bunch.

Aleix took a head count and frowned. "I make us as having thirteen in our company. I'm not certain I like that."

Roarke gave the man a solid nod. "All part of the plan, sergeant, but good that you noticed."

The soldier's brow creased with puzzlement. "I don't know that I understand."

The one-eyed man smiled easily. "If you were a Black Churcher, would you think anyone would mount an expedition to Chaos with thirteen in the company?"

"No."

"Then they won't be seeing us as much of a threat, will they?"

Hansen raised an objection. "That's all well and good, but we still have thirteen in our group. That's an ill omen."

I smiled. "Agreed, but you didn't count Cruach."

"The dog?"

Kit nodded solemnly. "Cruach's seen more trips to Chaos than any one of us. He's part of the group, and you know what they say. Had there been a fourteenth at the Shattering, Fialchar would have been stopped. Since we've got to deal with him and Chaos demons, having fourteen of us here is the way to go."

Hansen frowned. "What about her, the girl? She's not fit for this trip."

Before Xoayya could say anything in her own defense, Eirene swung back up into the saddle. "She's our trouble spotter. She tells you to check a cinch strap, you do it. She'll earn her keep with us, to be sure."

I looked around at the group. "Any other problems?"

Kit looked at his people, then shook his head. "I think we'll be fine from this point forward." He jerked a thumb toward the north. "We'll find all the trouble we need when we reach journey's end."

Everyone laughed politely in acknowledgment of his comment, then we set off. The two groups slowly merged. Roarke's acknowledgment of Kit as the group's leader eventually made Kit's people feel at ease. The Chaos Riders remained indifferent or amused with the soldiers, but gradually introduced themselves and did not make trouble.

The journey north to Chaos measured out to just under nine hundred miles on the map. Even given the remounts, the winter and lack of forage for the horses meant, at best, we could reach our destination in a month. Had we pushed the horses to the ragged edge, we could have done it much faster, but that was not practical because once we reached Chaos we had to travel further. Moreover, the conditions in Chaos were less likely to be hospitable than they were here, even in winter.

We headed almost directly north from Herakopolis for the first third of the journey. It took us a total of ten days, and we arrived at the Imperial Fortress in the foothills of the Bloody Dog Mountains with everyone in very good shape. At the outpost we replenished our supplies and checked for any messages that might have been sent from the capital for us by magickal means.

While getting information from and sending it to the capital was very important, we did not try to communicate with Herakopolis while we were in the field. Taci or Nagrendra could have managed it easily, but the use of magick could allow our enemies to detect us and pinpoint our location. It was better that messages into and out of the capital just appear as part of the normal traffic in messages going to and from outposts.

There was nothing from Herakopolis for us when we arrived, but by the next morning one small message had come in. It contained a report that indicated the ship that had run the blockade of the harbor had been found at a point on the Tarris coast, which put it roughly due east of us. The ship had been damaged, but there was no indication of the B*harashadi* or Fistfire Sceptre having been on it. On the other hand, there was no evidence to the contrary, either. If the Chademon was starting from that point, given the run of the coastline and the Bloody Dog Mountains barring his path, he would give up his head start in reaching his home.

We spent two full days at the fort resting up, then started off through Menal. While a straight shot to Chaos would have been the shortest route, we would have killed the horses by choosing that route. There was no way we could carry enough grain to feed them and, while the Menal plains made for excellent traveling terrain, open water was not that plentiful. Our course of travel was dictated by available resources, which meant we spent time stopping in various towns or at outposts along the way.

In many ways I did not mind stopping in villages for the night. Stabling the horses saved on our supplies, and a roaring fire in a tavern can do a body a world of good when traveling in the winter. Many folks shunned the Chaos Riders, but as we got closer to the border with Chaos, most folks accepted them, and some even sought them out.

During the day, when on the march, Eirene tended to take the lead and ranged well ahead of the rest of us. Among the other changes Chaos had made in her horse, it had incredible endurance. It seemed, as long as we kept it fed and watered, it would have been willing to carry her to the horizon and back without complaint.

Tyrchon spent much of his time working our backtrail, or positioning himself as an outrider to check what might be on the other side of a line of hills we were paralleling. The few nights we did camp in the open, he tended to shy away from the rest of us. Wolf packs that might have stalked us during the day disappeared at night, and I felt pretty certain that the howling we heard closest to us had come from our lupine companion.

Cruach tolerated the trip very well and, aside from occasionally growling at Tyrchon, seemed to like everyone in the group. He hunted for himself and managed to bag a fairly wide variety of animals, from hares to quail to rodents of all sizes. Best of all, for me, Cruach liked to sleep beside me, which meant my nights were warmer than those of my compatriots.

Despite the obvious hardships, Xoayya seemed to flourish on the trip. She split her time traveling with Eirene and Nagrendra. I don't know what she and Eirene talked about, but I sensed that Eirene set limits for her and made her operate within a code of conduct, or Eirene would just ride away. The Chaos Rider imposed a discipline on Xoayya that was reinforced by isolation if she did not comply.

The Reptiad discussed magick with Xoayya. Their conversations quickly carried them into theoretical areas of the art that were completely beyond my understanding. Nagrendra seemed to be able to provide Xoayya with simple, direct, and relevant examples to back up the discussions, creating a link between theory and practice. I don't know if he taught her some actual spells, but with every day we got closer to Chaos I hoped he had and that they were of the combat variety.

In Menal, about 250 miles from the border of Chaos, we made one last stop in the town of Imperial Plains. It had grown up around an Imperial Outpost and served to repopulate a city that had fallen into disrepair during its time in Chaos. As it had taken us twelve days to ride there from the Bloody Dog Mountains, we decided to remain for two days and trade for a few new horses.

Imperial Plains was home to the Emperor's Horse Guards, so Kit and his people reacquainted themselves with their old command. The Chaos Riders and I headed into the portion of the city roughly equivalent to Asylum, and Bishop Osane made her way to the Sunbird temple near the center of town. We found no tavern quite like the Umbra, but we did find a number of places willing to put us up for a reasonable amount of money.

From what little Kit had said of Imperial Plains while we were traveling toward it, I had thought the town would be a bit more sleepy than it was. A large number of men and women, Chaos Riders and not, had come to Imperial Plains, and I saw more and more of them arriving throughout our stay. Some looked to be refugees bringing children and everything they owned in overloaded wagons while others looked like mercenaries fishing for work.

When I saw Kit again in his barracks, he confirmed my suspicions about what was going on. "While we have been on the road, Garn Drustorn has started to raise an army. Colonel Grimands sent riders to all the villages in this district of Menal recruiting men and women for the expedition into Chaos. As generally happens when there is a call-up, some people panic and leave their homesteads for the safety of a larger town. They seem to forget the forces of Chaos cannot penetrate the Ward Walls."

"Until now."

Kit winced. "You may be right, but we have to remember that we have no solid proof the *Bharashadi* you saw came from Chaos. They could have been a clan living in the Bloody Dog Mountains or in the Menal forests for all we know. All we do know is that a *Bharashadi* has stolen the Fistfire Sceptre and is likely to be bringing it to Chaos. On top of that there is no evidence to suggest he has the power to cross the Wardlines."

"Granted what you say is true, Kit, do you want to bet that is not the case?"

He hesitated, and in that I sensed a resignation about what was really going on, but a terrible desire to deny it at the same time. If I was right and we failed, Imperial Plains would be wiped out. All of his friends and their families would die.

"Whether or not I'm willing to bet on which one of us

is right is really immaterial. In the absence of absolute proof, to assume the Chaos demons can breach the Ward Walls and spread that word would be criminal. It would cause a panic the like of which has never been seen since the Seal of Reality was shattered." He shook his head wearily. "People would flock to Imperial Plains for safety, food supplies would dwindle, and prices would skyrocket. Even *if* the Ward Walls were in jeopardy and were to fall, these people would be better off in their own homes."

There was no denying he was right. It was a point we had seen back in Herakopolis, yet here on the frontier the danger seemed much more immediate. "Your observation is especially true considering the fact that any large B*harashadi* army is likely to come and destroy Imperial Plains."

"I know, and I wish I didn't." Kit stood as someone knocked on his door. "Come."

Hansen opened the door and tugged off his woolen cap. "Tyrchon wants to see you, sir; your cousin, too."

"Is he here? Show him in." Kit swung a chair around from beside the door to the middle of the floor. "Tyrchon, welcome."

The Chaos Rider nodded, then waited for Hansen to shut the door. He rested his hands on the back of the chair, but did not sit. "I don't really like cities, so I've been doing some scouting around-abouts." His eyes narrowed, and he smiled. "I have some allies here and there, and I have heard of an attack on a wolf pack. I think it is the same one you talked about that first night out of Trickle Creek."

Kit nodded slowly. "All right."

"Well, whatever did that had a peculiar scent. Out away from here I cut a trail of fifteen horses with riders. They had two remounts each and went by about six hours ago now. They swung very wide of Imperial Plains—and avoided all contact with parties heading into the town. I would have missed them 'cept I had been directed toward them by my allies."

I felt a chill running down my spine. "And?"

"And the one they call 'Packkiller' is in that group."

I stared at him for a moment, processing what I'd heard. I looked over at Kit. "Do you realize what that means?"

My cousin nodded solemnly. "Without a doubt. The people we've been racing to catch left the capital after we did, and have been killing their horses to get home again."

21

Inside an hour we had all our people gathered up and out on the road heading north. Colonel Grimands agreed to lend us a fourth string of horses and sent three of his riders out with us. In an effort to catch the people Tyrchon had tracked, we rode these new horses hard for two hours, then turned them over to the riders from Imperial Plains, took to our own mounts, and set off again.

Four hours out, riding more conservatively, we stopped and huddled around as Tyrchon knelt in the snow to examine the tracks. With a finger he traced the edge of a track. "See, it's melted by the sun. I would say it was made five hours ago, which means we have gained little or nothing on them. Their strides are longer. If anything, they are getting faster."

I frowned. "But you said, pointing to earlier tracks, that the horses are nearly dead from exhaustion. How can it be? We've been on this track for four hours, and we have not seen them change mounts."

Nagrendra sat on his haunches and stared at the tracks. He passed a three-fingered hand over his eyes and I saw a blue-white flash from his palm reflected on his green skin. "Magick. They have used a spell to speed their horses."

"Magick?"

Nagrendra pressed his right hand over my eyes, and the flash from his palm momentarily blinded me. As my eyes cleared I saw a red-gold haze slowly evaporating along the line of tracks. It was as if those horsemen had ridden down a dry road and left a trail of dust hanging in the air.

"I see. Magick. Can we use a spell to catch them?"

Nagrendra's "Yes," collided with an emphatic "No!" from Taci.

I looked at the Reptiad. "Why 'Yes'?"

The large lizard-man shrugged. "The spell is not a terribly difficult one, and one oft used in Chaos to whisk Riders out of trouble. It could help us catch them."

I turned to the Aelf. "Why 'No'?"

Taci's face hardened. "That spell is fine for emergencies, but not for endurance situations. Tyrchon, aside from the lengthened stride, do you see any indication the horses are in good shape, or are they still tired?"

Tyrchon grinned up at her. "Tired. I think their riders are none too sharp, either."

The sorceress nodded. "The spell is speeding them up in part by making their passage easier. It is also demanding a great deal from them—the horses can travel faster, but they are still using their muscles to run. When the spell wears off, the horses will be much worse than if they had galloped that distance without magick."

Nagrendra shook his head. "If they maintain this pace, they could outdistance us rather easily."

"But they can't maintain this pace, Nagrendra, that is my point." Taci shook her head. "We have over two hundred miles to the Ward Walls, and if this is truly their line of march, we will be able to beat them to the goal. They will have to ride around to avoid two inhabited valleys while we can ride straight through them."

"And if they go into those valleys, steal new mounts, and push on?" Hansen nodded toward Nagrendra. "I don't really want to disagree with you, Taci, but this is a race we don't want to lose."

I held up my hands. "Perhaps there is another solution. Tyrchon, your allies have no love for Packkiller, right?"

"None whatsoever."

"Good. Why don't you ask them to harry Packkiller and his people. Nothing dangerous enough to get them attacked, but just enough to make rest difficult. If they can herd them away from settlements so they can't get new mounts, that would be perfect."

Tyrchon grinned. "Consider it done. No rest for the wicked."

Roarke nodded heartily. "Good. That will allow us to make up in shorter distances what we lack in speed. Remember, they just have to get to the Ward Walls. We have a long and difficult journey after that. A magick push makes sense if we close with them, but not otherwise."

"That's my read as well," Kit said, swinging up into the saddle. "Let's go."

Taci's prediction concerning the riders proved grimly accurate. As we were looking for a suitable place to stop for the night we found over a dozen horses half-frozen and mostly dead. They had been abandoned when the riders switched over to their other mounts. Urien spent the better part of the early evening trying to save even one of them, but he could not.

Sorrier-looking horses I had never seen. Lather had frozen against their skin. Their manes and tails were matted and full of ice. Oozing sores covered their backs, and their flanks bled from where they had been repeatedly spurred. They had been practically reduced to skeletons, and their deaths, which came hard, were a blessing.

The tracks at the stopping place told us quite a story. Tyrchon pointed out a large set of footprints as belonging to Packkiller. In comparison to the spoor left by the others, the B*harashadi* was in fine shape. "You can see by the crispness of his footprints that he's not tired and is moving well. His feet come up and out of the snow as he walks, and he hasn't stumbled."

Tyrchon knelt beside another set of tracks. "The others are shuffling their feet and have fallen down several times. This one is having trouble shifting his saddle from one horse to another without dropping it."

Everything Audin had ever taught me about tracking led me to concur with Tyrchon's read of the signs left in the snow. Packkiller's compatriots were exhausted. Part of me thought of it as justice for Black Churchers to be driven so hard by a Chaos demon, and another part of me rejoiced at how useless they would be in combat when we caught them. Despite that, however, I felt sorry for them because their delusions were putting them through such a trial and, at the end of it, would probably result in their deaths.

We worked hurriedly during our stop. Half of us fed and curried the horses while the others built a fire and prepared some warm food. We also melted snow into water for the horses and fed them from the grain we were carrying. After eating, we set up watches, and everyone managed to get four hours of sleep before we headed off again.

Shortly after dawn we found the place where our quarry had settled down for the night. One of their horses had been slaughtered for food, but from the butchery and the garbage they left behind, no one seemed to have eaten much of it. The rest of the horses had been fed sparingly and hobbled too far away from their fire to warm them. From the heat of the embers left in their fire Tyrchon estimated we had picked up two hours on them, but he doubted we would close much beyond that.

I agreed when, later in the day, we found five more dead horses and one of the riders. He had a hole burned through his chest and out through his back. The scorched area of his tunic reminded me of the burned ends of my sleeve, so I did not need Tyrchon confirming the stink of Packkiller being present.

"Taci, Kit told me of a spell you cast to locate the place where this Bharashadi killed the pack of wolves. It gave you a direction and time estimate, correct?"

She nodded. "Already worked it on a very low level. We are still four hours out."

I pointed to the corpse. "How powerful was the spell? Will having cast it interfere with his ability to speed the horses?"

"Strong, and tinged with anger." The Aelf pursed her lips. "It might force him to rest more or cast a spell of more limited duration."

Aleix squatted beside me and pointed to the corpse's knees. "See where his pants have worn through here and there up in the seat? Aside from his coat, he was not prepared for a long ride like this, especially through winter. I would wager he has been complaining for days and just threatened to head off to the nearest town unless they stopped. They did, and he died."

Xoayya's cloak puddled on the snow as she knelt near the man's head. She reached a gloved hand out and closed his eyes. "He was not terribly surprised when this Packkiller turned on him. This man was not the trusting type, nor did he engender the trust of others."

"That lack of trust killed him and isn't likely to make Packkiller's companions much happier about traveling with him." I shook my head, then looked up at Taci. "Taci, is there any indication the *Bharashadi* used the Fistfire Sceptre to cast this spell?"

She hesitated and chewed on her lower lip as she concentrated. "I felt nothing but pure Chaos and venom. I tried to locate the sceptre, but I got nothing." She glanced over at Nagrendra for confirmation, and he nodded silently.

"Well, at least he has not chosen to use it yet, but this close to the Ward Walls we have to assume he's preparing to put it back together." I smiled grimly. "I hope he is not saving it for us."

By pushing our horses, we topped the edge of the valley through which the Wardlines ran. I saw the shimmering, shifting wall of light from over a mile away, yet did not realize how tall it truly was until we drew closer. From where I first saw it, I thought it rose up perhaps half a mile, then ended. As I rode up to it, though, I discovered it was much taller, and, from near its base, the sky seemed to curve down to join it.

Any chance I had to speculate about what significance that might have was swept aside as we looked down into the valley. At the very edge of the wall we saw the riders we had been chasing. Amid them stood the black-furred Bharashadi I had seen in the sewers, and in his hands he held the Fistfire Sceptre. As I watched he screwed the gold fist clutching the black pearl onto the shaft.

The Black Shadow barked a command at his Black Church companions and they hauled themselves back into their saddles. Drawing steel or setting arrow to bow, they started toward us. Behind them the Bharashadi sorcerer began to whirl the sceptre much the way Fialchar had done with the Staff of Emeterio. Above him a glowing red-gold circle began to take shape.

Without a conscious thought, I drew my blade and spurred Stail forward. Behind me I heard others of our company draw their weapons, and Kit shouted something, but I did not hear if it was a warning or encouragement. I knew only one thing: I had to stop the Bharashadi.

The scouts' black arrows arced over me in a deadly rain. Two horses went down when hit, spilling their riders into hard landings amid the knee-deep snow. Another man rolled from his saddle when two arrows crossed in his chest, and a fourth was wounded. He fell from the saddle, then was dragged through the snow when a stirrup trapped his foot.

Roaring past me, Tyrchon's ears flattened back against his head. He set his spear and skewered one of the Black Churchers in mid-gallop. The crosspiece stopped the man from sliding up the shaft and blasted him back out of the saddle. Tyrchon cast aside the spear and his first victim, then drew his sword.

The Bharashadi arced the sceptre down and whirled its head toward me. The hollow circle of light spun madly as it swooped in my direction. Six feet across, with its edge a foot wide and of a snowflake's thickness, it crackled through the air, coming in at an angle that would burn it through Stail and me.

I hauled back and left on the reins, cruelly yanking the bit in Stail's mouth. The beast screamed and started to go down. I kicked free of the stirrups and let my momentum vault me from the saddle. I knew I would not land neatly or easily, but I wanted to be clear of Stail and the magick.

Above me a blue-white fireball jerked through the sky and slammed into the burning circle. They exploded, and the force of the blast hammered me solidly into the ground. The thunderclap deafened me, and I tasted blood running from my nose. A wave of heat flashed over me and vaporized the snow in which I lay. Pressing my left hand to the ground to push myself back to my feet, I felt soggy, grassy turf and looked down to find myself in a steam-shrouded circle utterly clear of snow.

As the mist curtain evaporated a Black Churcher launched himself at me. Clearly unschooled in the use of a sword, he held his sabre in both hands and had it raised for a crushing overhand blow. I sidestepped from the line of his attack, then whipped my sword across his middle. He folded around the blade, and blood sprayed from it in a crimson arc when it sliced free of his flank. He fell face forward in a snowmelt puddle.

Tyrchon, knocked from his saddle by the blast or on foot by choice, cut down another of the Black Churchers. Roarke rode through the cultist formation and split the head of one man with his ax. Osane, Eirene, and the scouts again sent a volley of arrows into the Black Churchers while our two magickers rode around the fighting to concentrate on the B*harashadi*.

Perhaps the smartest of all of us, Xoayya hung back and did nothing.

A cultist rode his horse straight at me and spurred hard to get the horse to ride me down. Thickly lathered, the horse seemed little of a mind to do his master's bidding, though he did enter the melted circle. There the horse balked, which, despite his rider's cursing, was a good thing because two arrows passed through where he would have been just one step forward.

My grandfather had ingrained in me the idea that fighting from the ground against a mounted swordsman is as close to suicide as I would ever want to get. I darted forward and grabbed the horse's reins real close to the bit, then ducked to the side as the cultist slashed at me. He drew his arm back again for another cut, this time on the side where I had taken refuge, so I shifted over to the other side. Again he missed, so he spurred his horse forward again.

I backed quickly, but tripped over the man I had killed earlier. As I went down, I lost my grip on the reins and the horse shied from me. This brought his rider around to attack me, but, luckily, I had fallen beneath his reach.

He straightened up and started to dismount, but never got a chance to complete his move. A streak of silver launched itself from the far side of the horse and toppled him from the saddle. Flashing teeth locked in the man's throat, Cruach carried the cultist clear of the horse and dumped him beside me. The hound shook the man once to the accompaniment of snapping and popping sounds, then dropped the man's body. The cultist lay still, with his head canted at an improbable angle.

As I got up again, I saw the *Bharashadi* stab the Fistfire Sceptre into the Ward Wall. The opal fire slowly slid up over the pearl and engulfed the shaft. The Black Shadow screamed when it touched his hand, and he recoiled as if snakebit. Then he hunched his shoulders, and his tail twitched. He stiffened, then again set himself as if hunting and waiting to take a boar's charge on his spear.

Starting with the sceptre's shaft, a red light pulsed out. It washed over the Chaos demon and clung to him as if he had been drenched in blood. The creamy opal light continued to swallow him, but it took on a pinkish hue as it did so. He straightened up and almost casually turned to face us. Grasping the sceptre in both hands, he raised it above his head and the blood-sphere expanded around him.

Through the space between him and the edge of the sphere, I caught my first glimpse of Chaos. In so small a view, and one filtered through the sphere, I could see none of the features I had studied so long and hard to recognize. I did, however, see something moving, but I could make no sense of it.

Xoayya could and did. "Archers! *Bharashadi* archers! Get down."

A flight of wickedly barbed arrows pierced the Ward Wall. They fell indiscriminately as the archers shot blindly through the wall. Horses fell and men went down, then those who were still able fled from the site of the first attack. A second overlapped the first to the far side of the battlefield, catching two more horses and one cultist.

Our archers returned a volley. From my vantage point I thought I saw two *Bharashadi* warriors fall, but I could not confirm my guess as the sorcerer stepped fully through the Ward Wall. It fell like a curtain to hide him, but did nothing to muffle his mocking laughter.

⌘　　⌘　　⌘

We quickly withdrew from the area back up to the valley lip. That gave us nearly five hundred yards of clear killing ground if the *Bharashadi* decided to breach the wall and send a raid out after us. As riding up the snowy slope would be much more difficult than charging down it, the Chademons would find challenging us very costly.

Of the fourteen cultists who had engaged us, half of them were dead, four were wounded, and three had surrendered without getting hurt. We also recovered twenty horses, but they were in such bad shape we knew they would be good for nothing for far longer than we could take to care for them. Even so, Urien prevailed upon Kit to let him tend to them, and we agreed to feed the horses from the grain we had brought for our own mounts.

Roarke proved very good at getting information out of the captured Black Churchers. He pointed to Nagrendra and told them, "Your mind is an apple, and what we want to know is cider. If you make it necessary, he has a spell that will work better than a cider press and get it. You'll be left with mush for brains, but that's not much of a concern for me. What will it be? Shall we let the Reptiad have the sort of fun we've denied him so far or will you frustrate him by cooperating?"

Unfortunately, as good as Roarke's technique was, the cultists had little to tell us. The Fistfire Sceptre had been broken down into parts and hidden in the personal baggage of various riders. A spy within the Imperial Guard had given the cultists the patrol schedules, and when one watch at Northgate was comprised of Black Churchers, the *Bharashadi* was smuggled out of the city. They had left over a week after our departure and had worn out two more sets of remounts over and above the ones we had seen abandoned.

Kit and I consulted with Taci and Roarke as we tried to make some very serious decisions. While the Black Churchers were guilty of crimes that would get them beheaded by Imperial officials, and Kit could carry out such a sentence here and still remain within his authority, I felt reluctant to kill them outright. "They know about people back in the capital who are Black Churchers. They know who helped put this theft into place, and, given how they were shot at by Bharashadi archers, their friend was killed, and that baker's family died in Herakopolis, they might be convinced to reveal the identities of their fellow conspirators."

"Fine, Locke, there is a reason to keep them alive. If we do, however, that means we bring them with us or send them back to Imperial Plains." Kit warmed his hands over the fire we had made. "We do not have the rations or people necessary to do the former. Sending them back to Imperial Plains means we have to send someone back with them, and I am reluctant to reduce our number. We were lucky that we only lost one of Roarke's horses to the Bharashadi arrows."

"It was more their mistreatment than our luck, Lieutenant, that let us get off so lightly." Roarke adjusted his eye patch with his left hand. "I am wondering, though, if we could not spare Urien to take the horses back and bring the prisoners with him as part of the bargain. He's a good scout, I'll grant him that, but he's been damned mournful at seeing how the Bharashadi treated these horses in getting here. If he doesn't like what he has seen so far, he surely will hate what he finds on the other side of the Ward Walls."

Taci agreed. "Urien is certainly distracted by how the horses have been mistreated. The fact is that we really should send a report back to the capital anyway, and he could take it with him to Imperial Plains."

The Aelf glanced over at where Nagrendra and Xoayya sat talking. "This is also the time to send Xoayya back."

I frowned. "Why do you say that?"

"She did nothing in the fight yesterday." Taci's expression sharpened. "Had the Black Churchers not been malnourished and exhausted, she might have been killed. We know that nothing we see on the other side will be that easy to kill. She's a burden we don't need and one that will cause us problems."

I arched an eyebrow. "And with Urien gone, she'll be the thirteenth member of our group, right?"

The Aelf blushed. "We're going into Chaos. There's no need to take unnecessary risks."

Roarke frowned. "If we leave Urien behind, we'll only be a dozen."

Taci pointed at Cruach. "What about the dog?"

Roarke laughed harshly. "Only an idiot would count the dog. Forget your superstition. Xoayya, in case you've forgotten, warned us about the arrows. She's part of our company, and that's the end of that. Right, Lieutenant?"

"Urien stays, Xoayya is going, and as much as I like Cruach, he doesn't count. It's a working plan." Kit looked over at the other, larger fire. "I will tell Urien. The rest of us better get some sleep. We will cross into Chaos tomorrow."

As we had agreed since the beginning, we wanted to cross into Chaos near Gorecrag. This meant a half-day ride to the east, which no one minded at all. The idea of crossing here carried with it the possibility of running straight into the *Bharashadi* with whom we had already exchanged arrow volleys.

Leaving Urien behind with the captives and their horses, we found a spot that, as nearly as we could reckon, would put us in the Gorecrag foothills when we crossed. Riding down into the valley, we watered our horses in the stream running through the meadow on our side of the Ward Walls. We all double-checked our gear and made certain our armor hung correctly. Weapons drawn, we rode toward the Ward Wall.

Xoayya brought her horse up on my left. Wisps of red hair floated free of her cloak's hood. The Wall's opal light illuminated her face and made her look more like a ghost than a living person. Her broad smile banished that thought immediately, however, for nothing that had passed from life could possibly look so excited.

"Xoayya, you really should wait. We don't know what we will run into on the other side."

She shook her head. "It doesn't matter, Locke. Whatever is on the other side, whatever happens to me, it's my destiny. Even if I drop dead on the other side, it will be because that is what is meant to happen. I don't know if there is a good reason or a bad one for it, but I am ready to accept it."

The open innocence of her declaration surprised me and scared me a bit. "I hear what you are saying, but I'd really prefer it if you would hang back. Wait for some of us to get through before you cross. I don't want your blood on my hands."

Xoayya reined her horse back. "As you wish, Locke. Understand this, though, whatever happens to me is beyond your capacity to control, change, or prevent. You and I differ in our thoughts about this, but I would not have you feel guilt over my fate."

"Thank you, Xoayya. I'll see to it nothing happens to you for which I need to feel guilt."

I turned back to face the wall as Stail walked into the magickal barrier. He approached it as if it were nothing more than early-morning fog. I braced myself as its red, purple, and white lights shimmered over me. I felt a tingle all over my body, then warmth—a warmth that made me want to reconsider crossing.

We pushed on and were rewarded by a sharp shock of cold. It hit me as I passed through to the other side—warning me of the dangers within Chaos. *This is the cold of the grave, something I am likely to find here.*

Despite those dire thoughts, part of me scoffed at the warning. *So this is Chaos. It feels as if I am home again!*

Before I could study my surroundings or figure out the feeling of familiarity that gripped me, an inhuman scream sounded from my left. I spun Stail to face it, expecting a Bharashadi ambush. I immediately feared Xoayya had followed me through and even now was being torn apart by a Black Shadow warrior.

What I saw, though nowhere near that horrible, still sent ice flowing through my guts.

The scream had come from Roarke. He clutched at his head as if trying to prevent it from exploding. The scream ended abruptly as he made it the rest of the way through the wall. Then Roarke slumped forward against his horse's neck, slid from the saddle, and crumpled to the ground.

22

I leaped from Stail's back and dropped to my knees beside Roarke's body. I felt breath from his nose against my hand and a strong and steady pulse in his neck. "He's alive." I looked at him, tugging off the mailed hood he wore. "No blood from his ears or nose. What happened?"

Tyrchon knelt on the other side of him while Hansen led Roarke's horse away. "The Ward Walls affect people differently. If this happened when Roarke first went through, it would explain why he has been reluctant to return. Let us get him back on his horse and get him to First Stop Mansion. If he lives to get that far, we can consider what we will do with him then."

I didn't like the sound of that. "Is it safe to move him?"

Kit came over and crouched beside me. "Do you think it's safer to leave him here?"

Taci looked down at the both of us. "I don't sense

any lingering spell effects, so it wasn't a magickal ambush. I don't want to use diagnostic spells here in the open, but I can if you insist."

I shook my head. "No, we don't want to let the others find us that easily."

"And find us they will if we don't get going." Kit stood slowly. "Everyone else got through in good shape. We know the Bharashadi are in the area, so the only way to guarantee our safety is to move. Roarke may not survive the trip, but none of us will survive waiting here for him to recover."

"You're right, of course." I scrubbed my hands over my face. "Let's move."

I grabbed one arm, and Tyrchon took the other. If Nagrendra had not gotten his legs, we would never have draped Roarke over the saddle. That accomplished, Tyrchon tied him in place and Hansen led the horse along, remaining in the middle of our formation for safety. Xoayya rode beside Roarke, reaching out to check his pulse from time to time.

Roarke's inexplicable problem undoubtedly colored how I saw Chaos, and it was probably a good thing, too. Throughout the whole trip I had been looking forward to leaving the womb. I wanted the distinction of having been to Chaos. I wanted the acceptance and camaraderie with the other Chaos Riders, and I wanted it as bad as a drunk wants liquor. In the Umbra I had been on the outside, and I hated it.

Entering Chaos allowed me to understand why Riders felt a race apart from the other people in the Empire. We rode from winter prairies to warm, dry redrock mountains. Unlike the Empire, greens and blues did not predominate here; instead reds and browns and purples made up the colors of the landscape. Verdant forests became hillsides filled with petrified trees and an undergrowth of bloody saw-edged grasses or purple prickly cactus-type plants. Rusty dust rose up from each hooffall. The rocks, from some fist-sized stones to boulders as large as a wizard's tower, dotted the landscape as if they were sentries opposing our invasion.

It occurred to me that Chaos looked exactly as the Empire might if the land were flayed down to the bedrock.

Despite the time spent viewing the model, this was all alien and new to me. I could have found myself wandering from one wonder to another, but the sight of Roarke hanging limp over the back of his horse killed all romanticism. Chaos might be the place from which heroes came, but that was because it was an unforgiving crucible. Here, in this forbidding terrain, we were the intruders. Everything on the Chaos side of the wall would do its best to destroy us.

Just as we would try to destroy anything of Chaos that came into the Empire.

Within two hours of crossing through the Ward Walls, we reached First Stop Mansion. What it once looked like, or might again appear to be if the Ward Walls were pushed out this far, I found it hard to imagine. In its present state it reminded me of nothing so much as a small fortress that had been crushed in a siege. Built into a semicircular plateau carved from the side of Gorecrag, the mansion originally had twin towers at the north and south corners of the main building. As its construction had taken place well before the peak had been baptized with its new name, it did not surprise me that the southern tower had collapsed, and the top of the northern one looked to have been burned away some time ago. The stone manor house stood two stories taller than the surrounding plain, but part of the northern wing had fallen into disrepair. Beyond it I saw what might once have been stables, but were now just a big pile of rubble.

Eirene rode into what would have been the paved courtyard in front of the mansion itself, then spun her mount and looked back out toward the west. "It looks clear, but keep an eye out for traps. The Bharashadi could have set them for Tsvortu or the other way around." She smiled grimly. "And other Riders could have set them for both."

Kit rode up to her side. "Hansen, get Roarke inside. Aleix, Xoayya, and Donla, help him. Taci, see what you and Nagrendra can do for him." He looked over at the wolf-headed man. "Tyrchon, if you want to scout the area, feel free. Holiness, if you would take watch in the north tower, I would be obliged."

"As you wish, Lieutenant," Osane replied, and rode off in the direction of the tower.

Tyrchon passed me the reins to his horse, then slipped from the saddle and ran back out of sight along our backtrail. Following the others, I rode Stail straight into the mansion through the main entrance and along an arched corridor to a central square courtyard with a working fountain. The horses' hooves clacked sharply off the cobblestones, and the sound echoed back at me from the mountain and inner walls. Because the inner courtyard was open to the sky, looking up to the east I saw Gorecrag.

The way the mansion had been built, the eastern portion had been carved out of the mountain, and a large archway opposite the front led back into the red rock. A covered walkway surrounded the courtyard, both on the ground level and one story up, but looked very unreliable where the north wing had crumbled. Still and all, the mansion's faded paint and the remnants of tile mosaics suggested it must have been very grand before Chaos swept over the world.

Eirene tied her horse's reins around one of the pillars supporting the upper walkway. "This is the first time I've been here, but others say it is very defensible. If worse comes to worst, we retreat into the mountain and hold them off at the doorway."

Kit glanced back at the dark opening. "There is no other way out of there?"

"No bolt-hole that I've heard of, but we should scout it out to make certain." Eirene stripped the saddle off her horse and set it on the low wall surrounding the courtyard. "We have water and an open killing ground in front of the mansion. We can last here for a while. If not"—she shrugged—"I can think of uglier places to die."

Hansen put Roarke in a south-wing room just off the courtyard. Taci and Nagrendra made him as comfortable as possible and worked on him while Kit, Eirene, and I watered and fed the horses. After I finished my work, I made to join them. I knocked on the closed door and waited patiently for someone to offer me permission to enter, since I had no desire to disturb sorcerers at work.

Xoayya opened the door and invited me in. Roarke lay on a makeshift pallet in the corner of a small, dark room. Cruach lay beside him and proved remarkably tolerant of Taci's poking and prodding of his master. Nagrendra stood at the foot of the bed, looking much like a stone statue. Only the flicker of his forked tongue and occasional nods in response to Taci's comments or questions showed he was alive.

Xoayya shook her head. "They have focused their

diagnostic spells down to limit detection. They don't think that has affected their ability to report results, but they can find nothing wrong with him."

Taci stepped away from the bed. "Roarke is unconscious and resting, but his body is at an incredibly low life-level." Taci looked utterly baffled by Roarke's condition.

"That room is not, according to the maps I have seen, a 'slow' zone." I looked at Nagrendra. "Do you have any ideas?"

"None." The Reptiad shrugged mica-scaled shoulders. "I suppose he could have some sort of sickness that only thrives within Chaos, but I have never heard of such a thing. Moreover, the diagnostic spells Taci and I used did not indicate a disease. As nearly as I am able to determine, he is healthy and recovering."

"That's good."

Xoayya nodded. "I feel odd saying this, but it feels to me as if Roarke is, well, *waiting.*"

I frowned. "Waiting?"

Taci idly tapped her baton against her left thigh. "Roarke's body seems to be reacting as if he is in a state of stasis. It's functioning, but at a reduced rate. It's not abnormal, but just subnormal. If it were a spell causing this, we might be able to modify it. If it were an organic problem, we might be able to heal it. Since we can't pinpoint the source, however, we don't know how to treat it."

"I see. So Roarke is waiting." I shivered. "Waiting for what?"

Tyrchon walked into the sickroom. "If he is waiting for Black Shadows, he has a day or so."

"This is important. Let's head outside and find Kit." I glanced at Roarke. "Let's give him a chance to recover in peace."

"Not much peace will be had here." Tyrchon led us out of the room and over to where Kit and Eirene were speaking in the center of the inner courtyard. I followed on his heels, and the others joined us. Xoayya was last, having pulled the door to the sickroom shut after the rest of us had left.

Tyrchon shared his scouting report with Kit.

"A day before they attack? How many?" Kit's head came up, and his expression changed as he assumed command again. "What can we expect?"

Tyrchon sniffed the air twice, then squatted down on his haunches. "I would assume, since the sorcerer saw how easily we dealt with his people and magick, they will send a hundred or so of their number after us. They will likely all be warriors, but one or two sorcerers may be with them."

"Do you think Packkiller will be one of them?"

Tyrchon shrugged in response to Kit's question. "I don't know, but I doubt it. He's too important to risk in this sort of operation. The Black Shadows will first try to spook us, then rush in and use swords or axes for close work. Any of you hunted by them?"

Eirene and Nagrendra shook their heads.

I shook my head. "This is my first time into Chaos. Same with Xoayya."

"That wouldn't preclude anyone hunting you, but it makes it very unlikely." Tyrchon sniffed the air. "How about Roarke or the bishop?"

Kit shook his head. "Unknown."

"Roarke may have tangled with the *Bharashadi* a long time ago." Eirene kicked a piece of paving stone loose from the courtyard floor. "You worried about *vindictx-vara*?"

"Worried, no. Wary, yes." The lupine warrior stood again. "I do not believe any of the Black Shadows will be coming after me, but it is possible. If you see a sword with my picture on it, that B*harashadi* is mine."

Aleix, the old sergeant, guffawed. "I will try to remember that as I shoot them full of arrows."

"You do that, Herakman. If you can." Tyrchon's voice dropped into a low growl. "Want to know what you will see tomorrow night? Close your eyes. Everyone, do it."

I complied and felt a rough cuff to the side of my head. From the startled shouts of others, I knew Tyrchon had hit them as well while we were blind. I opened my eyes again and saw Kit had grabbed a handful of Aleix's tunic to hold him back from attacking Tyrchon.

The wolf-warrior slowly smiled. "*That* is what you will see when they come for us—nothing. Black Shadows is a name the B*harashadi* earned through their stealth. In the night here you will not see them until they are on top of you. I hope you Herakmen get a chance to feather as many as you want, but you would do well to sharpen your swords, too."

Eirene nodded. "Tyrchon has the right of it, but this is a good place to defend."

"Lieutenant, if I might make a suggestion?" Nagrendra bowed his head to Kit.

"Please, Nagrendra, suggest away."

"Let us reconnoiter the mansion. We travel in groups and determine if any old traps are still in force or can be repaired. If each of us travels with a Rider, your people can be quickly introduced to this place. You and Tyrchon can then set up our defenses."

"A solid plan as nearly as I can tell." Kit folded his arms. "Hansen and Donla, you go with Tyrchon. Taci, get the Bishop. Locke, you and Xoayya will go with Nagrendra. Aleix, you stay here with the horses."

"Yes, sir."

I followed the Reptiad sorcerer and Xoayya as we walked out through the mansion to the front courtyard. The rooms between the exterior wall and the inner courtyard had long ago been stripped of furnishings, but some of the tile mosaics still could be seen beneath the red dust on the floors. Rubbish, paint chips, and bits of wood decorated the rooms now. As the dusk came on I could imagine skeletons lurking amid the shadows, but I had no real desire to go poking about to confirm my suspicions.

In the courtyard, Nagrendra's opal eyes became slits. "Locke, pace off twenty feet."

I took eight uniform steps from where I stood. "This should be it."

"Good even paces. Excellent." He turned to Xoayya and had her do the same. She smiled self-consciously as she ended up a foot back of where I stood, but Nagrendra did not seem to mind. "Close enough for what we will be doing. Xoayya, go out another forty feet. Locke, start over at the north tower and pace out ten feet, heading directly toward her."

He stood in the middle of the courtyard as we did what he told us to do. When I had taken my four steps out from the tower, he came to me and knelt down. He brushed the dust from one of the square paving stones in the courtyard, then told me to fetch a nearby rock. I did so and gave it to him. The Reptiad raised the rock in his fist and brought it down on the paving stone, breaking a triangle off one corner.

Drawing a dagger, he scraped the number one on the stone. He then surprised me by using the blade to nick his right thumb. Blood welled up in the cut, and he pressed his thumb first to the fragment of the rock and then to the stone it had come from. "Give me another twenty feet, Locke."

I marched closer to Xoayya, and Nagrendra repeated his actions. "What are you doing?"

"Please, Locke." Xoayya stared at me as if I were an idiot. "It's obvious, isn't it?"

"Patience, woman." The Reptiad dropped his jaw in a rough approximation of a smile. "He knows even less about magick than you do."

"I know about enough to fill a thimble and have room for the Empire left over." I gave Xoayya a smile. "And as my grandfather said, the first step to wisdom is acknowledging how much you do not know."

Nagrendra nodded, the dying sun painting red highlights on his stony flesh. "A wise man, your grandfather. In magick we deal with a number of laws. One of them is the Law of Contagion. It suggests that a part of something is tied to the whole simply by having come from the whole. Each of these rock fragments is tied invisibly and intangibly to the stone from which it has been taken. The use of my blood ties them directly to me. Twenty more feet, if you please."

I nodded slowly and walked to Xoayya's side. "Now I know what you are doing. Why are you doing it?"

"Because I want to kill Bharashadi." He looked up at me, and a clear membrane nictitated up and down over his eyes. "Each of these stone fragments becomes a focus for my spells, similar to using a magick staff or Taci's baton. When I cast a spell with my hand wrapped around one of these, the spell is all but guaranteed to take effect at the spot from which the stone was taken."

"And the spells you mean to cast have an effective diameter of twenty feet?"

Nagrendra smiled up at me. "You are quick, but I would expect that from one of your blood. Yes, I think the Bharashadi will find this courtyard a very dangerous place."

Xoayya plaited a lock of her red hair. "What could stop a spell from going where you wanted it to go?"

I winked at her. "I thought all this magick stuff was obvious to you."

"Intent is." She gave me a superior smile. "Technique, on the other hand, is not my strong point."

"That's because you've had little formal training. If you had, you'd know many things can make a spell go awry. Being distracted by a wound or being afraid. Anything that might cause you to lose your concentration in a battle will likewise cause problems for me." He anointed another stone with his blood. "Counterspells can negate any magick I choose to cast as well. Twenty more feet, Locke."

I paced it off, then chewed my lower lip. "You cast the counterspell that stopped Packkiller from getting me with his spell, didn't you?"

The magicker nodded solemnly. "I utterly mistook the strength of his spell. Luckily, he had chosen a physical focus for his magick, you moved to duck it, and I was able to deflect it. The two spells managed to annihilate each other, but the residual effect of his spell was enough to melt that snow and knock quite a few people from their horses."

"Well, thank you." I smiled. "It's kind of funny that your spell was erratic and blurry while his was so crisp and exact—no offense intended."

"None taken, but no amusement either. That is not funny because it is fundamental to the nature of magick." Nagrendra sat back on his heels. "Chaos magick demands that sort of precision because here, in a place of highly variable probabilities, order must be imposed on chaos to get the desired effect. Within the Empire, on the other hand, to obtain magickal effects, we must break the order imposed by the Ward Walls. In essence, creatures born in Chaos must use Ward magick disciplines to get what they want, and Imperial sorcerers must invoke Chaos to make their magick work."

"And the type of magick you do depends upon your training and where you were born?" I asked.

"To a greater or lesser extent." He held his hand up so I could see his mica scales. "I have been in Chaos long enough that were I to learn from a Chaos sorcerer, I could work their magick. This is how Black Churchers can learn to work Chaos magicks. Unlike them, however, I have no desire to see the Empire destroyed, so I have no incentive to learn the ways of the enemy."

Xoayya giggled nervously. "And the opportunities to learn from the enemy out here are not that common, I would imagine."

"A good point, my dear." The Reptiad straightened up and stretched his arms. "Both of you may also have noted that my spell had a blue or white tint to it, while the Bharashadi spell appeared more red or gold. The difference in color also marks the spells as being Chaotic or Imperial in nature. The last thing you want to see in the dark is the glint of gold eyes and a red spark."

Recalling my encounter with Packkiller in the sewers below the palace, I nodded and rubbed my right shoulder.

As night fell we worked more quickly. Nagrendra set up another line of defenses fifteen feet out from the front of the manor house, with only ten feet between them. He also took stone fragments from the lintel and each of the window frames on the front of the house. He marked each one and entrusted them to Xoayya so she could take them to Taci. "Taci will know what to do with these."

Xoayya nodded slowly, then shook her head as if to clear it after a clout. "After that, what should I do?" Her question came slowly and haltingly.

I looked at her. "Is something wrong?"

She shook her head again. "No, not really. It is just that I keep catching glimpses of visions. There is more here, to this place, than is readily apparent."

Nagrendra's jaw dropped open in a smile. "Not only have you a gift for Clairvoyance, but one for understatement, too."

Xoayya frowned at him. "I have the feeling there are tunnels and passages here."

"That the Black Shadows are going to come through?" I watched her closely. "We have to defend against that kind of covert attack."

Xoayya shook her head. "I sense no threat, just the potential of their existence. I might be sensing the past or the future, too, not just the now." She forced a grim smile onto her face. "If it is permissible, I'll do some exploring after I deliver the stones to Taci."

Nagrendra and I nodded. As she departed, I gathered up the other stones the Reptiad had prepared. He had me bear them to the top of the north tower—an excellent vantage point, with thick stone walls to protect us. He quickly set to work, and after a short time I could hear Xoayya searching around in the debris inside the base of the tower itself.

The effects of the fire that had taken off the roof of the tower could be seen in the charred wood and stone on the uppermost level. The creaky wooden floor looked none too safe to me, but Nagrendra picked a path around burned areas and ignored the groans of the wood. I followed him, knowing that any floor that could support his weight ought to bear mine, and I tried not to think about the possibility of our combined weight causing the floor to collapse.

Despite the unsafe conditions, the top of the tower was perfect for our purposes. Up there we had a spectacular view of the outer courtyard and some of the terrain beyond it. We couldn't see anything out there that indicated the Bharashadi were closing in, but Tyrchon's warning about their stealthy approaches meant the lack of signs didn't surprise me. They were out there, and we were setting up to give them a fierce battle.

Nagrendra crouched by a window in the tower's northern face. He set the first line of stones, the ones sixty feet from the manor, in a line on a low shelf. He arranged all six of them in numerical order so they all touched corner to corner in a line. The four stones taken from closer in he placed in a small alcove set to the right of his window. "This was once a shrine for a statue of the Earth Mother. I do not think she will mind its appropriation for this purpose."

I watched him arrange those triangles in a line, but he did not have them touching each other. "Is this going to be enough to keep the Bharashadi back?"

He shook his head. "No, not beyond the first night. The Bharashadi have absolutely no concern for their own safety. It probably has to do with this Necroleum you speak of as being our goal. If they truly believe they will be resurrected and their position after death depends upon their bravery before death, they will come at us without any concern for themselves. In fact, if they know the resurrection will be accomplished soon, they will be even more ferocious than normal."

"Why do you and Tyrchon think they will not hit us tonight?" I stood on my tiptoes and looked out into the night. "They were no further away than we were, and it only took us half a day to get here."

"Not true." Nagrendra drew a semicircle in the dust on the weathered wooden floor. "We were able to cut across the inside of the circle to get to this point. The Bharashadi had to traverse the exterior of the arc, and you should know that much of that terrain is quite inhospitable. The first night they will send a hundred after us. The next night it will be more. That will go on until we escape or are destroyed."

I moved to another window—one that had been enlarged by pulling stones out of the casement—and stared off into the distance. While my vantage point would give me an unobstructed view of the area to the west during the day, at night I could see little or nothing. The stars above barely twinkled at all and looked purple and green instead of the reds and whites I expected to see. "No moon in Chaos?"

The Reptiad shook his head. "No, there is one. It's just black. It will be coming up soon. You can spot it as it devours stars."

Off in the distance I saw a ghostly green light bobbing up and down as hills and rocks blocked my view of it. Despite the interference, I did see that it was moving very rapidly and coming in our direction. Along with it I heard the faint drum of hoofbeats.

"I think you're wrong about our not being attacked. Riders."

Nagrendra pushed me out of the way and looked out. "No, dammit, not again." He moved to the other side of the tower and cupped his hands around his mouth. "Eirene, lock up that beast you ride! The Emerald Horse is coming!"

Returning to the window I saw the light get closer. The sounds of galloping horses echoed from the plateau walls as the Emerald Horse led his herd up the trail we had used to reach the mansion. The light vanished for a second, then appeared again as the fabled creature trotted into the mansion's courtyard.

A more magnificent animal I do not think I have ever seen. Perfectly sculpted from glowing green crystal, the warhorse reared up in the courtyard and slashed his front hooves through the air. Muscles bunched and flowed fluidly on his semitransparent body. His mane and tail, though made of stone, flew as if hair. Landing on all fours he froze for a second and became a jewel-statue, then his nostrils flared and he neighed out a loud challenge.

Behind him came a host of animals as unique as the Emerald Horse himself. I could see that all of them had been, at one time, horses, but Chaos had changed them in a myriad of ways. Some looked to be zombi-creatures while others appeared as fully animated wooden hobbyhorses. I saw some with exoskeletons resembling the armor in which their masters had once encased them and one beast with a coat of quills like a porcupine.

The Emerald Horse again reared up and neighed. From within the mansion I heard our horses answer him, then Eirene's angry shout. As I watched, her mount burst from the mansion, leaping through one of the empty windows. It slowed as it approached the Emerald Horse, then ducked away from the nip he tried to give it and took up its place in his herd.

Eirene ran into the courtyard, sword in hand. The Emerald Horse turned and faced her, then charged, stopped, and reared. His hooves flashed at her, then he came down again and bolted off toward the west. His herd followed and galloped off along the trail leading north and deeper into Chaos.

Below Eirene sank to her knees and covered her face with her hands. I saw Kit come out and kneel by her side. I turned from them and looked at Nagrendra. "The Emerald Horse stole your mount as well?"

He nodded slowly. "The big horse with chain-mail skin, that was Seilide."

Despite the regret in his reply, and the obvious pain crushing Eirene down, something inside me would not see the Emerald Horse as evil. I wanted to whistle for him as I would for Stail and make him my mount. *On such a wondrous creature, I could not be defeated.* But even as I wanted to bring the Emerald Horse under my control, I knew his power could not be controlled unless he wished it to be controlled.

I glanced back at Nagrendra. "Do you wish you had her back?"

"Deny her freedom?" He shook his head slowly. "When you have been a Chaos Rider for as long as I have, you may understand this. I do not regret having lost her, I regret not having been able to go with her."

23

Eirene and I rode out of the mansion courtyard early in the morning. We headed off on the route the Emerald Horse had taken with his herd, but our goal was not to track him. His herd was gone and with it her horse. She borrowed a horse from Xoayya for our trek and seemed resigned to having to deal with it for the rest of our expedition.

The Emerald Horse's line of retreat led to a smaller, more treacherous path curving up around Gorecrag. Our goal was the top of the mountain itself, but I noticed Eirene seemed fairly intent on the tracks left behind by the Emerald Horse's herd. To Eirene's disappointment the Emerald Horse's herd left the path less than a quarter mile from the mansion, to run down a steep, rocky slope and off into the countryside.

"Eirene, I'm very sorry your horse went with the Emerald Horse. I . . ."

"Save it, Locke." She'd gathered her long hair into a

thick braid. "I should have known better. This mission, this place. I never should have let Roarke talk me into this."

Riding in back of her, I could not hear her curse, but I saw her body jerk with its vehemence. She wore ring-joined plate armor that had a dull gray sheen to it. From where I sat it looked as if the antler spikes she wore at her elbows and heels had become longer and sharper. She used the heel spikes like spurs to urge her new horse up a steep part of the trail.

I knew she felt bad about losing her horse, and even though she tended to keep to herself, I thought she might feel better talking about it. "So, what was your horse's name? I don't think you ever mentioned it."

She twitched in reaction to my comment as if it had been a barbed arrow that caught her in the spine. "He didn't have a name. If you name an animal, you get too attached to it, and it will be taken away from you. They said the Emerald Horse only takes horses with names into his herd." Eirene turned and gave me a toothy grin. "That's the same thing they used to say about your father's Valiant Lancers. The only Riders who became part of that unit were those who had made a name for themselves."

I ignored her attempt to deflect me by mentioning my father. "You never named your horse because you were afraid the Emerald Horse would take him away?"

"Six years ago, when I first became a rider, the Emerald Horse was known to raid Rider camps for horses, but I didn't believe it."

"Had you ever seen him before?" I got Stail up the switchback without having to resort to the use of my spurs. "Last night he was incredible."

"So says anyone who has not lost a horse to him." Bitterness and anger underscored her comment. "I saw the Emerald Horse once, a long time ago when he took a horse from a compatriot of mine."

"What happened?"

"The Drasacor were hunting us. They're the tribe people call the Mist Demons. They ambushed our group. My friend died because she thought my horse was not strong enough to carry both of us to safety. She made me go, and she stayed to act as a rear guard." She shook her head. "Chaos is not a nice place."

"This I have gathered."

"But do you *know* it, do you really *know* it?" She turned in the saddle and pointed out toward the limitless plains of Chaos. "Something out here killed your father. It killed Kit's father. Doesn't that make you afraid?"

I nodded. "It does, it scares me a great deal. But then *not* doing what we have come here to do scares me even more. I don't believe I have a choice."

"Congratulations, you are now a Chaos Rider." Eirene reined her horse back, then dismounted. She looped the reins around a spur of rock, then motioned for me to do the same. I did, and as I came forward, I saw what she had seen from further up the trail.

"By all the gods!" I dropped down on one knee. "Is that it?"

"That's it. That is where Fialchar lives." Eirene dropped a hand to my left shoulder. "That is Castel Payne."

Looming in the distance like a distinctly dark and brooding thunderhead, a spired castle floated above the ground. Given the rough, conical mound of dirt stuck to the bottom of it, the castle looked as if it had been ripped from the ground by the hand of a giant gardener pulling weeds. Indeed, the outer wall looked as if it had been crushed inward by external forces.

Even First Stop Mansion looked to be in better condition than Castel Payne's siege wall.

The interior castle, however, looked untouched. The outer spires glittered and sparkled as if a jeweler had fashioned them from green ocean water frozen into a vast block of ice. The whole thing had the complex transparency of emerald with the color of milky jade. The castle walls showed no crenellations or any other martial artifice to suggest it had been created as a fortress. Sunlight flashed from glassine edges that I had no doubt could slice like a razor.

Yet as beautiful as Castel Payne appeared to the eye, my soul ached because of the corruption and evil it harbored. There was a viper hidden among those jeweled towers. I remembered the Bear's Eve Ball and the ease with which he had manipulated all of us. My hands tightened down into fists, and I spat at the floating fortress.

"Take a bit more than spit to bring it down, I think, Locke."

I nodded, then laughed. "It's a start."

"True." Her face darkened as I looked up at her. "Still, this is not good."

I furrowed my brows. "What do you mean 'not good'? His castle is closer than we had dared hope, and it appears to be coming in this direction."

"We knew it would be close because that would be the only way he could have teleported into the palace, or so you said the Emperor's experts seemed to think."

"Right."

"But they expected him to be going away from the Ward Walls."

I saw her target. "So what does it mean that he is coming this way?"

Her eyes became slivers of opal. "I am not certain, but I do not like what comes immediately to mind."

"And that is?"

"He knows we are here, and he knows the *Bharashadi* are after us." She squinted at Castel Payne. "If he keeps drifting this way, he should be in a perfect position to watch the Black Shadows wipe us out tonight."

I whistled for Stail, and we mounted up. Eirene and I talked very little as we headed back down to First Stop Mansion. Our original plan had called for us to locate Castel Payne and, as nearly as possible, get right under it. Both Nagrendra and Taci were skilled enough in Conveyance magick to elevate half of us up to the flying castle. There we would talk with Lord Disaster, explain the problem he was going to have concerning lots of Black Shadows running wild through Chaos. He would give us the Staff of Emeterio, and we would go destroy the Necroleum.

The difficulty with that plan was that to implement it now would leave six people on the ground while the rest went up to Castel Payne. We had no idea what would happen to those of us who went up to beard Fialchar in his own den, but we had an excellent idea of what would happen to those we left on the ground. A comatose Roarke would do nothing to help the others, which left five people against a hundred *Bharashadi*.

Those were longer odds than anyone cared to take on, and if the dust cloud Eirene and I saw on the horizon was any indication, the *Bharashadi* might have sent more warriors than Tyrchon had estimated. Reinforced or not, the Black Shadow threat meant, for all practical purposes, we could not afford even one of our magickers to be used to send me or Kit up to have a chat with Lord Disaster.

"In short," I told the others as we joined them for an

early-evening meal of bean-and-rice gruel, "If we survive tonight, we can try to reach Castel Payne."

"We'll have to survive," Hansen declared as he put his wooden platter down. He waited until all eyes were upon him, then smiled. "Well, I would hate to think *this* was going to be my last meal."

After we finished eating we completed the preparations for the Bharashadi assault. The archers among us took up positions at the windows in the front of the house or, in Aleix's case, on the first floor of the north tower. Osane and Donla hid in the only good room on the northern side of the central corridor, while Kit, Eirene, and Hansen held the left wing. Tyrchon and I waited in the corridor to reinforce whichever side had Bharashadi reach it first. Because the opal eyes made night vision much clearer, Osane would call shots for Donla, and Eirene would try to direct Kit and Hansen.

I expected, by the time the Bharashadi got close enough for me to deal with them—opal eyes or not—I would be able to see them very well indeed.

Taci remained in control of our fallback position. We had placed our remounts back in the part of the mansion built into the cliff, but kept our own horses saddled and in the courtyard in case we decided that running was our only way out. I knew we all wanted to avoid that because it would mean, among other things, that Roarke would die.

Nagrendra had instructed Taci how to deal with the stones he had taken from the windows and doorway. We hoped whatever he told her to do would buy us the necessary time to fall back, if we were overrun. She agreed it would.

Nagrendra put himself in the highly hazardous position at the top of the north tower and would not allow

Aleix to be stationed with him. "I do not need anyone else getting in my way," he announced to us.

Xoayya tapped him on the shoulder. "I will not be in your way."

The Reptiad shook his head. "I will not have you there with me. You should be with Roarke."

"My place is not with Roarke."

"Your place is not with me." Nagrendra's membranes flicked up over his opal eyes. "Locke, convince her of this."

Xoayya looked hard at Nagrendra. "And if I convince Locke I should be there with you?"

That clearly surprised the Reptiad. His tongue snapped in and out of his mouth a couple of times, then he nodded. "I will abide by his decision."

I frowned at Xoayya. "Being with him will be too dangerous."

She grabbed my hand and led me away from the rest of the group. "Hear me out, Locke. If you can deny me after I explain, I will agree to what you want, but give me a fair hearing." Though she kept her voice low, she could not mute the urgency and passion in it.

"I'm listening."

"Think back to the night of the Bear's Eve Ball. You remember the magick Fialchar used?"

I shivered. "All too well."

"So do I." She hugged her arms around herself. "I don't know what you felt, but I have to guess it was what I did. I saw it in your eyes as I pirouetted past you. Fialchar's magick reached down inside of me. It touched something deep and primitive."

"I know." I blushed as I remembered what I'd felt. "Lust and fury. I was more an animal than a man."

"Yes, yes, that's it." Her blue eyes flashed, and I thought I caught a hint of *Chaosfire* in them. "For the first time in my life I felt something, experienced something that was of *me*. Prior to that I was always someone's daughter, or a tragic figure to be coddled and insulated, and when I wasn't that, I was having visions of futures that were not my own. Your suggestion about songs allowed me to begin to control my mind, but Fialchar's magick took me to where I could be if I mastered my mind and power."

She opened her arms, and her hands curled into fists. "For the first time I felt as if I was living my own life."

My face hardened. "If you're trying to scare me, it's working."

"No, Locke, not that at all." She stepped closer to me and rested her hands on my shoulders. "It is just that since I have come into Chaos I again feel alive. More importantly, I'm not seeing what will happen as much as I'm feeling it. I don't see myself in the tower with Nagrendra, but I know that's where I'm supposed to be."

"I still don't find myself compelled to put you in that danger."

"Look at it this way: as you explained to my grandmother, and she explained it to me, if there are multiple futures for me, switching between them happens at very select and important decision points." She pointed back toward the north tower. "Being there, tonight, is one of those points. Just as every decision you have made has defined who and what you are, this point will help me define who and what I am."

I glanced down at her. "You're abandoning your belief in destiny?"

"No, just explaining things in terms you will understand." She smiled. "Just as you feel compelled to come into Chaos and risk your life doing something your father failed to do, so must I be in that tower. My future is accessible only through that tower."

Her last comment sent a chill down my spine. I recalled Jasra's comment about her not being able to see more futures for Xoayya if she did not enter Chaos. Could it be that her future further narrowed to a choke point that only allowed one choice. If I did not put her in the tower, would I be killing her?

By putting her in the tower you most certainly will kill her.

Pain linked my temples with a lightning bolt. I wanted to deny her a place in the tower, but I didn't think I could do that any more than I could have denied her permission to travel with us. And the fact was that our chances of survival were so slender that to keep her out of the tower meant she would only survive a short while longer.

If she chooses to die in the tower, can I gainsay her the choice?

I sighed. "You can join Nagrendra in the tower. Don't interfere with him, or you could jeopardize the survival of everyone."

She stood on her tiptoes and gave me a quick kiss. "You won't regret this."

"You say that, but I know I will."

"It's my fate, Locke, not your fault." She winked at me. "You bear no guilt in what must be."

As night fell, we made the final preparations for battle. Taci cast several spells creating light to counter the Bharashadi advantages in the dark. She focused them on the front of the mansion, about two feet above the windows and doorway. She made them bright enough to illuminate the courtyard out to where Nagrendra had his first line of stones. Because of the location of the glowing white balls, they cast long shadows back into the windows and effectively helped hide our waiting archers.

As darkness fell we began to hear yips and screams. Fierce yowls ripped through the air, and I felt a shiver run down my spine. Tyrchon smiled at me from across the corridor. "Don't worry, Locke, these are *Bharashadi*, not *Jodlinaro*. The Screamers can hurt you with their voices, but not these beasts."

I glanced out through the doorway and saw golden glints in the night. They looked at first like fireflies, but I saw they moved in pairs and realized they had to be *Bharashadi* eyes. I found them just as haunting as what I remembered from the sewers. "I don't remember the *Bharashadi* sorcerer as being quite so tall."

"Old trick. You have one Chademon on the other's shoulders. The lower one has his eyes shut." Tyrchon half shut his eyes and nodded. "They are enjoying this because they know not everyone here is a Rider. Still, the warriors will be larger than your magicker."

"They won't employ their magick users in the first attack?"

"Unlikely, though you never know. Warriors usually make up the first wave they send at any target. Magick can come later. Remember, if you see red magick, it's them. Kill the sorcerer and save us trouble."

When they came, they came in a wave that flowed slowly in toward our position. With their manes shaved away from the sides of their heads, they were very tall and decidedly fearsome. Their muscles rippled beneath coats of short black fur, and tails twitched in anticipation of the battle. They crept through the darkness, inching up to the light's perimeter, wary yet charged with nervous energy. As they reached Nagrendra's first line of defense, my heart began to beat quicker. "Watch this."

The first one stepped beyond it and nothing happened. And then a second and a third walked over the line I had paced out. "What?"

Tyrchon growled at me. "Nagrendra knows what he is doing."

From either wing of the house our archers let fly. At such close range each shaft struck with deadly precision. Five B*harashadi* fell, but three of them got back up again and limped away. The other two, one of which was throat-stuck with Osane's gilded broadhead, left trails of blood as other Chademons dragged them off by their ankles.

Tyrchon backed to the doorways leading into the front rooms. "Gut shoot them. One arrow won't kill them unless you get lucky or have the Sunbird on your side. Make them hurt." He looked at me and my sword. "Get ready. You may only be an Apprentice with that thing, but you will do a Journeyman's work tonight. They will come fast this time."

The B*harashadi* broke from the shadows and ran at us like lunatics. They screeched and shrieked at us, brandishing swords and axes as if they were powerful talismans. In they raced, a tidal wave of ferocity. They sped past Nagrendra's first line of defense, and I tightened my hands on the hilt of my sword.

This is the first chance you get to prove yourself a hero, Locke!

Suddenly the world between the Chademons and us exploded. Huge fangs of blue fire erupted from the ground. They chewed through the front ranks of the B*harashadi*. Several Chademons dissolved in the magickal fire before my eyes. The bitter stink of burned flesh and singed fur nearly overwhelmed me as the acrid smoke made my eyes water.

I blinked the tears away and set myself as the flames died abruptly. While many of the Black Shadows fled burning, and others had been knocked sprawling by the blast, several leaped over charred corpses and ran on at us. Bowstrings twanged and B*harashadi* went down, but three kept coming.

I stepped into the north-wing room as a B*harashadi* warrior sailed through one of the windows, knocking Donla down. It turned on her, raising its sword to split her head, but coming from the side I parried the blow and let the Chademon's own strength carry my blade down into its left thigh. The B*harashadi* roared with pain as I slid my sword free.

It pivoted on its injured leg and aimed a backhanded slash at my waist. Twisting, I brought my sword up to the left and around, barely catching the blow in time. I parried the sword up and over my head, ducked beneath the cut, shifted my grip, and brought the blade down on its sword arm. I struck its left hand off, sending the blade flying.

I expected the Chademon to retreat from such a hideous wound, but it attacked instead. With a swipe of its right hand it tore away my armored face mask and started a trickle of blood from my right cheek. I stumbled back from its attack, belatedly bringing my sword up into a guard position. Before it could spring at me and take advantage of my misfortune, a golden arrow punched through its chest and pinned it to the wall. The Chademon clawed at the shaft, breaking it, but died as it tried to lever itself free.

I stared at the B*harashadi*. Cut and bleeding, with a hand gone and an arrow in its chest, it had continued to fight. "It should have been dead twice over."

Osane, nocking another arrow, shook her head. "B*harashadi* just require a lot of killing." She pointed to the hand still gripping the sword. "Pry that loose with your sword and toss it out onto one of the burning bodies. The Black Demons have to be whole to be resurrected, and I do not believe ashes are acceptable."

I did as she told me, retrieved my face mask, then returned to the corridor. Tyrchon looked at my blood-

ied blade, then nodded. I retied the face mask, reset-
tled my helmet, and waited. "What now, Tyrchon?"

"The magick surprised them. They will wait and make
us wait."

Wait we did. The B*harashadi* renewed their serenade,
and it began to make the horses nervous. That, in turn,
put us on edge again. My hands began to shake, but
Tyrchon explained that was merely the aftermath of
dealing with the excitement of the attack. He held his
right hand up, and it quivered like a leaf in a storm.

"You did fine, Locke. You will do even better."

When they came again, after two hours, I had no
choice but to do better. They ran at us again, and
Nagrendra triggered the spell using the outer set of
paving stones. In an eyeblink, a solid sky-blue wall
linked each of the stones. The leading edge of the running Chademons hit it and passed through, but fell and
thrashed on the ground as tendrils of blue lightning
caressed them. Their bodies began to smoke, then
burst into flame as the lightning died, and they lay still.

Then, suddenly, two things happened. One portion
of the magickal wall collapsed, creating a twenty-foot-
wide breach in our defenses. It looked to me as if the
blood spilled from one of the arrow-shot Black
Shadows might have trailed across one of the anchor-
stones. For whatever the reason, though, that section
of the wall flashed twice, then evaporated.

B*harashadi* poured through the gap at us.

Worse than that, behind them red-gold lines of magick drew themselves from the darkness to each of the
paving stones and on up the tower. They circled it like
ivy, then tightened around the top like a noose. A
golden flash pulsed up the magickal artery, crushing
the top of the north tower into dust and gravel. Debris
tumbled down into the courtyard, battering a few of the

Bharashadi, but more came in to replace them as the blue walls all fell.

"Magickers!" Tyrchon snapped. "Feather them, or we are lost."

The archers sent two volleys into the charging demons, then fell back as per new orders Tyrchon shouted. They sprinted into the central courtyard on either side of Taci as she stalked forward. Tyrchon and I stepped into the rooms the archers had occupied, and Taci's hands convulsed down into fists.

The spell she triggered exploded the window casings and door framing outward. Thousands of stone fragments flew through the courtyard, literally shredding the forward line of Chaos demons. Bodies tumbled back, and others fell over the top of them. The explosive thunderclap swallowed most of the initial screams of pain, but others echoed through the mansion.

The Bharashadi kept coming. Taci retreated down the main corridor, and a volley of arrows greeted the Black Shadows pouring in through the central door. One with an ax leaped into the room where I stood and chopped murderously at me. I sidestepped the diagonal cut, then closed and slashed at his belly. He tried to twist away, but I laid his flank open.

As he backed from me, pawing his wound, another Bharashadi leaped in through a window and collided with him. My first foe spun down and hit the wall while the other, who had his legs cut from beneath him, landed facefirst. He bounced up from the ground, and his neck looked broken to me, but I crushed his skull with an overhand blow to make sure. Bringing my sword back around, I beat down the first Bharashadi's ax and trimmed his skull down to the level of his eyes.

The terrible cacophony of battle swirled around me, as exhilarating and obscene as the tune Fialchar had played for the Emperor. Someone in the inner courtyard shouted about the horses while someone else cried "Up there!" I heard the wet thunk of an arrow hitting home, Cruach's bass barks, and the terrified neighing of horses. A scream ending in a gurgle marked the end of Aleix's life, though it vanished beneath a Bharashadi's victorious roar. Bharashadi voices howled in delight or pain, and the sound of steel on steel rang throughout the house.

I saw Bharashadi run down the main corridor, then another jumped over Aleix's body and into the room where I stood. He bore a black sword easily a foot longer than mine. Crystalline fangs flashed within a rot gray mouth as he smiled at me. I dropped into a guard and he laughed with the same choked snarl I had heard in a hundred nightmares. Taller and stronger than I, this was a creature deserving of life only in bad dreams, yet here it faced me with three yards of sharpened steel separating us.

The Bharashadi warrior hissed at me and brought his sword around in a diagonal slash. I blocked it and staggered beneath the impact, but remained on my feet. His blade came back to his right shoulder, and he brought it crashing down again at my left shoulder. This time I parried higher than before, having anticipated the attack, but I had no time to riposte before he tried the same cut a third time.

I parried high right, then slid forward and kicked at his right knee. He moved away, so my heel missed his leg, but my spur slashed across his knee. The wound surprised him, which made him hesitate a moment. I feinted an attack at his face, and he parried across his body. I shifted to my left, moving opposite his parry, and disengaged my blade from his. Sliding my blade forward, I hooked the tip in his right armpit, stabbed, and ripped the blade free.

Steaming purple blood pulsed from the wound. Any human foe I had struck that badly would have retired to staunch the wound before he died. I already knew better than to expect that from one of these monsters, so I ducked his return cut, then slashed from low left to upper right, nearly severing his right knee from behind. His leg bent funny, and he went down, though he still snarled at me defiantly.

Two more Bharashadi came in through the windows, and I knew I was done. Then I heard our horses running through the corridor toward the courtyard. In desperation I whistled loud and long for Stail, then set myself to try and kill the two ax-wielding Chademons facing me. As I did so Audin's words came to me: Men die *trying, but they* live *by doing*!

Stail burst into the room through the doorway from the central corridor. The Bharashadi on the horse's back smashed into the lintel, his head snapping back. He unceremoniously somersaulted from the saddle back over the stallion's rump and crashed to the floor. Bleeding from several wounds, the horse barreled into one of the two Chademons facing me, pitching him forward. I slipped to the left, then swung with all my might and chopped free through the Chademon's neck.

As his body fell beside me, the Bharashadi I had wounded in the armpit stabbed up from the floor, driving his sword up into Stail's chest. The horse shrieked and stomped both hooves through the Chademon's rib cage. Blood running from his nostrils and a pink foam on his mouth, Stail fell on his side, pinning the last Chademon against the wall. I heard both of the Bharashadi's legs break, then my slash struck all life from his eyes.

Not thinking clearly, I ran from my room and down the corridor to the inner courtyard. I saw Osane and

Tyrchon fighting a rearguard action. Behind them the others retreated into the more defensible part of the mansion, the one built into Gorecrag itself. I doubt any of them saw me because of the dozen or so Bharashadi between us, but even if they had, there was nothing they could have done. I was as far beyond their reach as Castel Payne was beyond mine.

I heard a hiss behind me and spun to face one of the largest Bharashadi I had yet seen. He looked at me and laughed, then hissed something I took to be a command. The Chademons broke off their attack on my companions and moved to surround me from one side, while the other Chademons in the corridor cut off that route of escape. I kept my sword in a guard and watched the Bharashadi warrior study the steaming blood dripping down over the blade.

Behind me my companions shut and barred the doors to their sanctuary. As I slowly turned a circle to keep the Chademons at bay, I saw the door to Roarke's infirmary still closed; but two smaller Bharashadi were heading for it. As last I knew Cruach had been left to guard Roarke, I figured the first sorcerer through the door would have quite a surprise waiting for him.

The big Bharashadi crackle-hissed. "You are a virgin from Wallfar. Your flesh will be sweet."

I turned around to face him. "And I will drink your blood before you taste my flesh." I reached up with my left hand and pulled my face mask away. "Before this night is done, you will wish you had my face on a *vindictxvara*." I looked around at the other Bharashadi, and they looked at me with what I can only imagine was awe at the audacity of my boast.

Their surprise bought me a couple more seconds of life, allowing me to see the pair of Bharashadi sorcerers open the door to Roarke's infirmary. Cruach's leap bowled the first magicker over, and I saw purple blood geyser onto the wall as the hound ripped his teeth free of the sorcerer's throat. Cruach then charged back into the infirmary after the second one. I heard a scream, then a thunderous, roiling ball of red-gold fire blasted back out the door and up through the roof.

As flaming bits of rafters and sharp fragments of roof tile started to rain down, I struck at my distracted enemies. My first thrust punched through one Chademon's belly. I yanked the blade free into a crosscut slash that disemboweled a second demon and thought I might even account for a third before one of the others buried an ax in my skull.

I spun, placing my back to the gap I had opened in the Bharashadi circle, in hopes of catching one of the Chademons coming at my back. One was, but not under his own power.

He stumbled toward me, his chest a ruin because of the emerald hoof that had kicked through him as easily as if he was dry-rot wood.

The Emerald Horse reared up and neighed defiantly, then slammed both hooves down, crushing tiles beneath them. Behind him, strewn along the corridor, I saw broken and dying Bharashadi, and yet the only blood on the jewel stallion came from their wounds. The Chademons in the courtyard melted away from him like night before the dawn.

Without a second thought I tangled the fingers of my left hand in his mane and leaped onto his broad back. His body felt warm and soft, as though it were living tissue not stone. I braced myself to be thrown off him, knowing that to lose my place was to die. To my surprise the Emerald Horse did nothing to rid himself of me.

In fact, he did nothing. He remained utterly still, as if he had become a statue.

I gently prodded him with my heels. "Go."

He remained motionless.

The Chademons began to recover from their fear.

"Get going." I tightened my knees and gave him some spur.

The Chademons began to creep closer.

"Go. Fly!" I slapped my left hand against his neck. "Fly, you stupid beast, fly like the wind, dammit!"

He reared and spun back toward the corridor with no warning. I barely got my grip on his mane again when he leaped away from the closing *Bharashadi* warriors. His ears pressed flat against his head, and with me hunkered down with my head along his neck, he raced back through the mansion. His hooves struck sparks from the stones as he galloped out into the courtyard. Faster and faster he ran, faster than any horse had ever run before. The rushing air made my eyes water, blurring the vision of broken bodies, burning demons, and crushed stone outside the mansion.

On he raced, acting in full accord with what I had commanded. His long strides carried us the length of the outer courtyard, scattering laggard Black Shadows. I laughed defiantly at them, then my laughter died in my throat.

The horse's speed increased.

The distance to the edge of the plateau shrunk.

I pulled back on his mane. "Whoa, stop!"

Neighing defiantly, my mount left me no doubt as to who was the master in our relationship. At once magnificent and terrifying, the Emerald Horse galloped off the edge of the plateau and carried me away with him into the night.

24

I realized we were actually flying when I no longer heard hoofbeats. The Emerald Horse kept galloping, but with each motion we rose higher and higher, as if he was running on air. I clung to his back and gently tried to steer him with pressure from my knees. He responded, and we slowly turned back around in a lazy spiral that took us up above First Stop Mansion.

The fireball that had killed Roarke had started the whole south wing burning. In its light I could see long shadows cast by *Bharashadi* warriors gathered around the fountain, and I took heart that I could see damned few of them. Another fire had started burning in the north tower, and scattered around it as if they were embers were the flaming *Bharashadi* bodies Nagrendra's magick had destroyed.

His loss—while no more tragic than Aleix's or Xoayya's deaths—was a great blow to our mission.

With Taci being our only remaining magick user, and she only being able to bring one other person with her to Castel Payne, we stood little or no chance of even getting to see Fialchar. *Given that she is locked away in the Gorecrag stronghold, there is no way we can even contemplate trying to reach Castel Payne until dawn.*

Then it occurred to me where I truly was. I squeezed my knees together and gently tugged back on the Emerald Horse's mane. "Up there, boy, take me to Castel Payne."

The horse's nostrils flared, then his front hooves reached forward as if we were climbing a hill. Up we went on a steep angle. The Emerald Horse's hooves sparked off the very summit of Gorecrag, then he leaped up into the void, and we sailed up to the castle floating in the air.

As he carried me toward it, I almost ordered him to turn away. It was completely stupid for me to try to face Fialchar alone. I had always counted on being part of the group that visited him, but I always saw Kit or Roarke taking the bit in his mouth and dealing with Lord Disaster.

"But they're not here, so that's no longer an option." The idea of facing Fialchar terrified me, but less so than the idea of the Black Shadows resurrecting their dead. If the stories of my father and Fialchar having reached a truce to let my father destroy the B*harashadi* were true— and I believed they were—then approaching him to continue that alliance of convenience was certainly the way to enlist his aid in stopping Packkiller.

We landed inside the ruins of the siege wall, and I slid from the Emerald Horse's back before the jeweled castle. My legs nearly collapsed when they touched the ground, and the evil I had sensed earlier pummeled me. I felt nauseous, but I refused to vomit. I leaned against the Emerald Horse as I steadied myself, then patted him affectionately on the neck. "Wait for me, please."

The horse tossed his head once, then locked himself into a statue that was the very picture of equine pride and arrogance. Despite where I was, I had to laugh. In the broad facet that made up his shoulder I saw my reflection. I flaked off some of the dried blood from where my face mask had been ripped away earlier, then homed my sword in its scabbard and mounted the steps to Fialchar's lair.

I had no idea what to expect. Though many bards loved to sing of the time when Jhesti the Lost Prince fulfilled his vow to pluck a hair from Lord Disaster's beard, they never described Castel Payne beyond the basics. Yes, they told how it floated in the air and sparkled like a jewel, but everyone knew that. Somehow I think that even if they made something up about the interior, they could not make it as horrid as I found it.

The castle itself reminded me in many ways of the Imperial Palace. The two buildings had been laid out with utterly different floor plans, but both showed the incredibly high degree of craftsmanship only available to those who could afford to hire the best. In many ways Castel Payne exceeded the palace in beauty because it had been fitted together from massive crystalline blocks, and light flashed from flaws in the stones. Those flaws created pictures locked away and only available to a viewer standing at one place at one time.

On the other hand, the nature of those pictures were what made Castel Payne obscene. Walking through the first corridor, I saw thousands of faces shrieking in terror. The jewels revealed their hearts to be graphic scenes of torture and abominations and crimes I could not have begun to imagine. What made them even worse was that I knew in my heart that each scene I saw was not just the depraved imagining of some lunatic artist, but a faithful representation of something that had actually happened.

I reached my first intersection and realized I hadn't a clue as to where to go or how to find Fialchar. I started across the intersection to continue in the first corridor and immediately felt a great sense of relief. I knew, then, that given the way my flesh crawled in this place, I had made the wrong choice. I turned and walked deeper into the castle despite a voice in the back of my mind screaming that I was a fool.

I shook my head. *If the quest was supposed to be easy, they would not have given it to someone who is supposed to be a hero.*

The Grand Hallway into which I stepped had no equal in anything I had seen in the Imperial Palace. The arches above me soared so high that the light sparking from the jewel's flaws appeared to be stars. The hallway's far end seemed a day's journey away, yet the sidewalls pressed me uncomfortably closely. I could not reach out and touch them, but they still felt as if they were inching together to crush me between them.

As I walked forward—with each step sublimating the desire to run screaming from this place—I decided this place had to be Fialchar's monument to himself. Throughout I saw trophies so grotesque they could have made a vulture vomit. One statue, for example, showed a naked Aelven lass caught running happily through a field. The artistry necessary to capture the love of life in her eyes had no equal to my knowledge. The statue displayed her virginal innocence, and I felt the same tightening in my chest that I remembered from when I learned Marija had gone out with Nob's grandson.

The statue would have been perfection itself except for the artist's choice of medium. He had rendered the work in meat—a fact hidden from view except when I came close enough to scare away the flies blanketing it. The pungently sour stench of rotting flesh, on the other hand, was unmistakable and inescapable.

Even more chilling were the huge, single block carvings of people set in the walls between the pillars. They had been carved from unnaturally large chunks of a milky, translucent stone. I thought at first it was opal, thereby to mock the Ward Walls. I realized that idea came because bleeding up from beneath the stony flesh of the carven figures I saw colors reflective of their skin, hair, and clothing. The statues reached out into the air with hands outstretched as if pleading with me to free them. One looked as if caught in mid-leap, and I could have sworn another shifted position as I approached it.

I knew distractions would make it harder for me to force myself onward. I focused on the darkened doorway at the far end of the hall and marched on toward it. As I drew closer it became more and more difficult to move. I felt as if I were caught in a blizzard, fighting both thigh-high snowdrifts and a hammering head wind. I gritted my teeth and pushed on, determined that I would not fail after having come so far.

Finally, in the arched doorway, the pressure against me stopped. I felt a moment's respite in the oppressive sensation of dread and even experienced some elation at having come so far. Then, suddenly, the overwhelming evil hit me again. I do not believe it returned with any more potency than before, but in contrast to my fleeting moment of happiness, it threatened to suck me down into oblivion.

I reached out and touched the jeweled wall. From its

cool solidity I drew strength and straightened up. I *have come too far to be sent running now*. I let my anger power me. I adjusted my breastplate and prepared to draw my sword.

I stepped into Fialchar's inner sanctum.

A thin patina of dust covered everything in the dimly lit room. Double rows of pillars held up a circular gallery. All around the walls of the main floor and the gallery I saw shelves with an incredible number of tomes on them. Some, in sets with like bindings, stood at attention and occupied whole shelves, while other, older books, leaned across gaps onto their neighbors. Some outsize volumes lay flat on a shelf with smaller books piled on top until the shelf itself began to bow under the weight.

Between the pillars I saw a number of small tables with all the things I would have expected to see in the libraries of the finest Imperial households. To my left I saw a chess game very near the end. Beyond it a set of crystal goblets and decanters both showed signs of the wine they had once contained having evaporated, caking them with brown residue. On the right I saw a sideboard with what, beneath the mold, might have been a round of cheese and a loaf of bread. Fuzzy, desiccated grapes sat on another tray that might have been silver had the tarnish been scrubbed away. Beyond that, books lay open on other desks, and a quill pen lay on a half-filled page.

All of these things I saw, but they dwindled to insignificance in comparison with the central feature of the domed room. A massive crystal ball, polished to perfection, hung suspended by invisible forces barely a foot above floor level. Directly beneath it I saw a hole in the floor that I had no doubt extended all the way through to the open air below. Surrounding it a hollow golden disc rested on eight gold pillars four feet tall. The pillars clutched the floor with dragon's talons, and arcane symbols twisted through a bizarre dance on the disc itself.

In the crystal globe I saw shifting scenes of Chaos. Rainbow cyclones whirled across the landscape, leaving disruption and altered terrain in their wake. Somewhere a black lake bubbled and burned, yet I saw huge stone ships sailing through it with impunity. Strange creatures, the like of which I had never heard of, stalked through jungles, and somewhere else two tribes of Chademons battled in the middle of a raging lightning storm.

Beyond it, staring into it, Fialchar leaned on the golden disc. I could see the hunch of his shoulders and top of his head outside the sphere's horizon. The sleeves of his robe hid his hands, but I took the twitching cloth to be a sign of his concentration on the sphere's visions. That was why he paid me no attention, and probably why I had gotten that far.

I swallowed my heart back down from my throat and clasped my hands behind my back. In my deepest voice I broke the silence. "I am Lachlan, son of Cardew. I am come on a mission for his Imperial Majesty, Thetys V. He has charged me with the duty of . . ."

Fialchar looked up, his black-emptiness stare skewering my brain. In a second I felt fear, then incredible agony, as if I had been torn into a million million pieces. Hellfire cauterized each of the shreds, then something else jammed us back together again. I felt myself falling, then landed on a strangely soft, squishy stone.

I found myself in a small room completely constructed out of the milky stone I had seen in the Grand Hallway. I pushed down with my right hand and found the stone gave beneath the pressure. It resisted me somewhat, but flowed away from my fingers as if it were some sort of molten pillow. It did not quite feel like living flesh, except in that it was warm, but came close enough to make me uncomfortable.

All but instantly I realized I had been trapped inside one of the blocks in the walls of the Grand Hallway. I shifted my shoulders to ease the residual aches of having been banished to this prison. "If that is how much it hurts to be teleported, no wonder Fialchar was so rude at the ball."

I laughed at my own joke and took a little pleasure in hearing it echoed mutely by the prison walls. I looked toward the front of the little box and saw a clear view of the Grand Hallway. Scrambling to my feet, and steadying myself against the shifting of the floor, I walked forward. I reached out with my right hand and, even though I saw nothing, I could feel the same sort of resistance that I got with the walls or floor.

Having seen, from the outside, the inability of various people to break through the wall, I drew my sword. I pressed the edge against the transparent panel and tried to shave away a thin layer. The blade skittered off the surface with no damage to it or the wall.

Shifting the weapon around, I tried to stab it into the clear panel. It met resistance, and the edge appeared not to cut the invisible barrier. I felt the wall pushing back against me and realized that I would be unable to maintain my pressure on it for very long. Dropping to one knee, I tilted the sword down and jammed the pommel into the floor. Trapping the blade between the floor and the wall, I let my prison push my sword against the clear wall.

Uncertain what to expect, but rather pleased with my effort, I tucked myself back in the corner of my prison. If the pressure proved too much, I knew it was possible my sword would shatter and spray the small room with metal fragments. Drawing myself up into a ball, I kept my right hand across the top of my knees and hunkered down so my armor protected my face.

Looking out between my thumb and forefinger, I could see no real change in my sword's position, but I did notice that the Grand Hallway seemed to be lightening. As sunlight poured down its length, I saw shadows shift faster than they should have. It occurred to me that Fialchar's prisons probably operated as slow zones, preserving the lives of his captives.

This did nothing to make me feel better, especially when I remembered some of the torture scenes immortalized in the castle's building blocks. Still, Fialchar had imprisoned me when he could have killed me, which meant he would be dealing with me eventually. Absent any means of escape, all I could do was wait.

Wait, as Roarke was waiting. The image of my friend being consumed by a fireball slammed into me. Part of me wondered if his death had been any easier than that of Nagrendra or Xoayya. I couldn't imagine what it must have felt like to be pulverized as the top of the tower contracted so violently. With any luck, or if the gods had any mercy, they all died so quickly they had no idea what was happening.

It struck me that could have been the case with Nagrendra and Roarke, but for Xoayya the situation had to be different. Had a vision of her future come to her a second or two before the stones ground her bones and flesh into paste? Or had she seen nothing and realized, as the red-gold tendrils snaked their way around the tower, that she had no future at all?

I snorted angrily, remembering all the times she told me that whatever happened to her was fate, fate for which I was not responsible. With a laugh and a comment she had absolved me of any complicity in her death, but that was easy to do. She was dead, and I survived. If not for me, she never would have been in a position to be killed the way she was. It might have been her destiny to die in Chaos, but I was left certain that she didn't have to die.

I wondered how things would have been different if Geoff had gone to Herakopolis, or if even Dalt had made the trip. Would they have let Xoayya come along? Would they have allowed her to be in the tower? How many of my slain companions would still be alive had someone else been making decisions?

As my thoughts took me further down into a dark spiral, piling up errors and compounding guilt, I realized I was finding I had failed in a test that had no right answers. As much as I could imagine my brothers doing different things, some of them with better results, I also had to acknowledge that other errors could have had more dire consequences. My frustration was not with what I had done or failed to do, but with my inability to control every little factor in the world. I wanted everything to be perfect and go my way, but I also knew that was impossible.

I needed to escape that black cloud of self-recrimination, so I forced myself to think about something else. As I had long ago learned to do, I cleared my mind and visualized a chessboard. I arranged the pieces in their proper places. I remembered Geoff's demand that I at least look at the board when I played him, and that brought a smile to my face. I slowly started to work my way through that last game with my brother, correcting his mistakes to make it last longer.

I found concentrating difficult and thought it might have been some enchantment placed on the prisons to prevent magickers from spelling their way out again. I closed my eyes, forced myself to focus, and even recited the rhyme that had saved me from Fialchar at the ball, but it had no effect. Then I realized that what was giving me trouble was that the last game I had with Nob kept bleeding over into the game with Geoff.

As I let those two games meld together I found myself returning to a board configuration I knew I had never played to, but I had seen before. I shook my head as I remembered where I had seen it. In *Lord Disaster's library*! *It's a wonder you have gotten this far, Locke.*

That game, I decided, was boring. The Imperial player, who, according to the position of the movestone had the next move, would win. All he had to do was advance his Empress two squares forward and he had Fialchar in checkmate. I felt fairly certain the game that had gotten the board to that point had been spectacular, but now the game only awaited the coup de grace to finish it. Were I playing Chaos, I would have resigned.

A sudden blast of heat from the front of my prison brought my head up and opened my eyes. A blue glow suffused with red lightning oozed over the transparent panel. The energy in it crackled, and I felt a tingle run through me. The square panel began to dissolve as if being nibbled away at all edges. Abruptly it shrank to a circle, a red-gold sheen coated it, then compressed it into a pinpoint sphere which vanished in a burst of white light.

I blinked my eyes in the aftermath of the flash and heard my sword clatter to the ground. I saw someone standing there in half profile, then rubbed at my eyes. "Roarke? You're dead!"

The Chaos Rider shook his head, keeping the left side of his face hidden in shadow. "I feel dead, but I am not—not by half. Let's get you out of there."

Something struck me as wrong about him. "Your eye patch. Where is it?"

He turned to face me. "I no longer need it."

His right eye, as always, was an arctic blue tinged with *Chaosfire*. His left, which had remained hidden beneath the eye patch for as long as I had known him, was a golden orb the like of which I had only seen in *Bharashadi* faces. "Your eye? What happened?" I slid from my prison and stood beside him. "How did you free me?"

"There are a number of things for which I must apologize, Locke, and deceiving you is one of them." He rested both his hands on my shoulders. "I didn't want to, but I had no choice, for reasons that will become apparent. As for what happened to my eye, well, I was with your father on his last expedition to Chaos. I have carried this eye with me since that time."

"You were with my father? What happened to him?"

"The story is too long for the telling now, Locke, and we have other things to do." He pointed down toward the end of the hallway. "Let us get the staff and get out of here. Think of it as what your father would have done."

I shivered, unable to decide if I could trust him or not. A wave of anger surged through me, but in its wake I realized he didn't have to come to Castel Payne, nor did he have to free me from my prison. *The mission comes first, which he's certainly kept in mind. Just as my father would.*

I picked up my sword and followed him toward Fialchar's library. "Roarke, at least tell me how my father died."

"I can't, Locke, because I don't know." I saw him shudder. "I never saw your father go down. All I remember is that we faced hundreds of *Bharashadi*, and I cast spell after spell after spell to defeat them. It was the last great crusade against Kothvir, and I cast spells until I was exhausted."

We marched into Lord Disaster's sanctum. "At battle's end I found myself pitted against a mortally wounded Kothvir. Your father had killed him, but the *Bharashadi* didn't know that yet. I shoved a dagger into him, and he tore my left eye out." Roarke raised his left hand to touch the scars on his cheek. "Kothvir collapsed on top of me, and I was ready to die happily, knowing he was finally dead."

"But it amused me to deny you that surcease!" Fialchar stood between us and the crystal globe. His hands hung at his side, holding the Staff of Emeterio across the front of his thighs and parallel to the floor.

Roarke stopped and regarded the bone-and-metal-faced sorcerer without fear. "Our host here found it funny to pluck for me Kothvir's eye and stuff it into my head."

"It has been a long time, Zephaniah. I always wondered what had become of you since you never deigned to visit my realm again."

"I take great comfort in knowing you were concerned for me." Roarke folded his arms across his chest. "Giving me Kothvir's eye meant my brethren in the City of Sorcerers were not very happy about me wielding magick."

"It pains me to think you were inconvenienced."

"Just as it pained you to know my possessing Kothvir's eye on the other side of the Ward Walls would mean your enemy would never trouble you again."

The ancient sorcerer nodded slowly. "I did find that an interesting side benefit to my act of charity."

"I know of another act of charity that should interest you, then." Roarke glanced at me. "Locke has come for the Staff of Emeterio. Give it to him."

Lord Disaster slowly shook his head. "Even a sorcerer of your paltry skills could understand why I will not give this staff over to him. Mind you, I believe Cardew's son had begun to state his request in a much more mannerly way than you. Have the years soured you so?"

"I will not play games with you, Fialchar, because this charade is beneath the both of us. You know I know of the Bharashadi Necroleum. You should also know the Bharashadi are preparing to resurrect their dead."

Lord Disaster barked out his maggot laughter. "Vrasha has long sought after a way to fulfill the Bharashadi bargain with their dark god, Kinruquel. As he has not the ability to pierce the Ward Walls, and as those of my Black Churchers it amuses me to grant him are incompetent, he will forever remain frustrated."

"Perhaps, then, it would *amuse* you to learn that while you were dancing with the ladies of the Empire, this Vrasha stole the Fistfire Sceptre from beneath your feet!" Roarke mimicked Fialchar's pronunciation perfectly. "While you threatened the Emperor and laughed to yourself here, he has brought the sceptre to Chaos."

That news clearly shocked Fialchar. "This is impossible! I would have known."

"Unless his possession of the sceptre shields him from magicks you focus through the staff."

Lord Disaster's eyes grew distant, and I sensed an involved discussion of magick looming on the horizon. I turned away from them and looked at the chessboard again. "Which side were you playing?"

The tall lich stared down at me with contempt. "You have to ask? Chaos, of course, and in my realm we move first."

"Oh." I reached out and pushed the Empress forward two spaces. "Checkmate."

"What have you *done*?!" Lord Disaster stalked across the floor at me, leaving the staff hovering in the air near the crystal ball. He grasped a pillar in each hand and gripped them so hard that the stone began to crumble. I saw flames shoot from his eyes in golden puffs as he looked down at the board. "Do you know what you have done?"

I nodded. "I won."

He looked at me, eyes still blazing, then snorted. "Cardew's son? Will you be as much of an impediment to me as he was?" He raised himself to his full height and folded his hands into the opposite sleeves of his robe. The staff floated to him. "I have no fond memories of your father."

"And I doubt he had any of you." I rested my hands on my hips. "I have come for the Staff of Emeterio because I will oppose the Bharashadi. I will destroy their Necroleum, and I will stop Vrasha Packkiller from invading the Empire. Give the staff to me."

The vehemence and commanding tone in my voice surprised me, and seemed to shock Lord Disaster. I braced against being sent back to my prison. His necrotic eyes narrowed, and the flesh around them screamed as it tightened. One clawed hand started from a sleeve toward my throat, but he restrained himself, and his expression eased.

"So brash, so young. So foolish." His hands emerged slowly from his robe in a gesture of openness. "It is my free choice and desire to lend you this staff. You may, in return, rid me of the nuisance Vrasha has become."

I reached out, and the Staff of Emeterio came to me. Its cool ebon shaft warmed to my touch and felt as I might imagine Marija's flesh would beneath a caress. I started to think of her as I had on the night of the ball, but that memory carried with it enough anger and disgust that it shocked me out of remembering. I looked up and caught Fialchar staring at me.

"Yes, Lachlan, this staff is full of dangers." With an effort he smiled almost beneficently. "It really is not safe in your hands. It could corrupt you."

"Whereas you are beyond corruption?"

"No, my dear child, I *am* corruption."

Roarke grabbed my arm and tugged me toward the exit. "Then we shall not detain you, oh Duke of Decay. When we are finished with your toy, we will leave it where you may find it again." He squeezed my arm. "Say good-bye to our host, Locke."

"Good-bye."

"So formal and final, Zephaniah. That is as you might wish it to be, but no, I think not." Fialchar stood there and watched us back out of the Great Hall. "Let us say 'Farewell, until we meet again,' for we *shall* meet again. Know it. Fear it."

25

Roarke all but hauled me bodily from Castel Payne. Once outside my mind began to clear, but before that I felt as if I had been there many times before. It felt akin to having seen some place in a dream, then seeing it again when awake. My confusion concerned me until I realized I had easily been a full day without sleep.

"Roarke, how did you find me?"

The Chaos Rider shrugged. "After I got out of the mansion's south wing, I saw signs of the Emerald Horse's passing. As I could not find you among the dead, and I knew we needed to get the staff from Fialchar, I decided to check Castel Payne. When I found the Emerald Horse here, I assumed you were here as well. As it turns out, Fialchar gave you the accommodations he had given me during my visit."

I walked through the courtyard to the Emerald Horse. "You have been here before?"

"After Fialchar gave me Kothvir's eye, he decided to keep me to see what the results of his experiment would be. I would be there still, I suspect, but Jhesti freed me soon after I had been captured."

I frowned. "Jhesti? He's just a legend." As I patted the Emerald Horse on the neck he went from being a statue to a mobile creature again.

"Just a legend, eh?" Roarke laughed lightly. "The Emerald Horse is just a legend."

"Blooded on the first thrust." I hauled myself up on the Emerald Horse's back. "So he helped you back to the Empire?"

"All the way to the capital, me and Cruach both. I did not fare much better going through the wall last time than I did this time."

"What did happen to you?"

The magicker shook his head. "I am not certain, but I know Kothvir's eye, because of the bargain the B*harashadi* made with their god, is still linked to him. Kothvir is dead, but alive and here, in Chaos, I know what he knew, and I can see what he has seen. Aside from feeling like a white-hot poker had been driven into my eye as I crossed over, I think I went unconscious to give my mind time to sort out everything. You know how it is said you should walk a mile in another man's boots before you judge him? Well, with this eye I'm walking around in two pairs of boots at the same time, and that is not easy to handle."

I nodded. "I think I understand." I looked toward the horizon and saw the sun slowly setting. "It is later than I thought."

"Time is slightly accelerated here on Castel Payne." Roarke squinted at the sun. "If we leave now we might be able to reach the mansion before the second wave of B*harashadi* warriors hits it."

I squeezed the Emerald Horse's ribs. "Go back to the mansion. Go. Fly!"

The horse did nothing.

Roarke, rising up into the air on a semitransparent red disc he'd created with a spell, laughed at me. "Some horses don't take their masters seriously."

I dug my heels into the Emerald Horse's ribs. "Go! Fly, damn you!"

The Emerald Horse leaped into the air and galloped along until he placed himself just slightly ahead of Roarke. During my captivity Castel Payne had moved a considerable distance from First Stop Mansion. Urging the Emerald Horse on, I knew we were not going to make it to the mansion before night had fallen.

I glanced over at Roarke and saw a blue glow covering his face like a featureless face mask. "What is that?"

"A spell. Through it I can see better. The Bharashadi are massing. The southern wing of the mansion is gone, but the doors leading to the interior are holding. It looks like the Bharashadi are trying to build a battering ram out of timbers taken from the north tower."

"Any sign of our people?"

"No, but I would guess the Bharashadi have doubled their number from last night."

I shivered, and it wasn't because of the chill in the night air. "How can we stop them?"

Roarke drifted closer. "Let me have that wonderwand Fialchar gave you. I'll have the Necroleum filled to overflowing in no time."

I started to hand it to him, then hesitated. I had known Roarke for only a relatively short time. While it was true he had never let me down in all that time, he *had* lied to me. Fialchar had warned me about how powerful the staff could be. Could it corrupt Roarke? Did he lust after its power? Would he give it back so I could use it to destroy the Necroleum?

The blue glow evaporated from Roarke's face. "I understand your confusion and hesitation, Locke. Just remember this: your father brought me along with him on what he knew would be the most dangerous mission he would ever undertake."

"And now my father is dead."

"Right, so let us make sure that doesn't happen to your cousin and the others."

I recalled the decision I'd made about him in Castel Payne and nodded. I held the staff out to him. "I trust you, Roarke. That's not because my father trusted you, but because I do."

"You'll not regret it."

Roarke's hands closed around the staff, and he stiffened for a moment. Then a grin grew into a smile on his face. The disc became more gold than red, then shifted to a green color. That color bled up into the smoky quartz at the top of the staff. "This is better than warm blankets on a cold night." He glanced down at the ground and started down in a slow spiral. "Can you whistle?"

"Whistle?" I puckered my lips and blew out a few notes. "Sure. Why?"

"Whistle me up some dancing music." Roarke jerked his head back toward Castel Payne. "Lord Ugly is bound to be watching, and I want him to see how a dance among your enemies should properly be arranged."

Roarke's flying disc descended to the ground in the center of the outer courtyard. Bright sparks ignited the half dozen Bharashadi upon whom he had landed, scattering them in a flaming panic. Roarke brought the Staff of Emeterio's heel down to touch the grounded disc. The disc shrank, intensifying the green tint in the quartz. It appeared as if the staff had sucked up the disc like a mosquito feeding on blood.

Roarke said something and hammered the staff's butt against the paving stones. At once a tangle of glowing green tendrils shot out of the top, draining the crystal of color. Each tendril struck a different Bharashadi warrior in the forehead. Roarke hit the staff against the ground again, forcing all the Bharashadi to slowly stand and turn to face him.

In time with the song I whistled, Roarke started the Bharashadi dancing around. As the Emerald Horse flew closer to the earth, I heard Roarke begin to sing.

> *Golden eyes aglow*
> *Spirits cold and black as night,*
> *Please take out your swords*
> *For now you're going to fight!*

At his command the Bharashadi bared their weapons. Cruel blades, hooked and barbed, somehow looked yet more sinister in the green light. The enchanted Bharashadi moved in a grand circle centered on Roarke. Many of them glared at him, furious at being trapped by his power, but impotent to do anything about it.

He sang on.

> *Find yourself a friend,*
> *Think not on your plight.*
> *Slash and stab so bright blood flows,*
> *To this slaying song tonight.*

The Emerald Horse set hoof to solid earth outside the killing circle. One by one, as Bharashadi warriors chopped each other down, the green lines winked away. The others, as victor moved at victor, wove together in a complex braid that slowly unraveled itself. Purple blood ran in torrents in the courtyard, raising a lavender fog that hid most of the hacked and cloven bodies.

Finally, only one Bharashadi remained. Roarke looked at him, then twisted the staff so that the line of power snapped free of his brow. The Chademon's head whipped around as if he had been punched. He shook his head to clear it, then looked at the carnage surrounding him.

Screaming in rage, he raised his bloody sword and charged at Roarke. The magicker held his right hand out, palm forward, fingers splayed, as if signaling the Bharashadi to stop his charge. Red power surrounded Roarke's hand, then the sorcerer clenched his hand down into a fist. The Bharashadi crumpled and fell, clutching at his chest. He died with violet blood bubbling up between his lips.

Roarke, picking his way between the bodies, held the staff out to me. "Very effective as a tool, but I do not want the burden of responsibility for what it allows me to do."

I accepted it back from him and slid from the Emerald Horse's back. The staff again warmed to my touch, but I ignored its message. "Let us see to our companions."

We ran through the mansion corridor to the interior courtyard. I would have continued running up to the doors leading into the mountain, but Roarke held me back. Before I could ask why, he gestured, and I saw a nebulous blue glow in the area before the doors. "What is that?"

"A *triggerfield*. It's like a *leechspell*, but bigger, and you don't have to do anything to make it work. It will suck enough energy out of whatever blunders into it to trigger some sort of spell. I doubt Taci had anything pleasant in mind." He pointed at the doors with his right index finger. I saw a blue nimbus surround his finger as he started moving his hand through the air.

From right to left on the door, blue flames ran in lines following the arcane symbols Roarke drew in the air. It took me a minute to figure out he was mirror-writing, which told me the burning letters had to extend all the way through the doors. His message, "All is well, Locke and I have entertained your guests," spelled itself out in letters a foot tall. By the time the last word had been written, the first had begun to fade, leaving no burn marks to show it had ever been there.

"An intriguing trick, Roarke, but they do not know you as a sorcerer. How will they identify the 'I' in your message?"

"Taci will know. If she does not, Nagrendra will."

I shook my head. "Nagrendra's dead."

"What?"

"The B*harashadi* sorcerers you slew first killed him. They crushed the tower."

"What about Xoayya?"

My shoulders slumped. "Gone, too. They never stood a chance."

"Yes, but from the carnage I saw, they sold their lives dearly. They went the way Riders are meant to die." He smiled weakly, then looked at the doors. "The *triggerfield* is gone. They are coming out."

I heard the sound of a bar being shifted behind the doors, then they cracked open. Streaking through them first came Cruach, who barked once happily, and headed straight for us. Roarke dropped to one knee to welcome the dog, but Cruach leaped over him at me. Unprepared for such an enthusiastic greeting, I fell over backwards and got a bar dexter splashed across my face with a big, wet tongue.

Roarke and I both laughed as Cruach jumped back and licked his face, too, but our laughter died as the survivors came out of the hole in the mountain. They all looked tired—Taci especially—and still wary about the possible presence of B*harashadi*. Everyone had soot stains on their clothing and faces, and more than one bloody rag staunched nicks and cuts. They all carried their weapons in their hands, except Kit and Eirene. Between them they bore a makeshift litter.

I scrambled to my feet and ran over to where they set Tyrchon down. In his right hand he clutched a dagger that looked much like those that hung on my wall in Herakopolis. It had the same hook cut in the back of the blade, and it looked to me as if a piece of it had broken off. The blade also had a line drawing on it, and the image I saw unmistakably represented Tyrchon.

Roarke knelt at Tyrchon's side and gently lifted the wounded man's left arm from the litter. He pulled open the leather jerkin and there, near the armpit, I saw a black hole in Tyrchon's chest. I nearly gagged when I caught a whiff of the suppurating wound—and was immediately reminded of the sculpture in Castel Payne.

Dark pus bubbled and oozed out of the wound. "Roarke, what caused that?"

He tapped the knife. "V*indictxvara*." He looked up at Kit. "What happened, Lieutenant?"

Kit hung his head. "After the first night and the explosion we heard, we decided we needed to scout the area. We had lost five people, you two, Nagrendra, Xoayya, and Aleix—six if you count Cruach. We had to try to find you before Taci could set up some defenses here, but . . ."

I held a hand up. "You did the right thing, Kit. We were beyond helping."

Kit gave me a thin-lipped smile. "Thanks. When we opened up again, Tyrchon and Hansen volunteered to go out and see what they could find. As nearly as we can determine, they ran into a group of Bharashadi and had a fight. Tyrchon returned with Cruach and this hole in him. Hansen did not make it back."

"We tried to find Nagrendra and Xoayya." Eirene shook her head. "The Bharashadi did an excellent job on the north tower. There's not a trace of them left."

I squatted and took a good look at Tyrchon's wound and the knife that caused it. "Roarke, that knife could have made a cut that would fit within that wound, but it couldn't have done that much damage. This looks like a cut that's been infected for weeks."

"Have you ever had poison ivy?"

"Yes."

"Vindictxvara does the same sort of thing. It is magically created to be antithetical to the person who is pictured on it. If the person who created it wounds the person for whom it is made, the attacker's hatred becomes like a poison. The weapon gnaws away at both the body and spirit of its victim." Roarke tapped the knife blade. "At least we have the vindictxvara that made the wound. I assume the wielder is dead?"

Kit nodded. "That much Tyrchon communicated before he fainted."

Taci shrugged her shoulders. "I know that should make healing him easier, but I am not that skilled in curative magic."

"Nor am I." Roarke shook his head. "There is no way we can get him back to the Empire in time for him to be healed. He has a day and a half at best, I would guess."

"Wait a minute, Roarke." I smiled. "Do you remember what you told me my father had done with one of his men on an expedition?"

"No . . ."

"You told me that he placed the man in one of the slow zones within Chaos. If I remember the maps correctly, there was one with a thirty-to-one ratio about two hours from here. We can put him there until we can get help for him, and we'd have a month and a half to get that help, too."

Osane frowned at the suggestion. "The ride will kill him. The terrain is too broken, too much jarring."

"Not a problem, Holiness." I whistled, and the Emerald Horse, head held high and mane flying, came trotting into the courtyard.

Eirene's face darkened. "What is that *thing* doing here?"

"Easy, Eirene, it's with me now." I turned to the Emerald Horse.

Roarke stood. "Good idea, Locke, but you cannot use your horse to fly Tyrchon to that spot." A red disc spread out from Roarke's feet and slid beneath the litter. "I will get him there, then join you on the road."

Taci leaped back from the disc. "Chaos magic! Who are you? What are you?" She raised her hands and seemed poised to cast defensive spells.

Roarke looked at her, and I noticed the rest of our company had likewise withdrawn from the red circle. Eirene somehow managed to keep her face impassive, but Osane and Kit both watched Roarke suspiciously. Cruach sniffed at the circle.

"I am, now, Roarke. I am still the person you have all known and, I hope, grown to think of as a companion on this journey. I was not always Roarke, however, and therein is the problem." He opened his hands to show they concealed no weapons, but that did not put Taci at ease.

"Twenty years ago I answered to the name

Zephaniah. In the City of Sorcerers I was known for being quick and not much on ceremony. My masters saw I was trouble from the start. They looked forward to my going into Chaos and dying. I knew that and limited myself to hunting down creatures in Menal and Tarris provinces."

The Sunbird Bishop slowly nodded. "I have heard other members of the Church refer to bounty-hunter magickers as 'Zefs.'"

"Ah, to be so fondly remembered." Roarke smiled, and that did begin to calm Taci. "Cardew and Driscoll had heard of me and asked me to join their last expedition. They figured *Bharashadi* warriors had made *vindictxvara* spears to kill all the sorcerers in the Valiant Lancers, so they wanted some new blood to surprise them. I agreed to go with them. You could hear the cheering from the City of Sorcerers all the way to Herakopolis.

"The fighting was nasty, and surviving it not that pleasant, either. Fialchar gave me Kothvir's eye to replace the one the *Bharashadi* warlord had taken from me. He thought that was funny. I found it meant all my magick was tainted with Chaos. You know about the paranoia concerning Chaos in the City of Sorcerers. I was not allowed to work magick there or anywhere in the Empire. You saw what happened when I crossed here, so returning to Chaos was not an option."

Kit nodded. "You picked up an ax and became Roarke the caravan guard."

"An ax is a fine weapon. Requires no skill, just brute strength." Roarke smiled broadly. "Given that Kothvir's eye could see through the patch I wore, I didn't even have a blind side. It even sleeps lightly, which is good given the sorts of places I spend my idle time. You all would do well to sleep while I take Tyrchon to the place where he can rest. We are half a day out from the Necroleum and will have to ride hard in the morning."

Donla shook her head. "I thought we were going to have to search for the Necroleum. How do you know how far it is?"

Roarke closed his right eye and stared at her with the gold orb. "I know because Kothvir knows. He can't be resurrected until he gets his eye back, and he's been waiting for its return for the last sixteen years. He wants it so badly he's been giving me directions to the Necroleum ever since we crossed over—my coma resulted from the battle of wills we were having over who would control my body on this side of the Ward Walls. I've won, and we have the staff. It's time to take him up on his invitation to visit the Necroleum and finish what was started on my last trip into Chaos."

26

Roarke gestured and the red disc floated up into the air. Bearing the sorcerer and Tyrchon on the litter, it rose above the courtyard, then dipped and sailed in a long, slow curve toward the south. As it sank from sight, the only light left in the courtyard came from the Emerald Horse's green glow.

Eirene scowled in Roarke's direction. "I certainly hope that disc can carry more than two. If not, we will not make it to the Necroleum in less than two days."

"Why not?" I glanced at the open hole in the mountain. "We put the remounts in there. They should have been safe."

Kit nodded. "Should have been. One of them stepped into a nest of blind *ghast-vipers*—or their chaotic equivalent. The herd lost four to snakebites and two others to broken legs as they ran wild through the dark. We do not know where the others have gone, but the ones we have recaptured appear disinclined to venture out into a courtyard awash in *Bharashadi* bodies and blood."

"Can't we do anything?"

Osane toed a dead *Bharashadi* with her right foot. "We can burn the bodies and withhold food from the horses. When they get hungry enough they will come out."

"But that will take too long and leave them too weak to be of much use to us." Kit looked over at Eirene and shook his head. "Either Roarke can work magick to get us to the Necroleum, or we have a long walk ahead of us."

I patted the Emerald Horse's right shoulder. "There is another solution, I think." Reaching up I stroked his neck. "Summon your herd. My friends need mounts, and on the backs of your herd they will ride into battle."

The Emerald Horse looked down at me, and his nostrils flared defiantly, then he nodded. I stepped back as he reared up on his hind legs and let out a neigh that was all but silent to the ears, but hammered through my chest like thunder. It echoed from Gorecrag like a phantom's ghostly whisper. His forelegs kicked out into the air, and he again called to his herd. His forehooves slammed down into the ground again, pulverizing more tiles, then he butted me with his head, and I stroked his neck.

Everyone looked around and silence fell in the courtyard as we strained to hear any sign his call had been heeded. Eirene's scowl lightened at first, but quickly deepened as we heard nothing. She folded her arms across her chest, then spat roughly in the Emerald Horse's direction. "Thieves never return what they steal."

The Emerald Horse's head came up, and he matched

her opalescent stare with one of his own. His tail swished through the air, the pace quickening as muscles bunched at the corners of Eirene's jaw. The Emerald Horse snorted once, then raised his head and broke for the tunnel out to the front courtyard.

Eirene laughed triumphantly. "Looks like you'll be walking, too, Locke."

My cheeks burned with a blush, but I met her stare openly. "We'll see."

"Sure, after our boots have worn out and our feet are blistered." Eirene shook her head. "It was a nice fantasy, Locke, but reality in Chaos is seldom that pleasant."

Kit placed his left hand on her right arm. "Wait, Eirene, I hear something."

Donla smiled. "I do as well. Dry thunder."

The sound of hoofbeats on the ground started as a distant pounding rhythm. I could not so much hear it as feel it, and that sensation grew as the herd approached. Like a sailor lured to a reef by a siren's song, I started out toward the courtyard. The others pressed in behind me, but Eirene broke through the knot of us and reached the courtyard first.

There at the far edge of the clearing, the Emerald Horse's herd drew up and arrayed itself in a battle line facing First Stop Mansion. As I and my companions left the building, we similarly spread out into a line to face them. In the middle, standing amid broken and bleeding Bharashadi bodies, the Emerald Horse waited. He glanced at Eirene contemptuously, then tossed his head up and down several times. He neighed and looked at Kit.

I figured out what the Emerald Horse was trying to communicate. "Kit, step forward."

When I spoke, my cousin did as requested. The

Emerald Horse stamped twice on the ground. From among the ranks of horses came one creature of dun fur and *Chaosfire* eyes. From his head curled a pair of horns that would have made any mountain sheep jealous, except they appeared to be burning. As the horse walked forward I noticed his forequarters seemed more powerfully built than his hind and that his hooves blazed the same as his horns did. He appeared to be in transition from a horse to a gigantic mountain sheep, but only in the way that Chaos could allow.

The mount came to Kit, and my cousin did not hesitate to climb up on his back. The creature started to rear up, but a neigh and feinted nip from the Emerald Horse put an end to that rebellion. Kit patted him on the neck, then smiled. "I cannot explain it, but I know his name is Curadh."

The Emerald Horse neighed and looked at Donla. As had Kit, she stepped forward from our line and waited. The Emerald Horse stamped once, and another of his herd trotted into the courtyard. Gray in color, a carapace covered the horse. It had the hooks and bumps and articulations that made me mindful of a *tsoerit* or crab. It came readily to Donla, and, even as we watched, the carapace shifted to form a saddle with a high cantle and stirrups incorporating a greavelike design to protect her legs.

She hesitated for a moment, then mounted the horse. "It's warm," she laughed. I saw her rub her hand along the creature's neck and the color changed from gray to blue there, then faded. "This is Gliomach, everyone."

The ritual repeated itself twice more. Osane received a horse that looked to be a mechanical construct hammered together from gold by a blacksmith. Lamp lenses replaced his eyes, yet they glowed with *Chaosfire* like the eyes of the other horses. He looked gangly and ungainly, yet I noticed he moved fluidly, and I heard no hollow ringing of metal on the ground as he pranced to her. She accepted him openly and announced to us his name was Grian.

Taci paled noticeably as a huge white charger answered the Emerald Horse's summons when she stepped forward. At first it looked normal to me, but as it approached the Emerald Horse I saw its mane and tail fell in ringlets that, while white, appeared made of chain mail. As I got a better look at the beast, I saw the whole of its flesh had the same texture as chain mail, and I had no doubt the hide would serve that purpose admirably. I felt certain I had seen it when the Emerald Horse stole Eirene's horse, but I could not figure out why I would have remembered it in particular.

Taci pulled herself up on its broad back. Their size difference made her look incredibly small perched on that huge animal. She slowly smiled and color returned to her face. "This horse's name is Seilide."

I nodded slowly. "She was Nagrendra's horse once upon a time." As I spoke those words, I wondered idly if my father had ever lost a horse to the Emerald Horse.

Eirene turned to me. "I guess, for my temerity, I get to walk to the Necroleum."

The Emerald Horse neighed arrogantly at her.

I gave him a harsh stare. "As magnificent as he is, I would think he can also be forgiving. Step forward."

Eirene did so, but the Emerald Horse neither neighed or stamped. He stood statue-still, one eye watching her and one watching his herd. No beast in the front rank moved, and I feared, for the barest of moments, Eirene had been right.

Then, from the back, a horse leaped forward and soared over the rank of horses between him and the courtyard. He landed solidly on the dusty cobble-stones, then reared up as the reflected light washed over his leathery skin. The mottled black-and-orange striping had taken on new dimensions, and the fangs in his mouth looked just a bit longer. Despite these changes, I had no difficulty recognizing the horse as Eirene's mount, and neither did she.

Eirene ran to the beast and hauled herself up onto his back. He nodded his head up and down, then proudly pranced past the other horses. Eirene hugged his neck, then smiled as broadly as I had ever seen her do. She glanced over at me and winked. "This is my horse, and I know his name is Trothgard."

The Emerald Horse turned toward the rest of his herd. He neighed, then charged toward them. They gave ground and scattered. A few stopped and turned back to look at him, but another charge sent them fleeing into the night. Rearing up, he neighed again, then came down on all four hooves and came to me.

I look around at the rest of our company. "Good, then we are prepared to travel tomorrow." I saw Eirene bring her horse in line with Kit's, and the two of them began to ride together. "Roarke suggested we get some sleep before tomorrow. We should set up a watch rotation."

Kit nodded. "Eirene and I will take first watch. We'll waken Taci and Donla for the second. You and Osane can have the last watch. We'll let Roarke sleep, so he can be at his best tomorrow."

I agreed. The Emerald Horse struck a pose and froze into immobility. I followed the others into the interior of the mountain and rolled my blankets out on a clear floor space. As I lay down, a full day's worth of exhaustion sank lead into my bones. I fell asleep before my head hit the bunched cloak that served as a pillow.

⌘   ⌘   ⌘

As tired as I was, I should have slept soundly, but I did not. I found myself locked into a dream of such clarity that I knew it had to be a nightmare. The second my eyes opened in that dreamworld I knew I wanted to quit it, but I also knew I could not. The feelings of desperation and doom I had felt in Castel Payne assaulted me again. Unable to resist, I let the dream carry me along.

Behind and around me I saw Chaos Riders of every race and from every province. They sat astride mounts as strange and unique as those the Emerald Horse had claimed as his own. Amid our company I also saw dozens of hounds, including Cruach. I looked to see Roarke, but no one matched his description to my eyes. I did, however, see a man with dark hair and *Chaosfire* eyes whom I took to be Marija's father, Seoirse.

All of us riders had been changed by Chaos in one way or another. My cheekbones had thickened, sinking my eyes deeper into my head. Looking down at my own hands, I saw bony spurs on my wrists and atop my knuckles. I also saw countless scars crisscrossing the flesh of my hands and forearms.

I looked up as a man reined his horse in before mine. He looked at me over two horns of fire, and I thought at first that he was Kit. The resemblance between the two of them was striking, but this man seemed taller and more thickly built than Kit. *As the dream has changed me, so has it changed him.*

"You have a report?"

"Our scouts say the *Bharashadi* have been drawn up into a host large enough to draw our attention, but not sufficient to defeat us."

I felt myself smile. "So Kothvir seeks to draw us into a battle with his army, then fall upon us with other forces."

"As you suggested he would, brother mine." Driscoll smiled, and suddenly I knew him to be my long-dead uncle, or a simulacrum of the same. This meant, in my nightmare, I had been cast in the role of my father. "The ravine you have inquired about is lightly guarded and, if we succeed in getting in there, the Bharashadi will have a difficult time defeating us."

"Good, then this ravine will be our goal. We will feint at their main force, then make for the ravine. Kothvir was wise not to defend it so heavily as to attract our attention, but his attempt to draw us off makes it too good a goal." I raised my right hand. "Let us ride, Valiant Lancers! Today the Bharashadi will die."

We rode forward, and I saw my dream had left me the Emerald Horse for my mount. Then, in a twist of the perverse logic nightmares demand, I rode around the corner of the trail and immediately found myself embroiled in a combat that raged across the landscape. Bharashadi came at us from all sides, and while I had seen no one ride past me, all my compatriots fought before me.

There, off on my left, I saw Driscoll and his horse swept from a ledge and my sight by an avalanche of Bharashadi warriors. I shouted to him, but I knew he could not hear me above the shrieking of the Black Shadows. At the same time I knew they had killed him, and I knew it was my fault.

Then in front of me I heard a challenge roared at me. I turned and saw a massive Bharashadi warrior striding forward through his forces. He held a sword, and I realized it was a *vindictxvara* meant to take me. I concentrated on trying to see the design worked on it, but the dream frustrated my attempt. It was enough that I knew the blade's mere touch would start my flesh boiling away.

Leaning down from my saddle, I tugged a spear free of a Chademon corpse. Kothvir broke through his own lines and brandished the sword he had forged to drink my blood. Raising his hands and the blade above his head, he bellowed at me. "Cardew, it is your time. You have long nettled me. Now I destroy you."

"Never!" I shouted back, and threw the spear.

It sailed through the air, then hit Kothvir in his rib cage with its full force. He laughed aloud at me, but I saw purple blood drip from his mouth. He pulled the spear from his chest and tossed it contemptuously aside. He never even probed the wound with his hand. He took one step forward, staggered, and fell.

Something heavy and hard slammed into the Emerald Horse. I kicked free of the stirrups as we went down. I hit hard, then bounced once and lay still. I smelled blood in my nose and tasted dust on my tongue. I tried to get up, failed, then slowly levered myself up and blinked my eyes.

In the few seconds that the battlefield had been hidden from my sight it had become a ghoulish wasteland. Men and B*harashadi* and horses lay twisted and locked in grotesque positions by death. Already carrion creatures had gnawed them to the bone, leaving only patches of flesh and wind-worn clothing covering them. Ivory bones stuck up from the red sand that half buried them. Lifeless skulls exhaled scarlet dust when the breeze blew.

I looked down at my own legs and saw they had been stripped of flesh and muscle. In horror I raised my hands to my face, but my bony fingers clattered against what was left of my skull. I rose unsteadily to my feet and slowly turned to see the skeletal evidence of the great battle surrounding me like a moat around a castle.

Then I heard the voice from behind me. "So you have defeated Kothvir, as it was foretold. Pity the *Chronicles of Farscry* say nothing of what I will do with you!"

I spun, and shouted, as Lord Disaster grabbed me by my shoulders. I fought him, but I could not break his grip. "Lachlan, Lachlan!" he shouted, and I wondered why he called me by the name I meant to give my next son.

I awoke with a start to find Kit gripping my shoulders. "Lachlan, wake up! You were screaming in your sleep."

I shivered, then loosed the death grip I had on his arms. "Forgive me, Kit."

My cousin stared at me intently. "What happened? Was it a nightmare?"

I nodded as images from the dream faded and evaporated. "I hope so. If it was an omen of what we will encounter tomorrow, I could see slitting my wrists tonight."

27

A strange company were we as we rode out from First Stop Mansion at dawn. Roarke floated ahead of us on his red disc. Its color, because it matched Chaotic magick, clearly made Taci uneasy. She gladly accepted a position toward the rear of our caravan, forming up the rear guard along with Osane and Donla. I rode at the head—more because the Emerald Horse would not brook competition than from any real desire on my part to lead—leaving Kit and Eirene to ride behind me.

Roarke, Kit, and I had all agreed about our route of advance. As Roarke's finger traced a path along a map, I remembered the narrow trail twisting along a ledge in the model's canyons. It made for an easier path than riding along the top of the canyon area, and, with Roarke flying ahead of and above us, we needed fear no ambushes.

Even so, as I remembered how that place had looked

on the model in the palace, I felt a chill run down my spine. Looking up, I saw how much Kit resembled the Driscoll of my dream, and I could not shake the feeling that we were as doomed as our fathers had been. They had died pursuing Kothvir, and the chances were that we would die chasing Kothvir's progeny.

Xoayya's loss returned to haunt me at this point because I would have valued her perspective on the dream. She was used to dealing with such visions of other places and times. What she found routine threatened to unnerve me.

I had mentioned the dream to Roarke, but he was unconcerned by it. "You'd not be the first person to see yourself as your own father in your dreams, Locke. Some dreams might be prophetic, but most just reflect fears we lock up in our hearts. You're afraid that this mission will destroy you the way it destroyed your father. That's a fear all of us share, but you have a lot more tied up in this than we do. You're hoping you are up to the challenge and yet, I suspect, you're a bit afraid of succeeding where your father failed."

"What?"

"Think about it, lad. Your father was a great hero. If you and Kit do what your fathers could not, you'll eclipse them. That will make the rest of your life difficult because you'll have to live up to your heritage. You're smart enough for that to terrify you. It would me."

I frowned at him, less because I disagreed with him than because I did not want to address the problem he identified. Every man's father is a hero to him, and I'd been saved seeing my father grow old and frail, so that heroic image of him never withered and died. But, as Roarke indicated, I could shatter that image by succeeding in my mission. Doing that would leave me without a goal to attain in life, and that was daunting enough a prospect to make me head back to the womb.

By succeeding I would cause as fundamental a change in my reality as had been caused by knowing a Black Shadow had crossed through the Ward Wall. I had to hope I had the strength to deal with that sort of change, but I didn't know if I could. *Still, Locke, it's not a problem you have to deal with until it becomes a reality.*

I looked up at Roarke. "What do you suggest I do about the problem?"

"Accept it." He smiled at me. "It's a pitiful child that can't go further than his parents, especially when they provide him the goals and support he needs. Some of that was lacking in your case, but no matter. Make your parents proud, do what they could not."

I nodded. "Makes sense."

"Oh, and one more thing."

"Yes?"

"Kill all the damned B*harashadi* you see."

As we headed out, I found two members of our group who appeared unapprehensive about this portion of our trek. Cruach trotted along quickly, crisscrossing our path and sniffing at various things I could not puzzle out. As hounds will, he marked our path quite well and occasionally ran ahead to rest in the shade while we caught up with him.

The Emerald Horse likewise seemed energized by our mission, and especially proud that I bore the Staff of Emeterio slung across my back. I had difficulty making him keep his pace slow enough for our other mounts. On more than one occasion he evidenced a desire to walk across air instead of following the trail where it looped deep into the mountains. While he did allow me to keep him on the ledge, he consistently walked about a foot above the ground just to show me he could.

The countryside through which we traveled varied little except where it became harsher and nastier. Acidic rains had eroded any topsoil from the red rocks through which we rode. By some mechanism I couldn't hope to fathom, twisted and needle-festooned plants clung to life in this bleak landscape, while their meager shade provided hiding places for scorpions and other venomous creatures.

As we rode on, the sun rose in the east and coursed like a furious red spark through the heavens. It brought with it great heat, and I felt myself melting beneath my armor. We had filled our canteens and waterskins at First Stop Mansion, so we were not overly cautious in our drinking. I think we all subconsciously realized that, given our goal, dying of thirst was the least of our problems.

The only wildlife I saw were vultures circling patiently in the sky. They did not fly over us, but remained over a place that I realized had to coincide with our goal. In many ways for vultures to be attracted to the Necroleum made sense, yet I took their presence as an evil premonition. Given the visions in my dream, I expected to ride around a corner on the trail and find myself in a bone yard.

Just past noon I recognized landmarks that told me we had made it very close to our target. I raised my left hand to stop our progress just shy of the last corner before the canyon we sought, then in the distance I saw Roarke's disc tip sharply up. A cube formed of thick red lines to define its outline surrounded him and spun quickly to trap him. He tried to steer his platform higher and away from the danger, but could not escape.

I dug my heels into the Emerald Horse's ribs, and he responded by leaping straight into the air. His head eclipsed my view of Roarke for a second as we scaled the sheer canyon wall, then we soared up and over the canyon lip. Galloping full force, the Emerald Horse's gluttonous pace devoured the distance.

When I spotted Roarke again, I saw the magical cube shift. The eight corners sought their opposite, passing through the center and again snapping into place. The action effectively turned the cube inside out, with Roarke caught in the middle. I heard him scream as the corners pierced his body, then the disc vanished. Hanging limp within the cube, Roarke's body began a descent that took it down into the canyon.

Reading my mind, the Emerald Horse vaulted over a large boulder and sailed down to the continuation of the trail we had been following. Down below, on the floor of the canyon, I saw Vrasha Packkiller with the Fistfire Sceptre held high above his head. He spun it around and pointed it in my general direction. A whirling red triangle bled out of the dark pearl and spun toward me. The Emerald Horse cut hard to the right, but even as he evaded the magickal attack, the spell veered off and sizzled past.

I turned and watched the spell as it expanded in flight until each edge had become man-sized. Spinning madly like a roulette wheel, it chopped into the canyon wall and sent shards of rock showering into the air. The spell sank into the stone, lay quiescent for a heartbeat, then pulsed out like an erupting volcano.

The canyon wall fragmented like hammer-struck crystal just as Kit and Eirene came galloping around the corner. I saw them, then a curtain of dust and rock obliterated them. I thought I heard screams, but the booming rumble of a rockslide silenced them. As I had seen in my dream, Kit had been swept away, never having a chance, never even knowing what had killed him.

Drawing my sword, I drove the Emerald Horse straight at the Bharashadi sorcerer. All around me I saw bits and pieces of my dream materialize in the canyon. Shades of those who had died with my father now returned to see if I could sell my life as well as he had. Screaming incoherently, I decided I would not disappoint them.

The Bharashadi warriors standing near Vrasha scattered, but the sorcerer held his ground. I gritted my teeth and drew my arm back for the blow I knew would split his head, uncaring that he swung his staff into line with me. I saw the red spark start from the pearl, but I ignored it. Nothing could stop me. Nothing would rob me of my revenge.

Ten feet from my goal, the red spark hit the Emerald Horse square in the chest. I felt my mount stiffen and go cold, then he stopped as if he were a hunter refusing a jump. With no saddle and no warning, I could not stop myself from flying forward. I slammed into his stony head, then tumbled forward, head over heels.

My unaided flight ended when my shallow arc intersected the ground. I landed hard on my tailbone, which numbed my legs and made it feel as if I had been split up the middle. I flopped down on my back, and my sword bounced free of my right hand. My helmet flew off, and I found myself staring up at the sky.

The Bharashadi sorcerer filled my vision. I saw him smile, then the Fistfire Sceptre's butt end smashed down against my face mask, and I saw nothing more.

28

As I came to I thought the thunder I heard in my ears came from the pounding in my head. I felt a throbbing ache centered on my forehead where Vrasha had bashed me with the Fistfire Sceptre. The armored face mask I had worn had lessened the force of the blow. Instead of actually having a split skull, my head just felt like it had been broken.

I opened my eyes and could see nothing. Panic rose in my throat, and I feared I had been blinded by my injury. I looked around in the darkness for anything that could help me determine if my sight had been stolen, but I found no reference points. Still, my eyes felt normal, and aside from the lingering ache of my tailbone and my headache, I had no proof of having been severely injured. I decided I could see nothing because there was no light.

Quelling that bit of anxiety allowed me to think a little bit more clearly. I tried to move and learned two things in that frustrated attempt. The first was that I had been restrained in a chair of some sort, and probably by magick as I could not feel the bonds that held me in place. Secondly, and more importantly, I learned I had been stripped of my armor and, as nearly as I could determine, wore nothing but a loincloth, my father's ring, and boots.

The drumming sound continued unabated from the black void into which I stared. By moving my head left to right and back, I determined that the drums, however many of them there were, had been set up in at least three groups. One lay straight forward and up a bit, while the other two were on either side of that one and higher yet. The echoes from the room also suggested to me that we were in an enclosure. The sound varied enough that I imagined my prison a natural cavern of some sort.

The air hung heavy and motionless in my prison. I could smell my own nervous sweat, but overlying that I caught the cloying scent of desiccated flowers and dry, dusty rubbish. The odors reminded me of opening a long-unused portion of my grandfather's sword school as a boy. I had stepped into a room that had lain undisturbed for over a decade and had the same musty lifeless smell to it.

In that instant I understood consciously what I had known in my heart all along. I had been brought to the Necroleum. Vrasha had gone to great lengths to be able to resurrect Kothvir and the other *Bharashadi*. It was with the highest irony that Vrasha Packkiller was able to deliver me, Cardew's son, to the Necroleum so I could witness firsthand the consequences of my failure and my father's failure.

I would be a sacrifice to that failure. They'd rip me open and read my entrails for omens concerning their coming invasion of the Empire. My death would be the first of millions as the *Bharashadi* dead exacted their revenge on the people of the Empire.

The drumming quickened as, high up and off to my left, I saw a reddish glow fill a tunnel. It approached at a steady pace, coming one step closer for every four pulses from the drums. On the light came, slowly, stately, as if borne by a priest fulfilling a role in an ancient ritual. I realized that my analogy was not very far from the mark because, if Imperial speculation was accurate, the *Bharashadi* would indeed be sealing a covenant with their god.

The full-maned sorcerer stepped into view at the tunnel mouth and revealed the source of the light to be the Fistfire Sceptre. On his wrists I saw bracers of gold. The red light flashed from the golden pectoral he wore, and the ruby in his gold circlet scintillated in the sceptre's glow. Raising the sceptre in both hands above his head, he hissed a word I did not understand.

From the dark pearl red rays shot out toward the ceiling. The scarlet strands wove themselves into a complex web of red light. The design started with concentric circles spreading out from the sceptre. After spacing themselves out evenly, drifting out at a pace with the drumming, the whole network sprang free of the sceptre. The origin point—a red-gold sphere burning like a miniature sun—drifted to the heart of the circles and centered itself above the dais where I sat. Positioned properly, it slowly brightened and filled the room with light.

I suddenly wished my wounds had rendered me sightless.

As the light grew I found myself trapped in the eye of a horror storm. I sat in a chair on a dais in the bottom of a gash that had once been sliced through the rock by an ancient, twisting river. All around me stalactites and stalagmites stood poised like teeth ready to tear hunks from waiting prey. Stone lay frozen in gentle terraces that sparkled with enough different and varied colors that this place might have been a wonderland to behold at another time.

But that time was not now because the cavern was part of the B*harashadi* Necroleum. On each and every terrace I saw knots of mangled and hacked B*harashadi* corpses. Flaps of hide had flopped open to reveal splintered ribs and dark organs nestled within the bodies. Skulls gapped where the fibers used to bind them together had long ago rotted away. Severed limbs, some nothing more than bare bones, lay as close to correct as possible next to the bodies of the warriors who had lost them. More complete corpses, these showing only slashes or puncture wounds or still having the shafts of arrows protruding from them, dangled from the ceiling at the ends of slender cords.

As hideous as that seemed, I found the display yet more vulgar because of the incalculable wealth scattered over the room. B*harashadi* bodies lounged on mountains of gold. Cascades of jewels lay splashed over them as if they were seeds carelessly spilled on rock by an idiot farmer. I knew all this had come from the cities and empires lost when Chaos o'erswept the world. I imagined they were the offerings made by fearful kin in an attempt to buy the good favor of the recipients when they returned to the world of the living.

In a chair at my left hand I saw Roarke. He had similarly been stripped to nothing but a loincloth. His head hung forward on his chest, but I saw him breathe regularly, so I knew he was not yet dead.

From him I looked up at the only other seat on the dais, and my heart caught in my throat. Monstrously enormous, the Bharashadi facing me sat in a throne carved from a single block of granite. I found the carvings decorating it as obscene as those in Castel Payne. At his left hand, fastened to the throne, I saw a scabbard containing a blade at least five feet in length and with a hilt long enough for him to wrap both of his massive hands around it with ease.

At his feet, near the middle of the dais, lay the Staff of Emeterio.

Most remarkable of all I saw that his left eye remained open and had been replaced with an opal of considerable size. Obviously dead, because he did not move and had two large holes in his chest, he stared at me with an artificial eye exactly like the real, one a Chaos Rider would have. Even though he remained inanimate, I felt a fearful thrill run through me as I looked at him.

So this is Kothvir. Staring at him I could not imagine how my father, having met the creature on more than one occasion, would have willingly sought him out again and again. If that sort of courage were required of heroes, I would gladly have returned to the Empire to live out my life in disgrace.

Even as that thought passed through my mind, I knew it was not wholly true. My father's encounters with this horror were motivated by something stronger than his personal fears. He saw Kothvir as the greatest living threat to the Empire and to his family. What he would have done by himself faded to insignificance in the face of preventing Kothvir from attacking the Empire.

Vrasha descended the winding trail of steps leading down from the tunnel to the dais. I noted ominously that another set of steps ascended the other side of the cavern and ended at what I perceived to be another tunnel. Clearly this was just one in a chain of similar caverns in which thousands upon thousands of *Bharashadi* waited for the ritual Vrasha could now perform.

In the dim light I saw the dozen drummers arrayed in three banks. Warriors all, I thought, because of their partially shaven heads, they hammered the drums in unison. They beat out a hypnotic rhythm with a martial quality that had my blood flowing hot. The music called for me to rise up and crush my enemies, something I had every intention of doing. I fought against my invisible fetters, but could not free myself, leaving me to snarl with frustration.

As I struggled I noticed something that disturbed me for reasons I could not instantly figure out. The boots I wore were not mine. They were old and worn down at the heel. They had been cobbled together in a fashion thought smart twenty years ago. Yet for all that they fit perfectly. Gooseflesh rose on my arms and legs.

I also took note of a peculiarity in the black velvet loincloth I wore. The ends of it were long enough to hang down to the floor in my seated position. I saw sewn on it the rank badges that had been affixed to the tunic I wore beneath my armor. Glancing over at Roarke I saw his rank badges had also been added his loincloth. *Why would Chademons go to such lengths with prisoners?*

Vrasha's advent on the dais gave me no time to puzzle out why an old pair of boots or loincloth decorations should bother me so. A large warrior trailed the sorcerer and remained one step down from the dais itself. He watched Vrasha very closely, but kept his hands away from the sword and dagger he wore. When he looked in my direction I saw contempt in his eyes.

The sorcerer stood in the center of the dais and raised the sceptre. A cone of red light shot down from the heart of the web overhead, then expanded at the top to become a cylinder that surrounded the dais. The crosshatched red lines in it formed a semitransparent screen around us and I felt the itch of magick on my flesh. The warrior, having been excluded by its creation, stepped through it without harm and onto the dais itself.

The lines paralleling the ground stood only a foot apart, and, as Vrasha gestured, they slowly expanded like clay on a potter's wheel. Each of them pulled a piece of the cylinder's vertical lines along with it, as if it were a wheel drawing spokes from the hub. They spread out until, foot by foot, they mirrored the web above, and every corpse in the cavern had been touched by the red light.

Pointing the Fistfire Sceptre straight at the ceiling, Vrasha wordlessly summoned one slender shaft of red light. It came from the center of the net and attached itself like a strand of spidersilk to the head of the sceptre. The sorcerer then slowly spun and touched the sceptre to Kothvir's brow.

The long-dead *Bharashadi* warlord twitched violently. Seconds later all of the other bodies in the room jerked, as if imitating their leader, but being distant from the core of the magic, their motion seemed subdued. Vrasha looked about the Necroleum, his needle-mouthed smile betraying his sense of triumph.

"The eye, Vrasha," hissed the other *Bharashadi*.

"I have not forgotten, Rindik!" Vrasha's eyes narrowed as he snapped at the warrior. "Recall, brother, it was you who doubted it would be returned, even though the *Chronicles of Farscry* said it would."

The *Bharashadi* sorcerer turned to Roarke and me, then gestured toward the web. "Through the magick inherent in what I am doing, you will understand all that transpires here."

Vrasha made it sound as if his granting me the boon of being able to understand the B*harashadi* tongue was a favor, but I knew it wasn't. He wanted me to understand because he wanted me to be frightened and to despair at what I was part of. I let my nostrils flare with disgust and watched him wordlessly.

Holding the sceptre in his left hand, he walked over to Roarke and tipped my friend's head back. Vrasha peered mercilessly down at him, then lowered his right hand to Roarke's face, letting his fingers rest against my friend's temple. He raised his thumb and held it poised like a scorpion's tail. I saw a black claw extend itself.

"No!"

With a wet *thwock*, Vrasha's right thumb scooped the eye from its socket in one razor-sharp motion. Roarke screamed in pain and twisted his head away. Blood flowed down his cheek and onto his chest as the Chademon brandished the golden orb triumphantly. I felt nauseous, and even the B*harashadi* warrior turned away.

Leaving the sceptre to float in the air, Vrasha pried the opal from Kothvir's face and stuffed the eye Fialchar had stolen from him back into his head. I saw a flash of red as Vrasha used magick to root the eye firmly back in its proper place. The sorcerer then turned, stepped forward, and caught Roarke's chin in his left hand. His talons left small cuts as the B*harashadi* jerked Roarke's head around to face forward. With deliberate care, he pried Roarke's left eye open and snapped the opal into place.

Roarke again snarled in pain. A blue light flashed over the socket, and Vrasha leaped back, then smiled as Roarke fought impotently against the magicks holding him in his chair. Roarke looked over at me and winked with his jeweled eye, but I took no comfort in his ability to manage that kindness.

For me the world had begun to waver and change in a manner that half made me wonder if I were not trapped in another nightmare. Throughout the Necroleum I spied *Bharashadi* warriors, and I knew where and how they had died. Just looking at one would let me see him in his glory and as he was cut down. I would have put this down to a link like the one that had allowed the others to know what their horses were named when they received them the night before, but the Chaos magick net uniting all the undead Chademons did not touch me.

Vrasha again raised the sceptre and another red line shot down to it. As he touched the sceptre to Kothvir's chest several things happened. Again the corpse jerked as if a cart had rolled over it. Seconds later the corpse host surrounding us did the same thing. Then the red light traced an outline around the two holes in his chest. I saw a bloody light burning deeper in the wounds, then it reached the outside, and the flesh pulled together seamlessly.

All around us this same thing happened to the other *Bharashadi* dead. The red light burned away the arrows that remained stuck in some bodies, dropping flaming bits of wood to the floor below. The red light fitted together shattered skulls as if they were puzzles. Bare bones became wrapped in scarlet flesh that solidified and made them whole. Detached limbs inched across the terraces to close the gaps with their bodies. Once reunited, the bloody light welded them together again.

Finally the ruby light crawled up Kothvir's chest and joined the first slender line. The red line went from the thickness of a piece of straw to that of my thumb, start-ing at Kothvir's brow and working its way up to the ceiling web. As if a worm were crawling through the line and plumping it, the energy spread throughout the network. When it touched the hanging *Bharashadi* the ropes holding them burned away, but the bodies did not fall.

Vrasha clutched the Fistfire Sceptre to his chest in both hands and rested his chin on the black pearl. He closed his eyes, and muscles on his forearms tightened as his fists contracted. The net glowed a bit more brightly, then its illumination rose and dimmed as the sorcerer spoke.

"It has been done as you instructed, oh Kinruquel. As was bargained when we, the *Bharashadi*, traveled through your realm to reach this world, we have kept this place sacred. In this, the Necroleum, we have enshrined our dead with the plunder of this world. We have tended to them and mended their wounds. We have made them whole once again. They are ready to receive your favor."

I felt the earth rumble beneath my feet. The *Bharashadi* warrior held his hands out at his sides to balance himself. Roarke scowled, and my mouth went dry. I had never heard Kinruquel's name recited in any heroic tale or as the name of a deity in any Imperial pantheon, but if invoking him could make the ground shake, I needed little more proof of his power.

Vrasha touched the sceptre's heel to the ground. "Come now, Kinruquel. Return to these your children, my brethren, that which was so cruelly stolen from them. This, in accordance with the covenant the *Bharashadi* struck with you, I demand!"

Again the ground moved, though this time the motion felt neither as strong nor as violent as before. The vibration thrummed through the air, and I saw the red lines of power begin to blur. They vibrated like lute strings strummed by a bard, deepening the tenor of the sound I heard. As the noise grew in intensity I clamped my jaw shut because it had begun to make my teeth rattle.

Up from the ground I noticed a newer, darker color seep into the power web Vrasha had created. The lines thickened again, as if a black, ashy mud was oozing up to coat them. This new power did not smother or supplant the magick Vrasha had cast, but it combined with it. In the cracks and beneath layers of the crust, I could see the scarlet fire still burning.

The crepitant power climbed up the cylinder, but did not spread out to any of the discs linking the dead *Bharashadi* with the dais. I wondered if something had gone wrong, but Vrasha showed no sign of being disturbed. Instead, he watched enraptured as slowly, inexorably, the power of Kinruquel despoiled his beautiful web.

It occurred to me at that point, that Vrasha's sense of beauty and mine might not coexist in any sphere of reality.

When the black power reached the top of the cone, it shot straight down the thick line to Kothvir. I saw the head snap back as if struck by the ray's increased physical weight. After it hit him, the power began to spread out through the rest of the network. It proceeded at different paces for each circle, so the black power would reach each of the *Bharashadi* at roughly the same time. As it did so, the nature of the sound it produced changed and became more organized and steady.

The sound focused down into a hammering thud that quickly split into a point-and-counterpoint rhythm. They remained paired, one a half second before the other, and gradually slowed. I knew the sound, but could not easily place it. By the time I recognized it as a heartbeat, other things I saw as more important made that discovery insignificant.

Kothvir moved.

At first I thought it was a trick of the dying light, but his chest began to swell and contract. His breathing came so shallow at first that I refused to believe I had seen it. As his lungs grew used to breathing again, I began to hear him breathe. My ears confirmed what my eyes had told me: Kothvir had returned to the living.

His hands convulsed, and his claws extended. I winced as I saw them, and Roarke squirmed uncomfortably in his chair. Muscles tightened on the creature's thighs, and his toes curled in. His shoulders dipped right and left as he loosened his back. His thick chest muscles heaved as he dragged his hands into his lap, then his arms flexed and bent at the elbow.

The power line withered as, finally, Kothvir brought his head up. His shaggy mane had been shaved away from the sides of his head in the manner of warriors. Red highlights played off the sharp angularity of his cheekbones and the strong line of his jaw. His nostrils flared with each breath, and his mouth remained open just enough to let some light flash from his teeth.

He opened his golden eyes, then blinked away the droplet of Roarke's blood. He stared forward at me and Roarke, but seemed to look right through us. He turned his head toward his left, and, when he saw Vrasha, his jaw began to work slowly as if he were speaking. He stopped, then tried again in a dry, harsh croak.

"You have done this?"

Vrasha nodded solemnly and raised the sceptre in his right hand. "As it was ordained to be done."

"You are?" Kothvir peered hard at him, ignorant of the other *Bharashadi* warriors slowly stirring.

"Vrasha, Father."

"Vrasha." Kothvir's eyes closed, and he sniffed the air. "You were the puling runt suckling born of a witch. I took your mother because it pleased me to displease her. I wanted to drown you at birth."

As much as I hated Vrasha Packkiller, my heart ached for him. I could never imagine speaking to a son of mine like that, nor did I think I would have lived through hearing those words spoken to me by my father. I looked at Vrasha to catch any outward reaction to Kothvir's comment, but he managed to hide his pain.

The Bharashadi sorcerer brought his head up. "I believed you had spared me for greatness."

"I spared you because your mother would have found it more convenient for you to be dead." Kothvir glanced over at the other Bharashadi standing on the dais. "You are?"

"The caretaker for your throne, Father. I am Rindik."

Kothvir smiled. "So you slew your eldest half brother to take my place."

"Actually, my lord, my mother poisoned your primary wife and her brood before you were a fortnight dead. I have, since that time, been very careful and have defended our realm against Tsvortu incursions."

"And you sanctioned Vrasha here in his attempt to resurrect us?" Kothvir's eyes narrowed.

Rindik did not even flinch. "I encouraged him. The timing was not what I might have desired, but the outcome was."

"Yes, the outcome." Kothvir turned back toward Roarke and me. "It has been a very long time since I have seen you. Even while I sat here, wrapped in death, I did not forget you. What you stole from me caused enough pain that I could not release it even after death. You killed not only me, but my dream of uniting Chaos and destroying the Empire. That is a crime for which you and all your kin should pay."

Roarke bared his teeth. "If that's a crime, recidivism would be a virtue." He struggled against the magickal bonds holding him in place. "Let your pet release me, and I will do it again."

Kothvir stood unsteadily, then pressed his left hand to the side of his chest where his wounds had been. "Even after this time I feel the pain. It is cold now, but it nests there to remind me. The years have changed you, but it makes no difference. I will finish now what I started years ago."

With his left hand he reached back for the sword attached to his throne. "I made this *vindictxvara* in the heart of a volcano, beneath a full moon, and quenched it in the river that runs through the most desolate parts of Chaos. There has never been a blade like this before. At its mere touch, you will burst into flame."

Roarke laughed all the more loudly. "Death has slowed you down. Not even a fair fight? Go ahead, slaughter me, your reputation will not benefit by it."

Kothvir turned on him, the blade yet undrawn. "Why do you prattle on so, wizard? I remember your knife—a splinter to the tree driven into me that day. This blade will kill you well enough, but now I use it on the one it was forged to slay."

With a hissing ring, Kothvir drew the *vindictxvara* and thrust it toward the roof. Red light ran like blood over the razor-edged steel. My jaw dropped open in complete surprise because there, staring back at me from amid the black tracery decorating the silvered blade, I saw my own face.

29

How could that blade be meant for me? At the time he had created the weapon I was nothing more than an infant. He had no way of knowing what I would look like when I reached adulthood. He could not have anticipated my trip to Chaos. It was impossible that he could have manufactured that *vindictxvara* intending to use it on me.

Yet even as part of me wanted to take refuge in the thought that the time Kothvir had spent in the Necroleum had rotted his brain, scenes from the nightmare and many others boiled back up into my brain. I had seen this Chademon before, I had opposed him, and I had defeated him. Never before by force of arms, but by tactically outsmarting him. I had known forever that to directly engage him would mean my death. Even throwing that spear at him in our last battle had brought me far closer to him than I had ever been before.

Kothvir took a step forward, and his tail twitched. "The *Chronicles of Farscry* reported my death at your hands, and so it has been. Now I will return to you the favor you showed me." With both hands wrapped around its hilt, he raised the sword over his head and closed to striking range.

I shook myself to clear my confusion. He was speaking to me as if I were my father. A confederate in his lunacy, I was letting nightmares bleed over into memories. How could he think me my father when Cardew was a hero, and I was too terrified to do anything to resist?

As the blade slashed down, a blurred bolt of silver swept across my sight and bowled Kothvir from his feet. Utterly unbalanced, the Bharashadi warrior scrambled to stay upright. In his struggle with the steel-pelted dog tearing at him, his feet kicked the Staff of Emeterio across the dais. Horror blossomed on Vrasha's face as the staff rolled toward Roarke and hit the legs of our chairs. In an instant the enchantment woven with the Fistfire Sceptre to hold us evaporated.

I leaped to my feet and dove toward a pile of loot to grab a weapon to use against Kothvir. Off to my left Kothvir roared in pain and stood. He held Cruach out at arm's length by the throat. A flap of the Chademon's pelt hung down from Kothvir's right shoulder, and Cruach's mouth ran with Chademon blood. The hound barked and bit at Kothvir's wrist, but the Bharashadi tightened his grip and choked off Cruach's voice.

Glancing over to make sure I was watching, Kothvir pressed the tip of the *vindictxvara* to Cruach's belly, then thrust the blade all the way through the dog. Cruach twisted in his grip and squeaked out a mournful howl. He looked at me, his opal eyes full of pain, but I could do nothing to save him.

Kothvir twisted the blade, then ripped it free of the hound's body. Finished with Cruach, the Chademon cast him aside as if he were a soiled rag. Cruach disappeared from sight on the far side of the dais, though his whimpers reached my ears easily enough.

Slashing his *vindictxvara* through the air, the B*harashadi* splashed a line of Cruach's warm blood across my chest. "Now I will do for you what I have done for your damned hound. Then I will destroy your beloved Empire!"

My hound. Unbidden and outside my control, memories of Nob—much younger and much stronger—presenting me the pick of a litter filled my mind. "For you, Master Cardew, a hound to be alert and be hunting the Chademons who hunt you." Cruach, the hound that had kept me safe during my expeditions to Chaos. The hound that had taken to me when Roarke said he was very particular about people. The hound who ran to me, not Roarke, when we returned from Castel Payne.

My hound. And the Emerald Horse, *my* horse. I scattered great handfuls of gold coins as my life and my father's life fused into an epic that could not have been all of one piece, yet I knew that was exactly what had happened. Madness began to nibble my sight down into a dark tunnel.

The words I *am my son*, I *am my father* echoed through my head without end.

"Locke, move!"

Roarke's yell freed me from my insanity. I dodged left as Kothvir's overhand chop sliced down at me. The blade pitched coins and jeweled baubles in every direction, then his backhanded slash at me splintered the chair that had been my prison. The force of the blow sent half the chair cartwheeling through the air. It clipped Rindik in the head, knocking him back off the dais and out of my sight.

I crossed to another of the piles of treasure gathered around the room and closed my right hand around the hilt of a sword. I had hoped for something strong, heavy, and straight, but I got a jeweled sabre. Kothvir leaped down onto floor level with me and let the *vindict-xvara* spin in time with his twitching tail. I got a hand and a half on the sabre's hilt and aped his hunched stance.

"You can make it difficult, Cardew, if you wish, but we both know the outcome of this fight." He dipped the point of his blade toward the loincloth and the rank insignia. "While I have lain dormant here, you have regressed. You could not have defeated me in single combat before. How can you have any hope now?"

I smiled at him with more confidence on my face than I felt in my heart. "Being in the grave for sixteen years hasn't made you any smarter, has it? You're the one bleeding. If *Farscry* says I am to kill you, and you do not want to count the time I've already done it, I am willing to oblige you again."

Beyond him I saw Vrasha and Roarke square off. From his side of the dais, Vrasha thrust the sceptre toward Roarke and sent a flight of four red balls shooting out at him like stones from a sling. With the Staff of Emeterio held in his left hand, Roarke muttered a spell that started a blue light playing along the staff. He slashed it through the balls' line of flight, letting the energy play out like a flag that engulfed and absorbed them all before vanishing.

Kothvir came in carefully, then beat my blade aside to the right. Sliding forward, he lunged, but I ducked beneath his sword and withdrew to the right, following my blade. He pivoted in my direction, trying for a horizontal slash that would have cut me in half. Holding my sabre in my right hand only, I blocked the cut and piv-

oted my body out of the way. I was ready for him to dis-
engage, but he surprised me by maintaining contact
with my blade.

That move shouldn't have surprised me. He brought
the *vindictxvara* up and over, carrying my blade with it.
As with fights with Dalt, since I couldn't counter his
strength, he intended to use it to power me into the
position he wanted.

Having learned from fighting with my brother, I
leaped away before he could push me back and got my
body out of the range of his blade. Dalt would have
bull-rushed me, allowing me to sidestep him and ham-
string him with a slash.

Kothvir did no such thing. He came in with a high
slash that I caught on my blade. Sliding to the right,
Kothvir shifted the direction of his attack away from me
and pressed it against my blade. I felt the jolt as my
sabre landed flat against the top of the dais and knew I
was in serious trouble. Kothvir's shoulders tensed, then
he brought the *vindictxvara* down with all of his power.

My sword's blade broke off with a brittle pop, leaving
me with three inches of sword attached to a beautiful
golden hilt.

"You are finished, Cardew."

"Don't mistake me for this sword." I whipped my
right hand forward, throwing the sword-crumb at
Kothvir's leg.

It hit him in the right knee and bounced off, doing
no visible damage. Kothvir snarled and brandished his
sword at me, splashing droplets of his blood and
Cruach's over the floor. "You'll have to do better than
that, Cardew."

"I'll do better once I find the right tool for the job." I
took a running step away from the dais and vaulted
onto the first of the cavern terraces. I skidded to a halt

in a shower of gold coins, then hauled myself up to the next level as the *vindictxvara* struck sparks from the stone below.

"Run, Cardew, run. You cannot avoid this blade forever!" Kothvir's tongue flicked out, and he licked some of Cruach's blood from the blade. "One touch. One nick, and you will die most horribly! I have waited in the grave for too long to be disappointed now!"

On the dais itself Vrasha and Roarke continued their sorcerous duel. With a wave of the staff, a flaming azure hawk materialized in the air. It swooped in at Vrasha, but the Chademon quickly described a square with the sceptre. A red cube formed itself around the bird, then fell to the ground. Both spells vanished in a violet flash, but Roarke spelled a snake to life in front of the Chademon, and it lunged at Vrasha.

As Vrasha spun one of his triangular spells to burn through the beast Roarke had conjured up, I knelt and found another sword. An inch or two longer than I preferred, the blade looked stout enough to stand up to one of Kothvir's blows. At the same time it felt light enough and well balanced enough for me to be able to put it to good use against him. He might not wear rank badges, but Kothvir was quite skilled with a blade. My new sword had a good edge, and I knew I would need it because, unlike the *vindictxvara*, my sword would require more than a pinprick to kill Kothvir.

I leaped down to the floor of the cavern and ducked beneath a crosscut slash. Staying low, I lunged at Kothvir, forcing him back. Drawing myself up to the right, I sidestepped and deflected an overhand blow to my left. Disengaging from his blade, I brought the tip of my sword up and through in a weak slash that managed to catch his left shoulder and open a small wound.

Kothvir backed away from me and probed the wound

with his left thumb. He sniffed at the blood, then tasted it. He smiled at me. "After so long, feeling even this is a joy." He wiped his hand clean on his chest. "Thank you for reminding me even the most tiny of pests can prove difficult."

The Chademon drove in, windmilling blows high left and high right. I blocked those I could not dodge and actually jumped above one low slash. As I landed, I lunged forward and stuck him in the right thigh. Pulling my blade free as he shouted in anger, I retreated but did not move quickly enough.

His right arm came around with a backhanded slash that caught me with more flat than edge. Despite the sloppy delivery, it sliced through flesh and muscles over the ribs on my right flank. In addition to opening up my side, the blow landed solidly enough to knock me sprawling and crack ribs. I fought to keep my sword in hand as I fell, knowing I would be dead without it.

But *he cut me with a* vindictxvara. I'*m dead already.*

Rolling to a seated stop, I clamped my right arm down over the wound. I felt my sweat stinging and burning in the wound. I slid my left hand beneath my sword arm and winced as warm blood oozed between my fingers. I could feel shredded muscles and bone spurs. Breathing hurt because of broken ribs, but that mattered not at all. I had been hit with a *vindictxvara* forged specifically to slay me! I had seen what a mere dagger had done to Tyrchon. Kothvir promised this blade would make me burst into flames. My left hand sought any spark, any hint of unnatural warmth kindling in my chest. *Maybe I can smother it.*

Kothvir had withdrawn and glanced down at the gash leaking blood over his right leg. He pressed his right hand to the wound as if anointing it with the blood from his shoulder would heal it. When it did not, he wiped his hand across his belly, then looked up at me. "Your last blow was a good one. You are better than I expected. Pity. I smell your blood from here. I cut you. Thus ends the story of Cardew, scourge of the Black Shadows."

He stared at me intently, as if he could make me combust by force of his will alone. I returned his stare, filling it with all the venom I could. I determined I would show him no fear, give him no satisfaction. It didn't matter who I was, or who he thought I was—I was going to die a man.

As I steeled myself against death, I realized I wasn't dying. I felt no fire in my wound. I felt nothing but the normal stinging ache of a cut and the sharp pain from broken ribs. I'd felt it before, and I knew I'd survived it before. I *may be going to die, but not right at this moment.*

I reached up with my left hand and grabbed the edge of the terrace behind me. I got a good grip despite the slippery blood and pulled myself to my feet. "That's where you're wrong. I am better than you ever dreamed. And I am *not* Cardew." I waved him forward with my bloody hand. "Come on, Kothvir, we have both outlived our rivalry. Let us end it now."

He stared at me, confusion swirling through his eyes and setting his face in a snarl. Wiping my left hand on my loincloth, I stalked forward. I could feel blood trickling down my side, but I felt no fear about the wound. I even let him glimpse it, taunting him with it, then I came at him as I had come at Dalt and Geoff and even my grandfather. I stole from him the role of executioner and forced him to play the victim.

I feinted high, then slashed low. Kothvir whipped his sword around in a circular parry. I pulled my tip back, sliding free of his parry in a hiss of metal, then stabbed forward as his blade passed. My point hit him in the upper chest on the right side, then I withdrew—but not far—as he swept his sword back in a late parry.

Wounded and bleeding, are you as strong as Dalt?

Kothvir grunted at the wound, then took a half step forward, placing him well within striking range. He lunged, and I parried. Sliding my sword up along his blade, I locked our hilts. Shoving upward, I drove our blades high, then I twisted my whole body and pirouetted beneath his right arm. His blood-slicked grip surrendered his sword and sent it spinning off into the air. Before it hit the ground, and before he could recover from his lunge because of his wounded leg, I thrust my sword through his armpit, skewering both lungs and his heart.

I released my sword and tried to jump away, but he spun and pitched me across the dais with a swat from his right paw. I hit hard and rolled to a stop on my knees, scraping them the way his claws had scored my chest. Weaponless, I balled my fists and waited for the *Bharashadi* to come after me.

Kothvir took one strong step toward me, then staggered and sank back. He slipped in his own violet blood and fell against the dais steps. A hideous cough racked his chest, and his last words pooled into lavender bubbles on his lips. Whatever he said, the magick did not translate for me, but it mattered not. His dying eyes filled with hatred, and I got his message.

Between us, the magickers' duel continued on the dais. Vrasha spun the sceptre into a circle and made a shield against the azure lightning bolt Roarke cast through the staff in his left hand. The two spells mutually annihilated each other in a brilliant burst of white light. Vrasha set himself for another of Roarke's assaults, then smiled as Roarke gestured with his right hand and a blue bat launched itself at the *Bharashadi* sorcerer.

Contemptuously, Vrasha brought the sceptre up in the square motion he had used to stop the magical bird Roarke had created. The cube cage flashed to life, but the bat sailed through the red enclosure and raked its claws across Vrasha's face. The Bharashadi sorcerer screamed and batted at the winged rat with the sceptre. The magical creature sank its fangs into Vrasha's right hand and tore off a bloody strip of pelt. The Black Shadow screamed in pain and lost his grip on the Fistfire Sceptre.

As it fell to the ground, Roarke leveled the staff at Vrasha Packkiller and murmured, "I want his heart." Tethered to the staff by a thin thread, a blue claw the size of my hand shot forward. It punched through the sorcerer's chest, then retracted. Disbelieving, the sorcerer looked down, probed the gaping wound with his hands. His eyes flicked up, then he reached for his still-beating heart.

Roarke smiled. "Allow me."

The heart burst into flame the second before Roarke stuffed it back into Vrasha's chest. The Bharashadi's scream ended in fiery jets shooting from his mouth and nostrils. Trailing smoke from face and chest, Vrasha teetered backward and crashed onto the dais.

Beyond him an unsteady Rindik rose up and stepped onto the dais with his sword raised. Before I could move, or Roarke could cast a spell to deal with him, two arrows sank to their fletching in the Bharashadi warrior's chest. I looked back up at the tunnel through which Vrasha had come into the cavern. Kit and Osane had already fitted new arrows to their bows while Eirene and Donla let fly at the other Bharashadi in the cavern. Two of the twelve drummers toppled from their perches, and the others died rapidly as the rest of our company picked them out from the slowly wakening Bharashadi dead.

Once they had eliminated the living threat, our compatriots started to come down toward the dais. I held my hand up to stop them. "No, stay there. We will come out to you. Secure the way."

I turned to Roarke, who knelt breathless on the dais. "You knew, didn't you?"

He smiled at me. "You mean about how no spell from the staff would get through defenses raised by the sceptre? Yes. That's why I pressed the attack and made Vrasha get careless. He was choosing defensive spells that had no relation to the attacks I made on him specifically because the defense didn't matter. When I made my warbat, I did not use the staff, and his defense failed."

"Not that, Roarke. You knew about Cruach, that Cruach was *my* dog. And about the Emerald Horse and why I knew where the Umbra was." I swallowed hard. "You knew I was Cardew all along."

Roarke nodded very slowly. "When Jhesti rescued me from Fialchar he took me to where Cruach stood guard over you. He said Fialchar had lured you into a zone where time ran backward, and that you had regressed to the age of two or so. We brought you back to the Empire, leaving only those boots behind for the *Bharashadi* to fret over.

"About what had happened to you, we told only a few people—Audin, Evadne, your wife Merle, Ethelin, and the Emperor. I think he has since confided in the Warlord. We needed you to become Cardew again, as you had become Cardew once before, so we tried to recreate your training and your life as exactly as we could."

I stared at him, speechless. "Why?"

"So you could fulfill the prophecy made in the *Chronicles of Farscry*."

"But I had already killed Kothvir."

The sorcerer shook his head slowly. "Not that prophecy, but another that indicated the slayer of Kothvir would destroy the Necroleum."

Suddenly uncounted coincidences and strange circumstances fell into place. Cardew and I both traveled to Herakopolis to attend the Emperor's Ball on Bear's Eve. We both had the same Bladesmaster, yet my training differed this time because Kit had left and Audin did not have two daughters to distract me from my studies. I was forced to read all the books my father had owned, but I was never allowed to see his journals. As a child I dunked a wooden horse in green paint because I remembered the Emerald Horse from when I used to ride him through Chaos, and the whistle to which I had trained him to come was the same I had used to train Stail.

It was an impossible task—to make me once again what I had been forty years before, when I first came to Herakopolis. Yet they undertook it because of its importance.

"I understand." I reached out and took the Staff of Emeterio from his hands. "Get them out of here."

Roarke hesitated, then stood. He picked up the Fistfire Sceptre and mounted the steps to the exit tunnel. I watched him stop and talk to the others, then they joined him and left me alone in the hall of the dead.

I walked over and picked up the *vindictxvara* Kothvir had so lovingly crafted to destroy me. I wiped it clean on his fur, then slid it through the loincloth's belt. Carrying the staff in my left hand, I stepped past Kothvir's body and knelt on one knee beside Cruach.

The hound looked at me, and I bit my lower lip to keep it from trembling. I reached out and scratched him behind his left ear. "There's never been as good a companion to a Chaos Rider as you have been, Cruach. The *Bharashadi* will have nightmares about you. Thank you for waiting for me."

He twisted his head around and licked at my hand. His tongue felt as soft as silk, but even that simple motion drained him of strength. His head sank back down, and he looked at me as if to ask forgiveness for his failing.

"You've not failed, Cruach." I stood and grasped the Staff in both hands. "You and I, we've just started. The *Bharashadi* will have nightmares about the both of us, nightmares to torment them for eternity. Anything that wants to get out of here will have to go past us. And between us, my friend, nothing gets past."

I closed my eyes and felt the seductive caresses of whatever Emeterio had placed in his staff for intelligence. As it had done before, it offered me incredible power. It would do for me whatever I wanted. It existed to serve, and it acknowledged me as its master. *I have done what was necessary to oppose the Sceptre. What will you have me do for you, Master?*

I brought the staff parallel to my waist and wrapped my right hand around the shaft. I willed the staff to show me a complete map of the Necroleum. It complied instantaneously, and I saw level upon level of caverns just like this one burrowed into the mountain. Each chamber had multiple links to others of them, making the mountain a virtual hive of *Bharashadi* dead. Our estimates of a hundred thousand dead *Bharashadi* waiting to be resurrected were as optimistic as they were wrong.

"It's grand guardian duty we will be doing, Cruach." I thought of Evadne, my *mother*, not grandmother, and how I would break my promise to her concerning my return. Likewise the promises both Cardew and Lachlan had made to Marija. "Forgive me."

I thrust the Staff of Emeterio over my head and tightened my grip upon it. I let anger seize me. I let my fury with the B*harashadi* and the grief over the deaths of so many pump through my body. I gathered every curse and indignity and mortification I had known in two life-times and used their venom to ignite a fire in my belly.

Fueling the staff with raw emotion, and wielding it with the careless abandon of someone unschooled in the ways of magick, I forced it to project all of its might outward. My flesh tingled as red and blue energies fused together into a roiling purple ball of fire. It expanded in stages, swallowing up the B*harashadi* bod-ies and using the energy in them to grow further.

In a handful of heartbeats it filled the whole of the cavern. I felt resistance, as if the magick could go no farther, but the very idea of failure infuriated me even more. *This will be done!* I ground my teeth and *pushed*.

By the strength of my rage and the force of my will, I sought to bring down the mountain above the Necroleum. The earth resisted, but I remained stead-fast. My arms quivered, but I held them aloft nonethe-less. I *will not be defeated*.

I heard it first, then opened my eyes. Looking up, up through the purple fire, I actually saw daylight through the cracks above me.

"I have won!"

The cracks widened and rocks fell as the magick fin-ished its task, then the dying mountain crushed me.

30

This is death?

The question occurred to me because the experience was not at all what I had expected. Yes, given the way I died I expected lots of pain, but it was the wrong type of pain. A *mountain dropping down to crush you should have a heavy, suffocating sensation to it.* Instead I felt as if the energy net Vrasha had created had returned. Made of razor-sharp blades, it sliced me into a thousand thousand little bits.

I decided that having that much pain linger forever also made a weird sort of sense, so I prepared myself for eternal torment. Inexplicably, my discomfort faded except for the pain in my shoulders and the stitch in my side. I felt as if I were floating, but my hands ached from holding so hard on to the Staff of Emeterio. That puzzled me, and I wished I could have seen my hands, but the darkness let me see nothing.

Then I felt hot breath on the back of my neck and I

opened my eyes. I found myself dangling by my hands from the Staff of Emeterio. Bracketing my hands I saw other, far larger and decidedly stranger hands. I released, hit the ground, and rolled away forward. Regaining my feet, I turned and faced Fialchar.

The sorcerer's black eyepits absorbed my stare. "I gave you permission to borrow my staff, not bury it."

"So you did." I glanced over at the huge crystal ball floating in the center of the room. In it I saw a cloud of dust settling in the region of the Necroleum. Black specks—vultures—circled and slowly descended to snap up any carrion exposed by the collapse. "You did let me borrow it, but in that you broke the agreement you and I made over twenty years ago."

Fialchar's quicksilver lips flowed back between his teeth. "That agreement was between your father and me."

"Please, do not mistake my earlier confusion for stupidity. You know I am Cardew. You caused me to age backward by transporting me to a place in Chaos where time runs in reverse. You probably planned to take me and raise me in your image. You would have used me against the Empire, which would have been the ultimate victory in your eyes. Jhesti thwarted your plan when he rescued Roarke and me."

I smiled casually. "The memories return slowly, but I recall the deal we had struck. You and I would play a game of chess—one move a month—and the winner would be able to ask any one thing from the other. The loser would have to comply. You told me early on you would ask for my son, Geoff. I never told you what I would demand, and your curiosity kept you at the game until I had you one move from checkmate. At that time you refused to allow me back into your lair because you knew my next move would win the game.

"This I did not mind at all, for that meant you left me and my people alone as we fought Kothvir and his *Bharashadi*."

"Far be it from me to interfere with a man performing an act of sanitation." Fialchar's eyes began to smoulder. "Your demand for the Staff of Emeterio could hardly have been covered in the agreement we reached concerning the game. I recovered it well after the game had been finished."

"No, Fialchar, the game was finished two days ago when I made the last move. The Staff of Emeterio could be mine if I demanded it. Your kind offer of letting me borrow it circumvented my demand, *and* reveals to me how much it means to you." I walked over to the gold ring surrounding the crystal ball and touched the globe with my right hand. The scene shifted slightly and showed me my compatriots safely up the canyon with a blue wall conjured by Roarke and Taci shielding them from the cavern debris. "I won the game, and I mean to have my prize."

Fialchar casually swung the staff in my direction. "And if I use this prize to destroy you?"

"You won't."

"And how can you be certain of that?"

"As I said, the memories return slowly. You could have killed me after I had destroyed Kothvir, but you did not. You took me away from him to frustrate his desire to end my life. You did that because you decided he was unworthy of being my slayer."

Little tongues of flame singed his eyebrows. "You flatter yourself."

"Do I? You could not then and cannot now abide the idea that I beat you in a game of chess. I even started with the Imperial side, which conceded to you the first move. You took me back to infancy to remake me so the person who beat you would never have existed. But I do exist, and I beat you."

As I spoke I realized that I had, in fact, been remade in my own image. The Emperor's conspiracy to have me grow up again in the same environment that had nurtured me originally succeeded on a basic level. It pushed me in the directions I had gone before, and quite well could have accomplished their goal except for one thing.

They trusted Audin too much.

He believed in his heart that he had failed both Driscoll and me. He had agreed I would come to the capital with the same rank badges I had held when I first traveled there decades before, yet he could not allow me to travel from him carrying the same seeds of destruction. While I only tested out as an Apprentice, I had the skills of a Sworder. Likewise my ability at chess far exceeded what an unranked person should have known.

Evadne had seen it when I arrived more slender than before. She knew Audin had violated the agreement, had strayed from the plan, but she said nothing. I think she, too, hoped I would overcome that which had doomed me before. She played her part, but also let me play the part that my reeducation had written for me.

I slowly began to smile as I realized how true had been the words I spoke to Kothvir after he struck me with the *vindictxvara*. Because of my grandfather, because Kit was not Driscoll, because of a hundred thousand other factors, I might have been Cardew in body, but I was not Cardew in spirit. The *vindictxvara* had been forged to capture Cardew's essence and destroy it, but the blade could not find it in me. Cardew had been supplanted by Lachlan.

I opened my hands and turned to face the sorcerer. "I offer you a choice. You may, if you choose, surrender the Staff of Emeterio to me. Or, you may heal my companion Tyrchon of the wound he received from a *vindictxvara* and grant my company and me safe passage to the Empire."

Fialchar let the staff hang in the air. "You ask of me two things whereas our bargain only allowed you one. Your safe passage with the Fistfire Sceptre *or* the well-being of Tyrchon, not both."

"Safe passage or the staff, your choice." I folded my arms across my chest. "I'll offer you something else for Tyrchon."

"You have nothing I want."

I smiled. "You'd deny yourself another chance to play me?"

The Staff of Emeterio dropped a half inch as Fialchar's concentration wavered. "Are the stakes the same as before?"

I narrowed my eyes. "Geoff is far too old to suit your plans."

"This I know, but I also know you will have another son." The staff floated to Fialchar's necrotic hand. "Is Lachlan now as brave as Cardew was then?"

"Braver. If I lose, you can take me back to the place where I became younger, and you will have me as your toy."

"Satisfactory. Your friend will be healed, but whether or not he or your other companions make it back to the womb will be entirely up to them."

"Companions?" Images of Xoayya and Nagrendra flashed through my mind. "Who else?"

"You have many companions who have been left behind in Chaos over the last forty years. I could not name them all, primarily because they are of no interest to me." Fialchar's face, all silver and ivory, approached a benign expression. "If you win our little game, what will you ask of me?"

If you won't answer my question, why would I answer yours?

"And destroy the suspense? No, you wouldn't like that. I will think of something as we go along." I smiled at him and bowed. "Good day, Lord Fialchar. I shall convey to the Emperor how helpful you were in this affair."

I backed out of his sanctum, and he filled the doorway to watch me go. "So cocky, little mortal. You leave because I choose to let you leave. Hereafter you will be nothing more than a fly caught in my web."

I nodded solemnly. "I hope the webmaster remembers that sometimes the buzzing in his web is that of a spiderhawk wasp. If he doesn't, he could be in for a nasty surprise, and you don't strike me as the type to like surprises."

The Emerald Horse, still as stubborn, prideful, and arrogant as ever, came when I whistled and carried me away from Castel Payne. I told him to find Roarke and the others, and he did so with a minimum of difficulty. We sailed over them, then slowly spiraled down toward the red earth as they came around a bend in the trail.

"Hail and well met, my friends."

Roarke, in the lead on his flying disc, laughed aloud and waved the others forward with a flourish of the Fistfire Sceptre. "You see, I told you he wasn't dead."

The smiles and laughs from my companions made me feel very good. Kit, on his devil-ram, rode forward. He looked a bit worse for his experience, with a cut on his forehead, but he seemed healthy nonetheless.

"I was glad to see, Kit, that Vrasha's magick did not kill you."

"Eirene and I would have died, but our mounts are well

suited to dealing with broken terrain and leaping clear of landslides." Kit swallowed hard. "Roarke told us some very strange things. Are you my uncle or my cousin?"

I clapped him on the shoulder. "By blood and kin reckoning I am your uncle, but in truth I am Lachlan. I am really no more Cardew than an actor playing him in a theatre might be. While I remember many things that he did, I am not he." I gave him a brave smile. "If you wish, though, I will tell you as much as I can remember about your father."

Kit took my forearm and grasped it firmly. "I would like that, Locke, very much."

We broke our grip and Kit rode on past. Eirene followed him closely, and they rode two abreast where the trail allowed. Behind them came Bishop Osane, Donla, and finally Taci. The entire road company looked weary, but victorious smiles lit every face.

Roarke drifted over to me. "So, Lord Disaster has his staff back again?"

"And we have free passage to Wallfar."

Eirene looked back. "We will have to detour to get Tyrchon."

I shook my head. "Lord Fialchar and I made an accommodation concerning him. It means Tyrchon will again be alone in Chaos, but that is a state he seems uniquely able to handle."

Roarke frowned. "What did Fialchar demand of you for that concession?"

"Nothing I hadn't granted him before." I shrugged. "The trade seems fair. We have the Fistfire Sceptre and the B*harashadi* threat is diminished if not destroyed."

The magicker nodded. "We definitely seem to have won the better of the deal."

"Even with Hansen, Xoayya, Nagrendra, and Aleix dead?"

"And Cruach."

I nodded as the lump in my throat choked off words. *And Cruach.*

Roarke forced a brave smile onto his face. "I think so, Locke. This mission was a gamble, but we accepted it. Some of us left our money on the dice table, and the rest of us walk away winners."

I kicked the Emerald Horse gently in the ribs and started him after the others. "A gamble it was, and against tough odds, too. I never thought we would survive, much less succeed. Did you?"

Roarke gave me a sly grin. "Survive, certainly. Succeed, I never had any doubt."

"What?" I narrowed my eyes and watched him closely. "We had the *Bharashadi* after us. We had to get Lord Disaster's most powerful tool away from him. We had to locate the place most sacred to the *Bharashadi* and destroy it while they were raising an undead army of millions? And you had no doubt about the outcome?"

"Of course not, Locke." He laughed lightly and brandished the sceptre triumphantly. "Things like that happen in Chaos."

ABOUT THE AUTHOR

MICHAEL A. STACKPOLE got his first rejection slip in 1964, at the tender age of six. He got the next one in 1976, and they arrived with more frequency after that. Clearly clueless about the fact that other folks didn't think he could write, he persisted. Shifting his sights temporarily, he moved into the game industry, writing and designing products for companies like Flying Buffalo, Inc., TSR Inc., Mayfair Games, FASA Corp., Interplay Productions, Steve Jackson Games, and West End Games. In 1987—self-deluded into believing rejection could no longer hurt him—he convinced the folks at FASA to let him write novels for them, which they did (the twelfth of which will see print later in 1998).

In the realm of fiction he is best known for his bestselling Star Wars X-wing Rogue Squadron novels. *An Enemy Reborn* is the fourth novel he has written in a universe of his own devising (or as some folks put it, this is his fourth "real novel"—save for those pundits in the SF industry who consider anything containing magick to be trash.) (And he'd live in terror that said pundits might see this sort of contemptuous remark and think ill of him, but he really doesn't care what they think).

In his spare time he plays indoor soccer (and at this writing has a three-game scoring streak going), rides a bicycle, and has actually cut down on his television watching (yet another sign of the coming apocalypse). He lives in Arizona with Liz Danforth and three Welsh Cardigan Corgis: Ruthless, Ember, and Saint.